Winner of the
HOLT MEDALLION AWARD

CIRCLE of LIGHT

NANCY J. COHEN

OGP
ORANGE
GROVE
PRESS

Prologue

Smoke billowed into the air, swirling and blending into a murky gray fog whose tendrils reached into every hidden corner of the city. Mantra remembered the pungent smell even though it had been ten months since he'd fled his home. A lot of good it did him to hide in the countryside. The deadly plague called the Farg had spread its tentacles until it reached him even there. The pestilence touched everyone, regardless of location or station in life. It was a great equalizer, as Mantra had come to learn.

Huddling in the shadows of a doorway, he clutched his cloak tighter around his trembling body. It wasn't the cold that concerned him. Mantra dared not risk being seen. The telltale ugly swellings on his thick tan hide would condemn him on sight. If he were caught, he would be sent to the pest-house. He wanted to die in his own bed, not in a chamber of horrors.

A paroxysm of coughing struck him, and he stooped, hacking and trying to clear the phlegm from his lungs. When at last he straightened, his face was red, his breath coming in short, painful bursts. In the dim light of the streetlamps, he could see the winding cobblestone street disappearing into the mist ahead. Only a few more blocks to go, then he would be home. With a stab of fear, he wondered if anyone was left to greet him. His mother and father… his sisters… had they all succumbed to the plague? It was selfish of him to return like this, to put them all in danger, but he craved one last glance of his loved ones before he died.

It was difficult to breathe the dry air after the relatively moist freshness of the country, and he had to stop every few paces to catch his breath. He was grateful that the streets were deserted. Public gatherings were forbidden, and all transportation had come to a halt. It was as though the very lifeblood of the city had stopped.

Sewage flowed freely in the streets, and even the wooden structures surrounding him seemed to lean inward with despair. Mantra cringed from the shrieks and lamentations he heard as he passed the homes still inhabited. Nearly everyone was affected by the horrifying visitation, if not themselves, then their dearest relations. The city had become a harbor of death.

Mantra's shoe slipped on a water-slicked stone. He flailed and caught his balance to avoid a dangerous fall. Voices ahead made a curse choke in his throat. He sagged against a wall, his heart thumping. *Go away!* he cried in silence.

A searcher and a chirurgeon hurried together on their gruesome mission to examine the dead. One of them held aloft a red rod, warning off anyone approaching not to come near. Mantra held his breath as they passed, for all the good it would do him. He was already infected. Soon he would become their next victim.

When the voices faded, Mantra stepped out and moved forward at a faster pace. His temples throbbed, and a wave of dizziness threatened to overwhelm him. He pushed on, determination giving him strength. He nearly sobbed with relief when he rounded the corner of his street.

What he saw made him stop short.

Oh, no. Was that a watchman with a halberd in hand guarding his front door? Mantra slowly approached. A large red circle was painted on the door with the piteous words scrawled across it, *HAVE MERCY UPON US!*

Terror struck his heart. "What is this?"

"You approach a closed house. Be gone," the watchman said. He was a stout fellow whose facial hair was thick and coarse. From the set of his shoulders, he appeared muscular beneath his robe.

"I must enter," Mantra replied, frantic with concern. "It is my home."

The watchman took a closer look. "By the sun, citizen, are you ill?"

"Aye." Mantra gave a wicked grin as he thrust up his sleeve to reveal a rash of purplish blotches discoloring his thick hide.

The watchman's eyes widened, and he stepped back. "You have the Farg!"

"Unlock the door. I wish to join my family."

The watchman withdrew a large key from the folds of his garment. He fumbled with the lock, swung the door open, and stood aside for Mantra to pass. "The faith be with you, citizen," he said, making the sign of the circle as Mantra went by.

"Mantra," his mother screamed as he entered. She flew down the stairs, and Mantra barely heard the door bang shut behind him, or the key turning in the lock a second later. He raced to greet her, flinging his arms around her and sobbing her name.

"Alas, I forget myself," he said, suddenly pulling back. "I am infected by the Farg."

"Mercy!" his mother cried.

Now he saw how haggard she looked as he stood back to examine her. Her hair, once her crowning glory, hung in stringy reddish-brown strands down her back. Her luminous eyes were dull and sad. Even her garment, a softly woven fabric in green to match her eyes, was creased and stained. A wave of guilt swept over him as he thought about how he had left.

"Who else is ill?" Mantra asked, afraid to hear the answer.

Malika's shoulders slumped. "Your sister Zunis. She has the fever."

"And Father?" His supply station should have kept them all well fed, at least until they were shut in.

Malika looked away. "He took sick all of a sudden. Two days didn't pass before the dead cart came to take him away."

"No," Mantra howled, rage and grief overwhelming him. He sank to the floor, squeezing his eyes shut to hold back the tears.

"Mantra, promise me you will not die, too," Malika cried, kneeling beside him.

"I'm so sorry. Mother." He gazed at her with sorrowful eyes. "I should not have left as I did. I ran at the first sign of the plague. I was a fool and a coward."

"Hush, my son." Her voice was gentle as she put out a hand to soothe him. "You were not the only one trying to flee. The streets were thronged with carts and beasts of burden, with wagons and goods, with people and baggage. You were lucky to get out before the barriers went up."

"The barriers are useless. The distemper is everywhere." Mantra ran his fingers through his rusty brown hair. "Curse this *maug* planet. If we lived closer to the sun, we might not be so horribly affected."

Malika straightened. "It is harmful to listen to rumors from offworlders."

"We have to ask the Coalition for help. It is the only way."

"The only way is for the Coalition to leave our planet alone. We joined for the trade only. Any other contact is forbidden." Malika's voice was firm. "This is an old discussion. Come to bed."

Mantra rose slowly, his limbs stiff and sore. He ached in a hundred places. "Joining the Coalition isn't enough. We need to become active members. We need to progress—"

"Progress brings corruption. We will talk no more of this." Malika peered at him closely, and her eyes darkened with anxiety. "You are trembling, and your face is a ghastly hue. How long have you had the distemper?"

"It's been five days since I got sick. The fever was the worst. It was not thought I would survive, but a kindly caretaker gave me a posset-drink, and I recovered." A rattling wheeze choked off his words, and he struggled for breath. His chest constricted as though a painful vise were around him, and he coughed, clearing the obstruction. "But as you can see," Mantra said, gasping, "the infection has spread to my lungs."

His mother's countenance paled. "Upstairs with you," she ordered, lifting her skirt and preceding him.

"Mantra, you have returned at last," his eldest sister Sita greeted him from the second landing. Her voice was cool, her expression disapproving. At least she hadn't suffered from their quarantine, Mantra thought. Sita's eyes were heavily made up in a rich lavender shade to match the silky cloth that draped her slender form. She looked as though she were ready to go out on a social visit. Mantra bet she hadn't lifted one finger to help Malika in the whole time he'd been gone. But then Sita had always considered herself first.

As had I, Mantra thought, feeling the familiar wave of guilt.

He regarded his sister calmly. "Where is Kairi?"

"Here." His next elder sister came flying out of the room she shared with Sita, book in hand. She was about to throw her arms around him when he stepped back, a look of warning on his face.

"Stay away. I have the Farg."

"Oh, no." Kairi's expression turned to horror as she observed him more closely. "You look terrible. Let me help you."

"Keep your distance," Malika said. "You girls must remain in your room. I will attend him as I do Zunis. Go now, quickly. I'll bring you both a sulfur balm as soon as I'm free."

Sita wrinkled her nose. "Not that awful stuff again."

"It's been an effective preventive agent, hasn't it?" their mother countered. "Now be off with you."

Kairi cast Mantra a regretful glance and followed her haughty sister back into their room. Mantra made haste for his own bed. It was as he had left it ten months ago, his possessions untouched, his bed made up as though he had just gone out for an afternoon. A sob of grief tore at his throat. If only he had seen his father one last time.

He made no protest as Malika turned back the coverlet and motioned for him to get into bed.

"Show me how bad it is," she demanded, leaning over him, her eyes soft with concern.

His modesty had long since gone. Mantra stripped, averting his eyes from the expression of horror on his mother's face when she saw the extent of his blisters.

"I'll check on Zunis, and then I will get you some poultices. The poison must be drawn from your body." She listened for a moment to his wheezing. "I will also brew a tea of *lalith* leaves for the congestion."

Malika bent down, and a tear escaped from the corner of her eye. "Rest, my son. I am glad you have returned." She squeezed his hand, and a brief expression of hopelessness flickered across her face before she turned away.

It was much later when Mantra was awakened by cries from downstairs. Throwing his cloak over his shoulders, he hobbled out of his room. "What is it? What's the matter?" he called.

Sita and Kairi emerged into the hallway, their frightened faces pale against the vivid blue hues of their nightclothes. "It is Zunis," Sita whispered. "When the fever spikes, she gets delirious."

"How long has she been like this?"

"Three days. The fever shows no sign of breaking."

Mantra frowned. That was a bad omen. "Is Mother tending to her?"

"Aye," Kairi replied in a low tone. "She won't allow us to help."

"I must go to her."

Despite their protests, he went down the stairs, stopping every few steps to catch his breath. The mucus in his chest seemed looser, so he coughed some of it up. A burning pain stabbed his lungs and Mantra winced, holding on to the rail and waiting for the discomfort to pass. Finally, the pain subsided into a dull ache and he was able to continue his descent.

"Mantra, please go to bed," his sister Kairi pleaded from above.

"Don't waste your words," Sita said to her. "Mantra never listens. He didn't listen when Father asked him to help out in the food station. Father might still be here now had Mantra been around to share the burden."

Feeling the blood rush to his face, Mantra whirled to face her. "Shut up, Sita."

"Go back where you came from," Sita hissed. "You're just more work for Mother. You're sick. You should never have come here."

Mantra took one glance at the shocked look on Kairi's face and suppressed his retort. Turning on his heel, he shuffled to the library which had been converted into a sickroom. He found his mother huddled over the writhing form of his youngest sister.

Mantra drew in a sharp breath when he saw the livid color of Zunis's face. Her eyes were glassy and wild as she thrashed about, muttering incoherently. Her reddish-brown hair, the same color as their mother's, lay tangled about her face. She looked like a different person from the last time he had seen her, a sweet young maiden about to breach her sixteenth year.

Malika straightened, and he saw she had been applying a wet cloth to Zunis's forehead. Instead of remonstrating with him for coming downstairs, his mother seemed glad of the company. She drew a weary hand across her brow.

"I know not what else to do," Malika said. "Either the fever must break, or it will take her. This goes on too long."

Mantra stared at her helplessly. He didn't know the ingredients of the posset-drink that had helped him, so he couldn't offer any advice. "The room is cold, Mother. Would a fire not help?" He drew his cloak tighter around his body.

"I think not. Zunis must be kept cool."

"But see how her limbs tremble."

"It is the distemper. Did you not find it so?"

"I suppose." He shrugged. "In truth, I was not aware of much when I passed through this stage."

Malika sighed. "I pray it will end soon. I grieve to see her suffering so."

Mantra stared at his sister, wishing he could will her to get well. She looked so frail as she lay there. He remembered her laughter, her happy innocence, and he thought how everyone's innocence had been destroyed by this onslaught of pestilence.

Returning to the hall. Mantra trudged up the stairs, knowing he would be more useful if he could recover his own strength. Kairi awaited him in front of his bedroom door.

"How is she?" Kairi whispered. He noticed she carried a book. Kairi was always reading, and he'd found he could talk to her about the things that interested him far more easily than with anyone else in the family. He supposed it was because Kairi drank up new ideas the way some people drank water.

"Alas, Zunis is not doing well. I fear for her survival." They commiserated a moment in silence. "Mother is worn out and needs a rest herself."

"I know. She nursed Father, and now poor Zunis. I wish she would let me help."

"Can you talk?" Mantra asked, suddenly eager for a sympathetic ear. "I promise to keep my distance."

At Kairi's nod of assent, he placed a chair for her in his doorway, and sat on his bed. Regarding his sister, he decided he liked the way she had braided her hair. It hung down her back nearly to her waist, while wispy bangs shaded her brow. Her face was a petite version of his mother's.

"I can't talk to Mother about these things," he began. "She doesn't understand. I heard a lot of talk when I was away… talk about the Coalition, and about the legend. It is said the time is right."

Kairi leaned forward. "How so?"

"The blazing star appeared in the sky as it was foretold, a full moon cycle before the onslaught of the pestilence. You saw it, do you remember? Its dull, languid color and heavy, solemn motion were supposed to predict a horrible judgment. So it has come to pass. The plague is slow but severe, terrible and frightful. And it's not happening just here on Tendraa. It is all over the galaxy, on planets not only similar to ours but different as well.

Don't you see?" His eyes burned with zeal. *"Death and confusion will reign throughout the heavens. And then the Great Healer will appear."*

Kairi gasped. "But it's just a legend."

"More than that," Mantra contradicted. "All that was predicted has come to pass—the Farg, the arguing factions within the Coalition, even the Morgots."

"The Morgots!" Her eyes widened with fear. "They are not in this sector, are they?" Mantra had told her about the warrior race from a distant solar system who had been attacking planets neutralized by the plague.

"The last I heard from Ravi, they were in the Quk system," Mantra said grimly.

"How long ago was that?"

"Six months past."

Their cousin Ravi was a renegade. He'd stowed away on a freighter to escape from Tendraa, then joined the Coalition Defense League. His prowess at flight school had earned him the prestigious position of first mate to Captain Teir Reylock. Mantra had secretly kept in touch with him, eager to hear the forbidden news from other worlds. But the spread of the pestilence had disrupted their communications.

"The Morgots could be anywhere by now," Kairi whispered.

"That is true. Ravi said the Coalition had their hands full just trying to deal with the plague. Their resources are limited. Even the ruling High Council is looking to the Great Healer for salvation."

"I wish I had such faith." Kairi's eyes filled with despair.

"Open your heart, Kairi. The prophecy will be fulfilled."

"But who is this savior? When will the Great Healer be revealed?"

"I don't know, sister." A paroxysm of coughing struck him, and as Mantra struggled for a painful breath, he gasped, "I only pray it will be soon."

Chapter One

"You want me to do *what?*" Captain Teir Reylock asked, scowling at his superior officer from across the man's desk.

Admiral-in-Chief Daras Gog glared back at him, aware of Teir's doubts. If it weren't for the captain's excellent reputation, Gog would rake him over the hot fires of Alpha Gomaran Two for his insolence. But Tier was the chief troubleshooter for the Coalition Defense League, and this mission demanded he recruit the best. He could overlook military protocol if Tier listened and obeyed.

"You heard me," Admiral Gog said quietly, fixing a steely gaze on the captain. "You are to deliver the Earthwoman to the High Council for her marriage to Lord Cam'brii."

"Just like that? The woman hasn't any notion of the legend. How am I supposed to get her to come? Should I tell her she's been identified as the wondrous Great Healer who will save the galaxy from destruction and despair?" Tier laughed, a harsh sound in the stillness of the office. "To her it will mean nothing."

"You'll manage." The admiral stood behind his desk and began pacing, his hands clasped behind his back. He was shorter than Teir, but with his military bearing and decorated uniform, he knew he cut an impressive figure.

"By the Suns, Earth isn't even a member of the Coalition," Teir said, his blue eyes stormy. He tucked his hands into his flight jacket pockets. "Considering how many years their civilization has existed, that doesn't say a whole lot for their planet."

Admiral Gog stopped and raised his eyebrows. "It is to your

advantage Earth is still in the primitive stages of development. Your small reconnaissance vessel can enter its orbit undetected."

"Reconnaissance vessel? What about my own ship?"

"Your spacecraft is too large. The vessel you will be assigned is small and swift. It is better for eluding radar."

"The hell it is. I take my own ship or I don't go."

"Captain Reylock," the Admiral thundered, losing patience. "Do you have any idea of the significance of this mission?"

"I don't believe in the legend of the Great Healer. You want me to do the job, I'll do it, but in my own way."

"By the moons of Agus Six, you'll obey orders! Do you want the plague that is devastating our galaxy to reach your home planet? Do you want the Morgots to enslave the few people who will survive? Worlds are falling one after the other, first to the plague, then to those accursed aggressors. The Great Healer is our only hope of stopping them both."

"An ignorant Earthwoman? Come on."

"All the signs point to her as being The One."

"Oh yeah? If anyone's going to save the galaxy, we have to do it ourselves," Teir stated. "The diplomats in the High Council argue like a pack of *borks*. We're facing two major threats, and the R.O.F. still calls for a vote to dissolve the Coalition. No wonder the Morgots are moving in. Dissension makes us ripe for takeover."

"Sarina Bretton—the Earthwoman—is the key," the admiral told him. "With the recent problems facing the Coalition, membership in the Return to Origins Faction has swelled, and the High Council is hard-pressed to focus its attention on external matters. If the Revelation occurs as predicted, the R.O.F.'s push for all species to return to their respective home worlds will be nullified. Coalition unity will be strengthened. That's why it's so important for us to retrieve this Earthwoman. The prophecy appears to be coming true. As it was foreseen, the harmony of the galaxy is disrupted by internal strife. Pestilence has struck us down. Hostile invaders are conquering our worlds. It's really happening, do you not see?"

"No, I don't. The only thing I see is religious fervor spreading throughout the galaxy. It's a distraction from the odds stacked against us. But I realize the High Council won't try to solve its own problems until the legend is proved false, so I'll bring the woman."

Tier didn't look happy by the prospect, but Gog didn't care as long as he did the job. "Good," the admiral responded, "and you'll take the reconnaissance vessel assigned to you."

Teir opened his mouth as though to protest, but at a quelling look from his superior, he pressed his lips together. "Aye, sir." He snapped a crisp salute, turned and left.

****

K'darr, chief of the Morgots, paced the bridge of the battlecruiser, *Krog*. The flagship of the Morgot fleet, the *Krog* had been named by K'darr himself. The word stood for demon in the language of his people. With his horned ears, ridged brow, and fiercely black coat of fine fur, K'darr appeared as the very Evil One himself, an image he liked. He wanted his enemies to quake at the sight of him.

"The Assimilation is going well, Your Eminence," said Grand Marshal Zen-Bos. He wasn't as tall as his leader, but since K'darr was over six foot seven inches in height, that wasn't unusual. Still, it made him feel awkward having to look up at K'darr, and Grand Marshal Zen-Bos didn't like feeling awkward about anything.

"Continue," K'darr barked. He stood with his hands inside the folds of his voluminous black robe, his one vanity being its trim of solid gold. He knew the robe made him look even more forbidding with his stiff posture and perpetual dark scowl.

Zen-Bos wished he could look into his leader's obsidian eyes without feeling a tremor of fear. But he'd heard too many stories about what happened to those who displeased his master not to feel a quivering in his gut. Still, he forced himself to meet K'darr's harsh gaze with a strong, determined one of his own.

"Two-thirds of the sentient planets are converted, Your Eminence. The satellite monitors are in place for the rest."

K'darr glared at him. "Then what are we waiting for? Set course for the Tendraan system."

What are *we* waiting for? The marshal swallowed. He'd thought K'darr was here for an inspection tour. His transport ship had arrived barely an hour ago.

"Sir?" he queried. A trickle of sweat itched beneath his light coat of golden fur, and he resisted the impulse to scratch it.

K'darr's mouth tightened. "I'll be coming along. Planet Tendraa is rich in flavium. If we secure the mineral's source, our new superweapon can go into production."

Zen-Bos nodded. He'd heard about the tectonic missile under development at the heavily fortified research center on Morgot. If the weapon could be implemented, their superiority over the Coalition alliance would be assured.

"A brilliant conception, Your Eminence. You may use my quarters for the duration of your stay."

K'darr's opaque eyes brightened. "I've already had my things moved in. You must come and view my plants."

The marshal shuddered. "I'll look forward to seeing them," was his careful reply.

He'd heard about K'darr's plants. The leader's collection traveled with him wherever he went. It consisted of the most exotic specimens from the planets they'd conquered—souvenirs, in their own way.

K'darr's favorites were said to be the vicious man-eating *thrum* from Antiguas Two, and the thorny swinging fodus vine from Souk. Zen-Bos remembered the report of the last warrior who had viewed the leader's collection. He'd annoyed K'darr by disobeying a direct order, and when he didn't show up for duty the next morning, a lieutenant had gone to check on him. K'darr had grinned and pointed to the pieces of fur and skin scattered about the *thrum* plant.

Zen-Bos gave the order for the change in course toward the

Tendraan system. "Will there be anything else you require, Your Eminence?" he asked in a deferential tone.

"Yes, step aside with me." K'darr drew Zen-Bos into a corner and lowered his voice. "You've heard about the legend of the Great Healer? I understand the time has come for the Revelation."

"I have heard rumors to that effect, Your Eminence."

"They are more than rumors," K'darr roared. Everyone on the bridge turned to look at him but just as quickly averted their eyes. "Intelligence reports that the Coalition has identified the one they call the Great Healer," he continued evenly. "It is an Earthling female known as Sarina Bretton. If there is any truth to the legend, she could pose a threat to the fleet. Teir Reylock has been assigned the duty of retrieving her."

"Reylock!" Zen-Bos had heard of the man's reputation. He itched for the opportunity to confront the meddlesome troublemaker. Eagerly, he watched his superior's face.

"I want you to contact Cerrus Bdan," K'darr ordered. "The smuggler has an old score to settle with Captain Reylock. He should enjoy this challenge. Tell Bdan we'll pay him well if he delivers the Earthwoman to us. He can take care of Reylock himself."

A slow grin spread over Zen-Bos's face. It made sense to let someone else do the dirty work for them. This way, nobody would suspect the Morgots were involved. "I will send the message at once, Your Eminence."

"Good. No one must interfere with our Supreme Plan. No one." K'darr swung around, his robe swishing at his feet as he headed toward the turbolift. His eyes blackened into two chunks of coal, and anyone in his path moved swiftly out of the way.

****

Sarina Bretton stared out of her office window at the dazzling cityscape below. The Miami skyline dipped and blended into the

14

pristine blue of Biscayne Bay. Numerous white sailboats plied the glistening sundrenched waters, and far in the distance, a barge chugged out to sea.

Her eyes glazed over, and in her mind she saw another scene from the space adventure film she'd viewed over the weekend. In her imagination, she became the pilot of the starship. With supreme skill, she evaded enemy laser blasts, dodged asteroids, fired photon torpedoes, and soared over new planetary horizons.

Sarina sighed and drew her attention back to the client list on her desk. As an attorney, she dealt in facts, not fantasy. To imagine herself in any other role was a waste of time. *Toughen up, girl.* Those were Mother's words, but she was right. Sarina always needed reminding to curb her soft side.

She attempted to focus on the work in front of her, but the viewphone rang before she could accomplish anything.

"Sarina?" Her boss, Hiram Simmons, looked harried as he stared at her from the monitor screen. "I've assigned you a new client by the name of Pierce Mitchells. He should be on his way there now. Can you come up to my office when he arrives?"

"Certainly, sir." She straightened her shoulders, feeling uncomfortable under the scrutiny of the gray-haired managing partner of the firm.

"I'll fill you in on the case once you're here."

"Okay, thanks." She was about to hang up when another call came through. Recognizing the number, she pushed the flash button. "Hello?"

"Hi, babe." Her fiancé's face came into view, his solemn brown eyes endearingly familiar.

Robert, one of the partners in the firm, had an office upstairs along with the rest of the upper echelon. Junior lawyers like herself were relegated to the lower floors. She'd been working here for over a year now and didn't even have her own personal assistant, but hopefully that would change soon enough.

"I got wind of the Goroka case," Robert said. "How the hell did you get involved in something like that?"

Uh-oh. She'd known he wouldn't approve. "I couldn't help it. The woman was so pitiful. She had nowhere else to go."

"She can't pay, for God's sake."

"I'm only giving her legal advice, and I'll work on it in my spare time. Don't worry, it won't cost the firm anything."

"That's not the issue. If you're going to be accepted as a full-fledged Associate, you must stop being a sucker for these hard-luck cases. This isn't the first time you've used your resources unwisely. Simmons won't like it."

Sarina's lips thinned. "Not everyone can afford the high fees he charges, you know."

"So let them go elsewhere. What do you want, a welfare job or a position that's going to pay your bills for years to come?"

"Some things are more important than money, Robert."

"Yeah, like what?" When she didn't answer, he went on. "You're up for the big promotion, sweetheart. Don't screw up now."

"Why? Are you going to delay our wedding again if I miss out?" Sarina asked. He'd already changed the date twice.

"I'm only interested in your career," Robert said, his tone sincere. "This week is crucial. Simmons is going to put you to the test."

"What do you mean?"

"He'll tell you he's sending you a client, but it'll be some wacko. Your reactions are what count. We all have to pass this nutty psych test to move ahead."

Her heart thumped with excitement. "Robert, Mr. Simmons called right before you did. He said he's sending in a new client, and we're to go to his office together."

Robert sucked in his breath. "This might be it, then. You can do it, babe."

"What should I expect?" Sarina's palms grew moist as her anxiety escalated.

"If your test is anything like mine, this 'client' will tell you a totally wild story. Simmons will be observing your responses, so act professionally. Go along with it and pretend like you believe every word. He wants to see how you'd handle a difficult situation."

"But I'm supposed to take the client up to Mr. Simmons's office. Won't he admit the ruse then?"

"Only after he's satisfied you've passed the test." Robert chuckled. "You might not exactly end up in his office either. I was led to a special suite of rooms he uses just for this purpose. It was decorated like a boudoir. The so-called client told me that if I handled his case satisfactorily, I could have my choice of any of the lovely ladies present. Of course, it was clearly a setup, but the women acted their parts convincingly."

"You never told me about this. So I can expect a really crazy scenario?"

"That's right. Just act cool and play along, but don't do anything that makes you uncomfortable."

Sarina couldn't imagine what might be planned for her, nor could she picture her staid boss getting his kicks out of games like these, but apparently there was a side to him she hadn't known existed.

"Good luck," Robert told her. "Call me later and let me know what happened."

"Wait." She wanted to ask him how he'd solved his own test situation, but he hung up before she got the chance. Damn the man! Now she'd have to struggle through on her own.

They'd been engaged ever since she graduated from law school and took the position at the firm. Robert's recommendation had helped her land the spot, and his influence was important in getting her promotion approved. She should be grateful to him, but gratitude wasn't what she felt. He kept postponing their wedding, saying she should concentrate on getting ahead. His attitude made her wonder which was more important to him—her job status or herself?

Their wedding was set for December, five months from now, and if Robert put it off one more time, she'd need to reevaluate their relationship. During the past few weeks, she'd felt increasingly dissatisfied. It was difficult to pinpoint the cause. Robert irritated her, but that could be because she felt pressured. She'd applied for Associate after he'd urged her to do so, and yet this job wasn't fulfilling her expectations.

She couldn't admit her doubts to Robert without starting an argument. Besides, she felt this problem wasn't the real issue bothering her. Something else tugged at her from beneath the surface of her mind, but she hadn't a clue what it meant.

Realizing the new client might walk in at any moment, she patted her French braid at the back of her head. It was still smooth and sleek, so she reached into her handbag to reapply her lipstick before he arrived.

Just as she was putting her mirror away, a loud rapping sounded at the door.

"Come in," Sarina called, her heartbeat accelerating.

The door opened and in strolled the most gorgeous hunk she had ever seen in all her twenty-six years. The man was tall and powerfully built, but the dominant feature that drew her was the strange color of his eyes. Never had she seen a blue shade so deep, so celestial. It was as though the sky was mirrored in his gaze. His eyes locked on hers as he approached.

"You are Sarina Bretton?" His masculine tone reverberated throughout the room and seemed to touch a chord within her very soul.

"Yes," Sarina stated as the man strode forward. She lifted her chin, intending to present a professional image.

He stopped directly in front of her and bent his head to examine the identification badge pinned to her crimson dress. Her I.D. picture showed her in a relaxed pose, her wavy blond hair hanging down her back, her gray eyes wide in an oval face. She knew her pink lips parted in a silly grin, but the photographer had been a friend who knew how to make her laugh.

She surveyed the stranger's thick black hair that grew long in the back, curling at his nape. His features were angular, firm and strong. Her gaze wandered down to the strange metallic silver jumpsuit that he wore. It molded to his powerful body like an animal skin.

"Excuse me—I had to make certain," the man said.

Sarina glanced at him, startled. He watched her with a flat expression. She searched his eyes for contact lenses but saw no telltale outlines. The intense color fascinated her.

"Certain of what?" she asked, wondering if his weird responses were part of the game set up by her boss.

"Of your identity." He grasped her right hand and turned it palm up. He touched the round area of pigmentation on her soft flesh. "You see? You have the mark as prophesied."

A shiver of delight ran through her at his touch. "That's just a birthmark," she said, withdrawing her hand. "Look, Mister, uh—"

"You can call me Teir."

Teir? She looked down at her desk where she'd scrawled the name Pierce Mitchells on her message pad.

"You are needed. I am to escort you," Teir explained, a hint of irritation in his tone.

"Escort me? Where?" But then she answered her own question. "Oh, you mean to Mr. Simmons's office." Obviously, this guy was the test case Robert had mentioned. Remembering her fiancé had advised her to play along, she stuffed a notebook into her handbag.

"You won't need that where we're going," Teir said with a bemused curve of his mouth.

"I may have to take notes. Shall we go?" She stood and smoothed her dress.

A look of astonishment dawned on the man's face, as though he hadn't expected her to be so cooperative. *Hmm, this test might turn out to be fun,* Sarina thought.

Grinning at the idea, she strode from her office and out into the carpeted corridor. Teir followed, his booted footsteps thudding behind her.

She waited until he caught up. "Has the initial data on your case been filed?" she asked as they walked down the hallway. The main bank of elevators was situated at the opposite end.

Teir didn't respond. Halfway down the hall, he came to an abrupt halt and pointed to a closed door. "This way. You can go first."

Sarina shot him a sharp glance. "That's a storage closet."

Wordlessly, Teir opened the door, and Sarina gasped. Facing them was an elevator car.

"A private lift? I never knew this existed. Where does it go?"

"Up," Teir said, without a trace of a smile.

It must lead to Mr. Simmons's penthouse suite. She'd better be on the alert in case her boss was watching them via hidden cameras. This had to be part of the test.

Chapter Two

At Teir's urging, Sarina stepped inside the padded interior. He entered the elevator after her, his tall muscular form seeming to take up most of the small space. Sarina's breath quickened at his nearness. She edged away until she bumped into a wall. Her apprehension rose when she noticed there was no control panel.

"How do you operate this thing?" she asked, her pulse racing despite her resolve to keep calm.

As the door slid shut and they began a slow ascent, Teir showed her a small remote-control device he held in his hand. "You'd better hold on," he said, securing the object in a previously hidden pocket of his jumpsuit. He slipped his hands into two loops protruding from the padded walls of the lift. "This thing starts slow, but it accelerates fast."

How peculiar. She didn't have time to speculate because just then a big thump rocked the elevator. Sarina grabbed for the two remaining loops on the wall and clung tightly as the lift shot upward at an incredible speed. Her stomach dropped, like it would in an airplane that suddenly developed lift. A whoosh of air sounded in her ears, and a smell similar to a pressurized cabin filled her nose.

Then just as suddenly as it had started, the acceleration stopped. An eerie sense of motionlessness gripped her.

"What happened?" she asked in a squeaky voice. Her head reeled, and she felt disoriented.

Tier gave her a solemn glance. "The antigravity device activated. We're out of the atmosphere now. That's the worst part of the ride, but thankfully, it's over." He did a quick calculation on his handheld device. "Another one of your Earth minutes and sixteen seconds and we'll be there."

Earth minutes? When Robert had said she'd be sent a wacko client, he really meant it.

The elevator swayed, and her throat constricted. She maintained her grip with frozen fingers. A gentle bump rocked the lift, and then the motion stopped.

She withdrew her hands from the loops. As she massaged the ridges they'd left on her skin, a buzzer sounded somewhere outside. The steel door slid open to reveal a short corridor with a blank white wall at the far end.

She peered out into unfamiliar territory. This was definitely not the penthouse suite where Mr. Simmons had his office, nor was it anywhere else in the building to her knowledge.

"After you." Teir jerked his thumb toward the exit.

"Right." Sarina swallowed, wondering where he was taking her. Would Mr. Simmons be waiting to join them? If so, she'd better not show any hesitation.

She stepped boldly forward. As Teir followed her into the corridor, the lift door closed behind them.

"Now what—" she began, but Teir prodded her ahead until they reached the white wall.

He pressed his hand against a raised panel, and a hidden door slid open with a hiss. Sarina gasped as a surreal vision unfolded in front of her.

They faced a space that reminded her of an airplane cockpit, with rows of switches and buttons blinking in various colored lights. The symbols displayed an unrecognizable language. But her attention didn't linger on the instrumentation. She swung her gaze to the wide viewscreen. In front of them was a blackness so profound she could only wonder at it. Pinpricks of lights twinkled in the distance, reminding her of the night sky in a planetarium.

"What is this place?" she asked in a hoarse tone.

"We're on my ship," Teir responded. He pointed to the two

modular seats facing the viewscreen. "Sit there," he commanded, indicating the one on the right.

When Sarina didn't move, he grunted with impatience and tugged her forward. Her knees weakening, she didn't resist when he pushed her down and buckled her into a safety harness.

"I don't understand. What's going on? Is this some kind of flight simulator?"

Surely Mr. Simmons wouldn't go to such extremes just to tap into her favorite fantasy. No one in his right mind would incur such exorbitant expense merely to test an employee. And for what purpose? This scenario had nothing to do with her legal expertise.

Come to think of it, Robert's hadn't either. He must have been tested to see if he would take a bribe, albeit in the form of seductive women. But Robert had at least known his location, whereas Sarina wasn't certain of anything.

"I think there must be some mistake," she said, wondering how to get back to her office.

Teir dropped into the pilot's chair beside her and strapped himself in. He released a lever and manipulated the steering column so a different view came into sight.

"Say farewell," he told her.

Sarina's mouth dropped open. That greenish-blue globe spinning against the dark backdrop of space looked very much like the planet Earth. Her mind going numb, she turned to stare at Teir.

"Firing thrusters," was all he said. He punched a button and a roaring noise sounded. A huge surge came from somewhere beneath them as their forward motion increased.

"Tell me what's happening," Sarina demanded, doubting her own senses. *I have to get out of here. Is this man the fake client my boss has sent, or is he not?*

The alternative was even too bizarre to contemplate.

Teir entered a code into the computer and then leaned back, folding his hands behind his head as though blasting from the atmosphere was all in a day's work for him.

"You want an explanation? Fine, I'll give you one. You've been identified as the legendary Great Healer. A terrible disease called the Farg is sweeping through the galaxy, killing billions of people. Those who survive are being enslaved by a warrior race known as the Morgots. You are destined to stop these horrors and save everyone."

He spoke in a sarcastic tone as though he didn't believe she could be a savior. "I'm taking you to the High Council where you will wed our esteemed prince, Lord Cam'brii of the ruling House of Raimorrda. Supposedly, the prophecy will be fulfilled through this marriage."

Sarina stared at him in disbelief. Obviously, this man wasn't Pierce Mitchells, the client Mr. Simmons had sent to her. Then who the hell was he?

Surely his story couldn't be true? No, it was too preposterous. This had to be a simulation, or some kind of theatrical set.

But even as she tried to find a rational explanation, her imaginative mind discarded it. That view of Earth had been much too realistic. She didn't know of any technology capable of producing such an effect. And if this setup was real, she had just been abducted by an alien in a spaceship.

She fumbled with her safety strap, desperate to find an exit.

"Stay in your seat," Teir ordered. "We're about to enter space warp."

Her anxiety escalated. She tugged at the buckle, but her hands shook so much she couldn't unlatch it.

"Nine seconds to go. Eight, seven…"

Her neck whipped back as the ship lurched forward. The stars became a kaleidoscope of color, a blur of passing images. She was pressed down into her seat.

The transition to real space came just as abruptly. Soon they were gliding smoothly through space again. Some of the stars seemed larger, closer than they'd been before.

She couldn't stand another moment of this uncertainty.

Wrestling with the catch on her safety harness, she finally unhooked it and jumped up.

"I want to go home. Where's the exit?" She peered around at the unfamiliar surroundings. Even if she did find one, she had no idea where it would lead. If this really was a spaceship…

"Get back in your seat," Teir commanded.

Ignoring his stern tone, Sarina charged for the opposite wall. Behind her, she heard a growl as Teir leapt up and chased after her. He grabbed her by the wrist.

"You're hurting me," she cried as the pressure of his fingers forced her to turn around. His use of force confirmed her suspicion that he wasn't an actor hired by her boss to play the part of a client. She wasn't even sure he was a man. Maybe he was an alien life form who'd taken on the shape of a human so as not to frighten her.

"Either you do as you're told, or I'll have to restrain you," Teir said in a dangerously quiet voice. "The ship's on autopilot right now, but there's some tricky navigation ahead. I have to pay attention to the helm."

"Let me go." Sarina struggled to free herself, but it was like fighting against solid rock. Teir maintained his tight grip on her arm, and even as she kicked and squirmed, he drew her against his body.

"You'll obey me, woman." As he stared into her defiant eyes, something within him softened. With a sound of disgust, he thrust her away.

As soon as he released her, Sarina raced to the door at the rear of the cockpit. She wouldn't be trapped here. The walls felt as if they were closing in on her. She searched for a means of activating the exit, hoping it would reveal the elevator or a familiar corridor on the other side.

"Storms of the sun, woman, get away from that wall. You can't go anywhere."

Realizing he spoke the truth, Sarina turned to face him. This man—or whatever he was—had lured her here and used her ignorance of the situation to his advantage. Now she was his prisoner. Her head reeled as she remembered what he'd said. She was needed. She had to marry someone. It didn't make any sense, but then, none of this did.

Glancing his way, she noted how his contoured muscles stretched the fabric of his silvery jumpsuit. From the demonstration he'd already given her, he could easily enforce his demands. She'd better do as he said until she learned what he had in mind.

Chapter Three

Teir noted the play of emotions on the woman's face. Her fear mixed with doubt and confusion. She might find this situation easier to accept if he gave her a fuller explanation.

"Sit down while I check our heading. Afterward, I'll answer any questions you might have."

Sarina pursed her lips but she obeyed, taking her seat while Teir dropped into the pilot's chair to verify their coordinates.

"Where are we going?" she asked in a matter-of-fact voice.

He regarded her with relief. At last, she was acting rational. His jumpsuit itched, and he scratched at a spot on his neck. He hated wearing it, but it was the standard uniform for sensitive missions. The sensory-laden material made him invisible to surveillance devices, enabling him to enter Sarina's building undetected.

He'd been amazed at how willingly she had come with him. He had been prepared to knock her unconscious if necessary, but she'd cooperated readily. She hadn't been anything like he'd expected. Gazing into her eyes had the oddest effect on him. Their silvery flecks reminded him of the mists of Quava Plain on his home world of Vilaran. He hadn't been home in ages and felt a sudden urge to return.

"We're on our way to the High Council," Teir said, pushing aside his musings about the softness of her lips. "According to the legend, your healing power will be activated when you fall in love with a member of the ruling family. Hence your marriage to Lord Cam'brii."

"The ruling family of what?" Sarina asked. No doubt she hoped to gain knowledge to prepare herself for the inevitable.

"Earth is not yet a member of the Coalition of Sentient Planets, an alliance of star systems in this quadrant of the galaxy. The House of Raimorrda has ruled the High Council for eons past. Lord Cam'brii is their most valiant noble. He was chosen to fulfill the prophecy."

Teir spoke with derision, not buying into the legend. It gave the politicians something to feed the dissatisfied masses.

She tilted her head. "Where do you fit in?"

"I'm an officer in the Coalition Defense League. I was assigned the unenviable job of transporting you to the High Council."

"You don't seem too happy about it."

"That's because this assignment is a waste of my ability."

"What is your normal role, Captain?"

He gave her a wicked grin. "I hire out my services."

"Is that so? What kind of services do you mean?" she asked, not responding to the sexual innuendo in his tone.

Teir focused his attention ahead. They'd entered a new star system and approached a large copper-colored planet. He punched a code into the computer and took over the steering column, guiding the ship around the planet's edge.

"I'm a troubleshooter," he replied after he'd completed the maneuver. "When the Defense League doesn't need me, other people pay me to solve their problems."

"What if I paid you more to take me home? I'll double your usual fee, whatever it is."

Teir shot her a disdainful glance. "No way, *princess,*" he said, using the title she would assume after her marriage. "The High Council has summoned you, and it's my job to deliver you to them."

"You don't have to reveal that you found me. Make up some excuse," Sarina begged.

His voice hardened. "Forget it. You're not going anywhere except to your wedding."

"Then you won't mind if I explore your ship since I'm stuck here for a while." She rose, her gaze noting the outline of a doorway on the opposite side from the escape hatch. Hustling in that direction, she ignored his warning grunt.

"Come back here," he said, annoyed by the inconvenience she was causing him.

He unstrapped his harness and stood, but she'd already ducked through to the next passageway.

****

Sarina found herself in a series of rooms that opened into each other, storerooms and gunnery lockers from the looks of them. At the sound of Teir's footsteps behind her, she glanced wildly around and grabbed a hefty rod-shaped object from a pile of tools on a shelf just as he raced through the hatchway.

"Don't come any closer or I'll brain you." She waved the object threateningly in the air. It was so heavy she could barely lift it, but she put on a brave front and faced him.

Teir took a step in her direction. "We're nearing the Yxon asteroid belt. I have to guide the ship. Stop this foolishness immediately." His tone was icy, his eyes furious.

"No! I want to go home."

He shrugged. "You've sealed your fate. I'm going to lock you up for the duration of the voyage."

"Over my dead body."

"Over your *unconscious* body, maybe."

Sarina swallowed a large lump in her throat. Her arm ached, and she couldn't hold the heavy rod much longer. She doubted she could swing it effectively to hit him anyway, but it was the only weapon she had.

"Will you stop waving that blasted electrifier around? It's dangerous."

Sarina lifted her chin. "Stop giving me orders. Turn this… this vessel back the way we came and take me home."

"You leave me no choice," Teir sighed. Setting his jaw, he pounced.

Sarina swung the rod, but Teir easily sidestepped the blow and chopped her forearm with the side of his hand. A sharp pain stung her below the elbow. The weapon fell from her numbed fingers and clattered to the floor.

He caught her by the wrists and forced her backward toward one of the cabins. As he shoved her around the corner, her braid loosened and her long hair came tumbling down.

"Inside," Teir commanded, his eyes glittering.

Sarina clung to the wall. He pressed his body against hers, trying to force her in the direction he wanted her to go. Her breathing shortened as she struggled, wrestling with him in the doorway. His thighs were muscular and strong, and he used them to push her sideways. She felt herself helplessly sliding.

The ship jerked, and she stumbled to the floor. He fell on top of her, pinning her down. With her skirt raised halfway above her hips, and her limbs tangled with his, she became acutely aware of his growing bulge against her legs.

Fury surged through her as she glared up at him. "Get off me."

"Look, princess," Teir said, "I never asked for this assignment. It's time you and I—"

Boom! Something impacted the ship. The hull shuddered, and another deafening *boom* followed.

Cursing, Tier rolled off her and sprang to his feet.

"What was that?" She followed suit, rising to face him.

"We're under attack. Stay here." He turned toward the cockpit, but just as he cleared the archway, a blast hit the ship. The area in front of him exploded.

Sarina screamed, throwing her arms up to protect herself as a cascade of fiery debris rained down.

Teir crumpled to the floor. When the ship stopped shuddering, she rushed to his side. Blood seeped from a jagged wound on his arm. His face was ashen, pinched with pain.

"Oh, my God." She stared at him as reality hit.

He'd been telling the truth.

She had left the planet Earth far behind. Everything she had ever known was gone. She was alone in a spaceship with a strange man, and hostile alien forces were attacking them.

"There are medical supplies on that shelf," Teir said, pointing. His finger trembled, and she wondered what she would do if he passed out.

"Get this blasted jumpsuit off me," he told her. "Hurry, I have to get to the controls."

Another thump racked the ship, and Teir ripped at his sleeve in his impatience. He stopped with a groan.

"Lie still," Sarina said. "Your wound needs to be treated."

She knelt beside him and tugged at the form-fitting material until his upper torso was bared. Her gaze swept over his massive shoulders, then down to the dark tangle of hair on his broad chest. The hair tapered and disappeared at his waistline. A warm flush crept up her face as she stared.

"Don't get shy on me now, princess." Teir's dark eyes bored into her.

Fortifying herself with a deep breath, Sarina yanked the jumpsuit down below his hips—and gasped. Dear God, he was naked.

"Stop gawking," he snapped. "My regular clothes are in the master cabin. You can get them after you dress the wound." He kicked the jumpsuit the rest of the way off by himself.

"Aye, aye, sir," Sarina retorted, saluting. Rising, she went to retrieve the medical supplies.

As Teir barked out instructions, she cleansed and dressed his wound. Part of her responded to what he was saying, and part of her tried to assimilate all that was happening. She still couldn't believe the spacecraft was real, until another shuddering *whump* reminded her they were under attack. A pungent odor remained in the air from the previous explosion.

When she'd finished bandaging him, Teir stumbled naked

into the cockpit while Sarina went to get his clothes. The sight on the viewscreen stopped him cold. Poised in space was a huge cigar-shaped vessel, its deadly weapons turrets aimed at his ship.

"By the corona, it's Cerrus Bdan," Teir muttered. A sinking feeling hit him as he realized he was facing his old foe. What rotten luck. Even if he didn't believe in the legend of the Great Healer, his mission was to deliver Sarina to the High Council, and Bdan's untimely appearance could put quite a crimp in those plans.

His jaw clenched as he thought about how he might have taken more pleasure from her touch on his skin. But there was no time for such indulgent thoughts now, thanks to his adversary.

He dropped into the pilot's seat and punched in the code to activate the ship's defenses. He should have done it before, but he'd been too distracted by Sarina. Now it was too late. The console refused to respond, and his shields remained offline.

"Blast." His fingers moved over the controls, but before he could activate a backup system, a flash erupted from Bdan's vessel and another resounding *boom* rocked his ship. One thought consoled Teir. If Bdan wanted to blow them out of space, he would have done it already. The smuggler obviously wanted them alive.

"What's happening?" Sarina asked, rushing in with his clothes in her arms.

She dropped them on his lap, averting her gaze from his nakedness to look at the viewscreen. Her eyes widened when she saw the armed vessel poised in front of them.

"Our main tangent beams are out," Teir explained as he stood to put on his pants and vest. "The laser cannons won't fire, and we've lost maneuvering ability." He glanced at her, his face expressionless. "We're defenseless. We have to wait for their terms."

"Terms?" Sarina's voice cracked. She stared at Teir as he fastened his trousers. The hip-hugging black pants and leathery vest were all that he wore. With a fresh white bandage around his muscular arm, a dark shadow at his jaw, and his unruly midnight hair, he made a rakishly handsome picture.

Teir seem unaware of her appraisal as he took his seat. "Cerrus Bdan owns that ship. He's waiting for our surrender. We're lucky, princess—we could have been dead by now." While there was still time, he keyed a message and transmitted it on subspace radio using a prearranged code.

"The stinking buzzard isn't even allowing us to negotiate." A shuttle had just cleared the enemy vessel and was turning in their direction. "I should have known Bdan wouldn't give us any options, especially not where I'm concerned. They're coming for us."

"Who is he?" Sarina asked.

"Cerrus Bdan is a notorious smuggler who deals in the slave trade. We haven't exactly been on friendly terms." Teir had disrupted a number of Bdan's illicit runs, and the smuggler had a grudge against him. "It's unfortunate he caught up with me just now."

"Will he kill you?" Her brow furrowed with concern. Not that she cared about the man, Sarina told herself, but he was her only protection.

Teir shrugged casually in response. He was more worried about what Bdan might do to her. Sarina's silky blond hair floated about her shoulders like spun gold. With her porcelain complexion, large smoky eyes, and full trembling mouth, she was more than pleasing. Add to that her curvaceous assets he'd felt earlier, and she'd bring a high price in the slave market.

Of course, Cerrus Bdan might decide to keep her for himself. Teir was fully aware of the smuggler's cruelty to his female slaves, and Bdan might take particular delight in tormenting Sarina if he thought she belonged to his old enemy.

Thrusting that unpleasant thought aside, he said, "There's no point in resisting. We'll plot our escape once we're on board their vessel." He only hoped that the plan he'd already set in motion would work without a hitch.

"What? You're just going to sit there and let them take us?" Sarina asked. If he didn't care about himself, the least he could do would be to fight for her freedom. "What kind of defense is this of your future… your future—" She couldn't remember what her title would be once she'd married Lord Whoever.

"Princess," Teir supplied. "Now listen carefully. Say nothing about yourself, or about why I brought you here. Let me do the talking, understand?"

Sarina nodded, and the anxiety in his expression made her fear increase. Before she could reply, a bump jostled their ship as the enemy shuttle docked. Teir rose and nudged her to do the same.

They turned to face the exit portal and whatever fate awaited them.

Chapter Four

The hatch slid open, and a formation of heavily armed troops marched inside. Sarina sucked in her breath. It wasn't the uniforms or even the shooters pointed in their direction that alarmed her. It was the strange blue hue of the soldiers' skin, the doglike appearance of their faces, and the floppy ears.

A husky officer stepped forward, barking out an order. His dark eyes looked small and menacing behind the wide brim of his helmet.

"What did he say?" Sarina asked, not really expecting an answer. The alien's voice was a harsh growl, and to her the sounds were meaningless and jumbled.

"He said we are to come with him to Bdan's ship."

"You speak their language?"

"No, I wear a linguist patch. It translates any of the known sentient languages." He pointed to his temple where she could see a slight scar. "You'll have to get one implanted. I didn't think of it before. Your disability could be an inconvenience to us."

She started to respond, but the officer—whose face resembled a vicious bulldog, she thought—snapped a few sounds that made Teir stiffen beside her. Touching her elbow, he urged her forward.

"Now what?" Sarina's voice trembled.

"He says he'll be more than happy to roast us for dinner if we don't do as we're told."

She gasped. "Would they really *eat* us?"

"Probably not, although cannibalistic tribes still exist on

their planet in the more remote areas. Bdan is a harsh taskmaster, however, and he wouldn't appreciate their doing away with us. He has something far more interesting in mind, I'm sure."

The alien soldiers flanking them, Sarina and Teir were marched through the airlock into the waiting shuttle. Standing beside Teir, Sarina tried to control her fear as the uniformed figures spoke in harsh, guttural tones.

A short time later, they entered Bdan's spacecraft. Although Sarina quaked inside, Teir appeared unconcerned, his stride long and his shoulders squared. Dear God, Sarina thought, how did he remain so calm?

In reality, Teir was worried as hell. As they headed down a long, utilitarian corridor, he wondered what Bdan had in store for them. He needed time to give his escape plan a chance to hatch.

They approached a set of double doors that hissed silently open at their approach. The officer of the guard barked a few commands, and Teir indicated to Sarina that they were to enter. Better they should separate, he thought, so Bdan wouldn't think she was his woman. Unable to explain his reasoning aloud, he strode past her, ignoring the look of surprise and dismay on her face.

"Well, if it isn't my old friend," Teir drawled, approaching the large figure seated on a dais. His peripheral vision assessed the number of attendants inside the chamber. The room was ringed with them.

The corpulent smuggler looked up from the naked slave girl he was fondling on his lap. She was humanoid and could have been obtained from any one of the pirate's illegal raids on Coalition vessels. Teir tightened his mouth to repress his rage.

"Captain Reylock. A gr-r-reat pleasure it is to gr-r-reet you again." Bdan's beady eyes shifted to Sarina who'd followed close behind. "And you br-r-ring with you such a lovely companion."

Sarina stiffened, not understanding his words but getting the gist of his meaning. Never had she seen a being so gross. With his bluish skin, hanging jowls, and large bulbous nose, Cerrus

Bdan reminded her of an ugly bloodhound. Even the sounds coming out of his mouth were a mixture of grunts and snorts.

"She doesn't understand you, Bdan," Teir said. "The Earthwoman lacks the linguist patch."

"Easily can we r-r-remedy that." Bdan rumbled his *r*'s with a guttural tone that made him even more unattractive to Sarina. She tried to keep her expression neutral as he pushed away the slave girl and beckoned with his finger for her to approach.

At an almost imperceptible nod from Teir, Sarina moved slowly forward until she was close enough to the fat smuggler to smell his foul breath. She cringed as he ran a stubby finger along her cheek. Turning his head, Bdan snapped out an order. A short-legged attendant whom Sarina thought resembled a dachshund waddled out of the room.

She glanced fearfully around, surprised by the luxuriously decorated chamber. The silken drapes and plush furnishings were in bright rainbow colors, but they didn't cheer Sarina. She could very well end up like that girl who was trying to slink off, unnoticed.

Bdan noticed the slave's movements and he let out a series of high-pitched barks that froze her in her tracks. An angry purplish blotch suffused Bdan's face as he screamed invectives at her. The girl looked terrified.

Sarina didn't dare move, but she felt Teir come up behind her. "What's the matter?" she whispered.

"He didn't give her permission to leave."

One of the uniformed guards withdrew an ominous-looking rod from his belted tunic. The girl shrieked and turned to run. The guard pointed the object at her. A crackling beam shot out, striking her in the back. She slammed against a wall and slithered to the floor. The guard strode forward, firing repeatedly as she writhed in agony. When she finally went limp, Bdan ordered her removal.

"Is she dead?" Sarina rasped, her throat so dry she could scarcely breathe. She'd recognized the rod-shaped object. It was similar to the one she'd picked up to use against Teir, the thing he'd called an electrifier.

"Probably," he responded, but shut up when he felt Bdan's glowering attention return to them. The dachshund-like attendant reentered the chamber, and after a rapid verbal exchange with his master, he headed toward Sarina.

"What's he doing?" she asked Teir, her voice rising in fear.

"Don't worry," Teir replied, knowing what was coming next but powerless to prevent it. This method was crude, but it would work.

As the dachshund approached, Sarina saw he held a tiny rectangular object in his hand. He grasped her arm and yanked her close. She cried out as he grabbed a handful of her hair and jerked her neck back at an awkward angle. He pressed the object against her temple. A loud snapping noise rang in her ears, followed by a blinding pain in her head.

The attendant released her, and after a few seconds, the discomfort passed.

"W-what just happened?" she asked, her tone tremulous.

"You have r-r-received the linguist patch," Bdan stated. "Now can we communicate. Aware am I of the reason for Captain Reylock's escort, your r-r-royalness. But the truth he may not have told you." The smuggler's dark eyes gleamed as he glanced at Teir. "The captain usually pursues his own agenda. Fortunate are you that I intercepted his ship."

A sly smile curved Bdan's mouth as he regarded Sarina. "Together shall we dine. Then can we discuss your disposition."

Teir smothered a curse. So Bdan knew her identity. There could be only one way the smuggler had found out. Someone from Defense League headquarters had leaked the information. No wonder Bdan had intercepted him so easily. Teir only hoped the rest of his plan hadn't been screwed up, or they'd really be in trouble.

Did Bdan intend to ransom Sarina to the High Council? Other than settling the score between the two of them, Teir couldn't see how else he would stand to gain.

"Bring him forward," Bdan barked, pointing at Teir.

Two husky guards grasped Teir's arms, ignoring his stifled groan of pain when one of them clamped a hand around his bandaged wound.

"I can walk, you animals." He twisted to free himself, but the movement only aggravated his wound, so he swallowed his pride and stopped struggling.

"Wounded in my attack, were you?" the smuggler said with glee. "Do not worry. Fix you we will… after you answer a few questions. Then have I other plans for you." His jowls quivered, and drool formed at the corner of his lip. "Looking forward to this have I been for a long time, Captain. I hope you decide to resist so we can prolong your interrogation. Take him below," he ordered the two goons.

"Hey, wait a minute," Teir protested, seeing the look of terror come over Sarina's face. But he was hauled through the doors before he had a chance to reassure her. He wasn't sure he could have done so with any confidence. The cards being dealt them were stacked in Bdan's favor. He only hoped Sarina could come up with a trump card.

As Sarina watched Teir being dragged away, she felt utterly lost. How could she defend herself against this repulsive creature? She turned to stare at the smuggler who observed her with a leer.

"What do you want from me?" She thrust her chin forward, hoping she sounded more confident than she felt.

Bdan gave a slight bow, making his pumpkin-colored caftan swish at his feet. "Your r-r-royalness, we wish only to please. Prepared have I proper quarters for you to refresh yourself and change into more appropriate attire. Then shall we dine together."

He clapped his hands, and an elderly female appeared. She must be from another species, Sarina noted. Her bent humanoid form was covered by a thin coating of a filmy substance. As she moved, her face shimmered. She wore a coarse sack-like garment.

"Come," the woman said in a flat tone. Sarina obeyed, following her through an adjacent room, then to a lift.

On a lower deck, Sarina was shown into a sumptuous dressing room. "A bath has been prepared for you, my lady," intoned the slave. The expression in her pale yellow eyes was vacant, making Sarina wonder if she were drugged.

"What are Bdan's plans regarding Teir and myself?" The smuggler might be giving her the royal treatment, but she didn't trust him. Surely there was more to his purpose in holding her than he let on.

The woman gave her a blank look. "The master honors you, my lady." She selected a gown from a large wardrobe and held the fabric up against Sarina's skin. "This suits your coloring."

"It's beautiful." Sarina fingered the silken material. The diaphanous gown was a vibrant tangerine interwoven with silver threads. It had a laced bodice, long sleeves, and a flowing skirt. Recalling the slave girl, Sarina could just imagine Bdan undoing those laces and putting his paws on her breasts. The thought made her shudder.

"I'd rather wear my own clothes, thank you," she said, thrusting the dress back into the older woman's hands.

The slave's expression hardened. "You will put this on after you are cleansed. Your water cools. Need you assistance?"

"Where is Teir?"

Receiving no response and realizing the woman was not going to budge until she bathed, Sarina stepped behind the partition indicated and quickly disrobed. She had to admit the warm water in the sunken bath felt good once she'd immersed herself. She hadn't realized how grimy she'd become since leaving her office.

Her office. God, that seemed ages ago. Was Robert worried about her? Was he trying to find out where she'd gone?

Tears sprang into her eyes. All that was familiar was gone. She was trapped in a strange place among hostile aliens. How was she ever going to get back home?

She sank deeper into the soothing water until it reached her chin and closed her eyes, letting her imagination bring Robert's comforting face into view. But it wasn't her fiancé's visage that appeared. It was Teir's. Somehow she had to help him.

"It is getting late, my lady." The slave woman stepped around the partition and lifted Sarina's clothes from the floor.

"How do I dry myself? I don't see any towels."

"You have merely to get out." The woman's shimmering features shifted, as though a hint of a smile had appeared, before she went into the dressing room beyond.

Sarina stepped out of the bath and waited. Instantly, the walls and floor began to glow. A pulsating vibration started, and her body warmed as waves of radiant energy washed over her. Seconds later, the vibrations stopped, and the stones went cold. As she looked down, Sarina saw that she was completely dry. Since she was also completely naked, she called out, "Excuse me, I need my clothes back."

"In here," the woman's voice commanded.

Sarina walked around the barrier, to find the slave holding up the tangerine gown. Her own clothes were nowhere in sight, and neither were her undergarments.

Having no choice, she allowed the woman to dress her. The silken material covered her down to her ankles, but it was so transparent she was sure Bdan would be able to see right through it. Naturally, that's probably what he had in mind.

The slave stepped back and studied her. "Suits you, this does. Now will I fix your hair."

She gestured toward a dressing table with a chair. Sarina took a seat, spreading out her gown on the carpeted floor. She watched in a mirror as the slave combed the hair back from her forehead and fastened it with jeweled clips, the rest cascading over her shoulders.

"The master will be pleased, but we need to add color to your lips," the woman said, examining her handiwork. She rummaged in a drawer and handed Sarina some cosmetics.

Sarina applied the makeup unwillingly. The last thing she wanted to do was attract the lascivious attention of that old dog.

As it was, she felt like a lamb being offered up for slaughter. She closed her eyes while the woman sprayed her with perfume. Her only hope was that Bdan would truly treat her as royalty. To that end, she'd have to play up the legend for all it was worth.

As she tried on the soft shoes the woman gave her, Sarina had a fleeting vision of Teir locked in a cell, his body sweaty and unwashed, his arms chained to a wall. Maybe they were torturing him even now. The idea filled her with horror. She shook her head to clear the vision, but it remained. She wanted so much to help him, but dear God, what could she do?

Cerrus Bdan waited for her in a room designed as a dining hall. An oblong table made from a white marble material was set for four. Crystals mounted on the walls provided a soft, muted light, while billowing purple and gold ceiling drapes added color. Gold glittered from the serving pieces to the tableware. Bdan sat on a throne-like chair at the far end of the table.

"Enter," Bdan commanded when Sarina hesitated in the doorway. He had changed his outfit and was resplendent in an olive military uniform, complete with rows of decorations.

Sarina lifted her chin and strode forward, then halted several feet from the smuggler.

"Come closer," Bdan said, his beady eyes gleaming. Drool ran down his chin as he leered at her. "The dress becomes you, it does."

"Are you expecting other guests?" she asked in a calm tone, while panic fluttered in her chest at his lascivious perusal.

Bdan leaned back against his cushioned chair, never once removing his eyes from her. "Arrf," he acknowledged. A side door opened, and an incongruous pair entered. His gaze shifted to rake them both. "Allow me to introduce my *gima*. This is Ava Bet."

A tall, stately female dressed in a shimmering jade gown nodded at Sarina, a look of displeasure on her face. She was heavily made-up, her green eyes rimmed in black. Her auburn hair writhed about her head as though it was alive. Her other, more unusual attributes were the four arms she sprouted, two from each side. Her twenty long, claw-like fingernails were polished in black.

Sarina could guess Ava Bet's function, which accounted for the *gima's* irritation at Sarina's presence.

"And this is Lieutenant Otis, my executive officer." Bdan indicated the uniformed creature beside Ava Bet. He, too, was humanoid in shape, but there the resemblance ended. His face was lizard-like and cold. Harsh onyx eyes glared at Sarina without even a nod of acknowledgment.

"Be seated," Bdan said, and as though by hidden signal, attendants appeared to wait on them.

Sarina sat opposite Ava Bet who stared at her, a low growling noise coming from her throat. Sarina folded her hands in her lap and waited.

"Tell me," Bdan roared at her, "how came you to be aboard R-R-Reylock's vessel."

Sarina jumped at the loudness of his tone. "Teir—Captain Reylock—came to my office and I went with him, thinking we were going to see my boss."

"Once on board his ship, did you not try to escape? Or were you already aware of the prophecy?"

Three pairs of eyes centered on her. Sarina decided to be honest. "I was not aware of it until Captain Reylock told me," she said quietly.

"Had no notion, did you, that you were the legendary Great Healer?"

"No." She lowered her gaze to her plate and the weird concoction that looked like worms squiggling on a bed of blue rice. She tightened her mouth as her stomach heaved and bile rose in her throat.

"And now?" Bdan persisted.

She wondered at the smuggler's probing questions. He glared at her eagerly as though he hoped she would make a mistake. No doubt he lusted to add her to his collection of slaves, she thought in despair. How could she get out of here to help Teir when she was trapped?

"The High Council wishes to wed me to Lord—um, Lord—" Sarina couldn't remember his name.

"Lord Cam'brii," Bdan concluded. "According to legend, fall in love with this nobleman you must in order for your power to be activated. Tell me about this power, your r-r-royalness. How does it work?"

Sarina looked him straight in the eye. "I have no idea. I don't understand how I was identified as this healer in the first place."

"The Auricle in the Great Hall glowed with the fire as it was predicted. An answering light came from Earth. From you, Sarina Bretton. So was I informed."

"Ah." Sarina nodded as though she understood. In truth, she didn't understand anything except that she wanted desperately to go home. She wanted to be with Robert, to return to familiar surroundings with normal people. Inside, she cried out for this to be a horrible dream. But it wasn't, and she was here, facing these repugnant aliens all by herself.

"Where is Teir?" she asked.

"Captain Reylock is being interrogated," stated Lieutenant Otis.

Throughout the conversation, he'd been staring at her, his expression unreadable. Ava Bet, on the other hand, was trying to pretend disinterest by noisily slurping her food.

"We are trying to determine Reylock's purpose in abducting you," the executive officer commented. He'd barely touched his food, Sarina noticed.

"Teir said he was ordered to—" Sarina stopped, biting her lip. Perhaps some of the information he'd given her was confidential.

"Take you to the High Council?" the lieutenant scoffed. "Told you this, he did. But what would he stand to gain?"

"For that matter, what do you want with me?" she asked point-blank.

Bdan spoke, ignoring her question. "Serves his own

ambitions, Captain Reylock does. He has r-r-raided my ship numerous times with his scurvy crew. Stole my cargo and sold it for profit. A thief, he is."

Sarina frowned. She wouldn't put it past Teir to do as Bdan said, but what other plans could he possibly have had for her? He seemed sincere about taking her to wed Lord Cam'brii.

"I want to go home." She addressed Bdan, who was stuffing his mouth with a green leafy food. "Maybe you can help me."

"An excellent idea," purred Ava Bet, taking an interest in her for the first time. She flashed Sarina a feline smile. "Why don't we just take her back where she came from?" she suggested, turning to Bdan and raising a hopeful eyebrow.

Bdan growled, "Not possible."

"Why not? Because your plans are every bit as traitorous as Reylock's?"

Bdan's blue face purpled and he rose in anger, knocking his chair over in the process. "Be silent! Overstep your boundaries, do you. I'll have your *mzips*—" he pointed at her writhing hair "—yanked out and served in my soup if you don't guard your tongue."

Ava Bet's expression turned sullen. "Then excuse me, my lord master. My appetite has suddenly vanished." With a swish of her skirts, she rose and left the room.

"Ar-r-r-r," Bdan snarled, turning his narrowed gaze on Sarina.

A rush of fear constricted her throat. But before she could find out what he intended, she became aware of a sudden silence. The engine noise had ceased along with the sensation of movement. What was going on?

Chapter Five

An armed guard rushed into the dining room and halted in front of the Souk commander. He offered a brisk salute.

"Report," Bdan snapped.

"Defense League forces have surrounded our ship, master leader. We are caught in a tractor beam. Demanding our surrender, they are."

"Find us, did they? How?" Bdan asked his subordinate.

Lieutenant Otis, who had risen, gave a snort. "You might ask your prisoner that question."

The corpulent smuggler glared at him. "Go to Security Level Six and ask him yourself." He pointed to Sarina. "Confined to your quarters are you."

At a hidden signal, the slave woman appeared to escort her out.

Like hell I'm going to my quarters, Sarina thought. This was her chance to free Teir. Security Level Six, huh?

Lieutenant Otis proceeded down the corridor while Sarina followed the warden to the lift. She kept a docile expression on her face, but inside her thoughts somersaulted. Somehow, she had to elude her guard. Then she had to find out where Security Level Six was located.

Then again, this ship's computer seemed to respond to voice commands. As long as authorization wasn't required, she should be able to get where she had to go.

She glanced down at her tangerine gown. It would be easier to move around if she could change into more practical clothing. These soft shoes weren't made for running, either. As her gaze lifted to regard the older woman, the glimmer of an idea dawned. By the time they reached the residential deck, she'd formulated a plan.

"Enter," the warden ordered, thumbing her into the same sumptuous chamber as before.

Stepping inside, Sarina noticed an inner door that hadn't been open earlier but now stood ajar. It led to an adjacent bedroom. Was there an exit from that room as well?

Pretending to be fatigued, she sat on the bed, trying the overly fluffy mattress. It appeared this suite had only one entrance through the dressing area. An odd arrangement, but given Bdan's predisposition for fondling nude females, she wasn't surprised he placed more emphasis on dressing or the lack of it.

"I'm terribly thirsty," she said to the female, who had taken a rigid stance in the archway between the two rooms.

A flash of sympathy showed in the woman's eyes. "Fatigued you must be. I'll get you a *sedit* beverage."

"What's that?"

"A drink to help you relax." The woman moved across the bedroom to an alcove by the wall. She punched in a code on the raised panel beside it. "Every stateroom on the ship has a fabricator unit like this one," she explained. "It can synthesize over three thousand foods with choices for different species."

"Why don't you order a drink for yourself?" Sarina suggested. "The air is so cool in here. Your throat must be dry."

She peered around the room, her gaze noting a piece of artwork. The rose-colored onyx pyramid sat on an accent table. It had a pointy tip and looked weighty enough for her purposes.

This was her chance, while the woman was occupied.

She slid off the bed and sauntered toward that side of the room. When a glance told her the warden wasn't paying attention, she grabbed the pyramid by its top and rushed at the slave with the flat side held outward. Sarina smashed her on the head, the crack upon impact making her wince. The woman crumpled silently to the ground.

Sarina dropped her makeshift weapon and knelt. She hadn't

hit the slave too hard, had she? She hadn't meant to kill the poor thing, just knock her out for a while. Risking a precious moment to feel the slave's pulse, she was glad to feel a strong beat.

She set about pulling off the woman's drab, sack-like garment. She'd determined that dressing as a slave would be a good disguise. With a grimace of distaste, she slid the coarse fabric over her head, only to see the tangerine gown peeking out from underneath.

Her dainty slippers would be a dead giveaway, too. Kicking them off, she decided to go barefoot. Then she remedied the other problem by tucking the silken gown up high under the slave robe where it wouldn't show.

Fortunately, no one was in the corridor when she tiptoed outside. She hastened to the turbolift and pressed the call button.

"Security Level Six," she ordered the computer once she was inside.

The turbolift shot downward, whisking her first vertically and then horizontally. She'd been afraid the computer might not respond to her, or that it would sound an alarm at her unfamiliar voice. Also, a special clearance might have been required for entry to the security level, but so far, her luck was holding out. She wondered if the computer would provide any other information. It couldn't hurt to ask.

"Is there a schematic available for this destination?"

A wall lit up with an illuminated diagram of the security sector. She peered at it closely, memorizing the details. There were six clusters of detention cells, each centered around a command quadrangle that featured guard stations, surveillance monitors, a staff lounge, and an armory. The turbolifts stopped right in front of each quadrangle. How would she get past the guards?

"Ah, computer, is there a rear entrance into the security level, by any chance?"

"That information is not available," came the toneless reply.

So, she was left with a dilemma. Sarina was still puzzling

how to solve it when the turbolift came to an abrupt halt, and the door slid open. Facing her was the command center for Detention Block Six, and it bustled with armed guards.

When she emerged, one of them detached himself from the group and strode over to her. His uniform was different from the others, and she assumed he must be the officer in charge.

"What are you doing here, *sumi?*" he asked, casting her a look of suspicion mixed with disapproval. His dog face wasn't hidden by a helmet, and his fierce features reminded Sarina of a bull terrier.

She wondered nervously what he thought about her appearance. Her bare feet might not be unusual for a slave, but her made-up face might arouse suspicions. At least she'd had the foresight to remove the jeweled clips from her hair. It hung loose, and she bowed her head so that long strands of hair shielded her face.

"The fabricator units in other sectors have been malfunctioning. I've been sent to check the ones down here." She slumped her shoulders in a subservient posture.

"Why was I not notified? Let me see your identification."

She fumbled inside a pocket. Something cold and hard met her touch. It was a rectangular object, like the one Teir had held in the elevator at her office building when they'd soared off into space. She handed it over.

The officer scanned the device. Then he looked at her again and frowned. "Verify your orders with my superior, will I. Wait here." He gave her back the card and marched away.

Left alone, she surveyed the area. None of the guards were looking her way. Her gaze swept to the other end of the command center. The beginning of the detention block stretched from there. How would she be able to tell which cell was Teir's? Would he be inside, or was he being interrogated elsewhere?

She didn't have time to consider her next move because a loud claxon clanged throughout the ship. "All stations, prepare for hostile boarding," announced the computer's disembodied voice.

The guards moved in a flurry of activity, and Sarina realized this was her chance. Keeping her head lowered, she shuffled around the command center to the other side. No one stopped her when she entered the detention block. Row after row of identical steel doors met her gaze. A wave of helplessness washed over her as she regarded them. Now what?

She reached an intersection and halted, unable to decide which way to go. Someone emerged from a cell off to her right. Startled, she recognized Lieutenant Otis, Bdan's executive officer.

Before he could spot her, she dashed down the hall to the left, rounded a corner, and hugged the wall. Booted footsteps stomped her way, changing direction at the last moment. She waited until the sounds receded before letting out a breath of relief.

Her knees shaking, she scampered down the corridor toward the cell Otis had just vacated. She remembered he'd been sent to question Teir, so hopefully the captain would be inside. But as she faced the massive door, her stomach sank. How did it open? She didn't discern a lock or a handle. She ran her fingers around the edges of the door but felt nothing unusual.

"Teir, are you in there?" she called. No response. The door was probably too thick for him to hear her.

Shouts came from the guard station, and Sarina froze. But after a breathless moment, she realized no one headed her way. The commotion must be due to the imminent boarding by Coalition forces. Turning her attention back to the door, she focused on a way to unlock it.

A sudden loud click resounded, and the door moved ajar as though a magnetic lock had been released. Or maybe Otis had been in such a hurry that he hadn't adequately shut it. In any event, Sarina didn't stop to count her blessings. She shoved the door wide open.

Teir was inside, stretched out on a cot, his eyes closed. He didn't seem any the worse for wear, but when she softly called his name, he twisted sideways with a groan.

She rushed over to him. "Are you hurt? I've come to rescue you."

His eyes snapped open, and he gave her a sardonic grin. "Well, aren't you a welcome sight. Then again, you don't look so great. What did they do to you?"

"This is just a disguise. We need to go if you can stand. The guards are occupied, but they might decide to check on the prisoners if we wait too long."

"What's happening outside?" He got to his feet, wincing as he leaned to one side. His face paled, and she noted a darkening bruise over one cheekbone. A fresh bloodstain marred his bandage. But it seemed to be his leg that bothered him the most.

"Coalition forces have surrounded the ship, or at least that's who Bdan thinks they are," she told him. "We're about to be boarded. Can you walk?"

He raised an eyebrow. "I could probably use some help."

She ignored her quickened heart rate when she put an arm around his waist. His body was as taut and strong as she recalled from rendering him first-aid. The memory brought a flush of warmth to her cheeks.

"My people will be looking for me," Teir explained as they hobbled toward the door. "I arranged for a backup unit to follow our route. When Bdan's ship intercepted us, I sent out a distress signal."

"So that's how the Coalition found us so fast."

"I thought it best not to take chances when I had such an important dignitary aboard." His tone was sarcastic, but his gaze held something more, making Sarina's breath catch in her throat.

"I'm sure Lord Cam'brii will be most grateful," she said, hoping to get a reaction.

He didn't have a chance. Just as they reached the doorway, two guards rounded the corner in the corridor. One cried out a warning shout as both reached for their weapons.

Teir shoved Sarina aside and threw himself into the air in a leaping kick that connected with one guard's nose, and then he punched the other on the downswing. The next minute, he dragged both their bodies in her direction.

"Give me a hand, will you? I've only got one good arm."

"What happened to your injured leg, for which you so desperately needed my support?"

"I had a miraculous recovery." He shoved the guards inside the cell and disarmed them. "Here, take this shooter," he said, tossing her a weapon.

"What? I don't know how to use this thing."

"Don't worry. The sight of you in that sack will stop any guard in his tracks. Seriously, grab hold of the grip like this, and point the energy emitter end forward. Your finger goes on the trigger. The setting should be on number three." He watched to make sure she understood. "Now let's go find my men." Gesturing for her to follow, he entered the corridor.

Sarina followed his lead. "Maybe Bdan was right. He told me you had your own agenda. You let me think you needed my help when you were faking it. Why?"

"I *did* need your help."

"Sure. And were you going to keep pretending if those two goons hadn't shown up when they did?"

A wicked grin lit his face as he halted to regard her. "Probably. Would you like to find out what my next move would have been?"

She lifted her chin. "No, thanks. Please keep your distance, Captain."

"Of course, *princess*. Now we'd better get moving, unless you want to be stranded here."

Panicked cries came from the command center where the enemy troops must have arrived. A thin figure charged around the corner and came to an abrupt halt upon spotting them.

"Sir, I was just coming to free you."

Sarina gaped as Teir and the tall stranger slapped each other on the back in greeting. The other male was humanoid but a different species. A thick tan hide covered his body, what she could see of it beneath his brown tunic and dark pants. His rust-colored hair was cut short.

"Alas, you have been hurt," the stranger observed, noting Teir's bandaged arm.

"Sarina took care of it. Let's move out."

The stranger glanced at her. His jade eyes had a luminous quality she'd never seen before. She looked back at him with interest.

Teir noticed their interchange. "My apologies, I am remiss in my introductions. Ravi, this is our wondrous Great Healer, Sarina Bretton."

Ravi flashed her a grin that lit his face. "*Mira,* it is an honor to greet you," he said, bowing. His voice was low and pleasant and she smiled in response.

"It's nice to meet you, too. You must be one of Teir's crew, I gather?"

Ravi glanced at Teir. "I serve as Captain Reylock's first mate on the *Valiant.*"

"Are there many of you?"

"Mistress?" He frowned, puzzled.

"Are there many crew members on board your ship?" She hadn't given up hope of going home. Maybe she could find a friend among his crew to help convince the captain to return her to Earth.

"You'll meet everyone soon enough," Teir said. "Where's Wren?" he asked the new arrival.

"He's supervising the cargo transfer. I am afraid I have bad news. Cerrus Bdan jettisoned away in a distress pod."

"Blast." Teir knew what that meant. Bdan wouldn't let him rest until he evened the score. Later, Tier would think about how to meet the smuggler's threat, but right now he had other priorities.

He turned to Sarina. "Come on, it's time to get you aboard the *Valiant.* Wait until you see her. She's nothing like that reconn vessel we were on before."

"Could you give me a ride home?" Sarina suggested

hopefully. Maybe he'd reconsider after this episode that had nearly ended his mission.

Teir gazed at her with a twinge of disappointment. "Your duty lies elsewhere," he said. Then he strode on ahead without another word.

Ravi fell into step beside her as they headed toward the exit. The first mate had a slower gait than Tier, so it was easy for Sarina to keep up with him.

"My cousin Mantra will be thrilled at your arrival. He has long been a believer in the legend. Seeing you, I can say my own doubts are relieved."

Sarina gave him an astonished glance. "How so?"

"I can see it in your eyes, *Mira*. The radiance of the true light is present."

"If you say so." She wondered how many people she was going to disappoint when her so-called power didn't materialize.

They entered the command quadrangle. Bdan's guards were lined up against a wall, disarmed, with their hands folded on their heads. A squad of uniformed Coalition troops held them at bay. One of them, an older officer who appeared to be in charge, snapped Teir a salute.

"Captain, the ship is secure. Our men are on the bridge."

"I understand Bdan has escaped." Teir toggled a switch on the control console. "Bridge," he said into the comm unit. "Lieutenant Rodan, how's the cargo transfer coming?"

"Nearly finished, Captain," came the immediate response. "The *Omnus* was carrying about forty thousand credits worth of calgonite ore. It's being transferred to the *Valiant* as instructed."

"Good. I'm going to take our guest to the *Valiant*. As soon as the transfer is complete, we're leaving."

"And Bdan's crew?"

"Place them under arrest according to regulation forty-two under the Treaty of Kidaren. You'll be responsible for securing the *Omnus* and towing it to the nearest starbase. I'll check in with you later."

"Do you wish to have an escort, sir?"

"No, we'll manage by ourselves. Reylock out." Teir turned to Ravi. "Let's go," he ordered his first mate, gesturing for Sarina to precede him into the turbolift.

She bit her lip and walked in, trying to keep her questions, of which she had many, for later.

The shuttle bay bustled with Coalition troops. Teir found a craft loaded with cargo and ready to go.

"Let's hitch a ride." He indicated the boarding ramp, then glanced at the men hauling ore into the other shuttles. "I'll bet that's not the only cargo Bdan is carrying." He turned to Ravi. "Give me your data link."

At the other's questioning look, Teir explained, "Bdan's guards took mine. And that reminds me—the reconn vessel needs to be returned to starbase also." He gave that order to Lieutenant Rodan, then patched into his crewmate Wren who was busy directing operations in the cargo hold.

"Wren, expand your search and see if you can find another type of cargo on board."

"Such as?" a melodious voice responded, making Sarina curious to meet this other crew member.

"Same thing we've caught him at before."

"I'll check it out," Wren stated. "We'll be back on board *Valiant* within the haura."

"Okay. We're heading over now. Reylock out."

The transfer went smoothly, and soon Sarina found herself aboard the new vessel. Compared to the luxury of Bdan's ship, the *Valiant* seemed austere with utilitarian corridors and metal bulkheads. Tier and Ravi went immediately to the bridge where they took their places in the command chairs.

Sarina stood behind them, staying silent as they flipped switches and punched in computer codes. The viewscreen in front showed Bdan's fat cigar-shaped vessel, the *Omnus*, poised against a backdrop of velvety space. Surrounding it were combat spacecraft with a round insignia she couldn't quite make out but assumed was the symbol of the Coalition.

Teir's ship was unlike any of those sleek, birdlike vessels. She'd gotten a glimpse of it through the shuttle window. The *Valiant* had an A-frame design in the back tapering off to a snub nose in front. Gun ports jutted out from various angles. It looked peculiarly menacing, reminding her of a porcupine.

"What kind of ship is this? It's different from the others," she said.

Teir swiveled in his seat to answer her. "This used to be a freighter, until I—um—acquired her. I've made a number of modifications."

"I see." She didn't, but she was glad to have found a subject to which Teir would respond. "How many crew members are there altogether?" She, Teir and Ravi were alone on the bridge, but other men must be working elsewhere.

"There are six of us to run the ship. Lieutenant Wren is our navigator. You'll meet him soon. He's supervising the cargo transfer from Bdan's ship. Wren is a Polluxite," Teir added with a grin, as though that meant something. "Then there's Datron, who's in charge of engineering and maintenance. Korox is our weapons officer, and Moff'tt handles science and systems control. They're down below."

"Perhaps the lady would like to refresh herself," Ravi suggested in a gentle tone. "Her experience with Cerrus Bdan could not have been pleasant. Have you assigned her a cabin? If not, she is welcome to use mine." His friendly green eyes met hers, and she couldn't help liking him on instinct.

"No, she'll take my stateroom. I'll move in with you." Teir's gaze raked her over, lingering on her legs. "I suppose you'll want to freshen up and change out of that slave outfit."

"Yes, thank you." She acted demure, although inwardly she was seething. He might think they were being kind to her, but this was, in effect, her newest prison.

Teir had made it clear he wouldn't accept any challenge to his authority, nor would he take her home. Sarina's only hope was to ingratiate herself with his crew and sway them to her cause.

So she smiled at him as though eager to comply.

"I'll show you the way," he said, rising. "Ravi, the helm is yours."

Tier strode to the rear of the circular bridge section. A turbolift was on one side and a hatchway on the other. As Sarina reached him, he pointed to a schematic on the wall.

"The *Valiant* has three decks. Level One contains the bridge, crew quarters, and conference lounge. Level Two holds the warp drive and sublight engines and deflector shield generators. Level Three is where we came in from the shuttle bay. It's also where our cargo hold is located." His face radiated pride. "She's tight, but well outfitted."

"I'm impressed," Sarina said. His ship wasn't as luxurious or as large as Cerrus Bdan's, but it suited Teir. Even in the brief time she'd known him, she could tell he didn't care about embellishments. His first devotion was to duty, and it showed in the functionality of his vessel.

It also showed in his attitude toward her. She turned her wide gaze on him. "Please, won't you reconsider and take me home? You've brought me here against my will. I don't know anything about your legends. The Coalition is wrong—I'm not the person they're looking for."

His mouth tightened. "I don't want to hear this again."

"But what about my friends and family? They'll be worried about me, and I miss them already. You can't just take me away."

"But I have, haven't I?" Teir gestured for her to cross the hatchway into a short corridor.

Afraid of making him angry, Sarina obeyed, peeking inside the first room off to the left. It held a long table and six chairs.

"That's our lounge," he said in a flat tone. "It doubles as a mess hall and conference room."

She was glad to see a row of windows lining the outside hull. The room would have been bleak otherwise with its plain gray walls. If he allowed her to come here, she could at least watch the stars while figuring out a way to get home.

"Crew quarters are up ahead." He threw open the first door further down the corridor and stood aside for her to enter. "This is my cabin. You can use it for the duration of the voyage."

"Will it be a long trip?" She wondered how much time she'd have to work on the sympathies of his crew. Getting friendly with them seemed the best course of action, as did learning all she could about this ship. She wasn't going to give up hope, not by a long shot.

"Bimordus Two is twenty-nine-point-four parsecs from this location. We should be there in about eighteen days if we hold maximum speed, and if nothing further interrupts us."

"You don't anticipate more trouble, do you?" she asked, noting the dark look in his eyes.

"I do not." He ended the conversation abruptly and went inside. The cabin was sparsely furnished but comfortable, with a low bunk, a single armchair, and a console with drawers. A compact computer sat on a separate small desk.

"Is that a fabricator unit?" Sarina strode to a recess in the wall and touched the raised panel beside it. "I thought you said the lounge was used as a mess hall."

"We prefer to eat together, but this device can supply all your needs in terms of food, clothing, and other necessities. You merely have to put in a request. Our matrix has a database from hundreds of worlds."

"Good. I can't wait to get rid of this ugly outfit." She began to yank the slave robe over her head.

He stared in astonishment as the coarse robe dropped to her feet, revealing the nearly transparent gown she wore underneath. His gaze traveled to her breasts, then dipped lower. The skirt flared out, seeming to float about her ankles. Her bare feet peeked out from below.

"By the corona, is that what Bdan gave you to wear?"

She stepped back at the fierce expression on his face. "Yes. A female slave brought me to a room to change, and she took my clothes. Later, I took hers." She smirked at the memory.

His fists curled. "I'll make Bdan pay for his crimes. His time is limited. But meanwhile, let's get you something decent to wear." He stalked to the fabricator and punched in numbers on the control panel.

Sarina watched as a shimmering haze descended upon the recess in the wall. The next moment, a pile of clothing, complete with shoes, materialized in the spot.

"Get dressed. I'll see you later," he said in his commanding tone.

He didn't bother to retrieve his personal belongings. Tier rushed out as though he didn't trust himself to be alone with her. Of course, she was probably imagining his reaction. The man wasn't the slightest bit interested in what she wore, other than to have her suitably attired for her presentation to Lord Cam'brii.

She picked up the items from the fabricator. How odd, then, that the captain had made the selection he did.

Chapter Six

Pajamas. That was what the clothes resembled. The loose-fitting black pants and long-sleeved top conjured up images of ancient Chinese peasants toiling in a rice paddy. Why on earth would Teir want her to wear these ugly things?

Frowning, Sarina spread the clothes on the bunk. It seemed to her as though Teir had deliberately chosen this shapeless outfit to make her look unattractive. But why?

An intriguing notion came to her. Perhaps this was a clever ploy on Teir's part to make Lord Cam'brii reject her. If that happened, she could return to Earth and Teir would have fulfilled his duty of delivering her to the High Council. But he'd be helping her at the same time.

Upon further consideration, she decided Teir wouldn't be so considerate. He was too bound by concepts of duty and honor to take any path other than the one assigned to him. In any event, if Cam'brii didn't like her, there was no reason why she wouldn't be paired with another member of the ruling family.

Apparently, the legend didn't specify Lord Cam'brii. It just said her healing power would be activated when she fell in love with a member of the House of Raimorrda. Doubtless there were other eligible males descended from the bloodline who could be mated with her.

But if Captain Reylock hadn't chosen these clothes to make her unappealing, why else had he selected them? Was this what high-born females normally wore in the Coalition? The only other members of her sex she'd seen had been the slaves aboard

Bdan's ship. None of the Coalition troops had been female. What about Teir's crew? She had yet to meet the other three members. For all Sarina knew, she could be the only woman aboard.

That's it! Captain Reylock simply didn't want his crew to be distracted by her feminine charms.

Damn the man. All he thought about was accomplishing his mission. Well, Sarina would decide how she'd dress, whether he liked it or not.

Turning to the fabricator, Sarina frowned. How was she to work the thing?

A loud knock sounded at the door. "Come in," she called.

"Mistress," Ravi greeted her with a friendly smile, "is there anything you require? I was passing on the way to my quarters and thought I would attend to your needs."

Sarina gave him a sweet smile. "I wish to learn how to use the fabricator unit."

"Ah. May I enter?" He cocked his head, awaiting her permission. Once again, she found his warm gaze comforting. Ravi didn't seem in the least surprised to see her in the silky tangerine gown. It was as though he'd accept anything from her because of who she was—or who he wanted her to be.

For the next few minutes, Ravi went over the basic instructions for using the fabricator unit. Each category had its own code. For example, food was preceded by a zero-zero-one prefix. Clothing was zero-zero-two, and so on. Then the requested item was typed in.

"How does it work?" Sarina asked after she'd selected a pair of jeans and a burgundy sweater. She picked them up and placed them on the bed next to the black pajamas. After Ravi left, she'd order some underwear. She was too embarrassed to do that in front of him.

"The method utilizes molecular alteration. If you wish a more complex explanation, you can access the files in our database. The computer responds to voice activation." Ravi ensured that she could initiate commands, then he gave her a stiff bow. "I will leave you now, Mistress. If you require anything further, pray ask the AI—artificial intelligence—to locate myself or the captain."

"Wait." She held up a hand. "Ravi, you know about this legend and the prophecy. Do you really believe it's right to force me into becoming the Great Healer, if it's not what *I* want?"

His luminous eyes chilled. "It is your destiny, Mistress."

"I don't agree with that. My destiny is on Earth, with my friends and family. People need me there. What gives you the right to take me away from everything I've ever known?"

"You will adjust," Ravi replied. "There are others who need you more. I will assist you in any way I can."

"Then tell your captain to take me home."

"That is not possible, *Mira*." And with those words, he left.

Disappointed, Sarina sank onto the bunk and covered her face with her hands. She hadn't met the other crew members yet, but no doubt she'd get the same reaction from them. They were all loyal to their captain and the blasted Coalition. Was no one willing to help her? Was she doomed to be separated from her loved ones forever? As she contemplated never hearing her mother's voice again, tears rolled down her cheeks and despair overwhelmed her.

After a while, her tears gave way to anger. Rage surged within her, giving her new strength. What right did the Coalition High Council have to change her life? On whose authority had she been kidnapped? How dare these faceless individuals interfere with her future.

Standing, she clenched her fists and vowed to find a way out. She'd scan the computer files to see what kind of information was available. If no one aboard this ship was going to help her, she'd have to rely upon herself to come up with a viable plan and learning all she could about her new environment was the first step.

Sarina ordered her underwear and dressed, perversely hoping she'd annoy the captain with her choice of clothing. She'd have to obey his orders until she figured out what to do, so this was the only way she could rebel. Meanwhile, as long as he allowed her access to the ship's database, there was hope.

She became so engrossed in the information the computer offered that she barely felt the vibration indicating their ship was underway. Nor did she hear the knock on her door until it had swung open. She whirled to see Teir facing her on the threshold.

"The crew is eating in the mess hall if you wish to join us," he said, without waiting for her to acknowledge his presence.

Despite her enmity toward him, Sarina had to acknowledge his masculine appeal. His dark hair swept low over his forehead. He'd shaved, and his jaw was taut and angular. Her gaze descended to the clean white shirt he'd put on under his black leather vest. He'd left it open at the collar, giving her a glimpse of a few dark chest hairs.

His glance boldly raked her body in return. She couldn't tell what he thought of the low V-neck of her sweater or the tight fit of her jeans, because his expression gave nothing away.

"I see you've been busy." He sauntered inside her cabin.

His cabin, she reminded herself, as heat rose in her cheeks.

She stood to regard him squarely. "This computer is a gold mine of information."

His gaze focused on her cleavage. "Is it?"

"I've learned a lot."

"I'll bet. You accessed the crew profiles. Did you learn everything about me that you wanted?"

She took a step backward, her heart thumping. "No, I… um… still have some questions."

"Such as?"

He was inches away now, his eyes glittering. Sarina, her throat suddenly dry, moistened her lips. His gaze followed her movements.

"You're from the planet Vilaran," she said in a hoarse tone. "You are human, but there's something special about your people—"

"Yes? And what is that?"

She bit her lower lip, unable to continue. She'd read about their mating instincts. Vilarans were highly sensitized to pheromones, chemicals produced by the body to stimulate sexual response. Once a Vilaran met a member of the opposite sex with a compatible scent, their body chemistries melded, and they joined for life. Staring into Teir's intense blue eyes, she wondered how he had evaded that fate thus far.

"I d-didn't get all the information," she said in evasion.

He smiled, reading the truth in her expression. By the corona, she was alluring in those strange form-fitting clothes, Teir thought. He should be angry that she'd discarded what he'd chosen for her. He'd purposely selected garments that would make him less aware of her feminine attributes. But her feisty independence attracted him even more, dissipating his anger.

He teetered on the brink of kissing her. Her soft, parted lips tempted him, as did the vulnerable expression in her eyes. Teir didn't remember ever feeling such an irresistible urge for a female before, and it confused him. Sarina was from Earth. Such a magnetic attraction should only be for one of his own kind.

Frowning, he stepped back. Regardless of how he felt about her, he'd never made it a habit to toy with another man's possession. Sarina belonged to Lord Cam'brii. Keeping his distance from her was crucial.

Sarina let out a sigh of relief when he moved away. For a moment, she'd thought he was about to kiss her. What was worse, she'd wanted him to. Disgusted with herself, she thrust out her chin and strode through the door. Loud male voices sounded from the lounge, men laughing and talking.

The crew looked up from their seats around the table when Sarina and Teir arrived. An awkward silence fell over the group.

"You already know Ravi," Teir said, gesturing. "This is Lieutenant Wren."

Sarina's mouth dropped open. The Polluxite was large, even bigger than Teir. Liquid hazel eyes were set wide over a straight nose, smiling mouth and firm jaw. His eyebrows were unusual in that they had three lines of color, a white streak between two chestnut layers. A thick thatch of brown hair covered his head. But what really astonished her was the huge pair of wings sprouting from his back.

She gasped at the sight. "Wings! You can fly?"

"No, and I'm sorry if they startled you," Wren replied. He pinched his face, and the wings folded, collapsing into his body.

"Where did they go?" she asked, oblivious to the titters among the others in the room. She walked behind the Polluxite to inspect his back but saw only his shirt with two narrow vertical slits. "Forgive me, I'm being rude."

She felt her face redden, but Wren just guffawed. Teir chuckled, too. Their entertainment at her expense riled her.

"You might have warned me," she snapped at the captain.

"And deprive my men of a good laugh? Your reaction was priceless."

She folded her arms across her chest. "Aren't you going to introduce me to the others?"

"Of course. Datron, Korox, and Moff'tt, this is Sarina Bretton."

She nodded to each one in turn. Datron and Korox appeared humanoid, whereas Moff'tt was small and elfin in shape, with large ears and a wide forehead. He was dressed in a short tunic. White tufts of hair in irregular patches covered his head. He looked so endearing that Sarina couldn't help smiling at him. He grinned back, his small white teeth flashing.

"You can choose your own food from the fabricator," Teir said. "A menu from your home planet has been entered into the basic programming. I hope you'll find something you like."

Sarina's stomach growled at the suggestion, and she realized she was starved. She hadn't been able to touch anything on her dinner plate at Bdan's ship. Standing before the fabricator, she requested a medium-rare steak, French fries, and a soft drink. Her mouth began to salivate as the food materialized.

"Meat," Wren commented, sniffing the aroma. "How barbaric."

Sarina noted his meal consisted of berries and nuts. "You're a vegetarian?" she asked as she took a seat. From the corner of her eye, she watched Teir order his own meal and wondered what he'd chosen.

"Plant food is nature's gift," Wren replied in his melodious voice.

"You may be right, but after the day I've had, I need something more substantial."

She cut into her steak, thinking Wren didn't appear to be undernourished. Maybe he consumed large quantities over the course of a day. That would account for his bulky size.

"What do you have to eat?" she asked Tier with a note of curiosity, after he'd taken a seat beside her. He named some items, then tried to explain what they were to her. She gave up attempting to understand. "Never mind. When I'm in the mood, maybe I'll taste them."

Bending her head over her plate, she tried to hide the sudden tears in her eyes. Everything was so *alien,* even the food. It only intensified her determination to return home, where all was familiar.

Her thoughts drifted to the people she'd left behind. Robert must be frantic, wondering what had happened to her. Mother would call her house. When Sarina failed to respond, she'd be worried to death. And her friends—Good God, she'd almost forgotten about Abby.

Every Sunday, Sarina visited her friend in the convalescent home, and Abby depended upon seeing her. She'd been injured a year ago in an automobile accident. Her legs had been paralyzed, and she was still undergoing rehabilitation. She wasn't expected to regain full mobility, but she looked forward to Sarina's visits as a morale boost.

Lifting her fork with a piece of juicy beef on the tip, Sarina pretended an interest in her food. She'd lost her appetite but knew she had to eat. No matter the cost, she *would* get home. She didn't have only herself to think about. Others relied upon her.

Of course, that was what Ravi had said about the Coalition citizens. What would happen if the legend were actually true? Would she become this Great Healer they all expected? She'd wanted to be a doctor but hadn't pursued a medical career because of her mother's objections. What if this gave her the chance to be a real healer?

Choking down the morsel of meat, she decided she didn't want to find out if it meant marrying a total stranger. No matter how noble he might be, she didn't care for the prospect one bit. All she wanted was to go home.

****

The days passed without further incident. As she got to know the crew better, Sarina recognized the deep respect they had for their commander. Teir remained an enigma to her, his behavior courteous but aloof. Never again did he allow himself to be alone with her, but Sarina didn't let it bother her. She focused on acquiring knowledge that would help her accomplish her goal of returning home.

To that end, she spent hours at the computer terminal in her room, absorbing history lessons and technical data easily processed by her analytical mind.

She questioned each crew member in turn, learning all she could about their roles in daily ship operations. For their part, they seemed to like her. Wary at first, they soon accepted her at face value and included her in their discussions. Moff'tt was funny, with an impish sense of humor that Sarina appreciated. He was always trying to make her laugh. Datron and Korox were the fall guys for a lot of his jokes, but they didn't mind because it relieved the boredom of the mission. Sarina was aware they all thought it was a waste of time—all except Ravi who couldn't seem to do enough for her.

His devotion warmed her heart and made her wish she truly was a healer, especially when she learned of the devastating effects of the plague called the Farg. Ravi told her what little he knew, including horrible tales of death and despair on his home planet of Tendraa. He'd lost contact with his cousin Mantra, who'd been supplying him with news. Ravi feared Mantra had become ill, and he was beside himself with worry.

"If the Liege Lord would ask the Coalition for help, it would improve matters greatly," he explained, seated beside her at the table one day. They were alone, and she sipped a fruit drink while he spoke. "Contact with the Coalition is forbidden on Tendraa except for trade. I can do nothing."

Sarina frowned. "Why is contact forbidden? Isn't Tendraa a full member of the Coalition?"

"Not really. My people are xenophobes—afraid of outsiders. Eons ago, Tendraa was much more technologically advanced than it is now. Trade with other worlds was widespread. We learned of many wonders from other cultures and made great progress, but our people were not prepared for so much so fast.

"A devastating civil war nearly destroyed the planet. The weapons used had been built with the knowledge we'd gained from other worlds. A new government arose from the ashes and decided it was progress that had led to our destruction. As a result, all trade was banned, and all contact with off-worlders was forbidden in order to avoid further contamination."

Ravi shook his head. "In my opinion, the life that ensued has been one of ignorance and suffering. Even now, we live in complete isolation except for the treaty, and that came about because our leaders got tired of smugglers raiding our mineral-rich planet. By making an agreement with the Coalition, trade is restricted and visitors are controlled."

He leaned forward, his expression brightening. "You are our only hope, Mistress, as well as a symbol that progress must occur. Destiny moves on the winds of change, and you are the force behind it. Do it, *Mira*. Show your power to my people and save my world from the Farg and its own oppression."

"How, Ravi? I don't think I'm this savior you're predicting." Sarina trembled at the expectations Ravi and his fellow believers had of her.

"Follow the prophecy. It will come true."

He spoke with such fervor that she wanted to believe him. "I'll do my best." But all she could think about was how in God's name could she aid his people when she couldn't even help herself?

Hoping to relieve the heaviness in her heart, Sarina sought out Teir the next day. Ravi was on the bridge, and she knew Teir was alone in the cabin they shared. She knocked lightly on the door.

"Come in." He leapt from the bunk on which he'd been resting when he caught sight of her. "Oh, it's you. What do you want?"

Sarina's face grew warm. He was bare-chested, and she'd obviously disturbed his rest, but he needn't be so rude.

"May I talk to you for a moment?" she asked, her tone hesitant.

Teir cleared his throat. As soon as he'd seen her outlined in the doorway, his heart had lurched. She looked lovely, her fair hair floating about her shoulders, a wistful expression on her face. She wore a royal blue chemise dress that vividly outlined the contours of her curves. He didn't need her to come any closer—his reaction to her was potent even at a distance.

"Sure. What is it?" he replied.

"I wanted to ask you about Ravi," she said, acutely aware of his proximity. The man seemed to radiate heat. She glanced at his muscled arm. His wound had nearly healed. His biceps bulged under the new pink skin.

Lowering her gaze, she stared at his dark swirls of chest hair. "I wish I could do something to help him and his people. Is there any way you can contact the government on his planet to find out about his cousin Mantra? Ravi is worried about him."

Teir ruffled his unkempt hair. "I've tried, but all communications are out. Our contacts are either dead or they've fled."

"Has anyone from the Coalition gone to assess the situation?"

"It's forbidden unless Tendraa asks for help."

"Couldn't you fly a clandestine mission?"

He stared at her, aghast. "Disobey orders and risk my crew catching the Farg? No way."

"You're no help at all," she snapped in frustration.

He moved forward and grasped her arm. "Don't criticize. You're out of your element here, and you know it."

Sarina twisted in his grip, frightened by his fierce expression. "Be careful how you handle me. I'll be a princess when I marry Lord Cam'brii, remember?" It was an idle threat since she planned to escape before that dreaded event.

"Poor man," Teir commented, rolling his eyes heavenward.

"Aargh!" She struggled to free herself.

He released her. "Why do you torment me?"

"Oh, come on. You've been avoiding me this whole trip. Are you afraid I'll convince you to take me home?"

"You can't convince me to do anything. You're nothing but a mere female."

"Well, this is one woman who's going to make a difference. And I'm going to start right here with your ship." Sarina felt like annoying him, and she knew saying anything disparaging about his spacecraft would do the trick.

"What do you mean?"

"This is the dullest vessel I've ever been on," she said, as though she'd flown in spaceships her whole life. "Nothing but gray everywhere. It needs color."

"Don't you go messing with the *Valiant.*"

"You can't give me orders. I'm not one of your crew."

"While you're on board my ship, you'll do as I say."

"Like hell I will." She saw his eyes darken and his mouth tighten and decided she'd better leave before he retaliated. She spun around and left.

The next day, Sarina conjured up some paints on the

fabricator and began work on one of the bulkheads. The cartoon mural took her several days to complete, but she thought the final effect was worth it—amateurish maybe, but cute. At least Sarina thought so. She grinned when she imagined Teir's reaction. Maybe he'd become so furious that he'd give in and return her to Earth just to get rid of her.

She actually looked forward to his angry response. But to her surprise, Teir took one glance and silently passed by. Disgusting man. At least he could have said *something.*

Still hoping to provoke a reaction from him, she decided to tackle the lounge next. The crew didn't object. Moff'tt even helped her select the colors. While she was painting, Sarina felt a sense of freedom she'd rarely experienced. Her mother had never approved of frivolity.

"You've got too much to learn. Study hard, and don't let your emotions get in the way if you want to succeed," was the refrain Sarina had heard ever since she could remember. Her mother hinted at a family curse that would descend upon her should she let her feelings take control. So she'd gone into law where facts were life and life followed rules—rules her mother approved of, just as she'd approved of Robert.

Now Sarina had no one telling her what to do, except for the captain, and he seemed to prefer ignoring her to confrontation. She kept hoping he would show his disapproval. At least then he'd be speaking to her again. It had been days since he'd uttered a civil word to her. The crew teased her, saying it was because the captain was smitten, but Sarina figured they had it all wrong. The man acted as though she didn't exist. He probably counted the hours until she'd be out of his hair for good.

Chapter Seven

"We're nearing the Bimordus system." Teir's terse announcement rang over the comm speaker one afternoon.

Sarina's heart sank. Nearly three weeks had passed since they'd left Earth, and not once in all that time had she been able to talk anyone into helping her. No matter how often she'd wailed that she didn't want to spend the rest of her life on some strange planet after being married to a man she didn't know, not one of them cared. She was not ready for her so-called destiny and would never accept it.

Her stomach fluttered as she gazed out the main viewscreen from the bridge. Teir and Ravi sat in the command chairs, maneuvering the ship toward a giant brownish globe while Lieutenant Wren worked the navigational console off to the side.

"That's Bimordus Two?" she asked in dismay. "It looks totally desolate."

Teir swiveled in his seat to regard her impassively. "The planet is barren of life. This site was chosen for the centrality of its location."

"What's that huge bubble in the distance?"

"A biosphere. The surface temperature of the planet is too cold for many of our member species, so an artificial atmosphere had to be created."

"Seems to me they could have chosen a friendlier planet somewhere else."

"This serves the purpose of neutrality." Teir eyed her attire. "You might want to change. You'll be presented to the High Council immediately upon our arrival."

"The ship will be landing?" She'd thought they'd take a shuttle down.

"Of course, at the spaceport. Bimordus Two is the location for our central government. There's a lot of traffic," he added in a patronizing tone.

"Is this where Defense League Command is located, too?"

"No." Teir compressed his lips, clearly refusing to say more. Despite her status, Sarina did not have security clearance.

"Will you be staying on Bimordus Two?" she persisted.

Teir shrugged. "Who knows? Depends on our orders." He turned his attention forward. "You'd better get a move on if you want to look presentable. We don't have much time."

Sarina glared at his back. She was damned if she'd change her clothes to please him or anyone else. Her ivory silk blouse and beige slacks were good enough. What did he expect her to wear, an evening gown and tiara?

She combed her fingers through her wispy bangs. She'd French-braided her hair, tired of wearing it loose. She knew Teir liked it down, so she'd done it on purpose to displease him. Now she felt an irresistible urge to annoy him further. She moved closer to his chair, standing behind him and slightly to one side so he could see her from the corner of his eye.

Teir was acutely aware of her presence. Irritated that she hadn't obeyed him and changed her outfit, he deliberately ignored her. It was a strategy that seemed to have worked for most of the trip.

"Activators coming online," he told Ravi, monitoring the automatic landing sequence. Sarina sidled forward for a closer look, her arm brushing his shoulder. Teir felt a jolt of electricity charge through him at her touch.

"Get away," he said. "You're in a dangerous position. If anything should go wrong, you need to be where the automatic restraints can hold you."

"You didn't say that before. You told me to go to my cabin to change."

He refused to be addled by her. "The chairs and bunk in your cabin are equipped with safety restraints should you need them. I suggest you go there immediately."

"I'll stay here, thank you. If anything happens, I'll hold on to you."

Teir gritted his teeth. This female infuriated him. He should give her a lesson she wouldn't forget. He jumped up and grabbed her wrist. "By the stars, do I need to lock you in your cabin?"

Sarina pressed herself up against him. "Why not? You seemed to enjoy it the last time you tried."

He jerked back, releasing her as though he had touched fire. "What are you playing at, woman?" He heard Ravi chuckle and turned toward him. "What's so funny?"

Sarina gave him a sweet smile and turned her back on him. "Let me know when we arrive. Captain. I'll check out the view from the lounge."

Teir stared after her, his body tense. "By the corona, I'll be glad when she's gone."

"Will you?" Ravi raised an eyebrow.

Teir didn't answer. Even though the mission had been successful, he didn't feel his usual exuberance.

****

Ravi came to get her from the lounge. "We have received clearance to disembark," he said as Sarina rose from her seat and approached him. He must have noticed the look of apprehension on her face, because he took her hand and held it gently. "If there is anything I can do for you while we are in port, pray call on me, Mistress."

Sarina gazed into his warm green eyes. "Thank you. And if I hear anything about your cousin, I'll let you know."

"May the faith be with you." Ravi made the sign of a circle, as though he were a priest blessing her. "Captain Reylock will see you off the ship. I regret that I cannot, but I must file our log entry before the rest of the crew can leave."

Letting go of her hand, he bowed deeply. "It has been an honor, *Mira.*" Then he left.

Sarina felt forlorn and alone. Teir's heavy footsteps proceeded down the corridor in her direction. She knew the sound of his steps by now, but instead of brightening her mood, his arrival saddened her more than ever.

"Ready?" he asked, a terse expression on his face.

She swallowed a lump in her throat. Why couldn't he be more friendly at a time like this?

"Yes, I suppose." She lifted her chin, determined to show poise and grace.

"Then let's go."

Sarina strode to the turbolift, her back straight and her head held high. Doubts swirled in her mind like a mist, all but blinding her. What if the High Council rejected her? Even if they did heed her pleas for compassion, would they send her back to Earth, or would they condemn her to some remote outpost where she couldn't reveal the existence of the Coalition to the people on Earth?

Knowing her fate hung in the balance, she stepped inside the lift with a deepening sense of dread.

****

Daimon, leader of the Return to Origins Faction and member of the High Council, adjusted his bulky maroon robe in front of the mirror. In just a few minutes, the woman from Earth would be presented in the Assembly Chamber. Everyone would see for themselves that the legend was a farce when they got a look at her. He should be glad. His movement would gain needed supporters.

Yet instead, Daimon felt doubtful. He stroked his peppery beard, narrowing his eyes. The Believers were strong. Their faith had spread throughout the galaxy, and it might take more than a powerless female to dissuade them. Their unifying force was in direct opposition to the R.O.F. Daimon would have to figure out a plan to counteract their rhetoric if the Earthwoman added any fuel to their fire.

"Daimon, come on," Ruzbee, his ally, called from the archway. "Their craft approaches the main entrance."

Daimon put on his pair of specially shaded glasses. They had been necessary ever since the ancient Auricle had begun to glow. The sacred stone was kept in a transparent receptacle in the rotunda of the Great Hall.

It had been nothing more than a cold oblong chunk until several months ago. Then suddenly it had begun to glow, increasing in brightness until special glasses became necessary for anyone in its vicinity.

An answering glow had come from Earth—from Sarina Bretton. Thus she had been identified as the Great Healer. Daimon couldn't wait to hear the rationale for this phenomenon from the subject herself.

He strode from the robing room behind the Council Chamber. Leaving the council wing, he crossed the rotunda, veering around the encased Auricle in the center, then entered the assembly wing on the opposite side of the building.

The Assembly Chamber was filled to capacity. Rarely was there a joint session of the General Assembly and the High Council, but today was an exception. Over five hundred seats were occupied. Daimon claimed his place among the other Council members in a semicircular row of twelve seats facing the Assembly. Behind them on a raised dais sat the Supreme Regent. The buzz of conversation was loud, drowning out the drone of the air filtering system.

Emu glanced at him from two seats down. The thin Sirisian was his most powerful opponent. "Our Savior comes," Emu said with a smirk, leaning over so Daimon could see him. His elastic body elongated as he stretched. "The Coalition will be strengthened, Daimon. It is inevitable. Your teachings will be disregarded as worthless ramblings."

"You worship a false god." Daimon craned his neck to glare at his fellow councilman. Emu had covered his bald head with a ruby turban. The deep red color made his pink skin appear dark, but it complemented Emu's maroon robe. "The Earthling has no power. She is nothing. The plague and the Morgots will destroy us unless we embrace our own kind. A return to our home worlds is the solution. We can only succeed against them if we fight for ourselves."

"Traitor. You cloak your words in rhetoric, but in reality you seek dissolution of the central government. You promote secession."

"The Defense League is too overburdened to do any of us much good. We're killing ourselves," Daimon persisted. "When are you going to admit the Coalition has grown too large for its own needs? You think this woman from Earth is going to save us? Bah! If you rely on her false powers, you'll doom us all."

"Gentleman," a stern voice interrupted from behind, "please be silent." It was Glotaj, the Supreme Regent.

Another voice broke in, quiet but with the force of authority. "You speak blasphemy of my bride, Daimon. I will not tolerate it. Her power will not be activated until she marries into the House of Raimorrda."

Daimon whipped his head around to view the tall blond man who had spoken.

"Pardon, my lord." He bowed from the waist where he sat. "You are correct, of course. I am only anxious for the ills that befall us to be eliminated."

Inwardly, Daimon cursed. He should have known Cam'brii's ears would pick up talk of the woman. He'd have to be careful.

Daimon sagged back in his seat, glancing at Ruzbee a couple of rows across in the Assembly. The Arcturian gave him a slight nod. He'd noticed the exchange. Daimon was certain Ruzbee would keep an eye on Emu and Cam'brii. And if the Earthwoman proved to be a problem, they'd deal with her as well.

****

Sarina's heart thumped wildly as she regarded the huge double doors at the top of the wide staircase. It had only been a few minutes since she'd left Teir's ship. A uniformed officer had whisked her away on some type of flying motorcycle and landed in front of the Great Hall.

The rectangular white building with immense columns and a raised portico in front housed the central Coalition government. She observed three separate entrances, one in the center and two on the sides. According to the officer, she was to enter the Assembly wing on the left.

From her studies aboard Teir's ship, Sarina had learned the High Council consisted of twelve members, and a Supreme Regent ruled over all.

She swallowed apprehensively, dismayed that she was not to be presented just to the twelve Council members as expected. Her escort had informed her that a joint session of the Assembly and the High Council had been called. Inside the Assembly Chamber, Sarina would face representatives from over five hundred worlds.

She glanced back at the officer. The bearded trooper was no youth, but his body was fit and strong, and his eyes held a kindly glimmer.

"Glotaj awaits your entrance," he said, naming the Supreme Regent. He gestured for her to move forward.

Maybe she shouldn't have worn pants after all, Sarina thought, her knees quaking as she mounted the broad flight of stone steps. A business suit might have made her feel more in control.

She stopped before the double doors as they were flung open from inside. Sarina caught a glimpse of hundreds of faces turned her way. A wave of dizziness assailed her, but she overcame it by taking several deep breaths. As she stepped inside, she crossed a short marble expanse before entering the Chamber proper. Everyone stood at her arrival.

She proceeded forward toward the impressively robed figure at the podium. She walked in a daze, awestruck at the variety of species represented. Teir's crew was nothing compared to this. Bird-like creatures, humanoids, snake faces, beings that reminded her of erasers with their elongated heads and rubbery limbs—all lined the aisles. Her mind reeled from sensory overload.

"Miss Bretton." The robed figure spoke, his voice rich and accented. "I am Glotaj, Supreme Regent of the Coalition of Sentient Planets. Welcome to Bimordus Two."

He was human, Sarina thought in relief, or at least he appeared so. She gave him a tentative smile in return. All the seats faced him, she noticed, except for a row of twelve that were turned toward the audience. Ah, the High Council. Which man was Cam'brii?

She furtively scanned the row of councilors. Only four were male humanoids. Lord Cam'brii had to be one of them. Was he the tall, handsome blond, the glowering one with a beard, the older fellow with white hair, or the young redhead with a puckish face?

She looked questioningly at Glotaj. He had observed her assessment, she guessed, noting the amusement in his brilliant blue eyes—eyes that suddenly reminded her of Teir's. A jolt went through her. The similarity was astounding.

Another pair of eyes burned into her. Glancing around, she noted the source. The tall blond councilman stared back at her. His eyes, too, were a celestial blue. The color must be commonplace here.

"We wish to ask you some questions," said the Supreme Regent, his voice booming throughout the hall. "Come up here where everyone can see you."

Sarina obeyed, her stomach churning. His black robe reminded her of a judge. She should feel comfortable in such a setting. The law was her profession, after all. But this was no ordinary court. Her life could be at stake. Sarina had no idea what they would do if she didn't fulfill the prophecy.

After the assemblage was seated, Glotaj addressed her. "How is it that you responded to the light from the ancient Auricle?"

Sarina remembered Cerrus Bdan mentioning this to her. It was the reason she had been identified as the Great Healer.

"I have no idea," she replied. "I knew nothing of the legend or the prophecy until Captain Reylock briefed me."

"Yet the glow came from Earth, from your specific location."

"I have no explanation. I don't understand it myself."

"Have you sensed any unusual abilities in recent times?"

"There's nothing. You must have mistaken me for someone else."

"No desire for healing?"

Sarina hesitated. As an attorney, she'd instructed clients to answer only the questions put before them and say nothing else, certainly not to offer any personal information. But in her case, if she gave Glotaj some insight into her character, maybe he would decide to send her home.

"I did think of becoming a doctor once, but my mother said I'd make more money as a lawyer. I wasn't even allowed to consider a medical profession."

"And now?" Glotaj's keen gaze held hers.

"Now I'm—I *was* an attorney. I was about to be offered a promotion when Teir—Captain Reylock—kidnapped me." Her voice ended on a sharp note.

Glotaj inclined his head. "We regret the need for subterfuge, Mistress. It was felt you might not be cooperative."

"And why should I be? What right did you have to bring me here against my will?" Sarina glared at the entire assemblage, as though it was their fault and not just the High Council's. "You took me away from everything that had meaning in my life. Why should I agree to anything you want me to do? I demand to go home."

"You will establish a new home here," Glotaj said, his tone firm.

She met his gaze. "Do you realize what it's like to be torn from your loved ones and banished to a place where everyone and everything is alien?"

"Your profile declares you to be intelligent and resourceful. We're certain you'll be able to adapt. And once you become the Great Healer—"

"I have no magic powers, Your Honor."

"Time will tell. According to the legend, you must first marry into the House of Raimorrda. You have heard of the dire situation our worlds are in?" At her nod, he continued. "Our planets are dying, one by one. The plague is taking its toll. Our scientists are working around the clock, but they are unable to find a cure."

His eyes burned with intensity, and his voice rose. "You are our only hope, Sarina Bretton. Let your power come forth. Heal the sick, and inspire our people to fight the aggressors who conquer us. By your marriage, you shall save us."

He turned to the audience. "Let the Rites of betrothal begin according to the customs of the bridegroom. Lord Cam'brii, take your place by your bride."

Before Sarina's stunned gaze, the tall blond man rose from his seat among the High Councilors. In several quick strides, he moved to stand by her.

"I accept my responsibility." He stood erect, his jaw resolute.

"Well, I don't," Sarina remarked.

Lord Cam'brii's clear gaze pierced her rebellious one. "Please, Mistress, be calm. This will all work out for the best."

"Not for me." Sarina studied him from under her long lashes. At least he was good-looking with his solemn, chiseled face and his full head of curly blond hair, but he lacked the rugged appeal of the *Valiant's* captain. And even though Lord Cam'brii's maroon robe stretched across his broad back and wide shoulders, she didn't get the same feeling of electricity that Tier gave her. How could she possibly marry this man?

Before she could utter another protest. Lord Cam'brii took her hand, turning her so they both faced the Supreme Regent. Glotaj raised his arms above them.

"By your marriage, I declare the prophecy is fulfilled. You are as one." He muttered an incantation in another language, then lowered his arms and smiled. "Go now and do your duty. And congratulations!"

Congratulations? Good God, were they married?

Speechless, Sarina stared at Lord Cam'brii in shock.

Chapter Eight

Lord Cam'brii strolled beside Sarina toward the council wing on the other side of the building. The assemblage had been abruptly dismissed, and she still wasn't sure what had happened. Was she wed to this tall, taciturn man beside her, or just engaged?

Glancing at his profile, she thought his noble lineage was aptly delineated in his refined features and his regal carriage. It was this ancestral heritage that had brought them together.

As they walked, various members of the government stopped to congratulate them and offer greetings to the Great Healer. The alien faces blurred in her mind, a mixture of colors and exotic styles of dress.

"Are we going to your office?" Sarina asked, feeling totally lost.

The filtered air felt cool, but it brought along a faint medicinal odor that was unfamiliar. Too many new things were happening at once. These people might be accustomed to meeting new life forms, viewing alien landscapes, and smelling strange scents, but to her, everything was like a dream.

Or a nightmare.

Her escort gave her a warm smile as though sensing her discomfort. "I wish for you to see the Auricle. It's just up ahead."

Sarina halted, stopping him with a hand on his arm. She ignored the robed officials scurrying around them.

"Tell me, my lord, are we married?"

He glanced at her in surprise. "Nay, Mistress. What gave you that idea?"

"Glotaj said we were as one, and everybody has been congratulating us." Sarina felt naïve. How was she supposed to know what the regent meant?

Lord Cam'brii regarded her with amusement. "He pronounced the words of betrothal according to the custom of my people. We are considered as one even though we are not yet wed. For the next sixty days, we are to be together. Then comes the marriage ceremony. The rituals are quite complicated. You'll need instruction."

"Where are you from? I mean, from what planet?"

"I'm from Nadira in the Regulus system, but my bloodline is descended from the House of Raimorrda."

"And that crosses planetary boundaries?"

"Correct. We are a human species, with minor modifications. But we live on many worlds."

"So these marriage rituals are those of Raimorrda?"

"Correct again. I am glad to see you have an interest in the subject."

Sarina just smiled. She wasn't merely being curious—she needed to learn all she could in order to find a way home. Maybe Lord Cam'brii would take her back to Earth after they'd gotten to know each other. He was bound to notice she wasn't happy here. But would her feelings mean anything to him? He probably considered it an honor to wed her and to serve the Coalition. Cam'brii might not understand how she felt. Worse, he might not care.

Feeling increasingly like a pawn in a game she didn't understand, Sarina was grateful that at least he was well-mannered. But even though the councilor was polite and his looks were attractive, being with him didn't give her the same thrill as Teir's presence.

A sad sense of loss weighed her down. Despite their disagreements, she missed Teir and wished he were here instead of Lord Cam'brii.

They walked on until they neared a wide circular area in the center of the Great Hall. Cam'brii paused to don a pair of dark glasses. "Forgive me, I forgot to get you a pair. Everyone who passes the rotunda must wear them. Wait here for a moment." He turned away, but not before she observed he spoke the truth. Everyone crossing through the area wore similar glasses, although no one had worn them in the Assembly Chamber.

"Don't bother," she called after Cam'brii. She moved toward the strange brightness ahead as a candle drawn to a flame.

She entered the rotunda. Directly overhead was a domed skylight through which bright rays streamed down. But that light was nothing compared to the radiance of the object standing in a cylindrical transparent case in the center of the marble floor.

"Sarina, step back. It will blind you," Cam'brii shouted from behind.

She slowly circled the guardrail as he ran up beside her. "Don't worry. It doesn't hurt my eyes."

He gaped at her. "How can it not? Others who view the Auricle without protection lose their sight forever."

She shrugged. "It glows, that's all. In fact, the effect is rather beautiful."

The smooth stone was about eight feet in height, oblong-shaped with a pointed top. It reminded her of something, but she couldn't think what it was. The fragment of memory nagged at her, but she pushed it away, awed by the phenomenon in front of her. The rock glowed with a pulsating fiery light that was oddly soothing.

Lord Cam'brii seemed stunned, as did others around them. Sarina was indeed the only person without special dark glasses.

"The Earthwoman truly is the Great Healer," someone cried, and his words spread throughout the Great Hall.

"I don't understand." She turned to Cam'brii for an explanation.

"This ancient glowstone is all that remains of a once great civilization on a planet called Shimera," he began. "The legend says that some of the Shimerans who escaped the planet before its destruction possessed special powers. It was prophesied that one of their descendants would arise in a time of great disaster, renew the power, and restore harmony to the galaxy. The Auricle would let us know when the time of Revelation was near.

"And so it has come to pass. After the Farg began to decimate the inhabitants of our star systems and the Morgots started their rampage, the Auricle lit with a fiery glow. It grew so bright that no one could look at it without going blind. One day our orbiting observatory picked up a signal, an answering glow, from Earth—from *you*, Sarina Bretton."

She shook her head. "But that's absurd. I sent no signal. And that business about Shimeran ancestry doesn't apply to me."

Sarina glanced around at the watching faces. This discussion shouldn't take place in public, but she wanted to hear more about the legend. Every bit of knowledge could prove useful.

"Could we go somewhere private to talk?" she asked Cam'brii.

"Of course, let's go to our quarters."

"*Our* quarters?" She gulped, wondering exactly what he meant.

"We are considered as one. That means we are to share everything."

Good God, did that mean she was to share his bed, also? Having no choice, Sarina followed him outside. The Great Hall stood on the crest of a hill, and the view was impressive. In spite of her anxiety, she looked around.

The late afternoon light, filtering through the crystal bubble that enclosed the biosphere, formed a hazy aura and cast a surreal light on the shimmering city spread out below. Sarina had been too nervous before to enjoy the dazzling sight, but now she appreciated its astonishing beauty.

Cam'brii pointed toward the horizon. "This biome is Bimordus Central. It's our lifestyle habitat. There are four other biomes besides this one on the planet."

"What's a biome?"

"It's a large-scale ecosystem that recycles its own air, water, and nutrients. I'll show you the other sectors over the next few days as you take breaks from your studies."

"My studies?" Sarina knew she sounded like a parrot, echoing everything he said, but she couldn't help it.

"You need to prepare for your new role. You have much to learn. Tomorrow I will take you to the study center and you can begin."

"Sounds like fun." She grimaced, thinking it sounded like law school all over again—learn the rules and abide by them.

"Today we shall endeavor to get to know one another," Cam'brii said.

It sounded suspiciously like an order. Sarina glanced at the councilor, but his face gave nothing away. She couldn't tell if the idea pleased him or not.

A squad of armed guards had been waiting for them and now escorted them down a curved footpath heading away from the Great Hall.

"I live in Spiral Town," Cam'brii told her. "It's not far from here. I hope you don't mind walking."

People turned to stare at them as they passed. Feeling self-conscious, Sarina moistened her lips. "Are you always guarded wherever you go?" She felt discomfited by the attention.

"Not until recently. Unfortunately, the guards have become a necessity in the past few weeks."

"Are you in some kind of danger?"

"Let's wait until we're alone for any discussions, shall we?" He smiled, his eyes crinkling. Sarina liked the way the smile transformed his face, but she wasn't interested in Cam'brii as a man. She was only interested in how she could use him to accomplish her goal of returning to Earth.

Her surroundings caught her attention, and she became fascinated when Cam'brii explained the methods of transportation. The wide, paved avenues bustled with flying speeders, slowly cruising airbuses, and crowded people-movers.

Sarina had never seen anything like it, and part of her longed to explore. But she wouldn't be here very long if she could convince someone to take her home.

"Spiral Town houses the members of the High Council," Cam'brii informed her as she quickened her pace to keep up with his long stride. "We each have our own apartment. Space is at a premium on Bimordus Two, so individual dwellings are not permitted."

"The buildings are lovely." She liked how the tall towers glittered and had a pinkish hue. When she asked what the exteriors were made from, Cam'brii told her it was marbelite mixed with a pink quartz-like stone.

"Here we are." He stopped in front of a building where residential units fanned out from a central spiral. Mirrored casements set into marbelite made the complex appear larger than it actually was. Each multilevel apartment was different from the next, giving the building an individuality all its own. Yet the design integrated the various parts into one fluid whole.

Sarina followed Lord Cam'brii to an entrance framed by large pink stone slabs. "Open," he commanded, and the door slid aside into a groove. "The guards will remain behind," he informed her, gesturing for Sarina to enter.

A spiral staircase rose from the central hallway, at the far end of which was a glass-enclosed lift.

"The lift or the stairs?" Cam'brii asked.

"The stairs, if we don't have to climb too far. I need the exercise after being confined to Teir's ship for so long."

Cam'brii shot her a questioning glance, and she realized that she'd sounded overly familiar with the captain of the *Valiant.* She supposed that wasn't proper in her present position.

Holding her head high, Sarina started up the stairs. On the third landing, Cam'brii pointed to a door on the right. "Daimon lives there. The less you see of him, the better."

Leaving her to wonder what he meant, he peered into a lens fixed in the opposite wall. The door to his residence slid open.

Inside, he had her do a retinal scan and showed her how to operate the security system so she could enter on her own thereafter.

Sarina felt like a mouse being led through a maze with a hidden exit. Danger was present, but she couldn't sense its direction. The only way to go was forward.

"Why, this is lovely, my lord." She glanced at the plush ivory carpeting, the curved furniture gleaming like iridescent mother-of-pearl, and the colorful splashes of paintings on the walls. Cam'brii had good taste.

"I'm glad it pleases you, Sarina, and please call me Rolf. Would you care for a beverage, or would you rather rest? I can show you to your room if you wish."

"*My* room?" Sarina asked, pouncing on the words. "You mean we aren't—I mean, we don't have to—you said we are to share everything."

Rolf's lips curved upward. "I am afraid you misunderstood. We are to use this period to get to know one another. The only hindrance I anticipate is the presence of your bodyguard."

"What bodyguard?"

"You're a valuable asset to the Coalition, and as such, you must be protected. Regretfully, I cannot be in constant attendance, since business occupies me during the daytime hauras. Your personal bodyguard will accompany you at all times, even when we are together."

"What about the troops outside?"

"Their responsibility is to me. Your man can assemble his own team if he wishes."

Sarina put her hands on her hips. "Why is it necessary for us both to be under constant protection?"

His eyes darkened. "There are those who do not want to see the prophecy fulfilled. They regard our joining as a threat. Once your power is established, I'm hoping the guards will no longer be required." A shadow crossed his face, as though he was contemplating telling her something more, but he remained silent.

"What if it doesn't?"

Rolf frowned. "Pardon?"

"What if my so-called power doesn't materialize?"

"It will. Have faith," he admonished in his deeply resonant voice.

"Yes, of course," she said sarcastically. How could she forget that she was supposed to fall in love with this man for the prophecy to come true?

"Sarina," he began hesitantly.

"Yes?"

"I know this situation is difficult for you."

"Do you? Do you really?" All her anger and resentment flared, and she glared at him.

"Please don't judge us too harshly. Sometimes over the course of events, new insights are gained. It would be unwise for you to act impulsively at this early stage."

She gazed at him in surprise. His eyes held a look of intense pain, as though he spoke from bitter experience.

"Your High Council didn't give me any consideration. They abducted me and delivered me to you against my will."

"I know, but your being here is important, my dear. I'll try to make it easier for you."

She turned away, annoyed by his response. His words were meaningless. The man sympathized with her plight but wouldn't do anything to change it.

"I'd like to get settled now," she said, wearily walking in what she hoped was the direction of her sleeping quarters. Each step on the carpet was accompanied by the musical tinkle of chimes. "What—?"

"That's the *aramus*." Rolf's serious mood had evaporated, and he was grinning. "It loves to be trampled. Each step is like a caress to the creature. We keep it warm, and it entertains us in return."

"How unique." Sarina studied him, thinking it would be in her best interest to learn more about him. She wondered how much time they'd have to get acquainted before their privacy was disrupted. "When is my bodyguard supposed to arrive?"

"There must be a delay. I'd have expected him to be here by now."

"Anyone I know?" she asked jokingly.

His expression sobered. "We are fortunate to be assigned the best officer in the Defense League—you've already met him. Captain Teir Reylock is to act as your bodyguard."

Sarina's mouth dropped open. Teir! *He* was coming to stay with them?

Her pulse raced with excitement.

****

Teir whistled low under his breath. "Loopa's here," he said to Korox. His weapons officer, a brawny fellow, had joined him for a drink in the bar at the Pleasure Palace. Teir took a sip of his Arcturian brandy. "What do you think he's up to?" He was interested in Korox's opinion. The man's mind was as sharp as a bzoran cat's claws.

Korox raised a bushy eyebrow. "Loopa usually shows up when he's after something. Watch it—he's headed this way."

Teir's hand dropped to his belt, where he kept his shooter. His body tensed as the Souk trader sauntered over. Loopa pulled up a chair, turned it around and straddled it.

"Captain R-R-Reylock, a pleasure it is to see you again."

"What do you want?" Teir asked. He wasn't happy to see the whippet face. Loopa always meant trouble.

"A job for you have I, if you are free."

Teir caught Korox's warning glance. "Oh, yeah? What is it?"

"Cannot tell you yet. If interested, I give first payment. Agree you must to the terms."

Teir leaned forward, narrowing his eyes. "I won't agree to anything without more information."

Whippet-face squinted. "Can tell you this much. A courier mission it is."

"Transporting what—slaves, illegal data cards, banned *pnimx* tusks?"

Loopa looked shocked. "Captain, concern myself only in legal cargo, I do! Good payment is offered. Give you cash now if you accept."

"How much?" The clever look that had entered Loopa's eyes intrigued Teir, even though he had no intention of accepting.

"Ten thousand credits, and twenty thousand more upon completion."

"Why can't you do the job, Loopa? You're a trader."

"Already have contract. Saw the *Valiant* on the manifest and your name gave to client."

"Who is your client? What's the delivery point?"

"Agree to terms first, then r-r-receive information."

"I'm not available under those conditions."

"Your ship in drydock is. Between assignments are you. Good chance to earn extra credits."

"The *Valiant* is being serviced. We'll be out of here in a few hauras."

The Souk trader grinned. "Not what I understand. Major r-r-repair needed. Stuck here are you for some time."

"Captain, may I have a private word with you?" Korox asked.

Loopa got up and walked away, stopping at a discreet distance from their table.

"I don't trust him," Korox whispered. "Datron hasn't checked in yet. Loopa could have done something to sabotage—"

"Nonsense! Datron's supervising the maintenance. He'd have let us know if anything was wrong."

"You're not thinking about accepting the offer?" His weapons officer looked at him askance.

"Of course not. But I want to know who's behind it." The Souks were known for their fierce loyalty to the commercial cartels that controlled the colonies. Loopa belonged to the one led by Ruel. Pasha of the largest cartel on Souk, Ruel was Cerrus Bdan's elder brother. Loopa could be working for one or the other Souk leader, or for someone else entirely.

Teir signaled for the Souk to come over. "I'll have to think about it," he said.

"Staying at the Visitor Tower, am I. Reach me there, you can. One haura I give you to decide."

Teir watched the trader leave. "I've got a bad feeling about this."

Korox grunted his agreement. Picking up his goblet, he swallowed the rest of his drink, a Flaming Starburst that burned its way down the throat.

Teir preferred the smoother glide of his brandy. He was about to raise his hand for refills when the data link in his pocket vibrated. He pulled it out and activated the receiver. "Orders are coming in from Defense League Command," he said with surprise, waiting for the complete transmission.

Korox's expression brightened. "You won't have to worry about Loopa now. We'll be shipping out. Let's hope we see some action for a change."

Teir's response was a sudden pallor. "Son of a belleek."

"What is it?"

"This can't be. I'm going to contact Datron." The engineer didn't respond to his alert signal. "Something's wrong. According to this, our ship is grounded for repairs to the power transfer conduits. We're temporarily reassigned to duty on Bimordus Two."

"What in Zor is wrong with the power transfer conduits?" Korox roared, drawing surprised glances in their direction.

"Moff'tt didn't alert us to any system malfunctions. You'd mentioned sabotage. You could be right. Let's find Datron and get to the bottom of this."

"If Loopa's responsible, he's out of luck. You couldn't accept his offer now. What's our reassignment?" Korox's tone was morose. He hated being stuck planetside as much as Teir.

"You're all to report to defense perimeter four."

"And you?"

Teir scowled. "I've been given guard duty of a different nature." He had to force the next words from his mouth. "I've been assigned as the Earthwoman's personal bodyguard. I'm under orders to stick with her for the duration of her betrothal to Lord Cam'brii."

Korox studied the look of dismay on the captain's face. Then his mouth opened, and loud bellows of laughter thundered out.

****

Cerrus Bdan was none too pleased when he heard Teir had been reassigned. "I thought the captain would be free," he snarled to Ava Bet while lying naked on his stomach on a lounger.

They hid in a safehouse on Starbase Alpha Ten, and the tiny cubicle that served as a sleeping chamber was far from comfortable. He'd managed to take Ava Bet and Lieutenant Otis off the *Omnus* with him while escaping from Reylock's troops. That he'd lost the rest of his crew rankled deeply and made him even more furious with the Defense League captain.

His *gima* murmured sympathetically, rubbing his back with her four hands. Her painted claws scraped up and down his skin in long, sensuous movements that made him squirm with pleasure.

"Loopa was supposed to interest R-R-Reylock in earning extra credits, but the imbecile failed to reach him early enough. Assigned another duty was the captain. He did not have the chance to accept Loopa's offer. Grrrr," Bdan growled. "Now shall I have to think of another way to get him."

"First things first. You have to get the *Omnus* out of impoundment," Ava Bet reminded the smuggler.

"I hired a squad of geckos. Good they are with informatics manipulation. They should be able to secure the *Omnus* for us."

Bdan sat up, and Ava Bet noticed that his beady eyes had taken on a malicious gleam. "Work on a new plan to capture the captain shall I. My agents are in place. Keep me informed will they. When the time is ripe, we will make our move. R-R-Reylock must pay for this inconvenience."

Ava Bet ran a claw along his jowl. "Don't forget the Earthwoman. K'darr will be angry with you because of her."

Bdan felt a pang of alarm. The Morgot leader was known to send assassins when an underling failed a mission, and Bdan didn't like to think that could happen to him. It wasn't his fault the Earthwoman got away. Captain Reylock was to blame.

"We'll figure out a way to get her, too. She's with Lord Cam'brii, but that is not a deterrent. Has plans for the r-r-respected councilor does my brother, Ruel." He saw the flash of surprise in her eyes. "Think you we would let Cam'brii get approval for his First Amendment? A major threat to the Souks is he. R-R-Ruel will take care of him. They've met before, though Cam'brii knows it not."

"How is that?"

"An incident in the past that does not concern us. Captain R-R-Reylock and the Earthwoman are our problems." With slow deliberation, Bdan pushed the thin straps of her sleeper gown off her shoulders. As his hand moved to her exposed breast, he said, "Vengeance is sweet, my love. Soon shall we have them. I look forward to inflicting pain upon them both."

He squeezed hard, bringing tears to Ava Bet's eyes. It was nothing compared to what he planned to do to Sarina Bretton.

Chapter Nine

Sarina had decided to send for the clothes she'd acquired on Teir's ship rather than outfit herself again from scratch. When the carrier containing her personal items arrived, she unpacked and checked out the facilities in Rolf's residence. The fabricator provided her with a quick meal, and now she was getting acquainted with the sonic clothes cleaner.

"You have a visitor," Rolf called from the shared living space.

"Who is it?" she asked.

"Your bodyguard is here."

Her heart skipped a beat. She'd half expected Teir to connive his way out of the assignment. She smoothed her metallic blue jumpsuit and pulled her hair out of its tight braid.

Over at the dresser, she grabbed a hairbrush and tamed her waves until they floated about her shoulders in the fashion that most pleased the dashing captain. After giving herself one last glance in the mirror, she entered the living room.

He stood by the doorway. His gaze briefly flickered over her, then rested on Rolf.

"Captain Reylock reporting as ordered," Teir said in a neutral tone.

The two men exchanged greetings. Their contrast in dress was remarkable, Sarina thought. Rolf had removed his robe of office and wore a belted topaz tunic over a pair of bronze-colored leggings. Gold braid appropriate to his princely status decorated his top, while a jeweled dagger hung at his belt. If he was a stickler for protocol, he might make her wear formal dress after they were wed. She'd have to increase her efforts to get back to Earth.

Teir didn't look happy to be here. Maybe he would help her now.

He wore a loose black shirt that was open at the chest, revealing a patch of curly dark hair. Her gaze lowered to his waist where the shirt was tucked into snug dark pants. They, in turn, disappeared into a pair of shiny boots. A belt strapped around Teir's hips held a shooter. With his shock of midnight hair falling across his forehead and his electrifying blue eyes, he was magnificent in a rugged sort of way.

He noticed her staring at him. "Nice to see you again, milady."

She realized he hadn't called her princess, the teasing term he'd used on board his ship. Somehow this cool attitude on his part left her feeling bereft.

"We are grateful you have been assigned to us, Captain," Cam'brii said. "Your reputation precedes you. I heard about the amazing feat you performed on Chanice's World. How ever did you locate the submerged ecolab with the ionic interference in the atmosphere?"

Teir's stance relaxed. "Lieutenant Wren, one of my crew, has exceptional navigational abilities. He pinpointed the site of the tsunami and figured out the possible range of drift. After he located the lab, we improvised a levitator."

"And just as you raised the tip of the observatory, another violent storm struck. I hear you went in alone and got the whole team out just before the lab was crushed by another tsunami. I trust you are fully recovered from the injury you sustained?"

Sarina gasped at this revelation. She'd had no idea his team went on rescue missions.

"Injury? You were hurt?" she asked in a mild tone to hide her concern.

He shrugged. "It was nothing compared to my wounded leg on Bdan's ship."

"What wounded leg?" she asked, confused. "It was your arm that—Oh." She suddenly remembered and flushed.

Rolf glanced between the two of them with speculation. "Would you care to discuss the security arrangements for my betrothed? Or can I offer you some refreshments to start?"

"Let's review the security details," Teir replied, avoiding her gaze.

"Sarina, if you are fatigued, you may retire," Rolf suggested, giving her a meaningful glance.

"No, thanks. I'll just sit here and listen." She settled on a lounger, reluctant to leave when she could feast her eyes on the captain. To satisfy her sudden restlessness, she nibbled from a plate of nuts on the table in front of her while the men spoke.

"I'll leave Sarina at the study center at ten each morning," Rolf said, after reviewing his own schedule. "I should return approximately six hauras later. You'll be solely responsible for Sarina's safety during this time."

Sarina sat upright. "Hey, wait a minute. I'm not going to study for six hours straight every day."

"You must acquaint yourself with the important issues facing us. There is no time for frivolity."

Teir held up a hand. "Pardon my intrusion, but I agree with the lady. Throwing too much information at her all at once will get confusing. She should become acquainted with our city and its people. If you want her to be on guard, she needs to be familiar with her surroundings."

"That's true," Cam'brii conceded. "Very well, you may show her around, providing that you take all precautions for her safety."

"I've handpicked my team. Councilor. They'll be unobtrusive, and they're tops regarding security and surveillance." Unfortunately, Teir's own crew hadn't been available, but they were too well-known anyway. He needed faces that could blend into the crowd.

"We can go anywhere in the city without fear," he added. "Sarina won't even notice my people are there."

"Fine. Just be careful where you go. You never can be too cautious, in my opinion."

"I'd like to see the medical center, if you have one," Sarina interrupted. "If I'm supposed to be a healer, I should familiarize myself with your advances in health care. And I need to learn about this plague everyone is talking about."

Even though she didn't intend to stick around for very long, she was curious. What if the Farg ever made its way to Earth?

"An excellent idea," Cam'brii agreed. "Take her on a visit to the Wellness Center." A melodious chime sounded, and a disembodied voice announced that Cam'brii had an incoming call. "Excuse me; I must receive this message at my work station. Help yourself to a beverage if you wish, Captain." With a purposeful stride, he disappeared around the corner.

Left alone, Sarina and Teir stared at each another in tense silence.

Finally, she spoke first. "Tell me the truth, Teir. How did you get stuck with this assignment? I'd have thought you'd be off on another mission by now."

He hooked his thumbs into his belt and leaned against the wall. "The *Valiant* is in drydock for repairs. There aren't any other ships available."

She lifted her eyebrows. "Repairs? What for?"

"The power transfer conduits are damaged. The circuits apparently overloaded and burned out. Parts have to be obtained. It could take weeks for them to get here."

"But there was nothing wrong during our trip."

"Exactly."

She noted the dark gleam in his eyes. "You mean—"

He nodded grimly. "Datron was overseeing the maintenance. He didn't check in as scheduled. When Korox and I went to investigate, we found him at the maintenance hangar, behaving oddly. He couldn't account for an haura of his time. I rounded up Moff'tt who said all systems were clear on the trip here. There'd been no warning indicators of any kind."

"But why? Who would sabotage your vessel?"

"I don't know. We're looking into it. In the meantime, I'm stuck here."

He'd thought Cerrus Bdan might have been behind Loopa's lucrative offer while he was between assignments. But someone else had to be responsible for his orders to remain on Bimordus Two and guard Sarina. Was that person also responsible for disabling his ship?

Sarina slid off the lounger and stood. "I'm glad you're staying. I need a friend here."

His pulse beat erratically as she approached. "You have your betrothed."

She shook her head. "I don't feel comfortable with him. I know the situation is awkward for us both, but…" Her voice trailed off. She couldn't complete her thought aloud. *But he doesn't excite me like you do,* she finished silently.

"You're going to wed him. You need to get to know each other." His glance fell upon the tendrils of blond hair feathering her face, then upon her soft, full lips. He looked away quickly, before his need for her overwhelmed his self-control.

"You're right, of course," she said dispiritedly. Those weren't the words of comfort she wanted to hear. She lingered, hoping he'd say more, but Teir kept silent. "Well, I guess I'll go to bed now. It's been a long day." When he still didn't respond, her shoulders slumped and she turned away. "Say goodnight to Lord Cam'brii for me. I'll see you tomorrow."

As she walked out of the room, she sensed Tier's gaze on her the entire way.

****

Early the next morning, while Sarina and Lord Cam'brii were breakfasting together, Teir headed for the Defense League station on the other side of town. Impatient for answers to his numerous questions, he entered the pink stone and marbelite building, which served as headquarters for troops stationed on Bimordus Two. He went straight to the comm center and requested to speak to Admiral Daras Gog at Command Central.

As the encrypted connection went through, he identified himself to his superior.

"Congratulations, Captain," boomed Daras Gog's voice. "You did a fine job of retrieving the Earthwoman."

"Thank you, sir. May I ask the reason for my reassignment?"

"By virtue of her position, the Great Healer has many enemies. You're the best man available for ensuring her security."

"I thought you might have something else for me to do, like—"

"A more active gig?" The admiral chuckled at the other end.

"I was hoping to go after Cerrus Bdan," Tier stated, compressing his mouth.

"He's headed back to Souk from what I'm told. We can deal with him later. This assignment is more important, Captain. We're at a crucial point in Coalition history. The Great Healer plays a pivotal role in what happens next, and you're the one who will be solely responsible for her protection."

"Surely any of the other officers stationed here could have taken charge."

"Not as well as you. You're the top officer in the Defense League. Your reputation alone is enough to scare off half the troublemakers in the galaxy. Besides, the woman already knows you. She'll be more comfortable with someone familiar to her. Or so I've been told."

Teir jumped on the admiral's words. "Then this assignment was not your idea?"

"Let's say a person in authority strongly suggested you would be the right person for the job."

"What about my ship, the *Valiant?* Was disabling her part of the deal?"

"I wouldn't know. You'd have received this assignment whether or not your ship was grounded. I can put in a priority call on repairs for you, though."

"I'd appreciate that." He paused. "I don't suppose you can tell me who recommended me for this job?" He wanted the name of the slythian worm who'd set him up.

"Look around, Captain. You might learn a thing or two while you're on Bimordus Two. And don't question your orders," Daras Gog said, then signed off.

Tier headed over to Cam'brii's residence, where he raised the subject with the councilor. Cam'brii was dressed for work in a royal blue tunic, navy leggings, and shiny black boots.

"Perhaps you could check into it?" Teir asked him. "I'd like to know who pulled the strings to keep me planetside." *And why,* he added silently.

Lord Cam'brii nodded as he stuffed a pack of data cards into his pocket. "I'll see what I can learn."

Sarina breezed into the room, hearing part of their conversation. "You're not in any danger, are you?" she asked Tier. "I doubt Cerrus Bdan will forget his defeat so easily. He might have agents here, waiting until the time is ripe to retaliate."

"You're the one needing protection," he told her, his gaze sweeping her lithe body from her silky blond hair to her sensible low-heeled shoes. He wondered if Cam'brii had noticed how her tight skirt caressed her shapely legs like a lover's kiss.

Sarina didn't notice his perusal. She worried about him. Perhaps Bdan had been responsible for his assignment. Stranding Teir on Bimordus Two would ensure his presence until the smuggler's henchmen were ready to attack. Her own safety wasn't foremost in her mind as they prepared to depart.

A short while later, they'd left Spiral Town and were heading down a wide paved street. Teir suggested taking a speeder, but Sarina preferred to walk and so did Rolf. The councilor gave orders to his guard to remain unobtrusive so Sarina could enjoy the outing. The troops fanned out, dispersing in the crowd. Sarina wondered where Teir's men were positioned, since she didn't notice any additional escorts. His team must be experts at surveillance.

As they strolled along, the glittering pink towers, flying vehicles, and alien inhabitants continued to amaze Sarina. Though part of her feared she'd be stuck here forever, another part of her wanted to gape and soak it all in. It felt as though her favorite science fiction movies had turned into reality.

Teir walked behind Sarina and Cam'brii. His posture remained one of alertness, his eyes wary and his body tense. The streets were crowded, and opportunities for a sniper were readily available at any one of the locations facing the main avenue. He had to rely on the scanners his team used to provide adequate warning should anyone aim a weapon.

Luckily, Sarina and Cam'brii didn't appear to be attracting too much attention. Most of the inhabitants were intent on their own business.

"I don't have to be in council chambers right away," Rolf told Sarina. "I can take you on a quick tour of the city, and then we can catch a speeder to the other sectors."

"That sounds great." She listened as he described the various sights they passed.

"This is the physiolab," he said, gesturing toward a low, rectangular building. "It has a full range of exercise equipment, an indoor pool, and a selection of fitness classes. I try to come here every day after work. Twice a week in the evening, I have fencing practice. You might want to schedule some sessions here."

Sarina simply nodded. She hoped to find a way home soon and establishing an exercise routine was not her top priority.

Behind her, Teir tried to focus on his job, but it was difficult not to notice how Sarina was hanging onto Cam'brii's every word. By the corona, he didn't know how he could cope with being in such close proximity to her. On his ship, he could occupy his mind with tactical operations. But now, he had to suffer while Sarina enjoyed the councilor's company.

"We'll have time for a quick tour of the other biomes. I'll show you more another day." Cam'brii squinted in the sunlight filtering through the crystal dome. The ceiling was so high, it appeared part of the sky. "We'll start with the Nutrition Pod. We use hydroponic and intercropping techniques to grow fresh produce. An aquaculture center raises farmed fish."

She glanced at him in puzzlement. "Why grow food when you have fabricators?"

He grinned, his golden blond hair gleaming in the light. It was still early morning, and the temperature was cold enough to chill Sarina's skin. She was glad Rolf had suggested she wear a shawl. The climate was temperature-controlled, he'd told her, but it was kept cool in the city during early hauras to reduce energy needs.

"Not all of our delegates consume nourishment created through molecular alteration," Rolf explained. "The less developed cultures prefer to prepare their own meals. Many of our ambassadors from non-aligned worlds, or new applicants to the Coalition, use this method. We find that when a culture's technology accelerates, the faster pace makes a fabricator more acceptable."

He studied her. "The surplus from our Nutrition Pod is offered in various natural eateries around Bimordus Central. Perhaps we should dine out tonight."

"I'd like that." Sarina smiled at him, pleased by the suggestion.

They entered a vehicle exchange station to pick up a speeder. Resembling a bullet-shaped, glass-bubbled car, it held up to four people and had the capacity to glide on wheels or fly through the air. A miniaturized bimanthium crystal reactor provided power.

Sarina gazed in wonder at the other types of transportation as Rolf described them. These included smaller-capacity speeders, flying motorized cycles, airbuses that cruised slowly just above the ground, and a people-mover that provided easy transport along the city streets. One didn't need to own a private vehicle on Bimordus Two. Everyone had free access to all means of transportation.

The station was bustling with morning activity, but Lord Cam'brii had no trouble requisitioning a speeder. Consulting briefly with his guards, he gave them his proposed itinerary so they could follow in a vehicle of their own. Teir used the communications mechanism on his data link to notify his team of their plans.

They proceeded to view the Nutrition Pod, Rain Forest, Marine Habitat, and Biogenesis Research Center. After they'd finished the tour, Cam'brii returned the vehicle.

Teir glanced around the station, unable to spot his men. He'd ordered them to wait there while he accompanied Cam'brii and Sarina to the different biomes. As the councilor led them back into the city, he hoped they were in position. The councilor's troops were good men but they were too conspicuous.

"This whole setup is so complex," Sarina said to Rolf. "Do other planets have these domes as well?" Teir walked behind them as they strode down a side street. He hadn't said a word during the entire tour, and she wondered what he was thinking. Rolf, on the other hand, seemed eager to answer her questions.

"Colonies have been built on previously uninhabitable worlds utilizing the biosphere technology," Rolf replied. "It allows for expansion of our population base, or for research that cannot be done elsewhere."

"Check this out." Teir strode past them and pointed to a tall obelisk in the center of a courtyard. The monument was covered with strange symbols. "It's a memorial to the *Musek*. The ship was a commercial passenger liner destroyed by the Korions one hundred and six annums ago."

Sarina had received her own personal data link as a gift from Rolf earlier that morning. Now she pulled it from her pocket and did a quick calculation. Bimordus Two rotated its sun every five hundred days. The disaster must have occurred circa 1929 according to Earth's calendar.

"Who were the Korions?" She'd thought the Morgots were the only threat to the Coalition.

Rolf took her arm and steered her toward a circular building with an exterior of translucent panels and pink stone. A large set of double doors loomed in front. "You'll learn all about it when you review our history. We've arrived at the study center."

Sarina glanced at Teir. He watched them with a pained expression on his face. But he didn't remain still for long. Pushing ahead with his quick stride, he reached the entrance before they did.

"I have reserved a seclusion space for you," Lord Cam'brii told them. "Captain, I assume your men will position themselves at strategic locations?"

Teir nodded. "I've given them their assignments. Some are already inside. Others will watch the exits."

"Remain alert, just in case. You can instruct Sarina on how to use the learning facilities." He paused. "May I have a word with you in private, please?"

A wary expression on his face, Teir stepped aside with the councilor. They were out of earshot of Sarina, but she observed them nonetheless.

"I've seen the way you look at my betrothed, Captain." Cam'brii narrowed his eyes. "Need I remind you of your duty? The woman is vulnerable. She is in a strange place surrounded by alien beings. Your job is to protect her. Mine is to woo her. Understand?"

Teir nodded, his mouth tightening.

"Good." Cam'brii turned away and approached Sarina. "I'll see you later," he told her with a smile. Bowing, he took her hand and kissed it. Then he was gone.

"What was that all about?" She'd seen the look on Teir's face, and he hadn't appeared pleased by whatever Rolf had said.

"Never mind," Teir muttered. "Let's go inside."

They entered the study center and Sarina was immediately struck by the cavernous interior filled by rows of empty cubicles.

"Where are all the books?" she asked, astounded. Not one volume was in sight.

"Books? Those are antiquated." He sounded amused. "Come, we'll find the seclusion space Lord Cam'brii reserved for us, and I'll show you."

A white robed caretaker who looked to be about two hundred years old led them to a private room at the rear.

"There's nothing here except for a couple of chairs," she said when they were inside surrounded by four blank walls.

"You simply have to make a request. Computer, show us the subliminal learning device," Teir commanded.

An alcove in the wall opened and a head mask slid out on a slab. Teir picked it up and handed it to Sarina. "You choose your subject, then put this over your head. Pictures will form in your mind's eye—ocean waves, waterfalls, and the like. Relaxing music plays in the background. While you're in a tranquil mood, images and sounds instructing you in the subject you've chosen will flash by at a speed too quick for your conscious mind to register. Those images become fixed in your subconscious. It's quite an efficient way to learn."

Sarina examined the device. It reminded her of the virtual reality headgear worn on Earth to play three-dimensional multimedia games. "Does anyone here go to school?"

He chuckled. "Of course. This just teaches facts, not problem solving or analytical thinking. You can only learn that through experience."

"So I have to wear this thing?"

"It's the quickest way to learn. Your other choice is the living picture method. A holographic display plays out the subject you have chosen."

Sarina nodded eagerly. "I'd like that one much better."

"Tell the computer what you want to do. It'll provide the rest. I'm going to check in with my team. Then I'll take the other corner to catch up on some reading." He saw her incredulous expression. "Yes, you can actually read. That archaic method is too slow for what you need to learn, but it suits me just fine. I need to catch up on the latest revisions regarding flight procedures, ship maintenance schedules, and news updates."

He showed her how to get started and then left her alone.

Chapter Ten

Sarina set about her studies with alacrity. First, she concentrated on the history of the Coalition, instructing the computer to calculate all dates in Earth-time so it would be easier for her to understand. Holographic images sprang to life, giving her the feeling she was living through the history as it played out.

Around 1860, first contact was made between Arcturians and Vilarans. By 1909, relations were established with four other worlds. A conference was held on Sinus IV regarding the formation of a coalition, but it ended in discord. It wasn't until 1919 that the Articles of Coalition were adopted at a consortium held on Bimordus Two. The Souk Colonies offered to join if they were paid a bonus of twenty billion credits. Their request was denied.

Five years later, a cargo ship operating near the frontier of Coalition space was attacked and destroyed by unknown aliens. The following year, another freighter was attacked by the same aliens who did not respond to any attempts at communication. Probes launched with peaceful messages did not return. The need for a Defense League became evident. A hasty force was assembled, and a squadron of twelve patrol craft was sent to obtain information. None was ever heard from again.

Then in 1929 came the incident with the *Musek*. The passengers and crew were all killed. Fear of pirates seriously curtailed cultural exchange activities. In 1933, a sneak attack by the aliens led to their identification as the Korions.

Time blurred for Sarina as events sped past. A devastating

war with the Korions resulted. Later, a peace treaty was signed followed by years of prosperity and expansion. The Souks signed a trade agreement. First contact with the Morgots became an armed conflict.

"It's getting late." Teir's voice broke her concentration.

Sarina's eyes burned from the holographic images dancing before her. At her command, the computer shut down.

Glancing at her data link, she saw it was almost time for her betrothed to arrive. "Rolf will be coming soon." She rubbed her aching neck.

"I know," Teir said. Sarina had been so absorbed in her history lesson that she hadn't paid him any attention, but he'd kept an eye on her. Cam'brii's warning stuck in his mind, and he respected the councilor's work enough not to defy him. He'd kept his distance on purpose.

Sarina regretted not having taken a break with Teir. As it was, they'd gotten a late start. The hauras had seemed to fly by. Now it was too late. She wished he were going to dinner with her instead of Rolf.

"Rolf and I are dining out tonight," she said, hoping to provoke a reaction.

"Does that please you?"

"He's quite attractive. I'm sure we'll have a good time." She was gratified when Teir's mouth tightened at her comment.

Before he could reply, the councilor arrived. Sarina stood and linked her arm through Rolf's with a show of enthusiasm.

"How did you fare today?" He flashed her an even smile as they strode through the exit.

She warmed to him, but not to the extent that she wanted to marry the man and remain here for the rest of her life. Their purpose in getting to know each other returned to haunt her mind and depress her spirit.

"I've been reviewing Coalition history. I got to the part where the Morgots enter the scene."

Her arms chilled in the twilight, and she drew her shawl

around her shoulders. Teir had gone ahead to check their route. Danger could come from anywhere. Rolf, too, remained alert, although the streets were quiet as most people had left work earlier. Their guards weren't visible, but Sarina was sure they must be around somewhere, keeping out of sight.

"You can carry on tomorrow," Rolf said. "I want you to become familiar with the current issues facing us."

"The history is fascinating, but I'm still unclear on my role. What happens if the prophecy is not fulfilled?"

"Have faith, Sarina. It will come to pass."

"You keep saying that, but what if it doesn't?" She hoped he would say she'd be sent back to Earth, married or not. He could always get an annulment if such a thing existed in this civilization.

"As you view our history, all will be explained," Cam'brii replied patiently.

"But what if my power doesn't exist?" Sarina persisted.

Rolf seemed reluctant to answer, so she stopped, hands on her hips, waiting until he responded. Footlights suddenly switched on, casting a muted rosy glow at their feet. She could sense Teir's presence as he stood guard behind them.

"It is understood that it may take some time for you to develop feelings for me," Rolf began, as a flush rose in his cheeks. "The legend states that you must fall in love with a member of the ruling House of Raimorrda for your abilities to become activated. Therefore, you will be allowed a grace period of one annum after our betrothal date to develop your power."

"One annum? You mean I'll have a whole year? But what if I don't fall in love with you during that time? Will I be passed along to another Raimorrdan to try again?"

The thought that she might be joined to one after the other of the nobility until her so-called power showed up appalled her. What if she never fell in love with any of them? And how could she, when she was already engaged to Robert?

"I have a fiancé on Earth," she told him. "My heart belongs

to him. It's useless for you to insist on this forced marriage when nothing will come of it. Please send me home, Rolf."

"I am sorry you were torn from all you hold dear," he said in a kindly tone. "But according to the signs, it is time for the legend to unfold. All that was predicted is coming true. You will understand someday that sacrifices are necessary."

"Why do we need to marry, if I'm just supposed to fall in love?" Sarina asked. "The two don't necessarily go together."

"The exact wording of the legend is this: *The prophecy will be fulfilled when the Great Healer marries a Raimorrdan who is highly placed and was born under the sign of the circle. The healing aura can only be activated by the power of love.*" Rolf spoke precisely so the meaning would be clear. "I am the only Raimorrdan of eligible age who meets these criteria. I'm the one destined for you to wed."

"All right, I understand that much." She was relieved that he was the only nobleman who met the legend's qualifications. At least she wouldn't get passed on to anyone else. But he still hadn't answered her initial question. "What if I don't fall in love with you? What happens if my healing power doesn't materialize after the given time?"

Rolf glanced away. "Unfortunately, there is an obscure edict that covers that possibility."

"And that is?"

He sighed, then squarely met her gaze. "The law was originally passed to discourage pretenders. It has never been repealed." He paused, and his next words chilled her blood. "Should you fail to become the Great Healer within the allotted time, you will be executed."

****

Rolf's words ringing in her head, Sarina was incapable of enjoying their dinner. The very thought of food made her want to choke. She decided she'd better study harder at the library the next day to learn all she could about their society and prepare, if possible, her own legal defense. Execution! How could they possibly accuse her of being a pretender? She hadn't deliberately chosen this path.

Lost in gloomy thoughts, Sarina's gaze roamed the restaurant. Sleek lines of polished iridescent furniture were complemented by etched crystal dividers and indirect lighting. It was a small place, and the patrons represented a variety of species. Their laughter and chatter pervaded the room, but the happy sounds only deepened her despair. These creatures were free to pursue their dreams and goals, whereas she was trapped. How could this have happened to her?

Feeling she'd better make an effort to get to know Rolf, she turned to him. He, too, had been silent, apparently attuned to her need to assimilate what she'd just learned. Sarina appreciated that and tried to force some enthusiasm into her voice.

"This place has a pleasant atmosphere. Thank you for bringing me here, Rolf."

They were seated in a private alcove. Teir had taken an adjacent booth facing the room so he could watch the entrance. The rest of their guards were positioned outside.

He signaled for a server. "Would you like a beverage?"

"Yes, I'll take whatever you recommend."

Rolf ordered, then cocked an eyebrow as he regarded her. "I want to please you, Sarina. It's important that we get along."

"For whose sake is it important? Not for mine. No one cares how I feel."

Rolf shook his head. "You're wrong. I understand how difficult this is for you and how frightened you must be. But your presence here is essential. The Revelation will strengthen the Coalition's unity and help get the First Amendment passed. The vote must go through."

"What's the First Amendment?"

"Let's just say that it's an issue that vitally concerns me." Leaning across the table, he covered her hand with his. "Stop worrying so much. Everything will work out for the best. Now let's drop the subject of politics for this evening. I want to find out more about you, Sarina. Tell me about your job on Earth. You were an attorney? I read your dossier but I'm not clear as to what that means."

Disconcerted by the warmth of his hand, she slid hers out of his grasp as she proceeded to tell him about her career.

"Nadira has a similar system of advocacy," he said when she had finished. "But you don't sound as though you were satisfied with your job."

"No, I really wasn't very happy there," Sarina admitted.

"Why did you not leave?"

"I wasn't ready to change." She was unwilling to reveal her fear of disappointing her fiancé. "How did you become a councilor? Has it always been an ambition of yours?"

"No. I was… persuaded to enter the diplomatic corps. Now it's my life's work."

"Do you enjoy it?"

Rolf shrugged. "I do what I must."

"What does that mean?"

He looked her in the eye. "I made a vow to someone that I must keep. It pertains to my work."

"What vow?"

"We'll discuss it another time. This night is for pleasure. Ah, here come our drinks." He leaned back as the server placed two crystal goblets on the table. "These are Moranian Flashers," Rolf told her. "Take a sip like this—" he half-sipped, half-inhaled "—and feel the effect. It's quite delightful."

Sarina peered at the bubbly golden liquid that frothed inside the crystal glass and nervously followed suit. She gasped as the effervescence tickled her nose. "Oh, my."

Rolf smiled. "It pleases you?"

"Yes, it's quite good." She took another sip, and the cool liquid flowed down her throat. It tasted vaguely of raspberries and champagne.

"I would be remiss if I didn't tell you how lovely you look tonight. I like the way you fixed your hair. I shall be proud to have you as my bride, and I look forward to getting to know you more… intimately."

The sensual tone of his voice and the warm, appreciative look in his eyes discomfited her.

Teir coughed loudly in the booth next to them, and Sarina's skin warmed. Dear God, he must be listening to every word, and Rolf had all but said he couldn't wait to get her into his bed.

"Isn't there anyone else, a girl from your home planet perhaps, whom you would prefer as your wife?" she asked hopefully.

A shadow crossed his face. "No, there is no one."

"Were you at least *asked* if you would marry me?"

"Yes, Glotaj did me that courtesy, but the dictates of the legend were such that I couldn't refuse. On the day of my birth, a supernova occurred in a nearby star system. The cataclysmic explosion created shock waves that traveled outward at an incredible rate—concentric waves, circles of radiation. A huge gas cloud erupted into space, again in a circular configuration.

"At the time, no one thought twice about these events. Interest in the legend arose when the predictions started to come true, and that only happened in the past few annums. A suitable Raimorrdan was sought. Given my status and availability, these natural events were interpreted as the Sign of the Circle foretold by the prophecy."

He smiled. "I am pleased by our proposed union, Sarina. When we wed, I shall assume the title of Prince on my home planet. It is only fitting that I marry you, a princess of the stars."

"Do you really believe in the legend?"

His eyes darkened to indigo. "I do. Your destiny is joined with mine."

Sarina wondered if all this might be true. She thought of Robert, of her mother and her friend Abby, of all the other people she'd left behind. Even if the legend were valid, could she sacrifice all she held dear for the sake of total strangers?

Hell, no. She didn't want to live the rest of her life in this strange place, light-years from home, regardless of how many wondrous things occurred. However, no one had asked for her opinion. If she became the Great Healer, would they listen to her then?

Who cares? Sarina thought. *I don't want to be here long enough to find out. If I don't fall in love with this man, I'm going to be executed within a year's time.*

She had to escape back to Earth before her marriage to Lord Cam'brii took place.

The next day in the study center, Sarina focused on the problems currently faced by the Coalition so she could better understand what she was up against. Foremost in her mind was the need to mount a legal defense against the execution decree in case she couldn't get home. She began where she'd left off the day before.

By 1998, Earth chronology, the Coalition included over five hundred worlds. It was becoming so large that only major grievances could be heard, a source of concern to many. The Defense League was hard-pressed to provide security for all. Then the High Council voted to impose harsh sanctions against Souk companies, ports and shipping interests that participated in the slave trade.

This angered the Souks, who were dependent upon slaves as a labor force. Bitterness against Coalition policy led members of the Souk Alliance, a syndicate of commercial cartels in the mineral-rich Capellan system, to conduct acts of piracy and aggression against Coalition citizens.

As a result, Lord Cam'brii proposed a First Amendment to the Articles of Coalition that would permanently ban slavery within Coalition boundaries and establish criminal penalties for transgressors.

Boycotting Souk ports was a controversial move that bankrupted a number of companies that relied on Souk trade. The Return to Origins Faction began on Arcturus II as a protest against Coalition policy. The Arcturians supported trade with the Souks because of the scarcity of minerals on their worlds, and they contended that the Coalition was violating its constitution by interfering in matters of planetary concern. By returning to self-rule, the R.O.F. claimed, member planets could make their own alliances.

The separatist movement became widespread within the Coalition as the crises mounted. The decimation caused by the Farg and the Morgot attacks further strained the resources of the Defense League, and the R.O.F.—now led by Councilor Daimon—said the central government had lost its effectiveness and should be dissolved.

"Why would Daimon oppose the Coalition if he's on the High Council?" Sarina asked Teir. He had been sitting with his back to her all afternoon, concentrating on his reading.

He swiveled in his chair and as his eyes met hers, Sarina couldn't help the swell of warmth that rushed through her. Gazing into his gorgeous cobalt eyes would never cease to thrill her.

"It's the old expansionist story. At what point does an organization call a halt to growth and put a limit on membership? The Coalition has grown too big and can't meet the needs of its members. Daimon believes each world could better function on its own. He might be right, but those who believe in the legend refute him. They say the Great Healer will eradicate the threats from the plague and the Morgots. Then the Coalition can focus on internal needs, and galactic harmony will result."

"So Daimon doesn't believe in the legend?"

Teir shook his head. "Nor does anyone else in the R.O.F. Their solution is isolationism."

"Are they a threat to Lord Cam'brii?"

"I don't think so. He has more to fear from the Souks. They don't want his First Amendment to pass the vote scheduled for next annum. An assassination attempt is likely, backed by the Souks or their allies."

Sarina gasped. "Is that why he needs to be so closely guarded?"

Teir nodded. "The situation is made worse by the plague. Let me explain." He moved his chair closer, and Sarina's pulse quickened in response.

"The Farg first surfaced on Tryst VI, annihilating most of the planet's population. When the Morgots moved in, they sold the survivors as slaves to the Souks. The plague spread, and so did the Morgot conquests. Pirate runs with slave ships have become a real nuisance for the force.

"Cerrus Bdan is a notorious Souk trader who specializes in slave transports. His brother Ruel is pasha of the biggest industrial cartel on Souk, which means he controls most of the home planet. Bdan keeps him well supplied with slave laborers and other contraband. I would guess they've made considerable profits from the Morgot conquests. Bdan and I have clashed several times, but always after we haul him in, he finds a legal loophole and is released. He's been a thorn in my side, one I'd dearly love to pluck."

"No wonder he wants you out of the way. He's probably tired of running into you, too. And after this last encounter, he'll really be angry," Sarina mused.

Tier's brows drew together. "I'm wondering if it's really me he was after. Maybe he meant to capture you."

Sarina shook her head. "Rolf is more important to the Souks."

"But you're a crucial factor in this whole issue. If the legend is true, it will reinforce the Coalition's unity. The First Amendment will be passed, and the R.O.F. will be out of business. When you eradicate the Farg, the Coalition will be able to concentrate on repelling the invaders. You'll help us to get rid of the Morgots. The Souks will lose a big source of their slave labor."

"So you're saying the Souks, the R.O.F. and the Morgots all have a reason to get rid of me?"

He nodded glumly.

"Well, they won't have to worry for long," Sarina said

bitterly. "My wedding date is only a few weeks away. After that, I'll have ten more months and then I'll be executed. The High Council will do the others' dirty work for them." She reached out her hand and touched his arm. "Teir, please help me escape. I want to go home."

His gaze narrowed. "I can't."

"But I'm not the Great Healer. I have no special power. Are you going to stand by and watch me die?"

"Gods, no."

"At least help me delay my marriage to Lord Cam'brii."

"Did someone mention my name?"

Rolf strode into the room, to find Sarina leaning forward, her hand on Teir's arm, a pleading look on her face. "What's going on?" he demanded.

Teir stood. "We've been discussing affairs of state. Sarina is concerned for your welfare."

Rolf looked at her questioningly.

"That's right," she said, regaining her composure. "It seems you have many enemies, and so do I."

"Indeed. May I remind you, Captain Reylock, that your purpose is to provide protection?" *And nothing else,* Rolf's stern expression implied.

"I am aware of my job. I'll scout the area outside before you leave." Tier pivoted on his heel and left.

Chapter Eleven

Out in the open, Tier cursed himself for letting down his guard. He'd allowed Sarina's fears to pierce his shield. Cam'brii had to remind him of his duty, and that must never happen again. Teir had to harden himself against her hapless situation.

He buried himself in his reading while Sarina studied during the days that followed. She switched to the subliminal learning method to acquire knowledge faster.

For her part, she focused on technical operations, linguistics, and law. Of the latter, she found nothing that would provide a valid defense against the execution decree.

According to the terms of the Ascension Statute, a pretender was defined as anyone claiming to be or *being presented as* the Great Healer, and who did not show evidence of any healing power within one annum of the Auricle's herald.

Teir explained it further. "The time limit was based on the legend, which states that the Revelation will occur within one annum from when the Auricle begins to glow. You've actually been given more time. You have one annum from the date you were betrothed to Lord Cam'brii."

"But who would pretend to be the Great Healer?"

"Many persons might do so, using trickery if necessary, but the severe punishment is an effective deterrent. The law was made to discourage unscrupulous people from seizing power either for themselves or in the name of another person purported to be the Great Healer."

As the ensuing weeks flew by, Sarina's panic as well as her

homesickness grew exponentially. Despair filled her as she anguished over never seeing her loved ones again. She even missed small things like her hologram collection and the certificate she'd won for an art contest. Everything and everyone she'd ever cared about were just memories.

Rolf introduced her to his colleagues, taking her out in the evening or entertaining callers at their home. She interviewed each one of them, hoping to find an ally, but to no avail. They were all believers in the legend and supported the preordained marriage that she dreaded more with each passing day.

Nor could Sarina expect any sympathy from Teir. He kept his distance except for once or twice when he took her along to meet his friends. Then he laughed and caroused, showing a side of himself that she longed to share. She especially enjoyed the visits with his crew. Ravi's lavish attention more than made up for Teir's lack of it.

In comparison, Rolf's friends were formally polite to her, treating her like the princess she was soon to become. Emu visited often, but all he could talk about was the legend. Most of the discussions Rolf held with his friends were political.

Sarina was desperate, but there was no one to help her.

"At last we are alone," Rolf told her one evening.

Teir had gone to check on the status of his ship, and for a change, they had no visitors. Rolf seated her on the wide lounger in the living room and brought her a drink. He'd dressed casually in a claret shirt and dark pants, his golden hair gleaming in the overhead lighting. At his voice command, the intensity of the light dimmed, and soft, melodious music began to play. It was the oldest setup in the universe, Sarina thought with dismay.

She smoothed her skirt and smiled nervously as Rolf sat beside her. He'd been pleasant whenever they were together, but they'd had few moments alone. She took a large gulp of her drink and then placed it on the low crystalline table in front of the lounger.

Rolf's thigh touched hers, and she jumped, startled. His steady gaze caught hers as he laid his hand on her arm.

"Sarina, I have been neglectful of my duty. It's time you and I got to know each other better."

His hand wandered up her arm and touched her face. As he stroked her cheek, Sarina's stomach churned in anticipation of what he would do next.

He traced her facial contours with his fingers. His hand played along her jawline, caressed her cheek, brushed lightly over her lips. He had a very tender touch, and Sarina sat very still, waiting to see if the physical closeness between them produced any effect. It did not. She felt nothing.

He caught her chin in his hand and tilted her face upward. "You are lovely, Sarina. I think we shall both enjoy our union."

"Rolf," she began, intending to discourage him, but his mouth descended upon hers, and the crushing pressure of his lips silenced whatever she'd been about to say.

His arms encircled her, pulling her closer. And then she felt his hand roving to the front fastenings of her dress. Pushing against him, she managed a strangled cry.

"I'm sorry. Am I going too fast for you?" Rolf pulled back. His breath was ragged, his face flushed.

Sarina's heart pounded. "Please don't touch me. I don't belong to you yet."

"But we are to be wed. It is expected that we are to join before marriage."

"I don't care what's expected. Keep your hands off me."

"You're just frightened. I'll go more slowly. I promise it will be pleasurable for you."

His curly head began to descend again, and Sarina jumped up. "You can't make me enjoy something I don't want. And I don't think it's something you really want, either. You have no feelings for me, Rolf. You view me as a symbol for the Coalition. Well, romancing a symbol won't work."

"Forgive me. This marriage is vitally important to me. I shouldn't force the issue."

He rose and began pacing, his hands clasped behind his

back. "It's not an easy situation for me, either. I'm trying to do my best, to fulfill the terms of the legend, but it's difficult for me to woo you when—" He didn't finish his sentence.

"When what?"

He gazed at her with tormented eyes. "We'll spend more time together," he promised, ignoring her question. "I haven't been devoting sufficient attention to you. I can see that now."

"Why don't you tell me what's wrong?" She'd seen that pained expression before and wondered what caused him such anguish.

"It's something I need to work out for myself."

"Let me help you."

"You can only help me by becoming the Great Healer."

So they were back to that again. It seemed to be the only thing he was willing to discuss with her.

"Come, we'll find an activity that's less... personal. I'll teach you how to play kather sticks." Rolf moved over to the fabricator.

"Kather sticks? What's that?"

He produced a set of colorful sticks with pointed ends and a pair of dice. "It's a game I used to play. I haven't had time for it in a while. I think I've forgotten how to have fun." He gave her a twisted grin. "Please, bear with me. I still think we'll do well together."

He seemed so earnest in his appeal that she nodded, albeit reluctantly. She didn't want to spend the rest of her life with Rolf, no matter how personable he was. Of course, Teir was another matter. If he had been here tonight, Rolf would never have made that pass at her. But if the captain had tried to kiss her like that...

Seeing the wistful expression on her face, Rolf interpreted it as being meant for him. Perhaps she was finally coming to accept her situation, he thought. She must be hoping, as he was, that things would turn out for the best.

Feeling a surge of affection for this woman who was about to become his wife, he took her hand and brushed his lips across the back of it.

Teir walked in just then and saw Lord Cam'brii bowing over Sarina's hand. Her hair was mussed and her mouth looked as if it had been kissed. The top fasteners of her dress were undone. Son of a belleek, what had he missed?

His face whitened but he said nothing as he went straight to his room and shut the door. Had Cam'brii seduced her? Was that why Sarina had such a dreamy look on her face? With a groan, he sank onto his bed. It was torture being so near to her and yet so far. The only thing that would get him through this *maug* assignment was to keep his mind on his job.

****

A couple of days later, Teir accompanied Sarina and Cam'brii to the Rain Forest biome. The other guards were to follow in their own speeders.

"There's a special place I want to share with you," Rolf told Sarina as they strolled down a winding dirt path in the jungle-like setting. "I think you'll appreciate it." His azure eyes lit with enthusiasm as he took her arm and propelled her forward.

She glanced at him, marveling at how handsome he was. Everywhere they went, feminine eyes riveted on him. Sarina knew those females envied her and would be thrilled to take her place. The councilor was both the best-looking and most eligible member of government in the whole city.

But Sarina didn't care how attractive he was or how much attention he lavished on her. She was not willing to die for him, and each day that passed brought her nearer the execution date.

Pushing aside her fearful thoughts, she listened to the sounds of exotic bird cries, rustling leaves, and scurrying wildlife from the thick foliage that bordered the path. Mist permeated the air, gleaming in the rays of light that penetrated the thick canopy of branches overhead. A rich earthy scent filled her nostrils, reminding her of home and bringing with it a wave of nostalgia.

Behind her, she heard the heavy tread of Teir's booted feet.

She felt his eyes boring into her, and her blood stirred. Why did he have the power to affect her so strongly when Rolf, for all his appeal, left her ice cold?

Teir didn't like the idea that they'd come here unprepared. Cam'brii had told him where they were going after they were on the way. With the councilor's permission, Teir had given orders for their guards to follow. But now they were alone, and he didn't know exactly when their backup would arrive.

He cursed himself for not placing a watch on the place since it was apparently one of Cam'brii's favorite haunts. The councilor was bound to bring Sarina here sooner or later. It surprised him that Cam'brii himself wasn't more wary. He appeared distracted this morning, intent only on impressing Sarina.

Whipping out his scanner, Teir surveyed the area. It would pick up any weapons, but not all species were evident to its lifeform sensors. Feeling an uneasy premonition, he shoved himself between the two of them.

"Be on the alert," he warned. "I've got a bad feeling about this place."

"Perhaps you should go ahead to check out the terrain," Rolf suggested. "I'll keep Sarina out of harm's way until we know the path is clear."

After giving a curt nod of agreement, Teir charged off to survey the secluded location Cam'brii was headed for. When all seemed secure, he retraced his steps. "I'll stay here and wait for our backup troops." His glance fell upon Sarina but he quickly looked away. With a scowl, he drew his shooter and stood guard.

Sarina wanted to remain in his company, but Rolf urged her forward with a hand on her elbow. Unable to think of an excuse to linger, she accompanied him along the twisting trail. The foliage was so dense, she couldn't see around the next turn. Finally, they rounded a curve and came to a halt.

Sarina gasped. A crystal-clear lake with a gushing waterfall sparkled in a magnificent panorama before them. Banks of flowers in a kaleidoscope of colors surrounded the lake, scenting the air with their perfume. Moisture gleamed on the leaves of nearby trees like tiny diamonds. But what made the scene even more exotic was the musical sound of chimes tinkling in the background.

"This is wonderful." She forgot her fears and resentments in the beauty of the moment.

Rolf smiled, the corners of his eyes crinkling with pleasure. "It's called the Rainbow Glen, a replica of the one on my home planet, Nadira. Those sounds you hear come from the tupella blossoms over there." He pointed to a bed of flowers with petals of orange and firecracker red. "I love this place. It reminds me of home." He sat on a large boulder and stared at the water.

Sarina lowered herself onto a flat-topped rock and dipped her fingers into the lake. The cool water felt marvelously refreshing. Her rust-colored suede jumpsuit, appropriate for the regulated temperature of the study center, was much too confining in the heat. She rubbed some water on her forehead, then picked a large round leaf from a nearby plant to fan her face.

"Tell me about your planet," she said to her betrothed.

Rolf gazed into the distance. "Nadira is a lush, tropical world with many areas of unspoiled wilderness. It's a popular vacation destination. We have many foods and wines not found elsewhere in the galaxy."

"It sounds delightful."

"When I entered the diplomatic corps, I had to move to Bimordus Central."

"Don't you miss your home? I miss mine terribly."

He shook his head. "I left nothing of significance behind."

"What about your family?"

"I am the second son of the Imperator of Nadira."

Her eyes widened. "But that must be a very important position. Of course, you said you'd assume the title of Prince when you wed. Didn't your father want you to stay home?"

He hesitated, then spoke candidly. "I was disgraced. You should know this before you wed me."

Sarina couldn't imagine Lord Rolf Cam'brii ever doing anything disgraceful. "What happened?"

Before he could reply, Teir shouted, "Sarina, look out!"

A beam of red light shot past her ear, and she heard a crackling noise. Rolf sprang up, slashing his blade through the air. The trees had come alive, Sarina realized in terror. Dark, hollow eyes glared from their trunks, and their limbs reached out to clutch at her.

She screamed as branches grabbed hold of her and began crushing the breath from her body.

Teir's shooter fired again, and the red energy beam hit the bark, charring a gash in the tree. With an unearthly howl, the tree bent, loosening its grip on her. The smell of burnt wood permeated the air.

Rolf battled two of the creatures with his blade. Teir tried to take them out with his shooter, but he was surrounded.

"Help!" she shrieked as a scraggly limb reached out for her. She ducked, grabbed a loose vine and ran around the trunk, wrapping the groping branch tight against it.

"Watch your back," Rolf called to Teir.

Teir whirled and fired, hitting his leafy assailant.

One of the tree creatures Rolf was fighting snatched up a rock and cracked it into the side of his head. Rolf went down as Sarina screamed.

Teir raced over to her. "Use this." He thrust his shooter into her hand.

"What—?" She didn't continue because she saw Teir whip out a hidden weapon. Before he could flick the control, a tree creature grabbed him from behind, lifting him off the ground. He flipped himself around in its grasp and knuckled it in the eye. With a moaning shriek, the attacker let go. Landing on his feet, Teir activated his weapon, aiming a fiery blast at the trees hovering over Lord Cam'brii.

Sarina fired the shooter as one cast up a limb to throw a rock at Teir's head. It toppled over with a hideous sizzling sound and a puff of foul smoke.

"Sarina, see if you can rouse Lord Cam'brii," Teir urged. "We have to get out of here."

As she scurried to obey, Sarina wondered what had happened to their backup. The other guards should have arrived by now. She knelt by the councilor's side, concerned by his pallor. A bruise marred his temple.

"Rolf, wake up." As she shook him, he moaned and opened his eyes not a moment too soon.

"Captain," he shouted.

Teir felt a stinging pain in his arm, the same arm that had been wounded before. He pivoted, thrusting a roaring wall of flame at the tree that had pierced his flesh. He jumped back as its bark caught fire and exploded, sending an intense wave of heat their way.

"Are you all right?" Sarina asked Rolf. He nodded and stood, wobbling in place.

She hurried to Teir. "Let me see your arm." Parting the tear in his shirt, she gave a sigh of relief. "Thankfully, it's just a scratch."

She probed the jagged edges of the wound. Her fingertips warmed as she smoothed away the blood.

"Don't worry about it. I've had worse."

"I know." She wiped her hand on a nearby leaf and glanced around. The tree creatures were vanishing into the surrounding jungle.

"Let's get out of here before more of them show up. Lord Cam'brii needs medical attention."

The councilor was swaying on his feet, and Sarina ran over to support him. With Teir's assistance, they made it out to their speeder. Still there was no sign of his men or of Cam'brii's contingent of guards. Concerned, Teir activated his data link.

"Sorry, sir," his squad leader said. "We're still at the vehicle exchange station. All transport was halted due to a systems malfunction. Communications have been jammed as well. We were unable to get through to you. The computer just came back online."

Teir gave a quick rundown of what had happened. "Meet us at the Wellness Center," he ordered. "We'll get to the bottom of this later. Someone must have been in league with the Twyggs, setting up an ambush."

****

Lord Cam'brii's injury was slight, the medic at the Wellness Center told them. He ran an instrument over Cam'brii's temple, and the councilor's blurred vision and headache cleared at once. Passing a shaky hand across his forehead, Cam'brii sat up on the examining table and turned to Teir.

"Thank you, Captain, for your vigilance."

"Just doing my job," Teir answered.

"What kind of weapon were you using, if I may ask?"

He grinned. "It's a Vilaran flamer. We use them against the jaegger beasts in the Uta Wastes."

"Quite effective," Cam'brii commented. "Who do you think sent the Twyggs?"

"Assuming they were after you, probably the Souks. But I'm not sure you were the target." Sarina and Cam'brii stared at him. "While you were at the lake, a couple of Twyggs jumped me. I fought them off and ran in your direction to warn you."

"They knew you were guarding us. They must have been trying to knock you out of commission before attacking us."

"Maybe. I can't help wondering which one of us was really their prey." Teir had a funny feeling about the whole thing, but he'd have to consider it later. He wanted to check on the transport system snafu. "I have to file a report, and I'd prefer to do it in person. My people are at their checkpoints outside and so are your men, Councilor. You should both be safe if you return immediately to Spiral Town."

"I'll show Sarina around the Wellness Center as long as we're here."

"Are you sure you feel up to it?" Sarina asked him, her brow wrinkled in concern.

"I'm fine." Cam'brii seemed pleased by her attention.

"Teir, have the medic look at your arm," she said. "That cut should be cleaned properly."

Teir gave her a curt nod before Lord Cam'brii led her out.

"Is it here, where your shirt is torn?" the medic asked a moment later. Teir grunted affirmation as the man probed his arm. "I'm afraid I don't see anything, sir. Are you sure this is the spot?"

Teir looked for himself. His skin was perfectly smooth with not even a trace of a scratch. "By the corona, you're right." He'd felt a tingling sensation when Sarina had touched him. The Great Healer—could it be possible?

A chill swept him. No, he didn't believe in the legend. Maybe some sap from the tree had made it look like an injury.

With a salute, he bade the medic farewell and left.

****

Sarina felt oddly drained as she followed Rolf around the Wellness Center. The medic rejoined them, showing her the diagnostic beds that probed a person's body with a sensor scan, then presented diagnosis and treatment options. Many diseases had been eradicated, including cancer. It was amazing they couldn't conquer the plague, Sarina thought.

Thinking about Abby at home, she asked if there was an effective treatment for paralysis victims. She'd seen the wards for patients with traumatic injuries and acute illnesses but had noticed nobody with chronic disabilities.

"Paralysis is no longer a problem," the medic said. He was a fresh-faced young man who wore an amber tunic over black trousers. The Coalition insignia was embroidered over his left breast. This appeared to be the standard issue uniform for medical personnel. "We can reconnect severed neurons or generate new ones, given the proper conditions."

"What? Can you show me how it's done?" Sarina asked

excitedly. If she were allowed to return to Earth, her friend could use such a gift.

The medic promised to teach her, and they left, soon arriving at Rolf's residence. Once they were in the living room, Sarina broached the subject.

Rolf's brows drew together in annoyance. "It's out of the question. You may not go home."

"I just want to see my family again and help Abby regain her ability to walk. Then I'll come back and marry you," she lied.

"Your duty is here," he insisted. "You must remain by my side."

"I'm sick of your attitude. You don't really care for me at all, do you? You ask about my home and family, but no matter what I say, your response is always the same. You might as well admit your interest in me is mere pretense. As far as you're concerned, I'm just a pawn in some great galactic game."

"A very important game. As Great Healer, you'll be in a position of considerable influence. Think what good deeds you'll be able to accomplish in your new role. In the meantime, it is imperative for you to support the First Amendment. You've reviewed our history enough to know the slavery issue is a pivotal point in strengthening Coalition unity. Your advocacy at this time is crucial."

"I'm never going to become the Great Healer, and I don't give a damn about your blasted First Amendment."

Anguish twisted his features. "We must end the terrorist attacks led by the Souks. Getting the First Amendment passed is critical."

"All you care about is your stupid job. No wonder you agreed to marry me. Probably nobody else would have you."

His face whitened, and Sarina felt a flash of guilt. It didn't last long, however. If she couldn't get home, she was stuck with this man who would never love her.

"My purpose is what drives me." he said quietly. "I cannot help being the way I am."

"What happened to you on Nadira? Something must have occurred to influence you so strongly."

"That is not your concern."

"Yes, it is. If I'm to be your wife, you should share everything with me, including your secrets."

"I can't." With those words, Rolf stalked out and slammed the door behind him.

Chapter Twelve

"The only thing I've heard," Teir said to Sarina the next evening, "is that there was some sort of tragedy in Cam'brii's past. No one will talk about it. Either they don't know what it is, or they won't say. He has loyal friends, and everyone speaks very highly of him."

Rolf had a meeting that night, so Teir had offered to take her out. They were on their way to the Pleasure Palace located on the outskirts of Bimordus Central.

Teir wore his usual outfit of a white shirt open halfway down his hairy chest, a black vest, and tight dark pants. His shooter was strapped to his hip. His gaze darted about as they strode down the dimly lit footpaths. He hadn't learned who was behind the Twyggs' attack, or which one of their group had been the actual target.

The transport system had supposedly broken down on its own, throwing the central computer off-line. Teir had mentioned that they needed to be cautious in case something similar happened again. His men were spaced at intervals along their route, watching from the shadows.

The chilly evening air had made Sarina don a long-sleeved dress for warmth. She'd fastened her hair on top of her head with a jeweled comb, completing her attire with a gold necklace and earrings that Cam'brii had given her.

She felt Teir's appreciative glance, and her blood heated. Rolf had left their residence without a single look in her direction. His demeanor toward her all day had been aloof. He didn't even seem to care that she preferred Teir's company to his own.

She gave the captain an encouraging smile. He noticed, moving closer in response. He took her hand, careful to keep his other arm free should he need to draw his weapon. Gradually he drew her nearer until his arm reached around her.

Teir groaned inwardly as she leaned into him. It was difficult enough, knowing she belonged to Lord Cam'brii. Being in physical contact with her was sheer torture. Her wedding was next week, and Cam'brii probably wouldn't tolerate him being alone with her afterwards.

The Pleasure Palace, a white-domed three-story marbelite building, loomed in front of them. Teir guided Sarina through the entrance and watched her face as she stared around in awe. The lobby was immense, with directional signs coded in Jawani, the official common language of the Coalition.

Teir pointed to one venue after the other. "The Showroom books the best acts from all over the galaxy," he explained. "The Natural Eaterie is a gourmet restaurant with fresh food prepared to order. The Lounge has a bar with over four hundred varieties of beverages, including specialties from most of our worlds. The Entertainment Center has interactive games where you become part of the action. And the Creative Corner is the real reason I brought you here. I think you'll be especially interested in what it has to offer."

"Then let's go." Sarina couldn't wait to have some fun. It was thoughtful of Teir to suggest this outing. Clinging to him more tightly, she squeezed his arm to show her appreciation.

Teir took a shuddering breath. She looked like an angel, with the soft golden wisps of hair framing her face, and her eyes flashing with silver specks. He desperately wanted to embrace her and press his mouth to her parted lips.

Instead, he strode forward to a sweeping staircase and led the way to the second landing. Here he drew her through a set of wide polished doors that hissed open at their approach. "The Creative Corner has several sections. I'll show you the one I think you'll like the best, and then we can explore the others."

They strolled through several rooms where other guests performed strange activities. A myriad of colors and sounds blurred in Sarina's mind until they entered a large hall lined with a series of private chambers, most of them with open doorways. A boxlike contraption was attached to the exterior of each chamber. A few of the spaces were sealed, and she heard laughter and voices from within.

"Go inside one," Teir suggested with a twinkle in his eye.

"Come with me."

"All right." He accompanied her into one of the chambers and ordered the door to close. Blank walls of white surrounded them, backlit so the room was bright. "Lift your arms, and face the wide wall away from the door," Teir suggested.

Sarina did so, and instantly, bright red light flooded the wall in front of her. "Oh, my."

"Try different movements."

As she waved her arms around, Sarina got the feel for what she was doing. Each movement produced a different color, and with finger motions she could direct the colors into lines. If she moved her entire body, a whole section might be filled in with whatever color she was using.

"It's an art form," she squealed in delight.

"You can print your work in different mediums. Just order it done."

She turned to him, her eyes shining with excitement. "This is wonderful, Teir. Thank you so much."

Apparently, the man had noticed her silly cartoon murals on the *Valiant* after all. It was a thoughtful gesture to offer her this outlet for her creativity. In a rush of gratitude, she stood on tiptoe and kissed him.

When she went to move away, he growled low in his throat, put his hands on her arms, and pulled her closer. His mouth brushed her hair. She felt his warm breath on her forehead, and then his lips were crushing hers. He tasted like heated brandy about to ignite.

She snaked her arms around his powerful shoulders and pressed her breasts against his chest. His muscles were rock hard and firmly contoured. She felt a bulge against her thighs that meant he was aroused. It excited her even more. Her knees weakened as she yielded to desire. She wanted to melt into him.

Rolf's kisses had never made her feel like this. Nor had Robert's, she realized with a shock.

Teir kissed her soft, creamy throat. Her moan of pleasure must have fueled his passion, because he put a hand on her buttocks as his other hand roamed to caress her breast.

"Oh yes," she whispered, warmth pooling within her as his fingers teased her nipple.

"By the Gods, Sarina, you're so beautiful," he murmured, kissing her again. She was everything he'd expected and more, but he wanted to make their first time special. He pulled back, regarding her dazed expression. "Let's find a more comfortable place to continue this."

"Wait, I'm not ready," Sarina protested, uncertain she wanted to go *that* far.

"Why not?" His heated gaze raked over her. "We're both enjoying this, so why stop?"

Sarina might be attracted to Teir, but she was engaged to two other men. The absurdity of her situation made her want to laugh or cry, or both. Robert was waiting for her back home. How could she face him again if she slept with another man? And Rolf would be furious if he found out she'd been unfaithful. She couldn't allow herself to give in, even though pregnancy wasn't an issue. Her birth control patch would see her through the rest of the year.

These thoughts took but a moment to flash through her mind. "I can't. It's not right. Lord Cam'brii—"

"Is a chunk of ice. I'm not." Teir reached out to grasp her, no doubt intending to dissolve her resistance with a kiss, but she stepped out of range.

"I said it's not right." It annoyed her that he was going

against the very principles of duty and honor he supported. "I'm sure Rolf wouldn't take lightly to his bride having an affair with her bodyguard."

"To Zor with Cam'brii. All he cares about is politics. You're just a means to an end as far as he's concerned. I'll make you feel more than he ever will."

"It's true that I feel nothing when I'm with him. But there's still Robert, my fiancé back home. You've conveniently forgotten that I had a life before you kidnapped me."

Teir yearned to take her in his arms, but she was suddenly erecting too many barriers between them. "You miss Robert that much?" he asked, conceding her point.

"Of course I miss him," Sarina proclaimed, but even as she spoke, the words sounded false to her own ears. "At least, I did at first," she confessed. "I'm not so sure how I feel now. Look, can't you at least help me get out of my marriage to Lord Cam'brii? I can't consider anything else with a wedding hanging over my head."

Her wide gray eyes captured his, and Teir felt his resolve weakening. Regardless of how she felt about her fiancé back on Earth, he cared enough about Sarina to want to help her now. Perhaps there was a way to assist her without defying the Coalition.

"I'll see what I can do," he agreed in a reluctant tone.

****

Two days later, Teir discussed the situation with Ravi. He'd returned to the Pleasure Palace with his friend to catch the latest Showroom act, a troupe of plumed Sumaran dancers.

"I can't jeopardize my position in the League," Teir said, cupping his glass in his palm. Seducing Sarina was one thing. Helping her escape her obligation to the Coalition was another. "Plus, I support Cam'brii's antislavery legislation. Sarina could be crucial to getting it passed if she marries him."

"You mean, if she falls in love with him. Are there any indications that this has come to pass?" Ravi asked, studying his captain.

Teir snorted. "Neither one of them cares for the other. Perhaps they need more time."

"Their wedding is less than five days away." Ravi pursed his lips. "A delay could prove helpful. Forgive me for changing the subject, but has the Mistress said anything about my cousin?"

"I'm sorry, she hasn't mentioned him." Teir's gaze remained fixed on the stage where a dozen costumed females kicked in unison.

"Could you remind her to make inquiries on his behalf?" Ravi persisted.

Teir turned his attention to his companion. "The situation on Tendraa is grave, my friend. No one is able to gain information."

"But Sarina is the Great Healer. She can do what others cannot."

Teir rubbed his thumb along his stubbled jaw. "Hmm, you make a good point. In fact, you may have just given me the solution we need."

"How so?"

"Sarina is the one person who could get permission to visit Tendraa. Your people, who won't allow any other Coalition repre-senttatives to come, would be overjoyed to greet their Savior. And a trip there would necessitate a postponement of her marriage."

"Do you think the High Council would give their approval?" Ravi asked with a hopeful note.

"I'll suggest it as a test. Maybe her healing power has already been activated. How would anyone know? If she visits the plague-scourged planet, it'll be an objective assessment of her ability. And while she's there, she can gather information for the Coalition."

"What about the risk of infection? If she hasn't developed her power yet, she could catch the disease," Ravi cautioned.

"She can wear a protective shield. And I'll bet I can get

approval to transport her." Teir liked the idea even better because it would give him time alone with Sarina. A ten-day trip in such close quarters could only work in his favor.

He rose from his seat. "I'll let you know what happens. May the faith be with you, my friend." His heart feeling lighter than it had in weeks, he left.

When Teir returned to Cam'brii's home, Sarina was seated in the living area with Mara Hendricks, whom she'd met at the Wellness Center during one of her visits. Teir knew Mara in her role as cultural attaché for the Department of Interstellar Relations in the Diplomatic Affairs Bureau. A xenobiologist, she represented new alien cultures applying for admission to the Coalition. Mara would often participate in interdisciplinary team rounds at the Wellness Center, offering her knowledge of alien customs as they pertained to medical care.

The two women were utilizing Cam'brii's personal entertainment system, watching a holographic Vyxian historical drama.

"Hi, Mara." Teir waved at the visitor. She was a looker but a bit too exotic for his tastes with her ocean blue eyes and thick raven hair.

"Captain." Mara inclined her head in acknowledgment. Rising from her chair, she turned to Sarina. "It's getting late, and I have an early consultation tomorrow. Let's meet again soon."

"That would be great." Sarina showed her friend out, then returned to Teir. "What's up?" she asked him.

"Up?" He glanced at the staircase. "I presume that's where's Lord Cam'brii is working in his study."

"That's not what I meant. It's an Earth expression. You look like you have something to say."

"I do, but please turn that thing off. The sound is distracting."

Sarina commanded the program to end. The colorful images stopped, and the room went quiet. "Raise lighting," she told the suite's A.I.

Teir sat on the sofa and she took a seat at the opposite end. "What's going on?" she asked, folding her hands in her lap.

"I may have a way out for you, or at least a delaying tactic." He described his plan.

Her eyes filled with hope. "It's a wonderful idea. Let's do it."

Teir jerked his thumb upward. "Will your fiancé agree?"

"Rolf is barely speaking to me. He seems deeply troubled, and I think it has to do with whatever happened to him on Nadira. I suppose he'll tell me about it when he's ready, but it might be good for us to be separated for a time. Maybe he'll work out whatever it is that's bothering him while we're apart."

She gave him a brilliant smile, and Teir knew without a doubt what she was thinking. If they got approval to go, she'd take every advantage of the opportunity to convince him to take her home.

****

Teir left to seek an audience with Glotaj. To his surprise, the Supreme Regent approved his proposal without delay. The Coalition leader had the authority to make decisions on his own, and he even went so far as to check on the status of Teir's ship.

"The *Valiant* is ready," he told Teir with a broad smile. "Fair winds on your journey."

Teir mumbled his thanks. Why was Glotaj making everything so easy? He didn't want to press his luck by asking, so he left and headed back to Spiral Town to inform Sarina.

Eight hauras later, they boarded his ship at Spacedock and awaited clearance to lift off.

"Too bad the rest of your crew couldn't come," Sarina said, glancing at him from the copilot's chair. Only she and Teir had received permission to visit Tendraa, so Ravi and the others had remained behind.

"We'll manage. Besides, it's better if they're not exposed to the Farg." He'd have her all to himself for the next five days. A quick visit to Tendraa, and then they'd be alone again. Ten days altogether.

He wasn't going to take advantage of Sarina since she'd stated her feelings so clearly, but it would give him the opportunity to enjoy her company. His every waking moment filled with her image, and he couldn't seem to get enough of her.

If he'd been offered the bodyguard detail now instead of six weeks ago, he'd snatch at it like a man dying of thirst would grab a carafe of water. She had become that important to him.

They reached orbit shortly after launch, and Teir entered coordinates for the Tendraan system. An escort of four combat ships accompanied them. He consulted with the squadron leader, then turned to Sarina who was perusing the controls. She wore her hair loose, he noticed with approval, his gaze wandering down her sleek form.

"Well, here we are," he said with a grin, relaxing for the first time in days. He'd activated the autopilot. Now he was free to give Sarina his full attention.

She glanced up at him from under her long lashes. "It was kind of you to do this for me, Teir."

"I said I'd try to help," he replied gruffly. "I don't know what this delay will accomplish, but maybe things will be clearer by the time we return."

"It will certainly give Rolf an opportunity to consider what's ahead for us. Whatever happened to him on Nadira has affected him greatly. I don't think the personal impact of our situation has hit him. Maybe he's realizing only now that he's about to lose his freedom and wondering if it's worth it."

"Do you think he'd back out?" Teir asked hopefully.

Sarina shook her head. "He's a man of honor. He'll do his duty. Besides, he believes in the legend."

Teir felt uncomfortable discussing her relationship with Cam'brii. "Shall we retire to the lounge? I could use a bite to eat."

"What are we going to do for five days?" she said, getting up to accompany him. "Will you always be busy with the ship? I can help, you know. I've learned quite a bit."

"I thought you were concentrating on health care."

"Yes, but I covered technical operations before that. The subliminal learning technique was quite efficient."

"Technical operations? For what?"

"Piloting and navigation."

He frowned, wondering at the extent of her knowledge and why she'd chosen that subject, when so many others would appeal to her.

"We won't need to work all the time," he said, entering the lounge. "Want a drink?" He suggested a mixed cocktail that he thought she would like. Her posture was tense. She needed to forget about Cam'brii and relax.

Sarina looked askance at the pale pink liquid sizzling in the crystal goblet. "What is it?"

"Go ahead and take a sip. Tell me what you think." He cradled his Arcturian brandy as he sat beside her at the table.

She bravely tried the strange beverage. "It tastes like cherries."

"And what else?"

She wrinkled her nose. "A straight shot of gin."

"Gin?" he repeated.

"A liquor we have on Earth. It doesn't bubble, though."

His fingers curled around his glass. "Oroxian Zingers are pretty potent, so be careful how much you drink. The carbonation magnifies the effects of the intoxicant."

"I see you kept my mural," she said, nodding to the colorful picture on the wall.

He shrugged. "It brightens up the place."

"You could have told me that when I painted it. You acted as though you hated me."

"On the contrary, I found you most desirable from the moment I first saw you."

Her heart pounded. "Don't, Teir. You know how I feel about things."

"Suppose you tell me again. How *do* you feel about me,

Sarina?" He got a whiff of her perfume as he leaned closer. The sensuous fragrance made his blood sizzle.

Sarina knew she'd be lost if she revealed how she truly felt. She wanted him, rather than her two fiancés. When had her affection for Robert actually dissipated? Had it been when he'd postponed their wedding until her promotion came through? Or had it been the disapproval he'd expressed about the welfare case she'd taken on?

Maybe she'd never loved Robert from the start. Teir, on the other hand, inspired a tumult of emotions she'd never experienced before.

"Is the question that difficult to answer?" he asked, his mouth compressing.

"I was thinking about Robert." She saw the flicker of dismay cross his face and hastened to reassure him. "It's not that I miss him. I was just thinking that I'm really not in love with him and wondering why I never realized it before. Maybe there wasn't much substance in our relationship from the beginning."

Teir didn't care to discuss Robert, but since Sarina needed to talk, he asked, "What attracted you to him?"

"Well, he's conservative, ambitious, intelligent, very success-oriented. I admired his dedication to his job. And my mother approved," she added with a wry smile.

"Did you make love with him?"

Sarina glanced at him, but his expression was impassive. "Yes, I did. It was expected."

"Was it—good?"

She took a moment before answering. "We only made love a few times, and I'd never done it with anyone else. I suppose it was satisfactory."

"That's all? Just satisfactory?"

Sarina frowned. "Maybe I've been missing something."

"I'll say you have! I could make you feel what neither Robert nor Cam'brii ever will."

"He's a lot like Rolf, you know," she went on as though she hadn't heard him.

"Who is?"

"Robert. They're both totally dedicated to their jobs. Mother always said you have to be ruthless to succeed."

Teir sighed and leaned back, folding his hands behind his head. "What else did your mother say?"

"That I have to ignore the sufferings of those around me and concentrate on achieving my goals. She expected me to marry someone like Robert. When I first introduced them, I saw instant approval in my mother's eyes."

Her mother must have wielded a lot of power, he thought. "And did you ever do what *you* wanted, purely for yourself?"

"What do you mean?"

"Hasn't it occurred to you that you've been following your mother's expectations all your life? What about your own interests and needs?"

She gazed at him, puzzled. "What about them?"

"You told me at one point that you wanted to be a doctor, but your mother discouraged you. She approved of Robert, so you got engaged. When are you going to follow your own heart's desire, Sarina Bretton?"

Sarina gazed into his perceptive blue eyes and thought she could get lost in them. Rolf didn't care enough about her to listen. His whole world revolved around the passage of the First Amendment. And Robert was part of her mother's legacy, which Sarina decided right then to cast away. He had been her mother's choice, not hers, she realized belatedly.

Feeling a weight lift from her shoulders, she regarded her ruggedly handsome companion. Teir was strong and courageous, yet he was also sensitive and kind. It was a potent combination. An urge grew within her to show her appreciation and to find out what she'd been missing all these years.

She tentatively extended her hand. "What if I start listening to my heart right now? Would you show me to my cabin?"

Teir's heart rate accelerated. Was that a spark of promise in her pearl gray eyes? "Of course," he said, rising.

Sarina stood and was surprised when the room swam in front of her. "Wow, you weren't kidding when you said that drink was potent."

"I'll help you." He came around the table and took her elbow, steering her toward the door.

"Whose cabin am I using?" she asked.

"You can have mine."

"That's very generous of you."

The glazed expression on her face brought out Teir's protective instincts. He drew her closer as they entered the corridor so she wouldn't trip over the steel ridging on the deck.

The ship's engines hummed beneath them, the vibration barely palpable. Sarina's pulse thrummed in unison. Just being alone with Teir was enough to send her sensitivity level spiraling. That he was accompanying her to her sleeping quarters sent waves of heat rippling through her. Her flesh burned where he touched her. She couldn't wait until they reached her assigned quarters.

Once inside, she twirled to face him. "Teir—"

"Sssh, *laria,* let me give you what you want." He bent his head and kissed her.

Sarina parted her lips. Teir instantly plundered her mouth as his one hand supported the back of her head, and the other encircled her waist. She swayed against him, overwhelmed by her need to be closer. He responded by rubbing his powerful body against hers. His broad chest brushed her nipples with teasing strokes, and she felt a hard bulge prodding her thigh. Knowing he was aroused fired her passion even more.

Stifling a moan, Sarina moved her mouth urgently under his. He tasted like brandy, and the strong flavor only served to inflame her desire. Her hands grasped at his hair. *So this is what I've been missing,* she thought in a haze of passion. But it wasn't enough. She wanted more.

Teir moved her over to the bunk. She didn't protest when he gently lowered her and stretched out beside her. His hot breath seared her neck as he whispered her name and kissed her throat. Sarina's head rolled back as he flicked his tongue across her sensitive skin, sending swirls of delight along her nerves. Then his mouth moved up to capture hers as his hand slipped inside her blouse.

Sarina gasped as he found her breast. He traced her curves, slowly running his fingers over her flesh and then down her cleavage. When his fingers brushed her nipple, Sarina moaned and grasped his back. Each time he stroked her, she could feel the muscular ridges rippling under his shirt. The ache between her thighs intensified into a raging storm of desire.

Unable to control his hunger for her any longer, Teir crouched at the foot of the bunk and pulled off her clothing. He buried his head in her triangle of golden hair. Her musky scent drove him wild. After kissing her there, he lifted his head, knowing his eyes must be half crazed with passion. Sarina's mouth curved into a smile of pure feminine power, as she opened herself to him.

She was more beautiful than he could have imagined. Touching her sensitive folds, he was gratified by her moan of pleasure.

As Teir continued to stroke her, Sarina felt herself spiraling toward mindless ecstasy. She was barely aware when he stretched himself across her, having cast off his clothes. His weight was a delight almost too great to bear, especially when he ground his hips against her.

"Take me in, *laria*. I can't wait any longer." With a forceful thrust, he entered her.

Sarina wrapped her legs around him, straining to get closer. His breath came ragged and fast as he surged inside her, and she joined him in the ageless rhythm of the universe. She gasped as he thrust harder.

Crying out her name, his passion exploded. As his molten heat pour into her, she reached her own ecstasy as shudders of pleasure wracked her body.

At last the spasms subsided. She lay still, too exhausted to move. A thin sheen of perspiration covered her skin.

Teir traced his finger along her breast. "I always knew it would be wonderful with you. We shouldn't have waited so long."

She gazed at him with a lazy half-smile. "You're mine for the whole trip. Now that I know what I've been missing, I don't intend to give you a moment's peace."

He responded with a kiss, afraid that if he spoke, he'd reveal his fears. When this voyage was over, he would lose her. She belonged to Lord Cam'brii and would become his bride.

Over the next four days, they spent time in desperate lovemaking. Sarina, too, realized their interval together wouldn't last. She didn't know what the future would hold, but she couldn't deny herself any longer where Teir was concerned. He filled her days and nights with ecstasy. Neither one said any words of commitment. It was understood they'd discuss the situation later, on the return trip.

That day got closer when the computer signaled their approach to the Tendraan system and Sarina had to face her destiny once again.

Chapter Thirteen

In the city of Ingorr on the planet Tendraa, Mantra drew his cloak tighter around his trembling body. He'd recovered from his illness, but now his family faced the danger of starvation. Shaking from hunger and fatigue, he despaired of the prophecy ever coming true.

He was foraging in his father's supply station, hoping to find food the looters had missed. It was the first time he'd been out since his return home, for the law stated that if infected persons did not die, their house must remain closed until four weeks after recovery to make certain everyone inside was well. Zunis had been taken to the burial pit some six weeks ago, but Mantra had slowly healed. Their household had just been certified free of the pestilence.

Not long after the Examiner left, another member of the family had fallen ill, and by not reporting Malika's sickness and Mantra's leaving the house, they were breaking the law. But his family was desperate for food and supplies, and he had to come to Father's shop. Their rations were barely enough to feed the four of them. How could anyone survive on tubers and a cruet of wine a day?

He also hoped to consult a caretaker if he could find one. The posset-drink that had soothed his distemper might be made available to his mother, and he needed to purchase more herbs to fumigate her chamber.

A horn sounded, and Mantra stiffened. When he heard it again, his shoulders slumped in relief. It was just a raker coming to clean the street. He wondered why they bothered. The stench of sewage permeated the city, and even the cold air couldn't dispel it. But the Baynor had ordered the filth to be swept away daily by the rakers, and along with many of the other laws issued by the city's leader to stop the spread of the contagion, nothing worked.

He stepped deeper into the shadows of the room until the scraping noises receded. The floor timbers creaked, and rats scurried about. *Soon we'll be forced to eat those horrid creatures,* Mantra thought dismally. The shelves were bare; there was nothing left. Only his father's secret cache remained to be checked.

Withdrawing a key from the folds of his robe, Mantra approached the hidden cupboard at the rear of the shop and swung aside the concealing shelf that had once held aromatic spices. A small wooden door set into the wall was still locked.

His heart thumping excitedly, Mantra fit the key into the hole and twisted it. The door swung open, and he gasped as he took in the stash of supplies. By the faith, now they could survive for another month!

Mantra cast a furtive glance over his shoulder. Seeing he was alone, he quickly stuffed the contents of the shelves into the wide sash he'd brought for that purpose. Then he tied it about his waist and drew his robe around him. No one would be the wiser should he meet anyone on the street. Not that there was much risk of that. The city was all but deserted.

He closed the hiding place and started for the front door.

"You, there. Who goes?" a voice called from outside.

Mantra froze in his tracks, realizing he must be visible through the broken glass in the front window. Someone must have spotted his movements in the darkened interior.

Terrified of being caught with his hoard, Mantra tightened his robe around his body. Then he stepped outside into the twilight.

"It is I, Mantra, son of Naars."

Three figures approached down the cobblestone street—two humans and one of his own kind.

Humans? Mantra's eyes widened. Inside their shimmering energy shields, they were strangely garbed, both wearing tight leggings and loose tops. The taller one wore boots. As they came closer, Mantra noticed the smaller one was female. Her golden hair was pulled into a tight braid down her back. And the Honorable Baynor himself accompanied them.

The Tendraan was lavishly dressed in a cloak and doublet of amber velvet woven with gold and decorated with ruffles of colbertine, with leather shoes to match his white silk hose, and a flowing silver wig. Around his throat was an elaborate lace cravat. The visitors must be important indeed to have lured the Baynor out of the sanctity of his keep.

"Come forward," the Baynor commanded. "Our guests wish to meet the populace, and no one else is available." He pressed a thick cloth to his nose and mouth to prevent contamination.

Mantra stooped as though his back hurt in order to hide the bulge at his midsection. He shuffled in their direction.

"Mantra, son of Naars, you have the supreme honor of meeting our wondrous Great Healer. She is the holy one who responded to the sacred light of the Auricle. Show your reverence," the Baynor ordered.

Mantra gaped at the female. Her large gray eyes looked back, steady and kind. In them he noticed a special spark, a ray of promise for his people. Truly, she was a princess of the stars.

He fell to the ground, pressing his forehead to the slime running in the street. "Oh, Great One, how we have prayed for your presence. Save us!"

"Please get up," her sweet voice crooned. "My name is Sarina Bretton. I wish to learn of your problems."

"Don't get too close," her companion warned. He was a dark-haired fellow with a stern face and piercing blue eyes. He looked intently at Mantra. "Are you by any chance cousin to Ravi, son of Shay?"

"Aye," Mantra said, rising. "What of him?"

"He has been frantic with worry. When communications terminated, he feared for you and your family." He must have noticed Mantra's wary look. "I'm Captain Teir Reylock of the *Valiant.* Ravi is my first mate."

"Captain Reylock!" Mantra was even more stunned at meeting him than Sarina. "It is an honor, Captain. Ravi is fortunate to serve with you. Has he accompanied you?"

"No. Only Sarina and I were allowed to come."

"We are so happy to see you are well," Sarina said. "Ravi will be relieved. What about your family?"

"Alas, my father and younger sister succumbed to the Farg. I, too, was afflicted, but I was fortunate enough to recover."

"Abide you near here, citizen?" the Baynor interrupted.

"Aye," Mantra replied cautiously. Despite the honor of meeting them, he didn't want his own transgressions discovered.

"The time of airing has passed?"

"It has."

"Then show us your dwelling."

"But—"

"I'd like to see how you live," the Great Healer told him with a smile. "And I'm sure Ravi will be interested in a full report… that is, if you don't mind."

Afraid to refuse, Mantra led them down the twisting streets. "In here," he pointed to one house, "all are dead, and the dwelling stands open. No one dares go inside."

He indicated several other houses as they passed. "A man and his wife and their five children are all gone in that one. Look across the street—the place is shut up. A watchman guards the door." His voice lowered. "I know the family inside. The son and I shared schooling in our younger days." And so he continued as they moved along, relating to the Great Healer the horrors of the Farg.

As they rounded the corner onto his street, Mantra's steps faltered. If the Baynor entered his home, he'd discover Malika was ill. He'd order the dwelling shut at once, and the occupants fined. It wasn't fair, Mantra thought. He'd survived the plague. He should be allowed his freedom.

At the doorway, he stopped. "It may not be safe for you to enter. We've just been cleared of the pestilence as of last eve."

Malika had taken sick that morn. She'd complained of a sudden violent pain in her head. Then a quarter of an hour later, she'd vomited. Putting her to bed, Kairi had noticed the fatal sign on her mother's thigh. Death had been known to occur within hours of such affliction, and Mantra feared she might already be dead.

The Baynor, who still held a scented cloth to his face, nodded in understanding. "The contagion is fierce, Captain Reylock," he said in a raspy tone. "Mantra may be right. The protective shields have not done much good on other worlds."

Sarina answered, her voice firm. "We accepted the risk in coming here, Your Honor. I want to meet the people, and I can't do that if I remain in your home or in the grand palace of your Liege Lord. Show us inside, Mantra."

Nervously, the Baynor glanced at the faded red warning circle painted on the door. "I'll stand guard out here. Don't linger too long. The noxious vapors might still be hovering about this wretched house." He stood firm, clutching the cloth to his face. His gaze darted about as though he could actually catch sight of the pestilence.

Mantra glanced at the two humans. The man's eyes flickered indecisively, as though he were deciding if it was safe to enter.

"Let's go," Sarina said, nudging him.

Mantra pushed open the heavy door. At once, he heard his mother's moaning from upstairs. A wave of relief washed over him. At least she was still alive. Hastily, he ushered the visitors inside and closed the door so the Baynor wouldn't hear.

"What's that noise?" Teir asked, as he felt the walls closing in on him. This had been a stupid idea. The Baynor was right— they had no assurance the protective shields would work.

Mantra turned to them with tears in his eyes. "I pray you will not tell the Baynor about my mother's illness. She has been afflicted with the Farg. Please, great lady, see if you can save her."

Sarina's own eyes moistened at his distress. What a sad world, desolate of life and joy, filled instead with sickness and despair. She prayed with all her soul she'd be able to help.

"Take me to her," she said softly.

Mantra led them up a flight of stairs. Sarina was aware of the risk, but it was worth it if she could help these people. She desperately wanted to be the Great Healer in their hour of need. Maybe the power *was* within her, needing only a powerful emotion to release it. That she had to fall in love might be a misinterpretation. She wouldn't know unless she tried to heal someone, and this was the best chance she'd ever get.

Flickering lamplight lit the way up the creaky wooden staircase. The moans increased in volume as they ascended.

A strange, foul odor met her nostrils at the landing, and Sarina hesitated. Maybe this hadn't been such a good idea after all. Behind her, Teir coughed. She glanced back at him and saw his glowering expression. She shrugged halfheartedly as though to say, *Sorry, but I have to try.*

When they entered the room, Sarina saw a frail female with scraggly auburn hair writhing on a narrow pallet. Her struggles and groans proclaimed her agony. A lamp burning on the floor cast a sickly illumination upon her anguished face. She rambled incoherently, mumblings that Sarina's implanted translator couldn't interpret.

The air in the chamber was stifling. Her protective energy shield acted as a filter for microbes but didn't provide a screen against the atmosphere in any other way. A fire blazed in the fireplace under pans and plates holding burning bulbs. Sulfur sticks smoldered around the room, emitting an odor of rotten eggs mixed with putrid smoke. Sarina raised her hand to her mouth to prevent herself from gagging.

A slender young female rose from the bedside. She'd been pressing a cool cloth to the older one's forehead.

"Kairi, what are you doing here?" Mantra cried. "I said I'd be gone just a half-sun. You should have remained in your chamber."

"Mother was in distress. I had to do something, brother."

"Where is Sita?"

"In her room, as usual." Her words were bitter, and Sarina gathered Sita was another sister. The girl's large emerald eyes rested on her. "Who are these strangers you bring among us, Mantra? Are they off-worlders?"

Mantra strode forward and clutched Kairi's arm. "This woman is the answer to our prayers. She is the Great Healer, sister."

Kairi stared in shock. "It cannot be."

"Truly, she has come from the stars to help us."

The girl fell to her knees and raised her hands. "Thank the heavens! We are saved."

"Please, get up," Sarina said. "Let me see your mother. How long has she been ill?"

"Since this morn," Mantra said. "She took sick of a sudden." Describing her symptoms, he said, "Now her body shakes as though the ground crust trembles. Alas, I fear she is lost unless you can heal her. Please tend to her, Great One."

"I'll have to shut off my bioshield."

"Sarina, no." Teir rushed at her.

She put up a hand to stave him off. "It's the only way. The protective shield might inhibit my power. I have to take the risk."

"We didn't come here for this reason," Teir reminded her in a low tone.

"I know," she said. Their original goal had been merely to postpone her marriage. But the excuse Teir gave to Glotaj was valid. She needed to be tested for her own peace of mind. "If there is any truth to the legend, we'll find it out now." Anything that could help her avoid the execution decree was worth trying.

Teir stared at her. If he were a believer, he'd have no qualms.

But he'd never given credence to magic or myths—at least, not until the cut on his arm had mysteriously healed after Sarina touched it. If she had developed her healing power, it must mean she'd fallen in love with Lord Cam'brii.

Although the thought was abhorrent to him, he said, "All right. But reactivate the shield as soon as you're done."

Sarina switched off the shimmering bioshield, then approached the sick woman's bedside. She put a hand to Malika's neck. Her hide was burning hot. The female's lips were dry and parched, her open eyes glassy. "What treatments are you using?"

"We are purifying the air with sulfur and other detoxifying herbs, Mistress," Kairi said. "And I have put a poultice upon her tumor."

"May I see it?" Sarina knew she would be upset, but she had to know what she was dealing with.

Gently, Kairi pulled back the coverlet and raised her mother's nightgown. A festering black boil covered her inner thigh. "Can you not heal her now?" Kairi asked, covering Malika.

Sarina sat on the bed, closing her eyes and taking the ill woman's hand. Ignoring Malika's tremors, Sarina prayed for her power to materialize. She clutched the woman's hand tighter. Malika still burned, still shook. The minutes ticked by.

Sarina's eyes snapped open. "I'm sorry," she said. "It's not working. There's nothing I can do."

"What?" Mantra cried, hovering above her. "You are the Great Healer. You must save her."

Sarina shook her head. "I have no special power."

"That is untrue. According to the Baynor, you are The One. You answered the light from the Auricle."

Sarina rose and placed her hands on his shoulders. "I am touched by your faith, Mantra, but it is misplaced. I am merely an ordinary woman from Earth." A deep pit of sadness yawned within her. "Truly, I wish I could help."

"Let's get out of here," Teir said. He must have been mistaken about the cut on his arm. Perhaps Sarina had seen bark fragments or sap from the Twygg on his skin, and in the frenzy of battle, she'd assumed he had been wounded and that it was blood. Her healing power didn't exist. Either she still needed more time to fall in love with Cam'brii, or the legend was false.

"Activate your bioshield," he told her, alarmed that she would catch the disease. "You've been exposed to the Farg."

"I need to wash my hands." Sarina glanced around the room, looking for a sink. The dim lighting cast parts of the chamber in shadow. Outside, a perpetual cold twilight was the norm, evidently due to Tendraa's great distance from its sun. What little rays there were couldn't penetrate the soot-covered windows. Flickering lamplight and the crackling fire provided some illumination, but the burning herbs and pungent smoke created a haze inside the room. Nonetheless, Sarina noticed the collection of dirt on the wood-planked floor.

A tall commode with a basin of water stood in one corner. She went over, grimacing at the brown flecks dotting the liquid's surface. A cup, half-filled with cloudy water, rested beside it. Sarina washed her hands—for all the good it would do without soap—and then grabbed a filthy rag to use as a towel. Conditions might be primitive by her standards, but they'd be considered prehistoric by the more advanced Coalition cultures.

Hmm, perhaps her knowledge could be useful after all.

"Come on," Teir urged. Fighting a known enemy was one thing, but lingering in a sickroom with invisible germs pervading the air was another. His skin crawled the longer they remained.

"Just a minute." Sarina approached Kairi and Mantra who had been conferring quietly at their mother's bedside. "I might not have any magic, but I do have some suggestions that could help. Can these windows be opened? You need more ventilation in here."

Mantra regarded her with skepticism. "We dare not," he replied. "If anybody heard our mother cry out, they would report us. We'd be quarantined again."

Sarina gave him a reproachful glance. "Suppose you tell me

about this method of dealing with the plague." When Mantra finished his horrifying pronouncements, Sarina promised her silence. "I won't tell the Baynor if you carry out my instructions."

She could understand the need for quarantine, but other methods of disease prevention might work better without causing so much suffering. Besides, four weeks sounded too long to confine the healthy with the sick. She'd have to learn more about this disease and the incubation period. Did it really take up to a month for signs of infection to show?

Kairi bowed her head. "Tell us what we must do, Mistress, and we shall obey."

"As I said, ventilation is important. It's very smoky in here. Try cleaning out the chimney in the house to see if that helps. Open windows if you can but avoid drafts and don't let your mother get chilled. Fresh, clean water is next. It must be changed more often. Where do you get your supply?"

"We have a well out back," Mantra responded.

Sarina instructed him in the technique of boiling water, stressing that the sick woman must be given frequent sips of cooled liquid. She suggested more sanitation measures, from housecleaning to personal bathing to handwashing.

"How is the contagion spread?" she asked.

"The air is corrupted by noxious vapors," Mantra said, giving her a look of surprise.

"Where do these vapors originate?"

"From the soil, of course. The poisonous efflux enters the air and is caught by the viscous humors of the body. This puts the blood into an immediate ferment and agitates the spirit."

"What do you mean by 'humors of the body'?"

Mantra glowered at her, as though everyone should know these basic facts. "The humors must remain in equilibrium for a person to be healthy. There are four—yellow bile, black bile, phlegm, and blood. They correspond to the four elements of the universe, which are fire, earth, water, and air. The sickness is brought about by a disruption of the elements. In this case, air."

"So how is catching the disease prevented? No one wears a face mask or takes any precautions against airborne transmission that I can see."

Mantra pointed to the fireplace. "The fire helps to fumigate the chamber. By their nitrous streams, the burning sulfur sticks change the nature of the poisonous efflux should it be received by the body. We carry cloths—" he pulled one from a pocket in his robe "—scented with the attar of flowers to refresh the spirit. Holding the cloth over your nose when you are outside helps to avoid contact with the corrupt air. But regardless of our efforts, nothing seems to work."

"I can believe it." No wonder these people were so sick. Their treatments were based on erroneous theories about the causation of disease. Since she wasn't sure what caused the Farg, she could only offer general advice.

"You've already had the disease," she said to Mantra, "but your sister hasn't. Keep her away from your mother. Wash your hands after every contact and get some fresh air in here. Stale air like this can encourage infection, not the other way around. See what happens if you follow my suggestions."

Someone stumbled through the doorway and Sarina whirled around.

"It's my oldest sister, Sita," Mantra said, stiffly introducing them.

The girl leaned against the doorjamb, a sardonic look on her face. Her features resembled Kairi's, but without any of the softness. Lines of strain showed under her heavy makeup.

"The Great Healer, is it?" Sita drawled, adjusting her garment, a canary yellow drape that clung to her ample curves. "Have you cured my mother yet?" She spoke to Sarina, but her interested glance was directed at Teir.

"I'm afraid not," Sarina replied, "but I've given some instructions that may help. I'll talk to the Baynor to ensure you receive adequate supplies."

Kairi came forward, her hands folded as though in prayer.

"Thank you, Mistress. You came to us without fear. That alone gives us hope."

"Perhaps you can convince the Liege Lord of Tendraa to consider a full partnership in the Coalition," Mantra offered, hope kindling in his breast. The Earth woman might not have any healing power, but she did have influence. The Coalition doctors might be able to teach his people newer methods for treating the distemper.

"I don't know," Sarina said doubtfully. "We only have permission to meet with your Baynor and view the city. But I'll see that Ravi gets your news. He will be happy to hear you are well." She switched on her bioshield and prepared to leave.

Thinking of Ravi reminded Sarina of all the problems she faced upon her return to Bimordus Two. As she walked back to the ship beside Teir, a mantle of gloom settled over her.

She'd be forced to marry Lord Cam'brii. Less than ten months later would come her execution. The latter event seemed inevitable after her failure with Malika.

She glanced at Teir's firm profile. His actions had shown her the depth of his feelings for her, even if he hadn't mentioned any words of love. Neither had she, because her emotions hadn't crystallized in her own mind yet. She only knew for certain that she couldn't accept a loveless marriage.

They'd put off discussing their future until the trip home. Well, now it was time. She wondered if Teir would agree to what she intended to ask.

Chapter Fourteen

"I feel as though microbes are crawling all over my body," Teir said when they were seated in the command chairs on the bridge of the *Valiant*. He monitored the helm controls as they left orbit at sublight speed. They'd removed their bioshields and taken decontamination showers upon entry to the ship. "That was the worst world I've ever visited," he added with a visible shudder.

Sarina grimaced. "The living conditions on Tendraa are primitive even by Earth's standards. I can't understand why their leaders would allow them to remain that way."

"It was a choice the Tendraans made years ago after the Techno War nearly destroyed their planet. You'd think they would have made some progress since then, however."

"According to what Ravi said, progress is anathema to his people." She brushed her hand through her hair. She'd untwisted her braid, and the waves fell down her back. The strands still felt damp from the vigorous scrubbing she'd done.

"Mantra wants more for his family, and there are probably others like him," Teir remarked. "Tendraa is rich in minerals, which is their main export product in the trade agreement with the Coalition. Where do you suppose all their profits are going?"

Sarina considered the Baynor's luxurious attire. "No way. Could the leaders be hoarding the riches for themselves and keeping the people in ignorance on purpose? That's horrendous, given the conditions on their world."

Teir shrugged. "Let's say I'm highly suspicious of their heads of state, not that it's any of our business. If I have any choice in the matter, I hope never to return there."

"Don't let Ravi hear you say that."

"He agrees with me. Ravi sees complacency as the problem, and unfortunately, it's one that is not confined to his planet. The R.O.F. came into being because too many changes were hitting the Coalition at once, such as expansion, threats from outsiders, and the Farg. The R.O.F. is responding the same way the Tendraans did—to retreat to an earlier era. They propose to dissolve the Coalition and let each species fend for themselves. It's isolationism and regression combined, and you've seen what that policy has done on Tendraa."

Sarina gazed out the large viewscreen. Tendraa was receding in the distance. From here, the planet appeared as a large yellowish globe. Cloud belts intermittently covered the surface. A huge brown spot was evident on the northern hemisphere, but a gaseous haze obscured the lower regions. It didn't offer much beauty, not like Earth. She missed the vast blue oceans and green forests of her home. Even Bimordus Central, the dazzling capital city, was built on a barren planetoid. All plant life there was artificially grown.

"Teir," she said, turning to him with a pleading look, "you've seen that my power doesn't exist. I'm not the answer to the Coalition's problems. I'll be executed just because I am nobody special. Please, take me home."

His gaze hardened. "You're forgetting what the legend has foretold. Your power will only be activated when you fall in love. You need more time."

"I'll never fall in love with Rolf. Why won't you listen? I thought you cared about me."

"I do, but it's not my place to interfere with the legend."

"Even if it means my death? All you have to do is transport me to Earth. I'm sure you can think of a way to elude our escort."

"We've gone over this before. My response is the same. The subject is closed." He set his mouth in a firm line.

"Then take me somewhere else that's safe," Sarina suggested.

He regarded her with a veiled expression. With desperation etched on her lovely features, she made him want to oblige her. But his duty was to deliver her to the High Council for her marriage to Lord Cam'brii. This delay had accomplished nothing except to cause them both more pain. Hoping to avoid further argument, he put off giving a direct answer.

His fingers flew over the nav pad as he programmed in the course coordinates for Bimordus Two and initiated the jump to warp speed. The *Valiant* shot into interstellar space so fast that Teir nearly missed the blip on his radar screen.

"Did you catch that sensor reading on your monitors?" he radioed to the squadron leader escorting them. The four combat ships had assumed position as soon as they'd left orbit.

"Briefly, sir, but I couldn't get a fix on it."

"I got the impression the range was rather broad."

"Meaning what? More than one ship has entered the system?" The officer's tone implied that was nothing unusual.

"Possibly." Teir frowned at his console. He hadn't received any communiqués indicating a large squadron of ships heading their way. He and Sarina might not have been given permission to go to Tendraa if that were the case. Was it possible Defense League Command didn't know about it? If so, where did those vessels originate?

Sarina left her seat, probably heading to their cabin to rest. After cutting off the comm link, he set the ship on autopilot and rose to follow her.

He forgot about the sensor reading as soon as he glimpsed her standing beside the fabricator. She must be hungry, since they hadn't eaten since that morning. He was hungry for more than food and moved to stand beside her.

"I've been waiting all day for this," he said, kissing her neck.

Sarina didn't appear to object, because she yielded to his ministrations. Four more days of passionate lovemaking commenced. Teir was content to enjoy her without worrying about the future.

On the last day of their voyage, Sarina found herself alone on the bridge. Teir had gone below to check a linear actuator on Deck Two. Her gaze wandered to the nav console, and she realized they'd never finished their talk about destinations. Wondering where Teir had decided to take her, she checked the coordinates.

Curse the man. They were still on course to Bimordus Two.

"I thought you'd listened to me," she told him upon his return to the bridge. "I don't want to marry Rolf. How can you condone that prospect after all we've shared?"

He halted, his back to her as he fumbled with a lever on a wall panel. "If there is any truth to the legend, you have to give the councilor a chance. Our personal issues don't matter."

It was his fault she was turning away from Cam'brii, Teir realized. Making love to her had satisfied his selfish need but it had impeded the prophecy's natural progress. In simpler terms, he was in the way. Did he really want to be the one responsible for the Coalition's downfall?

Wrestling with his conscience, he made a painful decision. It was time for him to step aside, and in so doing, give Sarina back to Lord Cam'brii. Though it grieved him deeply, he decided the easiest way was to pretend he didn't care for her. She hated it whenever she heard the word duty, so he'd use it against her.

"I cannot countermand my orders, and those are to return you safely to the High Council. It is your duty to marry the councilor."

"So you'd doom me to a loveless marriage. I thought you felt something for me."

Teir's gut twisted. It made him sick to think of her in the councilor's bed. But he merely turned toward her with a sneer. "I'll still be around when Cam'brii bores you."

"Bastard. You don't even care that I'll be condemned to die because I'm not the Great Healer?"

He steeled his heart against her, knowing he had to provoke her hatred in order for her to return willingly to Lord Cam'brii. "Your disposition is for the High Council to decide."

Sarina picked up a metal astro-compass and threw it at him.

He dodged the implement, wincing when it hit the console behind him with a loud clang. Sarina snorted in disgust and stormed from the bridge. With a sigh of relief, he sank into his seat.

Fortunately for his peace of mind, she remained out of sight until their approach to Bimordus Two. She surprised him by entering the bridge with two crystal goblets of wine in hand. His gaze dropped to her rose-colored gown that showed off her curves, and to her golden hair flowing over her shoulders. Her floral perfume drifted his way, teasing his senses.

"A peace offering," she said with a sugary smile. "I understand your devotion to duty, and I'm sorry if I upset you."

He regarded her with suspicion. "What's this about, Sarina?"

"I've decided our relationship doesn't have to end just because I'm going to wed Rolf. As you said, he'll probably bore me. Shall we drink a toast to our continued… friendship?"

Teir sensed she was up to something, but it was hard to concentrate when he could see her body through the thin material of her dress. Even one day without bedding her was like a lifetime of deprivation. He felt himself responding with an irresistible physical urge.

"All right," he said, standing and accepting the goblet from her outstretched hand. They clinked glasses and drank.

"Shall we retire to the cabin for one last time?" she suggested in a husky tone. Her long lashes shaded her eyes, and he couldn't read her expression. But her sensuous movements were unmistakable in their intent.

Teir took another sip. The honeyed wine was a bit too sweet for his taste. "We're about to enter orbit—"

"You don't have to initiate the landing sequence just yet. Can't it wait for one more haura?" Sarina rubbed up against him, sliding her leg along the outside of his thigh. Her warmth penetrated through his clothes. "I want you, Teir. I'll have you any way I can get you." She gestured for him to follow her.

Unable to resist, he switched on the autopilot and then trailed her from the bridge.

****

Hauras later, Teir wished he could push back the chronometer to the scene on the *Valiant* and change his response. He sat in the communications room at Defense League Station on Bimordus Central, a severe headache pounding his skull. But it was nothing compared to the rage consuming him.

"Captain Reylock?" Admiral Daras Gog roared over the comm unit. "Are you there?"

"Aye, sir."

"What in the fires of Alpha Gomaran Two is going on?"

Teir's mouth tightened. "Sarina slipped something into my drink, sir. She put me in a shuttle, probably by using the mini-levitator we have on board, and programmed it to land on Bimordus Two. I woke up when a technician in the shuttle bay broke open the door."

"And the *Valiant*?"

"She stole it. Apparently, Sarina tricked our escort as well. She used a digitized facsimile of my voice to order the squadron leader to follow the shuttle down." Or so he had been told after he'd regained consciousness.

What a fool he'd been. His head still reeled from the sleeping potion she'd put in his wine. He'd been right to be suspicious about her abrupt change in behavior. Her seduction scene was merely a ploy to throw him off guard. Now she'd stolen his ship and possibly ruined his career. Entrusted with her safety, he'd failed miserably. Teir wouldn't be surprised if a court martial was in order from the mess he'd created.

"I'll go after her," he stated. "Requisition me a fast patrol ship, and I'll get right on her trail."

"No, you won't," the Admiral answered. "The High Council has called an emergency meeting to decide what they want done.

You are to report to the Great Hall for a debriefing immediately after we sign off. They will decide what disciplinary action is needed." His voice lowered. "I'm disappointed in you, Captain. What would provoke the woman to do such a thing?"

"She's always wanted to go home, Admiral."

"If you knew that, you should have taken extra precautions to secure her return to Bimordus Two. You were extremely negligent in your duty."

Teir's hands curled into fists. "I'll make up for it. I can—"

"You'll do nothing. If the High Council releases you, I have a different assignment for you and your crew."

"What is it?" Teir replied in a cautious tone.

"We've had a distress call from the Matiaus system. The series of quakes on Mat Four have escalated, and the colonists urgently need a fresh supply of bimanthium crystals. Our only available source right now is on Lapis, and they're in a hostage situation. You're the only one who can defuse this fiasco and get the crystals to Mat Four on time."

"But Sarina—"

"I'll give you two weeks, Reylock. After that, the tectonic plates on Mat Four will start to separate. We don't have the resources available for a mass evacuation."

"Sir, let me detour to Earth first. I'm sure I can retrieve Sarina and then accomplish this mission." He couldn't believe what he was hearing. Not go after the woman? After what she'd done to him? Blast her to Zor!

Admiral Gog's voice came through loud and strong. "Understand something, Captain. Should you make any attempt to retrieve Sarina Bretton, you'll be dishonorably discharged from the Defense League." He paused to let his words sink in. "Now, do I have your cooperation?"

"Aye, sir." Teir signed off after promising to obtain the details of his new assignment.

A short while later, he approached the set of double doors at the right wing of the Great Hall. The entrance led to the Council

Chamber, where the twelve members of the High Council would debrief him.

Inside, the councilors sat in a semi-circle with Glotaj on a throne-like chair in the center. Teir was directed to stand facing them. Feeling like a criminal, he complied. From the corner of his eye he glimpsed Mara, Sarina's friend, standing off to the side.

"Report, Captain Reylock," the regent commanded. Glotaj's sharp gaze pierced his as though they could bore the truth out of him.

Teir told them what had happened, leaving out any hint of a personal relationship between himself and Sarina. He blamed her actions purely on her desire to go home.

Lord Cam'brii spoke first. The councilor's eyes were like two chunks of blue ice. "Are you certain nothing unusual happened on the voyage to provoke her actions, Captain?"

Teir sensed the underlying message, and his face flushed. "She was upset by the horrors on Tendraa. Her power didn't materialize, and she feared the execution decree. I suppose she felt her only viable alternative was to flee."

Emu shot up from his seat, his thin Sirisian body elongating as he bent forward. "We must retrieve her. The prophecy may still come to pass."

Daimon's hard-edged voice grated an answer. "I say leave well enough alone. She's not the Great Healer. Let her stay on Earth."

Emu's pink skin reddened as he bobbed his bald head in its ruby turban. "We will never know if she is the Great Healer unless we give her the chance to prove herself. Just because she failed on Tendraa doesn't mean she is not The One. According to the legend, she must fall in love for her power to activate. She probably needs more time. I say the marriage ceremony should take place as scheduled."

Daimon stood slowly and stroked his beard. "You would still wed her, knowing she has run away?" he asked Lord Cam'brii.

The blond councilor nodded. "Sarina is my responsibility. If she returns, I will fulfill my duty. Do we know for certain she is heading for Earth?"

"We'll find out. Mara, can you assess the situation for us?" Glotaj asked the woman.

Mara was a Tyberian who possessed empathic ability. She could sense another's emotions, but her power went beyond that. She could actually separate her spirit from her body and travel the astral plane to project herself into another's life space. This allowed her to see through the other person's eyes. She rarely used her gift, but since Sarina was her friend, she'd readily agreed to the High Council's request for aid.

She stepped into the brightly lit circle. "I am ready." She closed her eyes and tilted her head back. No one spoke. Teir noticed she held something in her hand—a jeweled comb, one like Sarina had worn. He recalled Sarina telling him that Mara needed to hold an object touched by the person in order to trigger her separation.

Through the comb, Mara homed in on Sarina's psychic vibrations. Her ability let her into Sarina's mind, so that she could watch events as they unfolded from her perspective. Mara couldn't picture what had come before or what would happen thereafter—only the immediate present was visible.

An image came to her. "I see what she sees," Mara intoned. "I am on the bridge of a ship, monitoring the controls. Now I am checking the settings." She rattled off a series of numbers.

"Those are the coordinates for Earth," Teir said excitedly.

"Captain, isn't there an emergency locator on your vessel?" Glotaj asked. "If so, notify Defense League Command to activate it. When we have confirmed the Great Healer's location, we'll decide what to do next. Mara, is there anything else?"

The Tyberian shook her head. "The viewscreen shows normal star space, Your Excellency."

Glotaj inclined his head. "Thank you for your cooperation. You are dismissed." After she left, the regent turned to Teir.

"Captain Reylock, you will receive a reprimand on your record. See that you maintain your vigilance in the future. I understand you are needed for another assignment. You may go, but first I'd like a word in private."

Teir's jaw gaped. That was it, just a reprimand? Gods, how lucky could he get?

Without waiting to see the others' reactions, Teir followed the Supreme Regent into his spacious office.

Glotaj shut the door, his black robe swishing at his feet. He took a seat at his desk while Teir stood facing him, hands clasped behind his back. It pained him to have caused that look of stern disapproval on the regent's lined face.

"Captain, would you care to tell me what *really* happened on your ship?"

Teir cleared his throat. "I don't understand, sir. I've given my report."

"Did anything unusual occur between you and Sarina?"

"No, sir," Teir lied.

Glotaj's sharp gaze studied him. "I want the truth."

Teir felt as though guilt must be written all over his face. "Sarina fled to avoid the execution decree, and I can't blame her. It makes no sense to put an innocent to death."

"You sound as though you don't believe in the legend."

"I'm not sure how I feel about it, but that doesn't matter. Sarina hasn't been treated fairly. She was torn away from her life on Earth and expected to adapt without any regard for her own opinion."

"You were the one sent to obtain her. As I recall, you didn't have any qualms about the assignment at the time."

"I didn't know her then, Your Excellency."

"Ah. And you know her better now?"

Teir moistened his dry lips, sensing a trap. Gods, they could accuse him of treason if they knew he'd been Sarina's lover. He sought a cautious reply. "As her bodyguard, I couldn't help becoming more acquainted with her, sir."

"Indeed." The regent studied him. Before he could respond, a knock sounded at the door. "Enter."

Lord Cam'brii stalked into the room. He glared at Teir, then gave a deferential bow to the older man. "I apologize for the intrusion, but I felt this was something that concerned me."

Glotaj sighed. "Very well. Perhaps it is best if the two of you air your differences. It is clear that hostile feelings are involved."

"Captain Reylock desires my betrothed," Cam'brii said. "I've seen it in the way he looks at her. It is dishonorable to covet another man's bride."

"Oh?" Glotaj turned a questioning glance on Teir. "I thought you said nothing happened during your voyage, Captain."

Teir's thoughts raced. If he told the truth, his career would be over. And who knew what punishment Sarina would receive if she ever returned? He'd have to lie to protect them both.

"I didn't touch her, Councilor. I'm aware of my duty. I would say if anyone was at fault here, it's you."

"How dare you." Cam'brii's face reddened.

"You've hardly paid her any attention. And when you do, it's only to talk about the First Amendment and how she can use her position to help you. You've made no effort to gain her affection. If she doesn't fall in love with you, the prophecy cannot be fulfilled."

To Teir's surprise, Cam'brii bowed his head. "I suppose you are right. To be truthful, I never expected her to be so keenly intelligent or so spirited."

"Not to mention beautiful, compassionate, and willful," Teir couldn't help adding. He glanced at Glotaj. The regent was staring at him, a peculiar look on his face.

"I've paid no heed to her feelings," Cam'brii confessed. "She accused me of treating her like a symbol, and I'll admit she was correct. I forgot the Great Healer is also a woman." He pursed his lips, and it was obvious he was uncomfortable with what he was going to say next. "If Sarina returns, I'll need your help, Captain."

Teir couldn't have been more astonished if Cam'brii had offered to buy him a new ship. "What do you mean?"

"I must win her love. You seem to understand Sarina better than I do. Tell me how to please her."

"Can't you figure that out for yourself? Forgive me, Councilor, but if you want to show genuine interest in Sarina, you have to make an effort to get to know her on your own."

Glotaj sighed. "Enough, gentlemen. Please be seated. Rolf, you must tell him. It would explain your difficulties."

Cam'brii's face paled but he nodded. He sank into a chair and waited for Teir to be seated opposite him. "This is not an easy story to relate. I hope when you hear it, you'll understand my viewpoint. Annums ago, I fell in love with a girl on Nadira. As Gayla was not yet of age, we faced a lengthy betrothal period, but we were too impatient to wait. We planned an elopement. We acquired a spacecraft and headed for the Hut star system where we could be wed in peace. Our ship was intercepted by Souk pirates."

His voice took on a note of anguish. "In the battle that ensued, Gayla was killed. I eluded the attackers and headed back to Nadira in our damaged vessel. I felt obliged to return Gayla's body to her parents. She was an only child, which made it all the more difficult for me to face them. As per our custom, I submitted myself for their punishment."

A long pause followed that Teir didn't dare interrupt. Cam'brii's eyes were glazed with pain as though he were reliving the terrible tragedy in his mind.

"Gayla's parents realized the elopement had been their daughter's wish as much as mine," Cam'brii continued. "They blamed her death on the Souks who attacked us and made me vow to dedicate my life to stopping the slave trade. I entered the diplomatic corps with the goal of getting legislation passed to eradicate slavery throughout the galaxy. Now do you see why getting the First Amendment passed is so important to me? We have to stop the Souk aggressors."

Teir could see the fervor burning in the man's eyes. He was driven by guilt and obsessed by the need for revenge. No wonder his goals were all that mattered to him.

"After I arrived at Bimordus Central," Cam'brii went on, "one crisis after another hit the government. Talk of the legend arose, and then the Auricle began to glow. I qualified as the Raimorrdan born under the sign of the circle. So I agreed to marry Sarina." His voice hardened. "My life is dedicated to destroying the Souks. The prophecy's fulfillment will help me accomplish that goal."

Teir leaned forward. "Why didn't you tell Sarina all this? It would have helped her to understand you."

Cam'brii looked away. "I should have confided in her. In fact, I'd made up my mind that I would tell her my story when she returned from Tendraa."

"I agree with your objectives," Teir admitted grudgingly. "I, too, would like to see the Souk pirates put out of business. But I would suggest you try to forget about them and the First Amendment when you're with Sarina. Tell her about your past and find out about hers. Learn to love her, Cam'brii, and she might love you in return."

Even as he said the words, a deep ache rose within him. Thinking of her in Lord Cam'brii's arms pained him beyond belief.

"I shall do my duty," the councilor stated. "Sarina is an admirable woman. I will woo her to the best of my ability. May I count on your support, Captain?"

Teir knew what he meant. "I won't interfere."

"Glotaj, you won't be reassigning Captain Reylock as Sarina's bodyguard, will you?" Cam'brii asked, apparently loathe to leave anything to chance.

The regent inclined his head. "No, his duties will keep him elsewhere."

What was this? Glotaj was responsible for his assignment to guard Sarina? Teir stared at the man. No wonder Daras Gog had told him to look around Bimordus Two for answers. Now he knew who to blame for his orders—the Supreme Regent himself.

Had Glotaj arranged for the *Valiant* to be disabled as well? When he gave Teir permission for the trip to Tendraa, his ship was functional again, so such a ruse was possible. But why go to such lengths to keep him planetside, and then allow him to take Sarina to Tendraa? It almost appeared as though Glotaj meant to throw the two of them together, but that made no sense.

Cam'brii was speaking about Sarina. "Should we send someone after her?"

"I don't think that would be the wise choice," Glotaj replied. "If she returns, it should be of her own volition. Her destiny will guide her if she truly is the Great Healer."

He glowered at them both. "By the way, we caught one of the Twyggs trying to leave Bimordus Two. His interrogation revealed the Souks hired his team. Their orders were to assassinate you, Rolf."

The councilor's brow furrowed. "Who gave this order?"

"All we know is that it wasn't Cerrus Bdan. We're still questioning the Twygg, however. If we learn anything more, I'll let you know."

Teir explained about the computer snafu that had set them up. "The whole transport system shut down," he said. "That's why our backup didn't arrive at the Rain Forest biome. The Twyggs must have been working with someone who had access to the grid."

"I've long suspected the Souks had an agent highly placed in our government," Glotaj admitted. "It would explain why Cerrus Bdan intercepted you and Sarina so easily when you first took her from Earth, Captain. It's my guess he was after Sarina, and not you. Interfering in the legend would prevent the First Amendment from getting passed. When this scheme ended in failure, one of Bdan's compatriots must have sent the Twyggs to murder Rolf. Killing either one of you would accomplish the same purpose."

Teir stood in alarm. "Then Sarina needs to be protected. If the Souks find out she's on her own, they'll send someone after her again."

"Or they'll decide she's of no value if she stays on Earth. Besides, if the legend is true, events will play out without our interference."

"But—"

"No buts, Captain. You have a new assignment on Lapis. See to it that you make no unauthorized detours." He stood and smoothed his robes. "Good day, gentlemen. You are dismissed."

Chapter Fifteen

Daimon and Ruzbee had their own conference about Sarina in the R.O.F. leader's private chamber.

"The Earthwoman is a rallying symbol for the Coalition and can only serve to feed the power-hungry Raimorrdans," Daimon said, regarding his companion.

Ruzbee's manner was quiet, but cunning lit his tawny eyes. An Arcturian, he was of medium stature with short gray hair. He wore the sand-colored cape of a General Assembly Representative, whereas Daimon was dressed in his maroon robe of office.

"What do you propose to do?" Ruzbee asked.

Daimon looked startled. "What am *I* going to do? Why, nothing. Let Sarina Bretton remain on Earth."

"The High Council may vote to retrieve her."

"I'll vote against taking any such action."

"Do you think Reylock will stay out of the way?"

Daimon nodded. "He usually obeys orders. Besides, the captain is scheduled for an important mission on Lapis."

"The hostage crisis?"

"That's right."

Ruzbee's eyebrows shot up. Cerrus Bdan would be happy to hear this intelligence. His payment for the information should be generous indeed. Unfortunately, Ruzbee hadn't known about the captain's mission to Tendraa in time to make a difference. Their small escort wouldn't have been able to protect them against a sizable Souk force had he moved faster. At least he could give Bdan the scoop on both of them now. Then the smuggler could decide what he wanted done.

"Emu could be difficult," Daimon mused.

"I'll keep watch on him," Ruzbee reassured him.

"If anything new develops, let me know. Otherwise, we'll sit tight."

Ruzbee nodded and left. Grinning, he thought what a fool Daimon was. The councilor figured Ruzbee was in his pocket. Instead, Ruzbee used Daimon as a source of information. The mineral-poor Arcturian worlds were dependent upon the Souks for trade. That the Souks used slave labor didn't bother Ruzbee in the least. His world needed the Souks, and he was glad to sell them information known only to the upper echelons of the Coalition government.

Occasionally he took a greater risk, such as hiring the Twyggs. That had been a fiasco. Never mind, something else would be done about Lord Cam'brii. Cerrus Bdan wasn't concerned about him anyway. The councilor was his other employer's nemesis.

Snickering to himself, Ruzbee put on his dark glasses as he neared the rotunda. He loved playing ball on different courts. It kept life interesting.

****

Mantra had his own concerns about the so-called Great Healer. Having expected Sarina to perform a miracle and cure his mother, he'd only gotten advice from her.

Malika had died the very same evening of the Great Healer's visit. Even his sister Kairi's words of comfort hadn't been able to dispel his gloom. Now Mantra was head of the family.

Would his sisters be taken by the dead cart next?

Desperate to ensure their survival, he'd adopted the sanitation measures suggested by Sarina. Already his breathing was easier since the smoky haze cleared from his house. It was almost a miracle in itself what those few changes had wrought.

Maybe, just maybe, the Great One's advice was the vehicle

for her aid. Mantra pondered this possibility and decided it must be so. In that case, he had to spread the word. She'd chosen him to be her disciple, and he had to have faith.

Fevered by his devotion, Mantra set out to see the Liege Lord of Tendraa.

****

"Open communications to the surface," K'darr ordered the communications officer from the bridge of the flagship *Krog*.

They'd just entered orbit around the outermost planet of the Tendraan system. The Morgot leader stood scowling at the viewscreen and the ice-encrusted globe spinning below. If this conquest went like all the others, it would take weeks to subdue the inhabitants.

"Wait," K'darr said, changing his mind. He needed to see how much time they had left before the prophecy came true. Maybe they should go directly to Tendraa. "Get me Cerrus Bdan on subspace radio."

"Er—the trader is back on Souk," the comm officer said nervously, afraid to be the bearer of bad news.

"*What?*" K'darr thundered. His black robe swished around his booted feet as he stomped over to the console. "Grand Marshal Zen-Bos." His gaze swept the bridge.

The marshal had been listening to the exchange, and he scurried over. "Sir?"

"I thought you had contacted Bdan to obtain the Earthwoman for us. What happened?"

"We didn't hear back from him. I figured he would get in touch when his job was done."

"It shouldn't take him this long." K'darr stroked the clinging aguar plant that hung over his shoulder. The leaves were crimson with a fuzzy texture. "If there's been a miscommunication, Grand Marshal, you'll be the one to pay."

Zen-Bos understood what he meant, and a shudder ran up

his spine. The aguar plant grew like a weed. One seedling had sprouted and taken over the whole recreation hall. K'darr loved the jungle-like effect and forbade anyone to remove it.

Besides, he used it as a fitting punishment for inefficient crew members. K'darr ordered them locked in the rec room for the night. The victims didn't look pretty when they came out. The plant secreted a slow-acting digestive enzyme that dissolved one's fur along with the underlying skin.

Trapped inside the room, the victim quickly became entangled in the voracious vines. Then the lights were turned off, and the enzyme went to work in the dark. Zen-Bos had heard the hideous screams himself when passing by.

"Cerrus Bdan is online," the comm officer announced.

"I'll take it in the ready room."

K'darr entered the private conference room adjacent to the bridge. Taking a seat at the table, he flicked the comm unit open. "I hear you've returned to Souk, Bdan. What happened to our contract? You were supposed to capture the Earthwoman and bring her to me."

The smuggler coughed. "A delay has occurred, master."

"A delay? What delay?" K'darr said with a low growl.

"We had the woman and then got away she did, helping Captain R-R-Reylock to escape as well."

"You stupid lyphound! I need to know if the legend is true. Reylock knows the location of the Blood Crystal."

"The mystical stone that can predict the future?"

"That's right. I must consult the Crystal. If it shows me this woman is truly the Great Healer, I will use her power to my own advantage. Capture them both and bring them to me—*unharmed,* mind you, or you'll pay the price for failure."

K'darr didn't hear Bdan's chuckle as they signed off. The smuggler had his own score to settle with the pair before he'd hand them over to the Morgots, if he handed them over at all.

****

Sarina breathed a sigh of relief as the *Valiant* reached Earth's orbit. During the long journey, she'd wondered how Teir had felt when he woke up and realized what she'd done. He'd be furious with her for stealing his ship, but it served him right. Did the man really think she'd return voluntarily to Bimordus Two to face execution?

All those sweet words he'd whispered in her ear—how could she have believed him? If he really cared about her, he would have taken her somewhere safe. Apparently, she meant nothing more to him than a sex partner. He'd even had the nerve to tell her, "I'll be around when Cam'brii bores you."

Sarina had thought of the sleeping potion as a last resort. Rolf suffered from occasional nightmares. Without explaining the nature of his dreams when she'd asked about them, he had mentioned taking a sedit beverage to get back to sleep.

After looking the drug up in the ship's database, Sarina had reproduced a supply of the sleep-inducing potion using the fabricator in Teir's cabin. Dissolving the powder in his wine had been easy, and her seduction act had worked.

Now she was finally home. Sarina admired the cleverness of the cloaking device. It utilized molecular alteration like the fabricators but in a different manner. By changing the speed of molecular motion, an object could be made to appear in any particular configuration. Teir had made the shuttle look like an elevator in her office corridor. She came down by the same method since it was already programmed into the computer. But before leaving the ship, she used the fabricator to produce suitable Earth clothing.

It was Sunday, and her office building was closed. She checked her space, surprised that her things were still present. Having been missing for so long, she would have thought her stuff would be gone.

Rummaging in her desk, Sarina found some money and her extra house key in a small purse she kept hidden in a drawer. After calling a cab, she went outside to marvel at being home again. The bright afternoon sunshine warmed her skin. A breeze blew off Biscayne Bay, salty and moist, ruffling the shirt that she wore over a pair of jeans.

It felt sublime to have solid pavement beneath her feet. Earth was a beautiful world, one she vowed never to leave again. Too bad many of its citizens didn't appreciate its uniqueness. Maybe she should consider studying environmental law.

Not knowing if she still had a home, Sarina directed the cab driver to her address and was surprised to find her favorite crimson potted flowers still blooming on the stoop of her townhouse. Realizing it might be futile, she took the key from her purse and fitted it in the lock, expecting it not to work. Surely someone else would have rented the place by now.

Stunned, Sarina stood there a moment when the key twisted as easily as though the lock had just been greased. Since she had been missing for so long, why hadn't her mother taken her personal belongings and canceled the lease? Confused, she shook her head. Her office, too, remained as though she still occupied it. By all standards, it appeared as though she had never left.

Stepping into the foyer, she peered around cautiously. Her umbrella stand still stood by the front door. And there was the blue umbrella she'd bought at Disney World during a downpour.

She tensed as sounds emanated from the kitchen. A feminine voice called out, "Who's there?" And to Sarina's astonishment, around the corner walked an exact duplicate of herself.

"Who are you?" Sarina said with a gasp.

"What are *you* doing here? I wasn't told to expect you," the other Sarina replied, looking as surprised as she felt. "Are you a replacement?"

Sarina peeked into the living room. Her furnishings and accessories were exactly as she'd left them. "What's going on here?" she demanded.

Her duplicate closed the door. "I'm Number 1468, revised series. Which are you?" When Sarina just stared at her, the other said, "You *are* an android, aren't you?"

"Certainly not. I'm human—the real me. *You're* an android?"

"The real Sarina? Oh, my." The android's gray eyes widened.

She looks incredibly human, Sarina thought. *I'd never have known if she wasn't supposed to be me.* "What are you doing here? I assume the Coalition sent you."

"I took your place when Captain Reylock came to get you. He transported me to your residence while he went to your office. My signature name is Kayo." She smiled proudly. "I have the new emotions module."

"I see. So you've been substituting for me?"

Kayo nodded.

"What about Robert?" Sarina asked.

The android raised an eyebrow. "He's quite a man." Her substitute began pacing the living room, and Sarina was annoyed to note the android wore her best clothes. "When I took over, your relationship seemed rather cool. After trying different types of behavior, I noted that I provoked the most positive response when I was pleasant every time we met. The two of you are very close now."

"Oh, no," Sarina groaned.

"Your mother's plans for the wedding are proceeding," Kayo went on. "She'll be sending the invitations out next week."

"Not if I can help it. What else have you done that I should know about?" Sarina stomped into her bedroom, followed by her double. The room was immaculate, neater than she'd ever kept it.

"I've been maintaining your business appointments. By the way, congratulations. You've been made Associate in the firm. You'll be moving into a new office with your own assistant this week."

"You mean I—you—we passed Simmons's test? What was it?"

Kayo grinned. "Pierce Mitchells took you out to lunch with your boss's approval. He plied you with cocktails to get you drunk, then tried to question you about one of the cases you were handling. The purpose, Simmons told me later, was to see if you'd leak information when you were under duress." She giggled. "Androids are not affected by alcohol. Pierce Mitchells was under the table before I'd even finished my sixth drink."

Sarina couldn't help laughing. "You know, Robert never told me the conclusion of his test case. Since you're so close to him now, did he mention it to you?"

"Yes, we discussed it after I passed mine—or rather, yours. He was tested to see if he would take a bribe."

"Ah, I thought so." Sarina went into the kitchen and opened the refrigerator door, to find it empty.

"Androids have no need for nourishment," said Kayo, watching her with amusement.

Sarina turned and looked into her own clear gray eyes. "Now that I'm back, you can switch yourself off. Or better still, I'll transport you to Captain Reylock's ship."

"The Captain escorted you home?"

Sarina regarded her a moment in silence. Maybe it wasn't such a good idea to send Kayo to the ship. She might signal the Coalition. "Not exactly," she hedged. "You'd better fill me in on what's been going on."

After an hour-long discussion, Sarina went out for her regular Sunday visit with Abby. She couldn't wait to see her friend. Kayo had been taking her place every week, and for that, Sarina was grateful. The thing that had bothered her most during her absence was how disappointed Abby would be when she didn't show up. Kayo had made sure that didn't happen.

Evidently, some sort of mind transfer had been deployed during the initial transport process in which Sarina's memories were imprinted onto Kayo's circuits, so Kayo had known everything that was on her mind. It had been easy for the android to step into her shoes.

Behind the wheel of her Acura, Sarina thought what a pleasure it was to drive again. Too bad these vehicles didn't take off into the air like the speeders on Bimordus Two. The traffic was congested with all the Sunday pleasure seekers on the road.

After parking at the rehab center, Sarina went directly to the paraplegic ward. Abby was sitting in a wheelchair, reading a book. Her long black hair was tied into a ponytail. When she spotted Sarina, her delicate features lit up. "Hi! You're early today."

"I couldn't wait to come." Sarina knelt beside her and lowered her voice. "I've got something for you, but we have to go to your room."

"Okay," Abby said. She pushed a lever and her electrically-powered chair moved under her direction.

Inside the room, Sarina closed the door and faced her friend. From her pocket she pulled out the neurojet unit she'd obtained from the Wellness Center on Bimordus Two. Mentally she ran over the procedure. *Examine the spine. Locate the damaged nerves. Repair or regenerate.*

"Lift your shirt and lean forward," she ordered. "I need to see your back."

Abby bent as much as she could, a look of puzzlement on her face. "What's that?" she asked when she saw the small device in Sarina's hand.

"Something I discovered that might help you. You must promise not to mention a word about this to anyone. It's top secret research, still in the experimental stage, and I'm not authorized to use it. Let's see if it works."

As she spoke, she glided the device up the middle of Abby's back and immediately picked up the signal that identified the damaged area.

"Here it is." Sarina pressed the unit against her friend's vertebra. She pressed a button, and the regenerating beam penetrated the skin with a radiating warmth.

"What are you doing? Ow!" Abby exclaimed.

"All done." Impatient to see if the procedure had good results, Sarina pocketed the neurojet unit. "It's a form of electrical stimulation," she explained in a manner that Abby could understand. "It works on certain kinds of nerve damage. You have to give it some time. Remember what I said. Don't tell *anyone* about this, okay? If anything, say you prayed for a miracle, and it happened. Not that I'm promising one," she hastened to add, in case this didn't work for Abby's situation.

"Whatever you say." Abby tilted her head. "You seem different today. Is everything all right?"

"Sure." Sarina frowned, wondering how Kayo had acted with her friend.

They visited for another half hour. Then Sarina hugged her and left. Tears moistened her eyes as she emerged into the sunlight. There was so much good to do here on Earth. She'd concentrated so hard on learning how to cure Abby's paralysis that she hadn't paid attention to any of the other medical problems plaguing humankind. Frustration tore at her until she remembered Mantra's family on Tendraa. Perhaps there were still ways to help using the newfound knowledge she'd gained.

She wondered if she'd have enough time to try. Teir could show up at any moment to bring her back to Bimordus Two. Or Cam'brii himself might come this time. His devotion to duty wouldn't let her evade him so easily. The passage of the First Amendment was too important to him, and he saw the legend's fulfillment as essential to Coalition unity.

Sarina considered going to the authorities and asking for protection. But what could she say? That she'd been abducted by aliens? She might offer proof by showing them Kayo or even taking them up to Teir's ship, but did she want to be responsible for establishing First Contact? That was too heavy a burden for her to bear. And if she had no proof, the police would just relegate her to the nut category, along with Elvis sighters and people who claimed to have out-of-body experiences.

What precautions could Sarina take on her own? She couldn't tell Robert—she didn't want to have anything more to do with him, and the sooner he found that out, the better. Her mother? Her friends? Who would believe her?

After stopping off to buy some food, Sarina went home to

eat and to decide what to do. Unable to come to any logical conclusions, she roamed the house, touching the treasured items she hadn't seen in so long—her books, her souvenir mementos, her family photos, and even her favorite clothes. She'd missed the stuffed giraffe she'd had since she was a little girl and the framed photograph of her parents from last Christmas.

She'd told Teir about these things, but she'd never asked him about his home, she realized. He didn't keep any personal items on his ship. Wasn't there anything special he wanted to remember? Biting her lip, Sarina told herself it didn't matter now.

Kayo wandered into Sarina's bedroom. "You haven't told me why you're here," her duplicate said, fingering Sarina's jade robe that lay on the bed. The android's blond hair hung loose in soft waves, whereas Sarina had bound hers in a tight braid.

She sank down onto the bed, weary in a way that went beyond fatigue. "I ran away."

Kayo's eyes widened. "You *what*?"

"I do not wish to marry Lord Cam'brii."

Apparently, Kayo had been briefed on Sarina's mission. "But you must fall in love and wed him for the legend to unfold."

"Then the legend will never come to fruition, because I can't fall in love with the man. It doesn't work that way. We have no feelings for each other. And in less than a year, I'll be executed if I'm not the Great Healer. The Ascension Statute doesn't allow for any exceptions."

"The law was meant to discourage others from usurping the political power that will rightfully be yours when you are the Great Healer," Kayo said. "You fear you are *not* the Great Healer, but the time may not yet be ripe for the Revelation. Events must fall into place as they are destined. You need to return to Bimordus Two."

"No way. I'm never going back."

"You aren't viewing things in a broad enough scope," Kayo persisted. "Your life has more meaning than mere existence here on Earth."

"This world is mine, Kayo. I *like* living here. I don't plan to ever leave again."

"But you are meant for greater things. Your life can have an impact on the entire galaxy. You must not cower here when you're needed by so many others. Where is your courage, Great Healer?"

"Do you have an off-switch, Kayo?" Sarina muttered. She was damn tired of hearing herself referred to as the Great Healer.

Her abrupt change of subject distracted the android. "Of course, it is located here." She pointed to her side.

"Then turn yourself off," Sarina snapped.

"You do not have the authority to direct me."

"Oh no?" Sarina leaped up and pushed the button herself. Kayo went limp. Sarina caught the android's falling body and gently stretched her out on the bed.

"That's better. I was giving myself a headache," she said with a sigh.

The viewphone rang just then, and her mother's image appeared on the video screen. Ellen Bretton's perfectly-coiffed blond hair and expertly-applied makeup made her look years younger than fifty-two.

"Sarina, dear, I just wanted to confirm our luncheon engagement for Wednesday."

"What?" Mother never called her *dear,* and Sarina wasn't in the habit of meeting her for lunch. "Oh sure," she said, recovering quickly, "but I forgot what time you said."

"Twelve o'clock. I'll meet you in the lobby. Is everything all right?"

"Yes, thanks." Her mother hung up before Sarina could ask which lobby she meant. Damn, this must have been Kayo's arrangement.

Glancing at the android lying on her bed, she decided to move her out of sight just in case someone should come to visit unexpectedly. After all, she had no idea what other plans Kayo might have made for her.

Grunting heavily, Sarina lugged Kayo over to her closet and set her inside. She spent the rest of the day at home, reviewing her calendar and the latest emails to catch up on her life. Tomorrow should be interesting at work, as Sarina had no idea what cases Kayo had been assigned in her place.

Chapter Sixteen

The next morning, Sarina headed to the office, apprehensive about what other changes the android had made in her absence. A call from Robert interrupted her in the midst of reviewing the papers on her desk.

"Hey, babe, they got the space cleared for you today. You can start the move."

She stared at his familiar face on the viewphone. "That's nice, Robert," she said, swallowing. Good heavens, how could she face him in person? She didn't know how far Kayo had gone in their relationship.

Realizing she had no idea where her new office was located, she cleared her throat. "Um, is my new assistant available yet? I could use her help with the move."

"Why don't you call *him* and ask for yourself?"

"I'm afraid I misplaced the number."

"Here, I have it written down." He rattled off the code, then frowned. "Say, are you all right? You look a bit odd."

"I'm fine, thanks. Just a little frazzled about the move."

"Well, don't work too late. Remember, we have plans later." He waggled his eyebrows suggestively.

Sarina's stomach clenched. "Sure," she said brightly. "I'll be ready. What time?"

"Come to my place after you're finished here. I'm already chilling your favorite wine, and the steaks are marinating in the fridge. It'll be a cozy evening."

"Sounds good. See you later."

After a short interval, the young male assistant arrived. Sarina sent him to her new office with a stack of papers. Taking a break from packing her things, she strode to the window and gazed at the sun-drenched scene. It wasn't very long ago that she was staring at the sparkling bay water below and daydreaming about space travel. Then her dreams had become reality when Teir Reylock walked into her life.

What was the captain doing now? Was he on his way to bring her back, or had he forgotten all about her? She would never forget him, no matter how badly he'd treated her. His tall, dashing figure, piercing blue eyes, and disarming grin were forever implanted in her memory, as were the kisses that made her feel like molten lava. Just thinking of him made her body ache for his touch.

Returning to her desk, Sarina opened a drawer and threw the contents into a carton the assistant had brought. The rest of the day passed quickly as she finished packing, met with Mr. Simmons to be briefed on a new client, and established her presence on the upstairs floor.

By the end of the day, her apprehension about confronting Robert had grown to new heights. Her palms sweaty, she stood in front of his condo building at six-thirty and pushed the door buzzer. They had decided she would give up her place when they were married. Although Robert had wanted her to move in with him earlier, she'd refused.

Despite herself, Sarina felt a surge of affection at the sight of him. Wearing a blue dress shirt and navy pants, he represented all that was familiar. She felt comfortable in his presence and regretted what had to be done.

As soon as he touched her, however, her reservations disappeared.

"Hi, honey," he said, giving Sarina a lingering kiss that left her cold. In his eyes was a look she knew too well, and her heart sank. This was going to be difficult.

"Come on in. Have a seat while I get the grill ready." Robert liked to barbecue steaks outside on the balcony.

"I came here to talk, not to eat, Robert. There are things we need to discuss, and they can't wait." She took a seat on the living room sofa.

As Robert approached, she wondered why she'd never recognized her true feelings for him. He appealed to her in a brotherly fashion, that was all. His touch didn't make her melt like Teir's did, and his kisses didn't turn her blood to fire.

Sarina smoothed her skirt, wishing there were a fabricator in the room so she could order a Moranian Flasher to calm her jangling nerves.

Robert sat down beside her and smiled. "I couldn't wait for you to get here," he said in a low, seductive tone. "To tell the truth, I'm not very hungry either." He edged closer and put a possessive hand on her thigh. "What do you say we head for the bedroom?"

Annoyed, she brushed him off. "Please, not now."

"What's the matter?"

Sarina gathered her courage, wishing she didn't have to hurt his feelings. "I've decided this isn't going to work between us."

He gave her a look of stunned disbelief. Then his expression cleared. "Of course, you're disturbed by all the postponements, and I can't say I blame you. I thought it best to wait until you were established in the firm. Didn't you always say one should forge ahead in life, career-wise?"

"That was before… I don't feel that way anymore." Clenching her hands tightly in her lap, she said, "Robert, I'm not in love with you."

He stared at her. "But we're perfectly suited as a couple. We're in the same profession, and it means a lot having a wife who understands the lingo. We're both ambitious. We like the same kinds of music and restaurants and shows. We've even joined the same health club. What more could you want?"

"I want a man who arouses my passion, Robert. I'm fond of you, but I don't feel that way about us. It's not your fault," she hastened to add. "I've changed, and certain things are more important to me now, like being in love with my life partner. Sharing similar interests isn't enough to base a marriage on."

Robert's eyes narrowed. "I don't get it. The last few weeks you've come on to me, and now you're suddenly telling me we're finished? It's another guy, isn't it? You've met someone else."

Sarina lowered her head. It might be best to tell him the truth. "Yes, that's it," she said, glad to have an excuse.

"But when did you have time to meet this fellow? We've been together every day."

Her mind raced for a plausible response. "It's, um, someone I used to know who'd moved away, someone I really cared for. He's back in the area now and eager to renew our relationship."

"Didn't you tell him you were engaged?"

"No, I'm sorry. I wanted to keep seeing him."

Robert's nostrils flared. "What about the wedding, huh? Your mother's sending out the invitations next week."

"We'll lose the deposits, that's all. I'll pay Mother back for her losses."

"*That's all*? This whole thing means nothing more to you?"

"I'll always be fond of you, Robert, but as a friend."

His lips thinned. "If you walk out on me, Sarina, this is it. I won't take you back if you change your mind."

"I understand. Forgive me for taking so long to make a decision. You're a good man, and it wasn't easy."

Robert stood and glared down at her. "It's going to be very awkward, being in the same office together. Don't expect me to defend you to Mr. Simmons anymore. You're on your own from now on. You'd better watch what you say, too. I've worked hard to build my reputation."

"I'll be cordial. You can tell people you're the one who decided it wouldn't work between us." It didn't matter to her who got the blame. Robert's feelings for her had always been guided by his ambition. Relief assailed her as she rose and gathered her purse.

She put out her hand in a friendly gesture, but Robert

brushed past her to the door. Swinging it open, he stood aside, his eyes cold. "Good-bye, Sarina."

She left, glad to be done with him. Now she only had her mother to face.

Wednesday arrived, and so did their date for lunch. Their meeting place turned out to be a hotel lobby at Brickell Point overlooking Biscayne Bay.

"So, daughter, tell me about your new position," Ellen said when they were seated in the restaurant. "I was thrilled when I heard about your promotion."

Slender and graceful, Ellen had dressed in a tailored linen suit with a diamond pin on the lapel. Her gray eyes were a reflection of Sarina's own.

Sarina described a few of her cases, but her lack of enthusiasm was evident to her own ears.

Ellen, however, didn't notice. As they ate, she raved about Sarina's promising future, then focused on the wedding. "I'm getting so excited. The invitations are perfect. Do you have any last-minute additions to the guest list before we send them out?"

It's now or never, Sarina thought. "I've called the wedding off, Mother."

"What?"

"I told Robert on Monday. I'll pay you back for the expenses you've incurred, and I'll take care of notifying the vendors."

Ellen shook her head. "I don't believe this. What happened?"

Sarina gripped her water glass for courage. "I realized that what I felt for Robert wasn't love. It was affection, like a sister might have for a brother, and that's not enough to base a marriage on."

"Love? Is that what's bothering you?" Her mother leaned forward and fixed her with a steely gaze. "Love has nothing to do with it. Robert is a sensible young man with excellent prospects. He's perfect for you."

"No, he's perfect for *you*." Sarina carefully folded her

napkin on the table, then looked her mother in the eye. "All my life you've told me what to do. Now it's time I made my own decisions. I hate the legal profession, and I don't want to marry Robert."

Her mother put out a comforting hand. "I understand. It's just a case of prenuptial jitters, dear. But you'd better set things straight with Robert before he finds someone else."

"Mother, *I am not going to marry him.*"

Her tone of voice made Ellen gape. "You're serious, aren't you?"

"Yes, I am."

"How can you do this to me? I like the man, Sarina. You're making a big mistake if you let him go."

"If you like him so much, *you* marry him," Sarina snapped.

"I've already got a husband," Ellen reminded her.

"Yes, and he suits you just fine."

Sarina had never liked her stepfather. William was a powerful, wealthy businessman who was generous to his wife but ruthless to his subordinates. He wasn't kind and compassionate like her own father had been. Sarina still missed him terribly. He'd died of a heart attack at the age of forty-six, and Ellen had wasted no time finding a new husband. Always practical, she'd cautioned Sarina against being too sentimental.

"By the way," Ellen said as they got up from the table, "I wanted to tell you about the investment possibilities of Anco Solar. The stock price is undervalued right now, so it's a good buy if you're looking to diversify your portfolio."

"Thanks, but I'm not interested." Sarina contributed her money for the bill.

"I'm more experienced than you are in financial matters, Sarina. Since you won't have Robert to support you, you've got to make the right choices now, while you're still young."

"You're probably right. We'll talk about it another time." Sarina gave her mother an obligatory peck on the cheek and left the restaurant without a backward glance.

Disgusted with her mother's opportunistic attitude, Sarina went home. Teir had been right in that she should have followed her own path a long time ago. She would have been a lot happier.

Her life fell back into a predictable, lonely routine. Each morning, her phone rang with her programmed wake-up call. She turned on the TV in the bedroom to catch up on the latest news, weather, and traffic conditions as she dressed.

On the job, she received a new identification badge that included a GPS chip in case anyone needed to locate her. She remained in her office most of the time to avoid running into Robert. The questioning glances of her colleagues didn't help. Everyone was curious about their breakup.

Meanwhile, she went through the motions of completing her work with little interest or initiative. It was something to do while deciding what other options were available to her.

The only thing Sarina truly enjoyed was shopping and being with people she knew. On her days off, she met her friends, and they strolled through the shopping malls. She had fun browsing in the shops and eating in the restaurants, ordering all of her favorite foods. An American cheeseburger had never tasted so good. She'd missed these amenities.

In a way, the malls reminded her of Bimordus Central, the shimmering pink and white city under a crystal dome. But Bimordus Central didn't have any shopping centers like here.

She'd strolled through the largest marketplace there offering exotic wares for visiting dignitaries to bring home. When Teir had taken her, Sarina had mentioned the malls on Earth and the diversity of items available. He'd promised to show her the modern emporiums on his home world of Vilaran if she ever visited.

A strange emptiness filled her whenever she thought about him. If only he were here, Sarina would show him around. She imagined them having fun together, sailing on Biscayne Bay, visiting Viscaya and Fairchild Gardens and the Zoo. She had to admit that her friends were beginning to bore her. They laughed and gossiped and had no concept of any world beyond their own reality.

But Sarina's eyes had been opened, and she found it impossible to close them again. Despite the feelings of resentment and betrayal she felt toward Teir, the captain's darkly handsome features remained in the forefront of her mind.

At least she'd been able to help Abby. Her friend had called excitedly to tell her she'd felt tingling sensations in her legs. The doctors said it was a miracle she felt anything at all. Sarina told her that was wonderful. Maybe the nerve damage wasn't as extensive as had first been predicted. A few days later, Abby phoned again. She was able to wiggle her toes.

Sarina was ecstatic, but it only increased her dissatisfaction with her job. Being a corporate lawyer didn't allow her to help people the way she really wanted. Her performance declined. She considered quitting her job, especially when Mr. Simmons began harassing her. Robert probably had a hand in that, Sarina guessed, but she didn't care. This might be just the push she needed. Her secret desire had always been to be a doctor, and that desire continued to grow within her.

She would go to medical school, Sarina decided at last. She'd learned a lot about medicine on Bimordus Two, but not nearly enough. She might not heal with a magic touch, but she could use kindness and compassion instead, and maybe that was more important.

She was sitting at her desk fingering her worry stone when she reached this momentous conclusion. It was a smooth stone passed down through the generations from woman to woman. Her grandmother had given it to her, feeling that Sarina's mother wouldn't appreciate the heirloom.

"This stone has been in the family forever," her grandmother had said. "Stroke it whenever you feel blue, and it'll help lift your mood."

Sarina liked to flick her finger over the pointed end. The last time she'd done it, a shock-like sensation had stung her hand.

She'd dropped the stone at once, afraid it contained a mineral that reacted adversely with her skin. The silvery-grey stone had lain untouched in her desk drawer ever since.

Until now. Sarina needed the calming effect she got from stroking the smooth surface. She grasped it in her palm and ran her fingertips over the rounded edges, avoiding the tip. As she thought seriously about changing careers, an odd tingling sensation spread through her hand. This time, instead of dropping the stone, she opened her palm and gasped.

The stone glowed with a pulsating light.

As she stared at it, her heart began thumping wildly. The glowing stone looked just like a miniature version of the ancient Auricle.

My God! Was this how it had happened? Was this the source of the answering light that had led Teir to her?

Sarina placed the stone on top of her desk and watched as the glow slowly faded. The last time she'd held it, she hadn't looked at it, hadn't noticed the pulsating light. The last time, she'd been having similar thoughts about being a doctor. Could it be that the legend was true? Could she become the Great Healer after all?

The implications boggled her mind. Kayo's words came back to haunt her: *You are meant for greater things. Your life can have an impact on the entire galaxy.*

There was only one way to discover the truth. She'd have to return to Bimordus Two, marry Lord Cam'brii, and try to fall in love with him. It was the only way to give the legend a chance.

Maybe if she supported Rolf's goals, he'd warm toward her, and their relationship would improve. She'd have to work at it, but the results could be worth the effort.

Her decision made, she moved with alacrity. She obtained a carton from her assistant and threw her personal items inside. Then she wrote a letter of resignation and addressed it to Hiram Simmons. She left it on her desk, departing the building without an explanation.

She'd call her mother and say she was going on an extended vacation. Mother could take care of her townhouse. She'd phone her friends, including Abby, to let them know she'd be gone. Leaving again would be painful, but hope filled her heart that she could accomplish greater things by her actions.

Kayo was the only problem she had left. If Sarina was going away, Kayo also had to leave. She'd have to bring the android along. To that purpose, she reactivated the robot and laid out her plans. Did Kayo know how to transport them to the ship?

Kayo, pleased by Sarina's desire to return to the High Council, retrieved the shuttle for her. Shortly after dark, it appeared in her driveway configured as a car. The android helped Sarina pack her favorite clothes, books, and treasured possessions into two suitcases, which they loaded into the shuttle.

Outside, Kayo paused. "Are you sure you don't want me to take your place again?"

Sarina shook her head. "That isn't possible now. I've told everyone I'm going away, and I've broken up with Robert. You're not needed here anymore."

"I suppose you're right, but still—"

"And another thing," Sarina went on. "You haven't been acting properly. You went against your programming by behaving in a different manner than I would have done under the circumstances. We'd better schedule you for a diagnostic exam."

"Maybe it's the new emotions module that is malfunctioning. All right, I shall accompany you."

Sarina was glad of the android's company when the two of them were back on board the *Valiant*. Kayo was excited. She'd found her experience on Earth fascinating, but she was eager to get on to new learning situations. She did agree, however, to submit herself for testing before getting reassigned. The Coalition ran a robotics center on Altara II.

"I am not programmed for ship's operations," the android said, gazing with bewilderment around the bridge.

"Fine. You can either keep out of the way or follow my

instructions." Sarina eased herself into the command chair. She tapped the control panel to initiate the sequence that would take them out of orbit.

It wasn't until Earth was receding in the distance that Sarina realized her danger. She'd been so focused on learning basic flight operations on Bimordus Two that she'd never taken the time to learn about the ship's defenses. No one had bothered her on Earth, probably because they were glad to see her out of the way. But now that she was coming out of hiding, any number of her enemies might be prepared to intercept her.

She glanced at Kayo, who stared out the viewscreen. The android could substitute for her in a pinch, but it wouldn't take hostile boarders long to discover their mistake. An android wouldn't read as a life form on their scanners.

Only one person could help her if she were in trouble, and Sarina had no idea where Captain Teir Reylock might be found.

Chapter Seventeen

Teir's mind registered pain as its first sensory input. At first, he felt a general ache throughout his body. Then the discomfort intensified until an agonized throbbing gripped his upper arms and drew him back to consciousness.

As the haze in his mind dissipated, he blinked open his eyes to regard a cave-like setting. He appeared to be inside a cavern, dimly lit by flamelights spaced along damp stone walls. Water trickled in the distance, overruling the faint hiss of the flames.

He replayed the final scenes he remembered—the completion of his mission on Lapis, the message from his aunt who had taken ill, his visit to her at the Wellness Center on Alpha Omega Two, where he'd learned she hadn't summoned him. Before he could guess what this meant, the ambush happened.

Several Horthas, huge bull-like creatures, trapped him in an alley, attacking him with their stun whips. The nerve-jarring pain had brought him to his knees, and his last memory was the sting of a syringe pricking his skin.

Trying to shift his position, he realized he'd been strung up by his arms. His wrists were bound above his head and secured to an overhead beam. He hung suspended in the air, his feet more than three decimeters above the packed dirt floor. Spasms of pain racked his shoulders, causing him to clench his teeth against the agony.

Heavy footsteps approached from the shadows. "Awake, are you, Captain?" gloated the guttural voice of Cerrus Bdan. "Welcome to the Souk home world."

The slave trader sauntered into his line of vision. The blue-skinned Souk wore a brightly colored caftan, an incongruity in the gloomy setting.

"Like you my dungeon? Long have I waited for the pleasure of bringing you here."

"You set me up," Teir accused, awareness flooding him along with a surge of rage. "I'll bet you sent the message about my aunt."

Bdan gave a slight bow of acknowledgment. "Waiting for such an opportunity was I. You've caused me much trouble, Captain R-R-Reylock." His eyes gleamed fiercely. "Now will you pay the price." He balled his hand into a fist and drew it back.

Teir saw the blow coming but could do nothing to avoid it.

"This is for taking the *Omnus,*" Bdan snarled, smashing his fist into Teir's jaw. "And for arresting my crew, here is another." He hit him again.

Teir's head snapped back with each assault. Combined with the aftereffects of the drug he'd been given, the blows made his head reel. "Given the chance, I'd do it over again," he rasped.

Bdan growled, his face taking on a purplish hue. "Answer my questions will you, or I'll see that you suffer greatly."

Teir heard a cough in the background. Scanning the shadows, he noticed Lieutenant Otis, Bdan's second-in-command, watching from a corner. He wondered if Bdan was going to ask the same things the lieutenant had when he'd interrogated Teir on the *Omnus.*

"I want the location of the Blood Crystal," Bdan said.

A surge of alarm went through him. Otis hadn't asked that question. Why was Bdan interested in it now? Moreover, who'd told him Teir was the one with the answer?

"Give me, will you, the troop deployments for the Defense League," Bdan continued. Teir felt better at this inquiry. He'd expected it from the smuggler. "In addition, Captain, ask you do I to r-r-reveal Lord Cam'brii's daily routine."

"Lord Cam'brii?" Teir asked, surprised. "Why?"

"Intimately familiar with his habits are you, and someone I know is interested." Bdan grinned, drool forming on his lower lip. "Let's start with the first question. Where is the Blood Crystal that can predict the future?"

"You won't learn anything from me." Teir's arm muscles ached unbearably. He attempted to shift his position, but the drug he'd been given had sapped his strength. He tried to ignore the throbbing pain that shot through his upper body and focused instead on his captor.

Bdan approached, hands curled into fists. Teir's stomach clenched as he anticipated another blow, but he looked the Souk in the eye, refusing to be intimidated.

"The Blood Crystal, Captain R-R-Reylock. Where is it?"

"Go to Zor."

"Defy me, will you?" Bdan's fat body shook with glee. "Enjoy this immensely, shall I." From a pocket in his voluminous caftan, he took out a golden orb. The shiny ball sat in the palm of his hand as he thrust it in front of Teir's face. "Know you what this is?"

"A Korion fireball. How did you get one? They were banned after the War."

"Your laws do not apply here, Captain. Know you how the device works?"

Teir nodded grimly.

"It burns the flesh where it touches." Bdan walked to a sideboard and picked up a heavy glove. Donning it, he activated the fireball in his gloved hand. The orb glowed as Bdan advanced.

"Where shall we start, Captain? On your face, by the eye? A nice scar on your temple would it leave. Or on your hairy chest? Or should I have you stripped and use it there?" He pointed at Teir's groin and laughed, an ugly snorting sound.

Teir knew the time for taunting was over. Bdan meant business.

"Talk, R-R-Reylock. Where is the Blood Crystal?" Bdan approached, raising the glowing orb.

Teir tightened his mouth, saying nothing.

With an angry snarl, Bdan thrust his hand forward, pressing the orb to Teir's chest where it was exposed by his open shirt. Burning heat tore at the layers of his skin. A sizzling sound rent the air along with the smell of burning flesh. Teir clenched his teeth to keep from screaming.

The searing pressure stopped, and as he inhaled a shaky breath, bile rose in his throat. Bdan was only a step away, watching him with a broad grin. Teir twisted his body, struggling to get free, but he only succeeded in swaying in place and doubling his agony.

"Talk," commanded Bdan, lifting the orb once again.

Teir spat at him.

"Guards!" Bdan shouted. Two Horthas rushed out of the shadows bordering the room. "Strip him," the slaver ordered.

Panic roiled through Teir's gut. His eyes fixed on the glowing ball outstretched in Bdan's hand, and he realized there was only one option. Raising his leg, he kicked at the Korion fireball. His foot connected, and the orb landed on the ground with a loud crash.

Bdan looked down at the smashed pieces, then up at Teir, his face mottled with rage. "That was the only one I had, you white-livered son of a belleek."

"Sorry," Teir said, forcing a grin.

Bdan punched him in the face. "Won't cooperate, will you? Perhaps a Morgot mind probe would unleash your tongue."

"You can try. I've been trained to resist them."

"Then how about this?" Bdan pulled a rod from the folds of his caftan.

"You can use the electrifier, but I still won't talk. You might as well kill me and be done with it."

Bdan growled, "One choice do you leave me. Saving this was I, but it is time." He snapped his fingers to the guards. "Bring in the girl."

The Horthas left. When they returned, the beasts lugged

between them a slender female dressed in a slave costume and wearing a restraining collar around her neck. As she was thrust into the light, Teir felt the blood drain from his face.

"Sarina!"

Her eyes widened at the sight of him. "Teir." She started to rush forward, but the guards held her back, grasping her by the arms.

"May I present my honored guest, Sarina Bretton," said Bdan, gloating at the look on Teir's face.

He stared at her, horrified. What was she doing here? How long had she been Bdan's prisoner? Why had he heard nothing of her capture?

She didn't look as though she'd been harmed, thank the stars. She wore a slave outfit but it was the skimpy bra and elaborately-gilded girdle of a harem girl, not the coarse cloth of a laborer. At least she hadn't been sent to the mines. Bdan must have been keeping her in reserve just for this occasion.

He returned his attention to the Souk, trying to moisten his lips, but his tongue was dry. "What do you want with her?" he rasped.

Bdan's eyes narrowed. "Owe you both, I do. But decided I have not what to do with the woman. You can help me make up my mind, R-r-reylock. Tell me what I want to know, and go easy on her, will I."

Seeing Teir made the situation clear to Sarina. She'd been captured by Bdan's pirates soon after she'd left Earth's orbit and had been imprisoned in his harem, without any explanation or demands. Bdan planned to use her to force vital information from the captain.

Her heart twisted. He hung by his wrists, looking more dead than alive. There was an ugly red blotch on his chest, and his face was badly bruised. His eyes were glazed with pain, but Sarina knew he would never give in if she weren't there. To save her, he would do whatever the smuggler asked.

"Teir, don't tell him anything," she urged.

"Be silent." Bdan thrust out the rod he held and a crackling beam of electricity shot forth, hitting Sarina in the side. She crumpled, held upright by the two Horthas gripping her in place.

Bdan pocketed the device and sneered. "Slaves speak only when given permission. Remember that, *sumi,* or use this to control you, will I."

The collar tightened around her neck, choking her. She couldn't breathe. Her eyes widened in panic as she gasped for breath.

Abruptly, Bdan released her from the choke hold with a movement of his hand. "Well, R-r-reylock? Reconsidering your response, are you?"

Teir saw Sarina's all but imperceptible nod indicating she was all right. The Horthas were still supporting her, but she could stand on her own. He refused to speak.

"Know you who else wants this woman. Captain?" Bdan taunted. "K'darr, chief of the Morgots. Shall I give her to him?"

"I don't care what happens to her," he lied, hoping Sarina understood his attempt to protect her. "I only followed my assignment in being her bodyguard."

"Is that all, Captain? My sources informed me there might be more going on between you two than you let on."

"What sources?"

"Like to know, wouldn't you? I could keep her here in my harem. Much pleasure would she bring me. Which is it to be— the Morgots, or me? Up to you is it. Make a decision."

Sarina was horrified by the alternatives. Either way, she faced an awful fate. Yet she'd almost rather be given to the dreaded Morgots than be manhandled by this ugly hound. Nonetheless, she didn't want Teir to reveal information because of her.

"Don't tell him what he wants to know," Sarina begged Teir. "Remember your duty. What happens to me doesn't matter."

Bdan barked an order for his slave foreman, Ixan, to take her away. She broke free from the guards and ran toward Teir. Ixan intercepted her. The whippet-face activated her collar. She fell to the ground, gasping and choking, her hands clutching at her neck. At a signal from Ixan, the Horthas dragged her away.

"Where is the Blood Crystal?" Bdan repeated, approaching Teir. "The female will suffer if you do not r-r-reply."

"Go to Zor. I'll never talk. I am sworn to protect the location of the stone."

"Time will I give you to think upon it. Consider the things I can do to her, Captain. Terrible, painful things."

With a flick of his wrist, he ordered Teir to be cut down. The agony of release was unbearable. Teir collapsed on the ground, clutching his numb hands to his stomach.

"Put him in the wasting pit," the slaver ordered another set of guards. "We'll see how well he r-r-resists after confinement. Enjoy your stay in my dungeon, Captain."

As the Horthas dragged him away like a helpless rag doll, Bdan's snorting laughter echoed in his ears.

****

The days passed without Teir knowing if it was day or night. Fear and anxiety occupied his waking hours as he wondered what had become of Sarina. Had Bdan hurt her? Or was the trader keeping her untouched as a prize for the Morgots?

Worrying about her ate away his strength, weakening him and leaving him with despair and guilt for company. If he'd told her the truth while they were on the *Valiant,* they might not be in this predicament. Sarina had wanted to go back to Earth to see the friends and family she'd left behind, but his refusal had compelled her to take action on her own.

If she'd known how much he cared for her, she might have stayed. Together, they could have found an alternative to the execution decree. It was his fault Cerrus Bdan had caught them, and so it was up to him to find a way out.

As though his mental torment wasn't enough, Teir's body

was further weakened by lack of food. He shivered in the cool dampness. The pit was lit by a single flamelight, but there wasn't much to see. A corroded chamber pot rested in a corner, contributing to the foul odor already present from previous occupants.

Resting on the packed-dirt floor, he considered Bdan's demands. By virtue of his position as Chief Troubleshooter for the Defense League, Teir had assumed the responsibility for guarding the mystical Blood Crystal's location. Glotaj and Admiral Daras Gog were the only others who knew its secret hiding place.

Fifteen annums ago, an unmanned alien probe had entered Coalition space from an unexplored region of the galaxy. The cylindrical vessel had no markings to reveal its origins or purpose. Inside, under a protective translucent dome, the Defense League force that investigated found a black crystal rock streaked with veins of red.

They reported it to Command and were told to take it to the nearest starbase. Twenty hauras after that first report, all communications with the patrol craft were cut off.

Another Defense League vessel was dispatched to follow up. They found the patrol ship intact, but all her crew were dead. From the destructive scene aboard, it appeared they had killed each other.

Thinking the crystal might have affected them in some way, the investigators encased it in a shielded container and took it to a laboratory at the nearest starbase. Analysis showed it to be made of a foreign matrix impervious to sensor scans. The scientists handling it began to have strange visions of the future.

Then the conflicts began. One scientist tried to steal it, hoping to gain great power by using its knowledge of things to come. Another was murdered over possession of the crystal. Its very presence seemed to drive men mad.

The head of the Defense League notified Glotaj of the discovery and the problems associated with it. Glotaj then discussed the matter with the High Council. They decided that the Blood Crystal, so named because of the spilt blood of its discoverers and the red veins in the rock, was a dangerous object. It must be hidden away where no one would be tempted to use it.

The Blood Crystal was put into the charge of whichever officer held the title of Chief Troubleshooter. This man would make biannual inspections of the guardian site.

So why would Cerrus Bdan be after it? Did he hope to discover the result of the First Amendment vote? Or maybe he meant to learn if the legend of the Great Healer was true before deciding what to do with Sarina.

The High Council had debated using the Blood Crystal to learn the Great Healer's identity once the signs of the prophecy appeared. They'd also considered consulting it to learn the outcome of the problems plaguing the Coalition. But the benefits of its use were minuscule compared to the evil it might unleash, and the risk was deemed too dangerous.

Teir himself had never handled the black crystal rock because he'd been warned how it twisted one's mind. In any event, he didn't want to know the future. But he took his responsibility seriously, and twice an annum, he journeyed to the guardian site to make sure it was secure. He must protect its location even now.

As time passed, he grew weaker. Parched with thirst, Teir eyed the mildew growing on the walls with a view to licking off the moisture. But then his meager ration of water would be pushed through a small, hinged opening at the base of the steel door, and his desperation would be momentarily forgotten. Gradually, he lost track of time and began mumbling to himself. His stomach went from gnawing hunger to where he thought he'd vomit if he ate.

Three times a day, when Teir got the water, someone peeked through a grate at eye level on the door. If he was ever going to attempt an escape, he'd better make it soon.

Mustering what was left of his energy, he took up a position beside the door, flattening himself against the wall. He stayed there for what seemed like hauras, his leg muscles cramping, clenching and unclenching his fists to maintain circulation in his arms.

Footsteps approached, then there was a pause as though someone were peering in. A grunt followed, and a rattle of keys. The steel door swung open. A Hortha guard entered, weapon poised.

Teir waited until his shadow had passed, then jumped him, desperation giving him the surge of adrenaline he needed. Before the guard could make a sound, Teir grabbed his shooter and locked him inside the cell.

Pocketing the prison keys, Teir surveyed his surroundings. He faced a spacious cavern with cells lining the circular walls. A trestle table with four chairs stood in the center. The room appeared to be unguarded, so maybe the Hortha had been the only one assigned. Teir wasn't going to wait to find out. Where was Sarina? He peeked inside each cell to make sure she wasn't imprisoned there.

Something cold poked him in the small of his back as he was peering into the last empty space. "Don't move," a harsh voice commanded. "You wish to find the girl?"

Surprised, Teir nodded. "Yes, I do." His voice came out as a dry rasp. He hadn't spoken aloud for days and didn't have the saliva to moisten his tongue.

"This way." The pressure eased from his back.

Teir whirled to see a hooded figure shuffling toward the exit. He hobbled forward, weak from hunger and lack of exercise.

"Who are you?" Teir couldn't make out the person's gender.

"A friend and believer in the legend. Follow me. I will take you to the Great Healer."

"How did you know I broke out of my cell?" Teir asked suspiciously. Maybe this was a ploy to get him to talk. He cradled the shooter in his hand, ready to use it if necessary.

"I have been waiting. If you had not made a move, I would have found a way to assist you. Be silent. We approach the armory."

Hortha voices emanated from an open doorway along with the smell of ale fumes. The beasts must be guards specially assigned to this section.

He and his rescuer crept past and then ascended to surface level via a set of steps. His companion had a key to unlock the upper door.

Above ground, the building took on a palatial grandeur. The maze inside Bdan's complex was like a labyrinth. Teir would never have been able to find Sarina on his own.

The Believer led him through a series of passages until they reached the harem.

"Your woman rests inside. Wait until daylight when she's likely to be alone. Other female slaves sleep here, and Horthas stand guard. I must leave you now."

"Wait. What about the collar she wears?"

"Aim your shooter at the seam, and it will break off."

"How do we find our way out of here?"

"Every sleeping chamber has an entrance to a secret passage at its north wall. Keep following the tunnels toward the right. They'll lead you outside."

This person must be high up in Bdan's hierarchy to be so familiar with palace secrets. "And then what? I have no idea where we are." Teir had been rendered unconscious after his capture, so he didn't know the location of Bdan's lair.

"The *Valiant* is secured at a spaceport some distance from here. I suggest you hide in the forest until you recover your strength and then devise a plan to board your vessel. My compatriots will look for you to render assistance."

From his voluminous garment, the stranger withdrew a hunk of bread. "Eat this. It contains carboplex nutrients and will give you energy. And here's some water." He added a canteen to his offering.

"Thank you." Teir took the items. "Who are you? I'd like to repay the favor someday."

"Free the Great Healer. That will be thanks enough." With a rustle of fabric, the Believer vanished around a corner.

Teir waited until the robed figure left, then he tucked the shooter into his waistband. He tore off pieces of bread and gobbled them like a ravenous animal. Finished with his brief repast, he gulped the water, careful not to guzzle too fast or he'd lose precious drops.

His stomach satisfied, he hunkered in a nearby alcove to wait for daybreak.

Chapter Eighteen

Sarina tossed restlessly on the cushioned lounger. The sleeping chamber held eleven other slaves besides herself, and the lack of privacy plus her anxious state of mind inhibited her ability to sleep. Horthas stood guard at either end, and knowing their watchful eyes were upon her didn't help. She turned on her side and contemplated her situation.

Two additional chambers could be reached through connecting archways. Altogether, thirty-six females of varying species inhabited the harem. Each of them, except for herself, competed for the attention of their master.

Ava Bet, Bdan's sole *gima,* threw a jealous rage whenever he spent the night with one of them, but gossip said Bdan liked to rile her. She was the only one chosen for that exalted position, so her title was fairly secure. She just didn't care to share his favors.

The surroundings were plush considering the women's status as slaves. Fabrics in bright multicolors billowed from the ceiling, and pillows in matching hues covered the floor. Bdan liked the setting to be pleasing to his eye when he strolled in to select his bed partner for the night.

Sarina cringed every time she saw him, afraid he'd choose her, but the others competed for selection. Privilege and power were granted to those so favored.

Meanwhile, Sarina suffered the most menial chores and frequent physical punishments. She had lost count of the times she'd felt the lash of Ixan's stun whip in the past few days. Each time the pain intensified.

Whippet-face took particular delight in tormenting her, and because the stun whips did no permanent damage, he could beat her as frequently as his cruelty dictated. He used the choke collar often, too, and a lingering sore throat was the wretched result.

This day had been particularly long, and she'd barely been fed. Sarina didn't know how much longer she could go on. She wasn't used to physical labor, and the work combined with the punishments were taking their toll. It became an effort to move. Her only consolation was that Bdan hadn't touched her yet.

She wondered why he waited. Maybe he planned to sell her to the Morgots after all. That would mean Teir hadn't talked, because Bdan implied he would keep her if the captain cooperated. Had Bdan tortured him? Was he still alive? Fear for him chilled her blood and made her shiver in anguish.

Suddenly the door blew open, and the room brightened. Cerrus Bdan sauntered inside, accompanied by his personal Souk bodyguards.

"You," he thundered, pointing at her. "Come."

Sarina curled into a ball, hoping he was looking at the Polluxite female in the next bed.

"Sarina," Bdan barked. "Do you defy me?"

She scrambled to her feet before he could activate her choker. "I obey, master," she mumbled, her head bowed.

The guards surrounded her and marched her out in Bdan's wake. Her heart thumped wildly, and she didn't dare glance around. She kept her head lowered, her eyes down. Where was he taking her?

Nausea clogged her throat as they wound through various corridors. The palace decorations became even more lavish as they neared Bdan's private quarters.

Her heart sank when he led her inside a sumptuous sleeping chamber dominated by a large circular bed raised on a dais in the center of the room. A moat of water surrounded this section. Mirrors covered the walls and ceiling, while muted lighting cast a mellow glow. A wide dresser was the only other furnishing.

Oh God, no. Sarina stared at the bed draped in gold.

Bdan turned to his bodyguards, sweeping his hand in an imperious wave. "Leave us."

The Souks marched out. Alone, she faced Cerrus Bdan. Drool dribbled down his mouth as he regarded her.

"What do you want with me?" she asked in a defiant tone, lifting her chin.

Bdan absently fingered his crimson caftan. "Wish I to see what you have to offer before I make my decision." His beady gaze slowly trailed down her body.

Sarina swallowed, realizing the skimpy bra and embroidered girdle she wore left little to the imagination.

"Let us get more comfortable," he said. *"Bridge!"*

A narrow path extended across the moat. He grasped Sarina's hand and yanked her to the edge of the water. "Cross," he commanded.

She had no choice. Trembling, she obeyed. Bdan followed her, then ordered the bridge to retract.

"The moat is not very wide, but it is deep. Creatures live inside it, tiny *flegymns*. Devour a human can they within seconds. Luckily, they do not like the taste of Souk flesh."

He snorted with laughter while Sarina cringed. She wouldn't be able to jump into the water to escape him.

Bdan's expression sobered. "Sample your wares, shall I. No Great Healer are you. A mere Earthwoman—frail, too." He looked her over appraisingly. "Killed a Vilaran female once, did I. Too thin, like you." He snickered, and Sarina's face blanched. "Tell K'darr, will I, that you were nothing special if you die. Off with your clothes."

"W-What?" She swallowed against a lump in her throat.

Bdan yanked her against his fat body. "Need I use the choker?"

"No, please don't."

"Then hurry. I grow impatient."

He was growing, all right. His organ protruded from beneath

the caftan, making a visible tent. "I can't," she said, her stomach churning.

"What say you?" he roared.

The collar tightened, constricting her neck so she couldn't breathe. She fell back onto the bed, clawing at the restraint. As she lay there, gasping and choking, Bdan's paws ripped away her garments.

Suddenly, a red beam of light pierced the air.

"What is—?" Bdan didn't finish the sentence. He toppled into the water and sank out of sight.

"Sarina," Teir's voice bellowed.

A surge of joy swelled within her. Rolling over so she could see him, she tried to call out a warning about the moat, but all she could do was gasp and yank at the cursed collar.

"Hold on," he said.

A moment later, he vaulted onto the bed using an electrifier rod he'd found propped against a wall. Casting it to the ground, he knelt beside her.

"Don't move." He twisted her head to the side. Then he aimed his shooter and fired. The laser beam severed the collar, releasing Sarina from its choke hold.

She gulped in shaky breaths of air.

"Are you all right?" His voice sounded raspy.

"Yes. What about the guards?"

He tucked the shooter into his waistband. "They're merely stunned. We have to get out of here before they wake up."

"And Bdan?" She stared at the water. No bubbles arose. There was no sign of him in the murky depths.

"Who cares? Let's go."

"Wait, there's a way across." Mustering her strength, Sarina shouted, "Bridge!"

The bridge extended, and as they hurried across, she got a good look at Teir. He appeared gaunt, his cheekbones prominent, his eyes darkened hollows. Purplish bruises on his face stood out against the pallor of his skin. His ragged shirt hung loosely on him, and she bit her lip when she saw his chest. The burn wound that blistered there must be painful.

"How did you make it this far?" Her throat still hurt, and her voice came out as a croak.

"I'll tell you about it later." Once across the bridge, he drew her to a halt. "You need something to wear," he said without commenting further on her lack of clothing. Then a bevy of emotions crossed his face.

Her heart swelled in response. He'd come for her. The man could have escaped, but he'd rescued her instead. This told her Teir cared for her more than he would admit, and it made her yearn to give herself to him in return.

****

Teir pictured the obscene bluish body of Cerrus Bdan hovering above Sarina, ripping away her clothes. He'd arrived just in time. Unable to deny his need for her, he pulled her into his arms. He only meant to hold her and to reassure himself that she was safe.

As she melted into his embrace, a strange tingling spread throughout his body.

"What are you doing?" He jerked away.

"I don't know what you mean."

Teir glanced at his chest. Instead of the ugly, raw sore, he saw a patch of unmarred, hairless skin. "The wound—it's gone."

"My God. And look at your face. The bruises have cleared."

"Sarina, how could this happen? Unless…?" He regarded her with awe.

A loud banging on the chamber door roused them to action.

"Quick, we have to go. Put this on." He grabbed a robe lying on a chair and tossed it to her. "There should be a way out by the north wall."

Sarina made the robe fit by tying it with the sash, then she joined him beside one of the mirrors. "Is this a crack?" she asked, pointing.

"You're right." Teir ran his fingers along the edges of a seam until something unlatched. He pushed on the wall, giving a grunt of triumph when a section swung open. "I'll go first." He drew his shooter and proceeded forward.

Sarina swung the section of heavy wall closed behind them. Tunnel after tunnel followed, then suddenly they were outside, at the west end of Bdan's complex. The spread of buildings covered a vast area over a desert-like terrain.

"Now what?" She shaded her eyes with a hand. The sunlight was so bright after being confined inside that it all but blinded her.

"This way," Teir indicated a range of forested mountains that rose in the near distance. "We'll hide in the jungle until we can figure out how to reach the spaceport."

Sarina gestured to a fenced-in yard. "That's where the beasts put me when I arrived. Those women must be new slaves, waiting for processing." Most of them would be sent to the mines. Only a few became palace servants, and on a rare occasion, Bdan chose one for his harem. "Can we free them first?"

"No, it might set off an alarm. So far nobody has noticed our escape." He started forward.

"Wait, Teir." He halted, and Sarina stood her ground. "We have the perfect opportunity to release these women. They're humans, like us. Some might even be from Vilaran, your home planet. How can you leave them? There's room in your cargo hold to bring them along, and it shouldn't be hard for you to take out the guards with your shooter."

"And what do we do in the meantime, while we're figuring out how to get to my ship? I'm not in good shape. I don't know where we're going to get food. We can't risk taking anyone with us."

"Teir, *please*."

Damn the woman, sometimes she took her compassion too far. "Look, Sarina, those women are being fed. They're alive. If we bring them with us, there's no telling what might happen. We could all end up dead."

Her shoulders slumped. "I suppose you're right. We might put the women at greater risk by bringing them along. Maybe we can do something later to help."

Loud sirens wailed, spurring them on. They dashed toward the woods. Dust kicked up at their heels as they sped across the dry, uneven ground. The nearest hill loomed closer, a thick tangle of vegetation marking its base.

Teir's head swam from the unaccustomed exertion, and his heart thumped wildly. The heat didn't help, either. They had to make the jungle before he collapsed.

Sarina kept pace with him, but it was a struggle for her, too. Her breaths came in short, hard bursts. Her bare feet hurt from pebbles on the rough ground. She hadn't thought to retrieve her slippers in Bdan's chamber.

The sun beat upon their backs, but they forgot their discomfort when the whine of engines sounded from behind.

"They're coming after us." Sarina glanced over her shoulder, and her breath hitched.

Speeders zoomed in their direction, driven by armed Horthas. The expressions on the beasts' faces struck terror into her heart.

"Hurry," Teir yelled.

The edge of the jungle neared as they stumbled forward. A mist rose like a curtain in front of them from the sudden increase in humidity. It felt like a fine sprinkle of rain as they reached the border of tall trees. The mist thickened as they penetrated deeper. Like a protective cocoon, it insulated them from the horrors behind. Thorns from twisting fodus vines ripped at their limbs and sticky spiderwebs netted them, but Teir didn't want to risk using his shooter to clear a passage—the radiation could be picked up on a scanner.

The heat combined with the humidity sapped their energy. Sweat soaked them both. Sarina's chest heaved with the effort of breathing. They entered a clearing, and the mist lifted. Sunlight filtered through the canopy overhead. A rich, earthy smell permeated the air. All around them teemed the sounds of the jungle.

A numbing fatigue entered Sarina's bones, and she faltered. "I have to rest," she said, leaning against a thick green stalk. Her chest ached, and her feet throbbed. She couldn't go much farther.

Something dripped onto her arm, and she jerked away from the plant. A brownish fluid had seeped onto her skin. For all she knew, the sap might be poisonous.

"We have to keep moving." Despite his words, Teir's steps ground to a halt several paces in front of her. He tripped over a root and toppled onto the soft, moist earth.

"What's wrong?" Sarina cried. She hobbled forward, her feet paining her with each movement. Teir lay still as a stone on the ground. Alarmed, she knelt beside him and felt for a pulse. The beat was rapid and thready. He was alive, but unconscious.

They wouldn't be going anywhere soon.

****

Teir had a marvelous dream. A glowing aura surrounded Sarina. The aura expanded, radiated, and became a blinding white light. It was the light from the sacred Auricle. Stories of the legend reverberated in his mind. An ancient people with special powers—from them would come a descendant—that descendant would be The One. When the signs were right, the Great Healer would be revealed.

In his dream, Sarina stroked his wounded arm. His cut skin healed. The burn on his chest disappeared when he held her in his arms. Her image shimmered in a halo of bright stars and then blurred. She called out his name…

His eyes snapped open. Sarina's face hovered inches above his as she spoke his name again.

"Sarina—" He tried to speak, but his mouth was so dry he could only cough.

She cradled his head and raised him, pressing a canteen of water to his mouth. He gulped thirstily.

"He's awake," she said to someone out of his range of vision.

Teir twisted his neck and saw two curious, wrinkled faces peering at him. Alarm surged through him. They were Crigellans, a crossbreed of humans and a lizard-like species. The taller fellow reminded him of Otis, Bdan's second-in-command.

"They are friends," Sarina said hastily, noting the look on his face. "Salla and her mate are Believers."

Teir didn't need any other explanation. The robed figure who had assisted his escape had said that helpers would look after them. A youth of about sixteen annums studied them. He was a fresh-faced male, with a thatch of bright auburn hair and an eager expression.

"How long have I been out?" he asked.

"For eighteen hauras," Salla answered. "The two moons of Souk have passed while you were still. Now it is morn, and soon the sol will be high in the sky. We must gather nourishment." The elder female narrowed her keen blue eyes. "We've left you some canna fruit. Eat and regain your strength. You are weak as a babe."

"What's the plan?" Teir asked. His limbs felt like gelatin.

"You will remain in the jungle until you are fully recovered. This place is called the Thicket of Bayne. Rising yonder are the Koodrash Mounts, on the other side of which is Ruel's territory. You don't want to go there. Bdan inhabits the Nurash Desert on this side, and he has secured your ship at the spaceport on the other end of his complex, beyond the Sand Pit. You'll need full use of your skills to get there safely."

She glanced at her companion. "Etan and I go now. Devin, the boy, will act as guard."

Teir nodded, deciding further questions could wait. The Crigellans marched off.

"I shall watch the clearing," Devin said. "There is a pond on the other side of that stand of trees if you wish to bathe."

"Thanks." Teir didn't have the energy to move, let alone scrub himself.

"Here, eat this," Sarina said, kneeling beside him. In her outstretched palm was a bulbous purple fruit.

Teir grabbed the offering and bit into it, stuffing the juicy morsels down.

"Not so fast," Sarina warned.

"Water," he rasped, incredibly thirsty again. She passed it to him and he gulped greedily.

The effort of eating took his energy and he lay back, resting his head on a makeshift pillow Sarina had fashioned from leaves.

"I'll help you wash," Sarina offered, reminding him that he must smell and look like a piece of vorax's forage.

"No, I can manage. I'll take a dip in the pond," he said, groaning at the effort of rising. It would be worth it to rid himself of the layers of filth he'd accumulated. He staggered off in the direction Salla had indicated.

The pond nestled in a small hollow surrounded by tall tropical trees. *Humma* birds sang in the branches, and colorful butterflies swooped low over the flowering bushes lining the earthen banks. A spicy scent tickled his nostrils but it was a pleasant sensation, like a woman's perfume.

Teir quickly stripped off his ragged clothes and waded into the crystal-clear water until it reached his chest. The temperature felt surprisingly warm. Relaxing, he stretched out on his back, enjoying the weightless sensation as he bobbed gently on the rippling current. Gradually, the soreness seeped from his limbs. He closed his eyes and let the warm water envelop him as he floated on his back.

"You can use this to scrub," Sarina's voice said close to his ear.

Teir pried his eyes open and stood, his feet resting on the sandy bottom. Sarina was waist deep and naked beside him in the water. In her hand was a spongy mass.

"I found this by the water's edge. Do you need help?"

He glanced at her full breasts. "Yes, I need help, but not the kind you have in mind," he said in a husky voice as his body responded.

"Not now," Sarina retorted. "First, we wash, and then we talk. You have a lot to explain."

"So do you," he said, remembering how she'd drugged him and stolen his ship.

"You're still weak. Let me do this so you can conserve your energy."

As she scrubbed his chest, his resentment drained, replaced instead with rising desire. Each stroke affected his skin like electric shocks. Her touch heightened his need, and he couldn't restrain the moan of pleasure that escaped his lips.

After commanding him to turn around, she tackled his back, taking an extraordinarily long time across his broad shoulders as though she were enjoying herself. Teir gave her a disarming grin when he faced her again.

"You can do the rest yourself," she said, holding out the sponge.

"Don't you want to finish me off?" His smile broadened.

"We're supposed to be getting clean, remember?" Despite her words, her lips curved upward.

Teir snatched the sponge from her fingers and proceeded to scrub his lower half while Sarina watched.

It's been so long, she thought, swallowing as he washed between his sturdy thighs. His shaft was hard and erect, and he glided the sponge up and down its length in slow motion, as if to excite her deliberately. When he stooped to wash his legs, she breathed a sigh of relief, but it didn't last long. As soon as he was done, he faced her again.

"Your turn," he said, that devilish grin on his face.

"I can wash myself, thank you." Sarina reached for the sponge.

Teir grasped her arm and whipped her around. "Let me do your back. It's hard for you to reach."

The sponge touched her skin. At first, he applied strong pressure, but then he lightened up. His fingers ran feathery movements across her spine, his touch eliciting a delighted shiver.

"Stop that." She squirmed when he passed the sponge over

her buttocks, and then again when he dared to touch between her legs. Pleasure flooded her as his fingers lingered there.

"Bend over," he said, applying gentle pressure to her back.

Too weak-kneed to protest, she complied. As he deepened his strokes, she shut her eyes in surrender. The intimate caresses continued until she felt herself blossoming with need.

"Turn around," he ordered, slowly rotating her body.

Sarina enjoyed the sight of him touching her private places. The sponge had vanished. All she could do was moan and thrust herself at him. His thumbs brushed her nipples, then he pinched them gently, sending exquisite sensations along her nerves.

"Teir, please." The ache between her legs had become unbearable.

"Don't rush it. We've been waiting for this for an eternity. Let's take our time and enjoy each other."

He licked her, and a sharp ache shot to her groin. She closed her eyes and groaned.

"Let's lie down," Teir suggested.

He led her to the water's edge and lowered her onto a soft carpet of moss. Teir crouched above her, breathing heavily. His midnight black hair clung wetly to his forehead. Several days' growth of beard shadowed his face. Those tender blue eyes, that mouth poised above hers, were all she'd yearned for and dreamt about during her time away from him. Talking could wait until later. Right now, this was all that mattered.

She reached for him, pulling him down on top of her, relishing the feel of his hair-roughened chest against her skin. Writhing under him, she eagerly sought his lips.

Teir clamped his mouth to hers, urging her legs apart with his strong thighs. He entered her carefully, gauging her reaction. When she didn't protest, he began his thrusts, slowly at first, and then more passionately. She was part of him, this woman, and he never wanted to let her go. He forgot everything except the incredible sensations spiraling through him.

Sarina clutched at his back. She wanted to be closer to him, joined with him forever. The future didn't matter as long as they were together. She moved her hips to match his frantic thrusts, all gentleness gone now. They'd been apart too long.

Waves of pleasure burst upon her. Spasms of ecstasy heralded her release, until at last, she was spent. Teir met his climax and then collapsed atop her.

She must have fallen asleep, because when she awoke, Teir was watching her. His finger stroked her hair splayed out on the moss.

"I want you again," he said.

That was all she needed to hear. This time, as before, their coupling was fast and furious, leaving them exhausted.

"I'm sorry," Teir said. "I wanted to take it slowly with you, but I need you so much. Next time, I promise it will be better." He leaned up on his elbow, smiling down at her.

She traced his cheek with a finger. "I enjoyed it just fine, thank you. But speaking of next time, what about now? I can't get enough of you."

A teasing twinkle entered her eyes as her hand roved to the curly hairs on his chest. She tweaked a silken hair provocatively.

"You witch." Teir sprawled on his back. "You've worn me out. I don't have any energy left to do anything else."

"Well then, I guess I'll have to wait. After all, you're supposed to be recovering your strength, not using it up."

He gazed at her, raising an eyebrow. "You're too much to resist, woman."

Sarina kissed him lightly. "Seriously, I'm supposed to be taking care of you. And Devin could return at any moment, come to think of it. We'd better get dressed."

She got up to wash their clothes. They'd have to wear them wet, but the heat should dry them fast enough. She didn't count on the blouse she'd been given by their friends to cling to her body in so revealing a manner.

"If that young fellow sees you like that, he'll want you for himself," Teir said as he put on his sodden pants, shirt and vest.

"I doubt it. He's too much in awe of me as the Great Healer. Speaking of which, I think it's time for our talk."

Teir made a face. He'd much rather talk of love than politics.

As soon as he thought the word, he frowned. *Love?*

Where had that notion come from? He stared at Sarina dazedly. What he felt for her was lust, not love, wasn't it? Then why had he missed her so much? Why had he felt as though part of him had been torn asunder when she left?

Now that he thought about it, he hadn't so much as looked at another woman since he'd met Sarina. She filled his thoughts to the exclusion of everyone else.

By the stars, this was a novel idea. Never having been in love before, Teir wasn't sure how it was supposed to feel. But Sarina still belonged to Lord Cam'brii, and the legend stated that she had to fall in love and marry him, not necessarily in that order, for her healing ability to be activated.

And yet twice now, she'd made Teir's wounds disappear. The first time, the cut on his arm had been mended after the attack by the Twyggs. Then in Bdan's complex, the wound on his chest had vanished and his bruises had disappeared. Her touch had healed him in both instances. Did that mean she'd fallen in love with Cam'brii after all?

Chapter Nineteen

Teir's mood abruptly darkened. "Yes, we need to talk," he agreed in a gruff tone. He found a moss-covered log to sit on, being careful not to get too near the ant garden on an overhanging branch. Spherical in shape and somewhat smaller than a kick ball, it was made of soil and masses of vegetable fibers chewed by the ants.

The garden bristled with small, succulent epiphytic plants that sprouted from the surface in all directions. If he got too close, the ants would swarm and spray him with a cloud of toxic formic acid.

Devin wasn't in sight, and there was no sign of the older Crigellans, either. His ears picked up the buzzing of paper wasps, along with bird songs and the whir of brambid wings. Occasionally, a kayoka screeched from the trees. Its cries echoed the torment in his heart.

Sarina waited for Teir to speak first. She wanted to hear his reasons for turning away from her on the *Valiant*. As the silence lengthened, she stared at the ground, wondering why he didn't begin. Maybe he was still angry at her for stealing his ship.

He had every right to be furious. She had acted in a deceitful and impulsive manner, and she could have cost him his career. By the passionate way they'd just made love, though, she had assumed he'd forgiven her.

What if she'd been wrong? Quelling her fear, she studied a beetle carrying a piece of rotten fruit.

At last Teir spoke, his voice low. "Twice now, you've healed me, Sarina. When I was wounded by the Twyggs, you touched me and my wound disappeared. We both know what happened in Bdan's palace. It can only mean one thing—you've fallen in love with Lord Cam'brii. Was that why you decided to leave Earth and return to Bimordus Two, because you realized how you felt about him?"

"Don't be absurd. I could never love that man."

"Is it Robert, then? Did seeing your fiancé bring back a flood of affection? Is he the one you're in love with?" It didn't make sense, according to the legend, but one of the reasons she had gone back to Earth had been to see Robert.

"I broke off our engagement."

Teir felt a swell of relief. "Well, you must have fallen in love with *somebody* for your healing powers to be activated."

Then again, the legend didn't actually state she had to fall in love with the Raimorrdan she wed, just that her healing aura would result from the power of her love. That could be interpreted in different ways. The High Council chose to believe it meant she would fall in love with Cam'brii, but maybe that wasn't correct. *Teir* was the one she'd healed, wasn't he? Didn't that mean something?

She gazed at him with apprehension in her lovely eyes, so he gave her an impish grin in response. "If it's not Cam'brii, and it's not Robert, I guess that leaves me," he said.

Sarina chortled. "I should say not. After the way you treated me? It was clear you wanted nothing to do with me."

"That was all pretense, Sarina." His expression sobered. "I knew you were destined for Lord Cam'brii. I really did care about you, but if I'd told you then, you might have chosen me over him, and that wouldn't have served the prophecy."

"I may have understood that deep down, but your behavior still hurt me."

"I get that now. I'm sorry. I should have told you how I felt and relied on you to make the right choice."

"Do you forgive me taking your ship? I hope you didn't get into too much trouble."

He brought her up to date on his activities while they munched on ripe sulu berries from a nearby bush. The bushes grew on Vilaran, so Teir knew the berries were safe to eat.

"You say your aunt raised you?" Sarina asked, curious about his background. Until now he'd never talked much about himself.

Teir nodded. "Aunt Catharta said my parents died in a reactor accident when I was small. She and Uncle Jeb were my only living relatives. We traveled around a lot. Uncle Jeb's business took us to different planets, but then we settled in a small hamlet on Vilaran. Having had a taste of travel, I hated being confined to one location. But Uncle Jeb's health was failing, and Catharta thought we should stay close to home."

Sarina read the distress on his face. "You weren't happy, were you?"

"I didn't fit in. All the other kids seemed to have such narrow concerns, while I had a different view of life. I wanted to roam the stars and have grand adventures. For some reason, Aunt Catharta discouraged my views. She gave me the impression my dreams frightened her. She became reclusive after Uncle Jeb died, never inviting anyone over, and that made our life even more dismal. Yet for all that, she loved me as though I were her own son."

"It must have been difficult for you. What made you join the Defense League?"

"The chance to travel and see some action. Aunt Catharta, surprisingly enough, approved. She'd realized that I couldn't be restrained to one world."

"I understand that feeling." Ever since Sarina had a taste of touring the stars, she wanted to explore further.

"I didn't have any trouble getting into the Academy," Teir went on. "Aunt Catharta had a connection with Glotaj, and he recommended me."

"What connection would that be?"

Teir shrugged. "She never explained. I remember the conversation they had about my joining the Defense League. It was all very secretive. When I asked Aunt Catharta about it, she said to forget I'd ever heard the Supreme Regent's name. There's more, now that I think about it. I got the strange notion that Glotaj meant to bring us together by assigning me to retrieve you from Earth and then to act as your bodyguard."

"But why would he do that? The High Council has chosen Lord Cam'brii as my husband."

"I don't know. If Aunt Catharta recovers, I'll ask her. She was in isolation at the Wellness Center when I last visited. Healers feared she had the Farg." He paused, preferring to change the subject away from the painful topic of his aunt's illness. "Did you see everyone on Earth whom you'd missed?"

Sarina nodded, warmed by his interest. She moved to a low stump and sat on the flat surface. "I told you about Robert. Mother was disappointed by our break-up, but that's her problem. The most exciting thing that happened to me involved my friend, Abby." Sarina described the results of her treatment.

"So because of the glowing stone from your desk, you're returning to the High Council?"

"Yes, I must see if the legend is true. I really do want to be a healer, Teir. There's so much good I could do in the role. Abby was just a small example, and I used a neurojet unit in her case. Think of what I could do if I didn't need tools." She'd hidden the lustrous stone on Teir's ship, but she didn't share that news with him.

Teir regarded her thoughtfully. How far would she go to test the legend's truth? Would she marry Lord Cam'brii?

"You'd asked me once about Cam'brii's background." He swatted at a buzzing insect. His skin itched, and perspiration trickled down his neck. The rising sun made the jungle steamy hot. "I found out his secret. It explains his behavior and his antipathy toward the Souks."

When he'd told the story, Sarina nodded. "That does explain a lot, but it doesn't change how I feel about either of you."

"What were you planning to do when you returned to Bimordus Two?"

"I'll wed the councilor if it's necessary to activate my

power. As for loving him, I never will. Nor will I be a pawn in his political games."

Teir tilted his head. "How do you feel about me, then? Is there an explanation for why your healing power only seems to work on my injuries?"

She brushed a strand of hair off her face, confused by the jumble of emotions his question aroused. "What I feel for you is probably what I should be feeling for Lord Cam'brii."

He went over and knelt by her side. "Say it, Sarina. Tell me how you feel." He desperately wanted to hear the words.

She reached out and smoothed the hair off his forehead. He caught her hand and turned it palm up, kissing her soft flesh. She gasped as his tongue darted out, licking the cup of her hand with circular movements that sent thrills down her spine.

"Teir, you're making me want you again."

"By the stars," he said, his voice holding wonder. "Look at the circle on your hand."

The circular birthmark on her palm had a faint glow.

"The Great Healer bears the sign of the circle," she repeated from her studies on Bimordus Two. "The sign will glow like the ancient Auricle." She withdrew her hand from his grasp, stunned by this further proof of the prophecy.

The circle reverted to a flat birthmark. Sarina stared at her palm. What was it about touching Teir that inspired her powers?

They stared at each other but were startled by shouts coming from behind the thicket.

"Quick! Bdan's men are closing in on your location." Devin crashed through the brush. The youth had a panicked expression.

"Where are Salla and her mate?"

"They fight them off."

"How many are there? Are they Horthas?" Teir bolted to his feet and reached for his shooter at the same time.

"No, they are Souks, armed with stun whips. But there is one among them who is a champion fighter. Salla's mate has no hope against him. You must flee."

"I'll not abandon them. Take Sarina to safety."

"No." Sarina jumped up from her perch.

"It is not wise for you to fight," Devin warned Teir. "You are still weak from your ordeal. You need rest and food."

"I've just had both."

A high-pitched scream sounded and spurred Teir to action. Ignoring Sarina's cry of protest, he set off, crashing through the ground cover. Fallen tree trunks impeded his path and matted cobwebs brushed his face. Pressing on, Teir came to the clearing just in time to see Salla being manhandled by a giant Souk. Her mate lay on the ground, deathly still.

"Release her," Teir shouted, aiming his shooter.

Before he could fire, something sharp stung his wrist from behind. His numbed fingers dropped the weapon. Whirling, Teir saw he'd missed the two rear guards who were poised in low-hanging branches. They swung their stun whips in his direction. He easily sidestepped them, but by now the giant had dropped the helpless Salla and lumbered toward him.

Teir faced the scowling dog face. So it was to be hand-to-hand combat, was it? He gave a quick glance backward, but Devin and Sarina were nowhere in sight. Either they were hiding, or the boy was already leading her to safety. Somehow he knew, though, that Sarina wouldn't leave him. He hoped she wouldn't cry out if he got hurt.

He faced the Souk champion and mustered his strength. Muscles bulged on his opponent's arms, broad chest, and sturdy legs. Teir searched for an obvious weakness but couldn't find one. Being shorter than the Souk meant he would be more agile, but that wasn't a great advantage. In his weakened state, a few punches could easily bring him down.

Teir assumed a fighting stance and readied himself by bouncing back and forth on the balls of his feet. The Souk neared, drops of spittle on his lower lip. Scuffling noises sounded from behind Teir, as though the other guards were getting into position should their champion fail.

The Souk lunged, his right knee bent forward, his fist swinging. Teir feinted to the left but was too slow. The blow caught him in the ribs. With a grunt, he kicked and caught the Souk sideways on his legs. The Souk cursed and twirled around, jabbing at Teir with a stiff hand to the neck.

The blow hit him on his collarbone, forcing Teir to his knees. The Souk advanced again. Teir bent his head and butted the champion in the stomach, but it was like banging against a stone wall. The Souk chuckled and grasped Teir under the arms. Lifting him, he encircled his chest and began squeezing.

The air rushed from his lungs. A wave of hopelessness washed over him. They were all going to be captured. He only prayed Sarina was safely away. A strange buzzing sounded in his ears as his vision began to dim. *Not again,* he thought as he lost consciousness.

****

Sarina watched from the vantage point where she and Devin crouched behind a clump of trees. They remained a safe distance from the guards. She'd thought Teir was doing well when he kicked the giant, but the champion had brought him to his knees. Her heart skipped a beat at the expression of pain contorting his face.

"We have to help him," she told Devin.

The youth glared at her. "You think we stand a chance against two Souks armed with stun whips and their champion fighter? We should flee while their attention is diverted."

Sarina watched in horror as the Souk fighter lifted Teir and squeezed his ribcage. Teir's jaw slackened, and then he went limp and hung lifeless in the giant's embrace.

"He's killed him. Oh, my God. Devin, he needs me."

"He still breathes. See, his chest moves. He is merely knocked out."

The Souk laid Teir out on the ground next to Etan, Salla's mate. The guards hovered over all three of them, stun whips crackling as they swung them menacingly close to the older woman. Salla's face showed no fear. Her expression was calm as she huddled beside her companions.

"I can't leave them." Sarina surged to her feet.

"Don't be foolish. You can do nothing." The red-haired youth stood, his height taller than hers.

Ignoring his warning, Sarina put a foot forward. She'd do anything to save Teir.

"I'm sorry, but it is my duty to take you to safety," Devin stated.

A sharp blow impacted the side of her head. With a cry of pain, Sarina lost her balance. She tumbled to the ground as blackness swallowed her.

****

Teir pried his eyes open to view an unwelcome sight. He was back in Bdan's gloomy dungeon, strung up by his wrists in the same manner as before. Only this time, Salla and Etan kept him company in the cavernous hall.

A smoky scent permeated the air, clogging his nostrils and making his painful intakes of breath even more difficult. That giant must have cracked some of his ribs. Shadows played in the corners of the room, so he couldn't see who else was there, but buzzing noises indicated the presence of Hortha guards.

He wondered who had ordered his recapture. It must have been Otis, the smuggler's second-in-command. The lieutenant hadn't been harsh during his interrogation of Teir on board the *Omnus*. Perhaps they could strike some sort of bargain for his freedom. Hope surged in his chest, only to be dashed the next moment.

A figure stepped from the shadows and approached. Flamelights flickered along the damp stone walls, providing meager illumination. It took Teir a moment to identify the individual.

"You!" he said, stunned.

"Welcome back, Captain," Bdan crooned.

"Where did you come from? I thought you were—" Teir had a vision of Bdan vanishing from sight in the moat surrounding his sumptuous bed.

"Thought you I was dead. Captain? The *flegymns* in my moat do not feed upon Souk flesh, and an escape hatchway have I underneath. I simply vanished below and reappeared in another section of my complex. A tiresome journey it was, however. Another reason for us to even the score." The smuggler snarled, baring his teeth. "Finding it irritating, am I, to keep hunting you. Simpler would it have been had Loopa succeeded in snaring you with his offer."

"So *you* were backing him. Was he responsible for sabotaging my ship as well?"

"Most definitely. Unfortunately, Defense League Command reassigned you before you could accept his proposal." Bdan's brow furrowed. "Disappointed, am I, to see the Earthwoman is not with you. Where is she?"

"Sarina is long gone," Teir lied.

"Gone where, exactly?"

"You won't get any answers from me."

Bdan whipped an electrifier out of his robe and hit Teir with a low, but painful, voltage. "Not waiting around for you to talk, am I, this time. Monitoring all flights have I been. The woman has not been seen at the spaceport. So I repeat, where is she hiding?"

"Go to Zor," Teir replied.

The Souk struck him again, adjusting the power level one notch higher. "Talk will you, Captain R-R-Reylock. Or maybe your friends would rather speak than watch your suffering." He turned his attention to the other captives. "Lieutenant Otis."

Otis scampered from the shadows. "Master?"

"Know you these two? Crigellans are they, like yourself."

Otis's lizard face was impassive as he regarded the pair. "No, sir. I've never seen them before."

"Good, then mind not will you when they are executed. Found any trace of the Earthwoman, have you?"

Otis's face pinched. "Not yet, sir. My men are working on it. However, there is something I want to show you that is of interest."

While Otis drew Bdan off to the side, Teir glanced at his companions. Etan was awake but appeared woozy. Salla was strung up between the two males. She watched Teir, her expression inscrutable even though she must be suffering considerable discomfort.

"I'm sorry," Teir told her. "If I had been stronger, I might have been able to defeat the Souk champion. Now you're here because of me."

"Do not apologize for your weakened condition. You should have listened to Devin and left while you had the chance."

"I don't abandon my friends. I'm just sorry you're involved." He glanced away, avoiding her gaze. "It seems I've met nothing but failure lately. Even on Lapis, our mission succeeded but lives were lost. And now it seems we're doomed. I don't understand what's been happening. Before Sarina came along, my crew and I had no problems. We finished all of our assignments without distress. Now, things keep going wrong."

He hung his head, his body throbbing in a hundred places. His arms felt like they were pulling out of their sockets.

"Do not sound so hopeless, Captain," Salla said in a gentle tone. "Sarina is safe, but you must complete a quest before you see her again."

"What do you mean?"

They were in a no-win situation as far as he could tell. If Sarina had escaped, he didn't fathom how he would ever see her again. Bdan would put him to death so he couldn't cause any more trouble.

"The legend has yet to be fulfilled, and you are the key to its attainment. The Blood Crystal will reveal what must be done." Salla winced as a spasm stole her breath.

Her aged limbs must be tearing apart, Teir thought, anguished because he had caused her pain. Beside her, Etan squirmed, but his wrists were securely bound above his head like theirs. Teir wriggled his fingers that were going numb.

"Listen carefully," Salla said. "My energy seeps away, but there is more I must tell you. It is you, Captain Reylock, who is destined to marry the Great Healer."

"What?" Teir sucked in a sharp, painful breath.

"Consult the Blood Crystal," Salla repeated.

"How is it that you know so much?" He lifted his head, his gaze narrowing. Maybe this was a trick of Bdan's to get him to reveal the location of the magical rock.

Salla nodded at her chest. "I wear an amulet around my neck. It is a glowstone, Captain. We are of the people—you, I, and the Earthwoman. There are others like us—"

"R-R-Reylock!" Bdan roared, marching over to them. "What means this?" In his palm he thrust out a data link. On the display were the entry codes for the *Valiant*.

Teir looked him in the eye. "It's not mine. You emptied my pockets when you captured me the first time."

"Is Sarina on her way to your ship?"

"I told you she's long gone. Where did you get that?"

"Found at your hiding place in the Thicket of Bayne was it, according to Lieutenant Otis. Who does it belong to, then? These two?" He turned his furious face to the Crigellans.

"It is not ours," Salla replied quietly. "We would not have advised the Captain to return to his ship. It is too heavily guarded."

"Where is the girl?" Bdan bellowed. "Talk, or kill you one by one, will I." He boosted the power level on his electrifier, clearly incensed enough to carry out his threat.

"Wait," Teir said, when he took aim at Etan. "You still want the location of the Blood Crystal?"

If he could divert Bdan's attention from Sarina, she'd be one step ahead. And Salla had advised him to consult the crystal. How better to serve both goals than to take Bdan there and elude him? For the first time, hope glimmered in the future.

Bdan stuck his ugly face in front of Teir's. "Decided to cooperate, have you, Captain?"

Teir assumed a defeated expression, which wasn't hard to do. "I'll take you to the Blood Crystal, but only if you let my friends go free."

"Give me the location," Bdan snarled, raising the electrifier.

"No, I have to go with you. The guardian will only open to me. We can take the *Valiant*. She's fast, and the coordinates are already in the computer."

"Trying to trick me are you. There's no reason to take you. Analyze the files we can ourselves to get the information."

"The data is likely encoded," Otis interrupted, his gaze thoughtful. "And you don't know anything about this guardian, sir. You could take along the captain's friends to ensure his cooperation."

"Good idea." Bdan returned his attention to Teir. "Very well, agree to your proposal, do I. However, your friends will be released only after I have possession of the Blood Crystal."

Teir would deal with this complication later. "We go in the *Valiant,* then?" This was a crucial part of his plan.

"So be it." Bdan barked an order to the Hortha guards, and the three were cut down.

Giving them no time to rub the circulation back into their tingling limbs, Bdan commanded them to move out.

Soon all three captives, Bdan and Otis, and a contingent of mixed Hortha and Souk guards, advanced through a series of tunnels.

They emerged into the blazing desert sun. The *Valiant* was secured in a hangar complex a short walk away.

Teir's heart swelled at the glimpse of his ship. She'd help him escape, this great galactic bird of his. He only had to get access to the controls.

Bdan wasn't about to let him get off so easily, however. He

made Teir and the two Crigellans sit in the lounge while he and Otis piloted the ship. The three prisoners sat around the conference table, a silent group, ringed by guards. The viewing ports were closed, apparently under Bdan's orders. Teir could tell when they were underway by the vibrations.

At last Bdan waddled into the lounge. "Need some information do I, Captain."

"You want our destination? I'll have to use the ship's computer to set the coordinates. I can use that terminal." He nodded to a corner of the room that held a small console.

"Tell me, will you, and I shall enter the data."

"That won't work," Teir explained. "The system will only respond to me. This particular entry is voice activated. Security, you understand."

"I see." The Souk appeared to consider. "All right," he agreed with obvious reluctance, "but watching you, shall I be. No tricks, R-R-Reylock."

Bdan lumbered over to the console after him to observe over his shoulder. Teir was careful to keep his expression bland, but as his fingers flew over the control pad, his heart soared. He coded in the sequence that would repel unwanted intruders from his ship. This wasn't the right time to activate it, though, not with Bdan watching him so carefully. He'd have to wait for a better opportunity.

As an added precaution, he ordered the computer to record Bdan's voice in case he needed to fake the smuggler's gruff tones in the future.

That left one more thing to do. If they were going to take the shuttle down to Taurus, Teir would need a remote unit to gain control of the vessel from his getaway point. That way, once he escaped Bdan and his guards, he could summon the shuttle himself.

"What are you doing?" Bdan snapped.

"I'm opening the path for voice commands," Teir replied, finishing on the keypad with a flourish. "Computer, locate coordinates for code name Onyx, authorization Reylock, Gamma Alpha Two Zero Six."

Coordinates ready, responded the computer in a sultry female voice.

"Lay in a course," Teir ordered.

Course locked in.

"Activate."

Course set for location code name Onyx.

Teir let out a long breath. "Voice activation off."

"Where are we heading, Captain?" The smuggler hovered over him, his rolls of bluish flesh quivering as the ship rocked. He put a paw on the wall to steady himself. The skirt swayed on his purple and gold caftan.

If Teir had been flying, there would have been no sensation of movement at all. He knew how to fine-tune the controls, but Otis wasn't as familiar with ship's operations. He might be able to use that in his favor.

"Our destination is the planet, Taurus," he answered.

"That's in the Quantum sector. Weeks will it take us to get there."

"Not if you go at warp eight. It should take us ten days at the most. I assume you checked the fuel capacitators?"

"Fully charged are the crystals."

"Then we'll have no problem. Tell Otis to increase power."

"Know the location now do I. Expendable are you," said Bdan with an evil chuckle.

"No, I'm not. You still need me to get past the guardian, remember?"

"Grrrrr," the Souk growled. He passed on the order to Otis to increase speed, then apparently decided his stomach took precedence over further action. He lumbered over to the fabricator and conjured himself a snack. Joining the Crigellans at the table, he ranged his bulk across two chairs and sat alongside them.

"May I have permission to use the sanitary?" Teir asked.

Bdan studied him through narrowed eyes. "No harm can you

do from there, I suppose. Geemus will accompany you to make certain you behave." He nodded to one of the Souks standing guard then slurped up a mouthful of live Rigelan slugs.

Teir washed and shaved, then entered his stateroom. Under the close supervision of his vigilant guard, he changed into a fresh blue shirt and navy pants with a black leather vest.

When the ship rocked again, causing the Souk to momentarily glance away, Teir's hand shot beneath the slight overhang of his desk. He grasped the small rectangular object taped in place. Bending over with a pretended cough, he slipped the remote unit into his inner vest pocket.

Back at the lounge, he offered Salla and Etan some refreshments, then sat down himself with a bowl of nourishing stew and a drink of his favorite Arcturian brandy. He would need all his strength for the ordeal to come.

Bdan, who had gone to the bridge to consult with Otis, sauntered back into the lounge. He bombarded Teir with questions about the ship and insisted on a tour. Teir rattled off a series of technical instructions that would confuse even Datron as he led the fat Souk through each deck. He pointed out only the obvious, keeping secret the hidden compartments and security details.

The next days passed with agonizing slowness. Bdan took over Teir's cabin, and Lieutenant Otis occupied Ravi's. That left the remaining two cabins with double bunks for Teir and the Crigellans. Geemus, the guard, was assigned to share with Teir. Bdan wasn't taking any chances of leaving him alone.

Teir was careful to keep his remote unit on his person at all times. He changed his shirt and pants each day but kept the same vest. Geemus never saw fit to frisk him, and Teir made sure the guard's suspicions weren't aroused.

Confined for the most part of the journey to the lounge, he spent time in conversation with Salla and Etan.

"I hope Sarina is well," he told them, mentioning her name for what must have been the hundredth time.

"What is meant to be will come to pass," said Salla. She and her mate played a game of Boks using a backlit board and colored tiles on the wide table.

"Are you sure she got off Souk?" he asked in a low tone so they wouldn't be overheard. "Where is she now? Do you think she is trying to find me?"

Endless questions plagued him. If only he knew for certain she was all right. If only he could speak to her or hear her voice.

"She'll be all right," Salla reassured him, patting his hand. "In fact, I sense she will soon be with friends, and one person in particular who cares about her."

Teir's head jerked up. A friend who cared about her? Who could that be, unless it was Lord Cam'brii? Was Sarina returning to him after all?

A terrible fear took hold of him that he might lose her to the councilor. By the corona, she could even now be preparing for her marriage.

His escape took on a new urgency, and he counted the hauras until they reached Taurus.

Chapter Twenty

On the planet Tendraa, Mantra faced his own challenge. He'd requested an audience with the Liege Lord. The whole future of his disease-ravaged planet might depend upon what happened during this interview, so he had to think carefully about what to say.

The journey from Ingorr had been long and arduous. He'd joined a caravan leaving from the posting station at Cameron. They passed through the icy Kougar Chills without incident. Weeks later, their group reached the capital city of Lazore on the coast of the Bazmayan Sea. At least it was warmer here. Mantra's breath merely steamed instead of freezing in his nostrils.

Cold and tired, he had put up at a local inn to wash and rest. Then he'd presented himself at the palace gate, armed with a letter from the Baynor of Ingorr and endorsements from other town leaders he'd met along the way. Word had traveled fast. Those cities that implemented the measures suggested by the Great Healer were already showing declines in the disease rates. Thereafter, Mantra's advice had been sought all along their route. He'd had no trouble getting an appointment with the Liege Lord.

He stood nervously in an anteroom, unable to appreciate the gilded wallpaper, carved cornices, or plush draperies that decorated the space. Part of him wondered where the credits had come from to furnish the palace. Mostly, he kept busy by rehearsing his speech.

All rational thoughts flew from his mind when he was ushered into the grand presence of their ruler, Cyng Navin. The

Receiving Chamber shone from crystal chandeliers reflecting the gold trim. He squinted at the brightness as a pageboy led him forward toward a raised dais.

The Liege Lord seemed almost dwarfed by the immensity of the throne he occupied. Mantra bowed deeply, and it wasn't until he heard the command to rise that he was able to study his leader at length. He noted the Liege Lord's sharp brown eyes, his shock of coal black hair, and his rangy physique.

Cyng Navin regarded him just as intently. Mantra knew that Navin hadn't become the leader of Tendraa by virtue of his birth alone. He had been born into the ruling dynasty, but it was his charisma that had propelled him to dominate planetary politics. He'd risen through the ranks and had been proclaimed Liege Lord at a younger age than any of his predecessors.

"The faith be with you, citizen," said Cyng Navin, making the sign of the circle with his hand as though giving a blessing. "What brings you to us?"

Mantra cleared his throat. "I have seen the light, Your Worship. The Great Healer herself came to me."

"Aye, I have heard of your good deeds. You spread the word even as you travelled to our esteemed city. What is it the Great One revealed to you?"

"She gave us the means to help ourselves, Liege Lord." He rattled off the sanitation measures Sarina had suggested, then told of his own implementation and the positive results. "Neither of my sisters have fallen ill. We breathe easier, and our hide has thinned to its former softness. The Great Healer has spoken. We must heed her word throughout the land."

Mantra dropped to his knees and clasped his hands together. "You have never seen such sweetness and compassion, Your Worship. The woman called Sarina is like a miracle come to life. Truly, she represents the Ancient Ones as prophesied in the legend. The sacred light shines in her eyes. I myself saw this wondrous sight. If we do not follow her decrees, I fear our people may perish."

Tears came unbidden to his eyes. "I lost both my parents and my younger sister, Zunis, to the Farg. I pray we do not see a resurgence of the horrifying visitation. Kairi is very dear to me— another sister, sire. I could not bear to lose her, too. Everyone must do as the Great Healer says in order for us all to be protected."

"Why does the Great Healer not cure the sick?" asked Navin, his brow wrinkled in thought. The bejeweled crown on his head bobbed when he spoke.

Mantra rose to his feet. "That puzzled me at first, sire. But then I realized it was a test of faith for us to heal ourselves." He let his gaze fall pointedly to a side table holding a crystal goblet of wine and a silver bowl of exotic fruits. "Surely we have the resources to make widespread change."

"Change is what caused our downfall in the past," Navin reminded him.

"That's because we were not prepared, and the changes came too fast for us to adapt. These are smaller, attainable measures that I propose."

"Hmm." The Liege Lord rubbed his cheek as though wondering what it would feel like to have soft hide again. The smoky haze that permeated the cities wreaked havoc on one's outer skin, and although Navin's hide was smoother than average for someone his age, it still might feel rough to his touch. Also, because of the Farg, their leader had been mostly confined to the palace. Perhaps he'd like to stroll the streets again and shake people's hands as he had in the early days of his reign.

"We'll give it a trial," he agreed to Mantra's delight. "We can start in Lazore. If I see positive results, I'll issue a decree. In the meantime, Citizen Mantra, I have a mandate for you."

"What is it, Your Worship?" Mantra asked, as an inner glow spread within him. He'd achieved his main purpose in spreading the gospel of the Great Healer.

"I've been thinking about this long and hard, and I feel the time is right. We need a representative in the Coalition so we can keep abreast of news regarding the Great Healer. She might have more of these pronouncements to make. Since she chose you as her contact, I now appoint you to be our ambassador."

Mantra's mouth dropped open. Ambassador to the Coalition! How could this be? It was a dream come true.

"Are you thinking of applying for full membership?" he asked in some confusion.

"No! We do not want interference with our policies, just information."

"But—"

"You will follow my directives, citizen, will you not?"

"Of course, sire," Mantra said with a humble bow.

"I have a piece of news you must take with you." The Liege Lord pushed himself up from the throne and began pacing the dais, his hands folded behind his back. His voluminous robe swished at his feet as he walked. "We have advanced technology that was preserved from the Techno War. Our palace houses a communications center. We have been monitoring the long-range sensors. They have picked up an alien force orbiting the outer planet of our system. It appears their intent is hostile."

"The Morgots are here?" Terror struck Mantra's heart. Finally they had a handle on one problem, and now another threat arrived.

Navin looked him in the eye. "Tendraa is rich in flavium. The Morgots will want to use the mineral to produce weapons of mass destruction. We've forbidden the mining of flavium for that very reason. Now the Morgots have come to steal our resources."

"We must ask the Coalition for help," Mantra stated.

"I don't want the political bungrats on Bimordus Two getting their claws into our system. That's what led to the Techno War the last time we sought partnership in the Coalition. You will ask the Great Healer for assistance."

Mantra saw the Liege Lord wouldn't budge on this issue. "Very well, sire. When do you wish me to leave?"

"Immediately. My daughter, Tami, will assist you with

preparations." His gaze swept over Mantra's worn tunic and baggy pants. "You'll need to see Popus, keeper of the royal wardrobe. As our representative, you must be properly dressed."

He tapped a hidden gong by the throne and a door at the rear of the chamber slid open. In walked the most beautiful girl Mantra had ever seen. Her age could be no more than eighteen annums, he figured. She was of medium height, slightly shorter than him, with a slender figure draped in a metallic jade cloth. The drape complemented her luminous green eyes and provided the perfect backdrop for her long russet hair.

Gazing at her delicate facial features, Mantra thought he'd never seen a complexion so lovely. The creamy beige of her hide was smooth and unflawed. High cheekbones and a slightly upturned nose went perfectly with her pouting mouth. He wondered insanely what it would be like to kiss her, then abruptly cast the thought aside. As a commoner, he stood no chance with a princess of the realm.

"Citizen Mantra, may I present my daughter, Tami," said Cyng Navin.

Mantra bowed deeply. "My lady, it is an honor." He was glad the Liege Lord had ordered him to be suitably attired for his journey. He wanted to look his best in front of this woman.

"Your transport has already been arranged," Navin continued. "Everything you need will be aboard. I'll expect your first report within seven days after your arrival on Bimordus Two."

Dismissed, Mantra understood he was to leave with Tami. He followed her out the rear door and through a series of corridors into a salon.

"Please be seated," she said in a musical voice. Every movement she made was dainty and graceful.

Popus, the keeper of the wardrobe, shuffled in to take his measurements. When he was finished, the portly gentleman stroked his beard. "You maintain your weight well, citizen. I have many excellent garments that will fit you." Turning to Tami, he asked, "Shall I have them sent directly to the spacecraft, Your Highness?"

"Yes, and please make haste," she said.

She ordered refreshments. After the small cakes and carafe of wine had been delivered, she smiled at Mantra. "You have a brief time before the transport is scheduled for departure. Do you have your own belongings that you wish to bring on the trip?"

"Aye." Mantra gave her the name of the inn where he'd left his baggage.

Tami gave instructions to a servant to retrieve Mantra's bags. "Now, Mantra, tell me about this mission you undertake."

Mantra knew her mother was away visiting relatives, so Tami was taking her place as hostess. Still, it felt strange to speak so freely to a young lady in such an unaccustomed manner. They were alone, the servants having withdrawn and Popus having hurried off to complete his task.

"I go to seek the council of the Great Healer," he said. Noting the interest on her face, he proceeded to tell her of his own experience with Sarina.

"I have prayed for the Great Healer to save us," Tami responded. "I am sorry she was unable to help your parents and sister."

Her compassionate reply surprised Mantra. "What's important now is that the legend is coming true. Peace is in our future. But achieving it might be difficult. Alas, I fear the Great Healer may not be able to help our people overcome the latest threat. The Morgots are on their way to strip our planet of its resources and enslave our people. Your father refuses to ask the Coalition for aid."

Tami's eyes widened. "Surely the Morgots won't come while the pestilence still afflicts us."

"That is exactly the sort of situation that benefits them. For some reason, the Morgots are immune to the sickness. According to my cousin Ravi, they've been conquering planets whose people are stricken by the plague."

"That's horrible. What are we to do?"

Mantra wanted to take her lovely hand in his and comfort her. "Help your father realize we cannot fight this alone. We must request the assistance of the Defense League. He wants me to ask the Great Healer for aid. I shall do so, but I fear her powers will not be enough. Tami, for the sake of our people, talk to your father about this issue and get him to change his mind before it's too late."

She nodded emphatically. "I shall follow your advice, Citizen Mantra." She glanced at the doorway, where an attendant had signaled her. "And now, I believe it is time for your departure." She stood, and Mantra followed suit.

The words escaped his lips before he could stop them. "Your Highness, may I have the honor of calling upon you when I return?"

"Yes, that would please me, but you must call me Tami when we are alone."

"Only if you call me Mantra."

She raised her delicately arched eyebrows. "We have too many inequalities on Tendraa. Things have been static for longer than is wise. Change is inevitable."

Mantra couldn't help himself. He stepped over and took her hand. "It warms my heart that you feel as I do about these things. Perhaps we can talk more of this at a later date."

Tami blushed and lowered her eyes. "I shall be monitoring the communications room for your news."

"Then I shall be certain to report in as often as possible." He held her hand a moment more, then released it.

The attendant entered to show him the way.

"Lightspeed on your journey, citizen," Tami told him.

"The faith be with you, lady." Mantra bowed, turned on his heel, and left.

Soon he entered the cockpit of a space transport with only a two-member crew for company. As he readied himself for his initiation into space travel, his heart thumped with excitement.

Wonder of wonders! He was going where his cousin Ravi had gone before him.

He strapped on his safety harness and stared out the viewscreen. His life was about to change, and he hoped to be the one to usher in a new era of enlightenment. The Great Healer had chosen him to serve her and implement her pronouncements. Somehow, he'd deal with the Morgot threat as well. His faith would guide him along the right course.

In his pouch he held a parchment from the Liege Lord. It was a letter of introduction, authorizing him to represent the people of Tendraa. He'd have to present himself to the General Assembly for ratification of his appointment. Once that was done, he'd seek an audience with the Great Healer. And if his cousin Ravi was on Bimordus Two, they'd enjoy a warm reunion.

Hope filled his heart for a brighter future, and it glowed with faith and love almost as brightly as the light from the ancient Auricle.

****

Sarina blinked once, then several times more, as she returned to consciousness. She lay flat on her back and could see nothing despite the fact that her eyes were wide open. Forcing herself to remain calm, she waited for her vision to adjust to the dark. A throbbing headache told her she was alive. The last thing she remembered was Devin warning her that his duty was to bring her to safety. Then he'd apparently cracked her on the head to ensure her compliance.

So where was she? Raising a hand, she gasped when her palm met a smooth wall. She traced the outline with her fingers, alarmed to discover the surface seemed to enclose her. When she tried to roll to her side, the tight space obstructed any further movement.

Oh, God! She couldn't see or hear anything. This box surrounded her like a coffin. Had Devin knocked her cold and left her for dead? Or had he placed her inside knowing she was alive and breathing? Maybe he was a spy for the Souks after all.

She banged her fist on the hard surface. How was it possible that she could breathe? She listened intently and then heard a faint hissing noise. So there was air in here, or at least a vent somewhere.

"Help!" she screamed, banging more fiercely until her knuckles hurt. It might be wise to conserve what little air was present. She was hyperventilating, breathing in short panicked breaths. If she continued, she'd pass out. Then again, that might be a blessing.

"Teir," she said, craving the comfort of his presence. "Where are you?"

A vision of the Souk champion hovering over the captain's prostrate body came to mind. He must be a prisoner, too. Was this to be their fate? They'd die apart, never to see each other again? Good Lord, it was too much to bear.

A squeaking sound invaded her thoughts. She yelled out, afraid of vermin sharing the space with her. That idea made her bang on the hard surface with renewed desperation.

Suddenly a square hatch opened above her, and bright light streamed in. She squeezed her eyes shut against the glare.

"Hush," said a male voice. "You must remain quiet."

She cracked her eyes open. The eraser-pink face of a Sirisian peered at her. "Who are you? Where am I?"

"You're on board a cargo vessel bound for Bimordus Two. You were smuggled aboard from Souk several days ago."

"Several days ago?" It seemed like she'd just seen Teir and the others. "What about my friends?"

"Devin remained behind. He fights for freedom with other Believers on Souk. Of the rest in your party, I know not. No one else on this vessel is aware you are here. I gave you a drug to keep you quiet for most of the journey, but we arrive at Bimordus Two within the haura, so it was necessary for you to awaken. You must remain inside the container until we land and off-load the cargo. The other crew members are sympathetic to the Souks."

"I'll die if I stay in here much longer," Sarina protested.

"Do as you're told, or I'll inject you again and put you back to sleep. You endanger us both by making noise. Your ordeal is nearly at an end. Please try to stay calm."

"Wait!" Sarina thrust out a hand as he went to close the hatch, but he waved her back and sealed the lid.

Blackness overtook her once more. *If I just lie still, I'll be all right,* she told herself. *Think about the legend. Believe in it, and everything will turn out all right. Believe…*

Time passed while she lay there, allowing her mind to drift and trying to assimilate all that had happened to her.

She'd been about to doze off when the hatch popped open again. The Sirisian reached down to assist her out of the container. Her knees buckled when she stood, and she swayed against him.

"Easy, Mistress, you are free now. Give yourself a moment to adjust."

"What is this place?"

"We have arrived at the Spaceport on Bimordus Two. The cargo is being unloaded. You have to go before you are noticed. I regret that I cannot accompany you, but my absence would be noted."

She peered at her rescuer. He wore a belted tan tunic with a yellow turban on his bald head. "Thank you for helping me. Your name is…?"

"It does not matter. I am honored to help the Great Healer. You have much work to do. The universe is torn by strife, and disease is rampant. You are the star we have prayed for to lead us away from the darkness and into the light. Here is a cloak for you to wear," the Sirisian said, handing her a dark brown cape. "You need to blend into the crowd."

Gratefully, she wrapped the garment around herself and drew the hood over her blond hair.

"Come, I'll show you the way out." The Sirisian took her arm and led her through another storeroom to an exit. "The faith be with you, Mistress. I shall pray for your success."

"Thank you for helping me."

She advanced toward a section bustling with activity—spaceships taxiing to and from hangars, cargo being off-loaded, uniformed officers shouting instructions.

Afraid of being spotted, she slunk through the shadows until she came to a transport terminal that would take her into the city. There she boarded a tram, trying to remain as inconspicuous as possible. She found a seat and scanned the directory display. She'd go to Rolf's place. Would he welcome her return? She had nowhere else to go.

As the tram emerged into the daylight, she figured it must be early morning. Maybe her betrothed would still be in his quarters. If he rejected her, she'd seek sanctuary with Glotaj.

Twenty minutes later, she stood at the entrance to Spiral Town. The sergeant in charge of the perimeter troops greeted her with surprise. No doubt she looked a wreck, given how she'd escaped from Souk and spent days on a spaceship confined in a box. He maintained his professional mien as she requested entry into the building. When she asked him not to notify the councilor of her arrival, he agreed, albeit with obvious reluctance.

As the officer led her into the lobby, she wondered how Rolf would react to her presence. He might be so upset by her behavior that he'd order her to leave. Her body trembled, more from fear of his response than from her ordeal of the past few days. She pressed the button for the lift while debating what to say.

She'd made up her mind to go through with the marriage if that's what it took for the prophecy to come true. Initially, she'd wanted to become the Great Healer to cure people like her friend, Abby. Now, she hoped to use the political clout of her position to help free Teir from the Souks. She'd do anything for him, even if it meant sleeping with the councilor.

She approached Rolf's door and placed her eye in front of the retinal scanning device. Thankfully, it was still programmed for her parameters. After a brief flash when the scanner read her eye, the portal slid open.

Rolf was doing sit-ups on the living room carpet, wearing a pair of shorts and nothing more. Seeing her framed in the doorway, he leapt to his feet and gaped at her.

"What are you doing here?" In two long strides, he stood beside her. His gaze raked her up and down. "By the stars, what's happened to you? Where have you been?"

Sarina averted her gaze from his muscular chest. "It's a long story. May I come in?"

"Of course." He stood aside while she passed and seated herself on the double lounger at the opposite end of the room. He ordered the door shut, grabbed a towel and wiped himself dry, then turned to face her. "Let me get you a drink. You look terrible." He brought her a cool beverage, then hovered protectively over her.

Sarina gulped down half the drink before she could speak again. Her body must be parched from dehydration. "I'm sure you have a lot of questions," she began when her thirst abated. She placed the glass on a side table.

"I've been worried sick about you. Talk to me." He sat beside her and patted her hand.

"Perhaps I should start at the beginning." She gave a long sigh, partly out of relief. At least he wasn't angry with her. "I left because I was afraid of the execution decree, and I was also anxious to see my friends and family. I took advantage of the opportunity to escape and go home."

"You made a fool out of Reylock."

"Teir deserved it. Anyway, let me tell you what happened when I went to Earth."

"What do you mean, he deserved it?" Rolf said, picking up on her words. "For weeks, I've been wondering what happened between the two of you. Did Reylock seduce you? Is that why you ran away, because you'd been dishonored?"

"No, you've got it all wrong. He wanted nothing more to do with me. Teir explained later that he—"

"Later? The captain was ordered not to pursue you. Where is he?"

"He's a prisoner on Souk—I hope."

"You hope?"

"Either that, or he's dead."

"What in Zor are you talking about?"

Sarina wished he'd put on a shirt. She was all too aware of his nearly naked body beside her. He certainly maintained a virile physique. With his tall height, curly blond hair, and piercing blue eyes, the man was undeniably attractive. But for all his appeal, she felt no desire for him. No matter how hard she tried, Teir was still uppermost in her thoughts.

After fortifying herself with a deep breath, she described her sojourn to Earth, her experiences with Abby and the stone, her capture by the Souks, and her reunion with Teir in Bdan's dungeon. She was about to tell him about healing Teir, but then thought better of it. Rolf would see it as confirmation that something significant had occurred between them.

When she had a chance, she'd inform Glotaj. According to Teir, the regent had seemed interested in their relationship, and she needed to talk to him anyway.

Rolf frowned and stared at his hands folded in his lap. "Before you left for Tendraa, I didn't relate to you on a personal level. Nor did I treat you with the proper respect. I realize now that it was the wrong response. I should have been more caring. Now that you've returned, I'd like to make amends." He shot her a hesitant glance. "If you will have me, I still wish to wed you. We'll spend time together and get to know each other better."

"Yes," Sarina said, trying to put some enthusiasm into her voice, "the marriage ceremony can be rescheduled. I am ready now to fulfill my obligations." The councilman would understand that much.

Rolf rose and drew her to her feet. He grasped her hands and gazed intently into her eyes. "With you by my side, we can accomplish anything. We'll make this work, my dear."

Sarina closed her ears. She wanted to be at Teir's side, not the councilor's. Why couldn't she have stayed with him on Souk?

At least then she would have known what happened to him. This way, she suffered the agony of uncertainty.

When she saw Glotaj, she'd ask the regent to investigate his status. Right now, Sarina didn't feel like going out again. People would ask questions, and she was content to let Rolf handle them for her. All she wanted to do was rest.

Rolf dressed in his business attire and left to report to the High Council. In his absence, Sarina luxuriated in a hot shower, ordered a cheeseburger and fries for lunch on the fabricator, and caught up on the news on Rolf's entertainment system.

He returned by dinnertime and beamed at her. "The High Council rejoices at your return. They seek an audience with you tomorrow morning so they can hear about your experiences. Our wedding date has been set for seven days hence. Glotaj will officiate at the ceremony, which will take place in the Assembly Chamber. It's the only place on Bimordus Two that can hold so many guests. A reception is planned in the large conservatory located in the Nutrition Pod."

"Will your parents attend the ceremony?" Sarina asked, wondering what her future in-laws would think of her. Meeting them was not a prospect she anticipated with any joy.

His mood change was abrupt. "I doubt they will come."

Sarina noticed his downcast expression. "Teir told me about the tragedy in your past. Surely they don't still hold that against you?" His silence gave her the answer. "But you are second son to the Imperator. You told me yourself that you would assume the title of Prince after we wed."

"My position in the family does not change, only my father's attitude. According to our law, he does not have the authority to disinherit me. It is enough that he has never spoken to me since my disgrace."

"And your mother?"

"She has never defied him. I have sent word to my elder brother, but the journey would take too long for him to get here in time."

"I'm sorry."

"Don't be. I shall have my revenge when the Souks are defeated. I live for that day."

Troubled by his family grievances, Sarina sought to distract him by serving him his favorite dish. She got a plate of pastagillo noodles with vegetables for herself and joined him at the table.

Rolf's words had indicated that revenge was still his driving force. He might plan to use her to achieve his goals, but then, she was using him, too.

"I hope our marriage serves its purpose," she told him. "I want the legend to come true."

"Even if it doesn't, Glotaj has requested a repeal of the execution decree," Rolf told her between bites. "The vote is scheduled to go before the General Assembly next month, and then the High Council must ratify the statute."

"Do you think it will pass?" Sarina asked, praying for that outcome.

"There are still those to whom your presence is a threat, and they may vote against the measure."

"You mean Daimon and his followers in the Return to Origins Faction?"

Rolf gave a glum nod. "The R.O.F. has been gaining power in your absence. I have ordered a new detail of guards to escort you around town. You must maintain caution and be aware of your surroundings at all times."

Chapter Twenty-One

The next day, Sarina made her report in person to the High Council. Emu was ecstatic when she related the account of the stone.

"It glowed while you were thinking about being a healer," the Sirisian counselor proclaimed. "This is truly a sign that you are The One."

"Do you have this object with you?" Glotaj asked, his demeanor solemn. He wore a purple robe with gold trim that made him look regal.

She stood in the center of the semicircle, facing him. "I hid it on Teir's ship when the Souks captured me. It might still be on the *Valiant.* Can't you send someone after Captain Reylock? He could fly the ship to the nearest Defense League outpost. I'm sure he knows a way to get on board and elude the Souks' defenses."

Glotaj shook his head. "You don't even know if the captain is still alive."

Emu spoke up. "Pardon me, Your Excellency, we could consult Mara. She gave us direction when Sarina went away."

"Please, ask her to help us." Sarina recalled her friend's special ability to see through the eyes of another.

"The captain's disposition is the concern of Defense League Command," said Glotaj coldly. "I'll notify Admiral Daras Gog. This falls under his jurisdiction. We have more important matters to pursue. Council is dismissed."

But when the meeting was over and the regent turned to leave, he cocked an eyebrow at Sarina, indicating he wanted to see her outside.

She told Rolf to wait for her in the antechamber while she entered Glotaj's private office.

"Please be seated," said the regent. He closed the door and turned to her with a smile. "I didn't mean to be so brusque, but there are things we must discuss that are not for everyone's ears. I want you to know that I *am* concerned for Captain Reylock's welfare."

Hope swelled in her heart. "Then you will send someone after him?"

He held up a hand. "We don't have enough information. I would suggest you consult Mara on your own. Your Tyberian friend may agree to use her power to aid you. She helped us when you stole Reylock's ship. From her, we learned you were on your way to Earth. But do this quietly. If you get anything definite to go on, let me know and I'll pass the word to Admiral Gog."

"Why can't you consult her?"

Glotaj's eyes darkened, and he began pacing, his hands folded behind his back. "Remember the attack on Lord Cam'brii by the Twyggs? We learned they were sent by the Souks." He told her about the central computer snafu that had brought the whole transportation system to a halt and prevented their backup guards from reaching them. "We suspect the Souks have an agent here who is a highly placed government official. The agent would have been responsible for hiring the Twyggs and sabotaging the computer network."

"So you don't want this spy to know you're interested in Teir's situation?"

"Oh, the spy knows I'm interested, but not that I'm doing anything about it. When Reylock disappeared after visiting his aunt on Alpha Omega Two, Admiral Gog put a tracer on him. Eventually, the homing beacon on the *Valiant* led to Souk. But how or why the ship ended up there when you had supposedly commandeered it and gone to Earth, we didn't understand. The signal terminated, so we assumed the Souks deactivated the device.

"We'd heard rumors of an underground movement on Souk, but they weren't confirmed until you told us your tale. We still don't know how to contact these people. Occasionally, captives have escaped, but there's never been an organized pipeline. I think the assistance you received was because of your renown."

Sarina's blood ran cold at his admission. "I hope I haven't hurt Teir's chances of survival by mentioning Devin and the others in front of your councilors. Do you suspect the spy to be one of them?"

Glotaj's brow furrowed. "I do not wish to make guesses at this point. I have some suspicions but haven't been able to fix them on any one person in particular. However, you do understand why I wanted to pursue this topic in private?"

"Yes, and I'm sorry. I didn't realize—"

The regent waved a hand. "If the resistance leaders on Souk want to establish contact, they'll have to make the first move. The only thing I can do at this point is to pass information along to Admiral Gog."

Sarina, seated in an armchair facing his desk, folded her hands in her lap. "Tell me, Your Excellency, why did you have Teir assigned to retrieve me from Earth and then to act as my bodyguard? You also allowed us to go to Tendraa together. Was there some reason why you wanted us to be together?"

The regent regarded her impassively. "Captain Reylock is a top officer in the Defense League. I simply thought he would be the best person for the job."

"Why did you recommend him for the Defense League Academy? Teir told me you knew his aunt."

"That is not your concern," Glotaj said, a flicker of emotion in his expression that was quickly hidden.

"Everything about Teir is my concern. Is there something you're trying to hide?"

"I am merely attempting to protect Captain Reylock. Do not inquire further into his background. It could be dangerous for him."

"Why?"

"I can tell you no more."

"I healed him," Sarina blurted. "Twice, I made his wounds disappear."

"What?" When she described the occurrences, Glotaj rubbed a hand over his face. "So, it comes to pass," he said in a barely audible tone.

For a long moment he didn't say another word. His expression showed a shifting of emotions, as though he had to make a weighty decision.

At last he regarded her, his face a cold mask. "Speak of this to no one and proceed along your present course. Let me know what you learn from Mara."

"What about the wedding? It's scheduled for six days from now."

"Destiny will show you the proper path, child."

"Let's hope you're right," Sarina said. Rising, she wondered if protocol demanded that she bow or curtsy. Deciding to do neither, she left.

Rolf was waiting for her in the antechamber. They exited together. Once outside, Sarina paused on the hilltop, gazing at the brilliance of the city below and feeling a flash of comfort. Was this place becoming her home? *No,* her mind answered. *Your home is with Teir.* Her heart cried out for him, wishing he were there beside her instead of the polite councilman.

Rolf turned to her. "What did Glotaj want?"

"He just needed a few more details about the Souks, so I went over my story again," she lied. She wasn't about to tell him they had spoken about Teir.

"I think you should put the past out of your mind and try to relax. Let's go to the Pleasure Palace. I'm free for the next couple of hauras."

Sarina had no desire to waste time at the city's arts and entertainment complex, but she didn't want to offend Rolf. There would be time enough to see Mara afterward.

"All right," she agreed.

Rolf requisitioned a speeder, and they zoomed toward the massive structure. He parked in an adjacent terminal.

"What would you like to do?" he asked, obviously eager to please her.

"I don't know," Sarina said, remembering the last time she had been there. Teir had made her happy by appreciating her love for art. Thinking of him suffering on Souk, she didn't feel like having fun.

Noting her unenthusiastic response, Rolf suggested they have a drink in the lounge. He asked about her family and friends on Earth and what she had accomplished while she was home.

Sarina told him about her life there and the people she'd known. Somehow, the subject drifted to Robert.

"You didn't regret leaving him this time?" Rolf asked, studying her.

"No, because I realized he'd lost his appeal to me. He's too rigid in his views. All that matters to him is his job."

"His dedication sounds admirable."

"I suppose it would, to you," she said. When she saw the pained look on Rolf's face, she hastened to add, "I'm sorry. I didn't mean—"

"Yes, you did. My role is extremely important to me. But so are you, Sarina. I promise to give you the attention you deserve."

Seated beside her, he leaned close and brought his head down. His warm lips pressed against hers. She fought an urge to pull away. She had to fall in love with him if she wanted the legend to come true, and that meant enduring his physical advances. The councilor wasn't displeasing. He just didn't arouse her passion the way the captain did.

As soon as Rolf left for a meeting with the High Council, Sarina contacted Mara and asked if they could meet. She chose a public eaterie, so the guards following her would think she was enjoying herself with a friend. She didn't know if they reported her movements to Rolf or not, but the fact that they surrounded her wherever she went inhibited her freedom. She was grateful for their presence, though. Too many different political factions opposed her and Rolf, and Teir was no longer available to act as bodyguard.

She spotted the tall, raven-haired woman approaching the restaurant. They exchanged excited greetings and then went inside. Sarina requested a corner table so they could watch the entrance. She'd learned a few things from Teir in terms of security.

After ordering a light snack, Mara fixed her knowing gaze on Sarina. "So, you've returned to Bimordus Two, my friend."

"I think the legend might be coming true after all." She filled Mara in on events.

"I helped locate you after you escaped from Captain Reylock's custody, you know."

"Yes, Glotaj told me."

"I sensed you were not happy."

"You were right. I was angry with Teir." Realizing what she'd let slip, Sarina hastened to cover up. "I mean, the captain wouldn't help me get home."

"He was dutybound to obey his orders."

"I know. He's an honorable man." She compressed her lips, reliving the memory of her suffering over his callousness. Then the purpose of his behavior came to mind. He'd been sacrificing his own happiness to push her back to Rolf. How ironic that she'd returned to Rolf of her own accord. Now she was the one making sacrifices for Teir. "Mara, I need your help. I want you to find information on Teir's current situation."

Mara took a sip of her wagmint tea. "How much do you know?"

"Not a whole lot. I've asked Glotaj for help, but the government has no contacts on Souk. I haven't anywhere else to go. I just want to make sure he's all right." She didn't mention Glotaj's interest in the matter, or the regent's suggestion that she pursue this avenue on her own. "I understand you need an item of his, something he's touched. Could we meet later, maybe at your place?" She'd kept his shirt, unable to discard the one item of Teir's she had left.

"That's fine. How about coming by at twenty hauras?"

Sarina agreed, and they parted ways after chatting for a bit more. Outside, she hopped on the people-mover, chuckling at the curses of her guards as they scrambled to follow her. She headed for Spiral Town, hoping to get some rest before she met Mara again.

Her heart sank to find Rolf waiting for her.

"I'm sorry I had to leave for that meeting," he said, trailing her into the bedroom. "I would have liked to spend the day with you. Where did you go?"

Standing before the mirror, she untwisted her long braid. "I met Mara for a snack."

"How is she?"

"She's good. She invited me over to her place later. I'd like to see where she lives." Sarina picked up a hairbrush and brushed out her hair.

Rolf placed his hands on her shoulders, and she stopped, the brush poised in her hand.

"Why do you resist me?" he said, breathing into her ear from behind.

"Pardon?"

"You know what I mean. Every time I touch you, you cringe. Reylock isn't coming between us, is he?"

"How could he? The man isn't even here."

"He's in your thoughts. I will not tolerate disloyalty, Sarina."

Pivoting, she faced him. "You have my allegiance, and I'll support your goals. Isn't that enough?"

"No, it's not. I may have felt that way before, but things have changed. You're going to be my bride. I'll need your full attention, in all ways that matter."

"You have my attention. Just remember that affection can't be forced."

"But you're making it difficult for me. I want the legend to come true, same as you. If I'm willing to work toward that end, you have to do your part, too."

"You're right," she said, chastised by his words.

Rolf tilted her chin and kissed her. Sarina endured his caresses as his hands roamed her body. She tried not to think about Teir, but she couldn't help herself. As Rolf's mouth moved over hers, she wept inside. It wasn't his embraces she wanted.

After dinner, Sarina left for her meeting with Mara. Luckily, Rolf was busy with a conference call so he didn't argue when she said she was going out. Tucked beneath her bulky maroon sweater, she wore Teir's shirt. Hopefully, her guards wouldn't notice anything unusual.

Mara let Sarina into the apartment she shared with Hedy, a medic from the Wellness Center. Sarina greeted her roommate, and then the two of them went upstairs to Mara's study.

"I wore his shirt under my sweater," Sarina said with a grin, pulling the outer garment over her head. She unbuttoned the shirt and took it off, replacing the sweater.

Mara took Teir's shirt from her. "Do you want to begin right away?"

"If you don't mind. Rolf might get upset if I'm gone too long."

"He is attractive, Sarina. There are many females who would like to be in your position."

"I know. I wish I could feel differently toward him."

"The captain still holds your affection?"

Sarina grinned weakly. "More than that."

"What about your wedding?"

"The arrangements have been made." Her gown had arrived, and the dress was stunning. She'd felt guilty trying it on, however. This marriage to Rolf didn't feel right.

Glotaj had told her destiny would be her guide. It seemed to be moving her straight toward the ceremony that would bind her to Rolf. Unless something miraculous occurred, Sarina supposed she'd have to go through with it.

"But if you don't want to wed Lord Cam'brii—" Mara said, confusion in her dark eyes.

"I want the prophecy to come true, Mara. I'll do whatever it takes to fulfill the terms."

"You're supposed to fall in love with him."

"The legend states I must marry a Raimorrdan who is highly placed and was born under the sign of the circle. The power of my love will activate my healing aura. Those are the exact words, Mara. They don't say I have to fall in love with the Raimorrdan I wed, do they?"

"Well, no, but—"

"I never thought about it before, but maybe the meaning is different from the High Council's interpretation. Maybe it isn't Rolf I'm supposed to love. Maybe it's—"

"Teir?" Mara supplied.

"I've healed him, Mara. Twice now, I've made his wounds disappear."

"How could that happen unless you're in love with him?"

Sarina stared at her friend. "Good God, why have I never realized it before? No wonder I don't feel anything toward Lord Cam'brii. Teir is the only man I want. Maybe I *am* in love with him. I think about him constantly. I can't wait until we're together again. Oh Lord, I hope he's all right."

"But what of the legend that states you're supposed to marry a Raimorrdan?" Mara asked, her gaze radiating sympathy.

"I don't know. Glotaj seems to think everything will work out in the end." She narrowed her eyes. *Wait a minute.* What had the regent meant when he said it was dangerous to inquire about Teir's background? Was it possible…?

No, surely Glotaj wouldn't let her marry the wrong man.

"Let's begin," she said to Mara. "Tell me about Teir."

Mara clutched the shirt tight against her chest. Her eyelids fluttered, and a distant glaze came into her eyes.

Sarina waited, her heart racing. What would they learn? A wave of dizziness broke over her. She uttered a choked cry that broke her friend's trance.

"What is it? What's wrong?" Mara demanded.

"I don't feel well. I think I'm going to—" Sarina dashed across the room to the sanitary and vomited into the toilet. Moaning, she sank to her knees.

"You are ill," Mara said, her voice tinged with concern.

"My head hurts." Sarina held her hands to her temples. Her vision swam dizzily, and her body felt as if it were burning up. Feeling her stomach heave again, she propped herself upright and leaned over the bowl.

"Hedy, come upstairs," Mara shouted to her roommate.

"What's the matter?" the medic asked, rushing up the flight of steps.

"I don't know. She got sick all of a sudden."

"I'll get my mediscan." A few minutes later, Hedy returned, holding a triangular object. She used it to survey Sarina's body. A gasp of horror escaped her lips when she read the diagnosis.

"Lord Cam'brii must be notified immediately," the brunette said in a voice laden with fear.

"What is it?" Mara asked.

"If these readouts are correct, the Great Healer has contracted the Farg."

"Oh, no. Then that means… we've all been exposed."

****

Mantra heard of Sarina's illness the moment he set foot on Bimordus Two. The whole settlement was talking about it. Belief ran rampant that the disease would spread, even though she'd been quarantined in the Wellness Center.

Murmurs of doubt had arisen about her ability as the Great Healer, for if she possessed the power, why hadn't she healed herself? The High Council was in a turmoil, and Mantra had to wait to be presented as the new ambassador from Tendraa.

At last, he gained an audience and received approval for his appointment. The High Council was greatly pleased that the Liege Lord of Tendraa had assented to sending a representative, and Mantra was authorized to sit in the General Assembly. He beamed with pride when he received his sand-colored cape of office. Because of Tendraa's status as an associate member, however, he was not permitted to vote.

Glotaj was shocked when Mantra informed them about the Morgots. "Why have we received no intelligence to this effect?" he demanded of his councilors. "Lord Cam'brii, contact Admiral Gog and find out what's going on. The Morgots must not be permitted to take Tendraa. If they get hold of the flavium resources, the Coalition is doomed."

"Pardon, Your Excellency," Mantra said. "My Liege Lord expressly forbid me from asking the Defense League for assistance. He requested I consult the Great Healer for her advice in this matter."

Glotaj waved a hand in the air. "The Great Healer is not available. You can tell your leader the entire Coalition is threatened by the Morgot presence. Upon my authority, a force will be assembled to oppose them. You've done well, Ambassador. If we are successful in repelling the invaders, you can take credit for saving your world."

Admiral Gog was astounded by the news when Rolf contacted him later via the comm unit at Defense League Station.

"Have the Morgots learned how to expand the molecular alteration technology to cloak their vessels? We haven't been able to convert anything of that size. I don't understand how their fleet got past our sensors otherwise. Be assured, Lord Cam'brii, I'll get on this at once."

"Any news of Captain Reylock?" Rolf asked. If he could bring Sarina a positive report, it might help her recovery. He was terribly concerned about her prognosis.

"Not so far. Our intelligence in that region is limited. We sure could use his help, though. Reylock's our best strategist."

Rolf had to agree. The captain was a formidable opponent in the art of war. His unorthodox tactics and brilliant maneuvers had made him the youngest captain in the League.

"Keep me posted," he told the admiral. "Cam'brii out."

Chapter Twenty-Two

Mantra was just leaving Defense League Station after inquiring about his cousin Ravi. The duty officer had informed him Teir's crew members were due to return later that day. Surprised to see Lord Cam'brii striding by, Mantra hastened to his side.

"My lord, may I accompany you to see the Great Healer?" he asked, falling into step beside the tall, blond man. With his regal carriage and noble profile, Lord Cam'brii made an impressive figure. Mantra felt small in comparison.

"I'd be honored by your company," Rolf said. "I understand you met Sarina on Tendraa?"

The two exited into the bright afternoon sunshine and turned onto a busy walkway.

Mantra related all that had occurred during her visit, including the effects of the sanitation measures she'd suggested. "It is truly a miracle what those few changes have wrought. The Liege Lord has agreed to mandate the orders throughout the land. I've come to seek Sarina's advice."

"I fear she can give you none. She is gravely ill."

Having already had the pestilence, Mantra didn't need to don the protective energy suit like Lord Cam'brii. He could walk right into her cubicle and sit at her bedside.

Her appearance shocked him. Her livid complexion and red, blazing eyes told him she was indeed smitten by the plague. A flicker of surprise lit her face when she saw him.

"Mantra," Sarina whispered through cracked lips.

"I have been made an ambassador to Tendraa, Mistress," he

told her, gently touching her forehead. Alas, she was burning up. "I am to seek your counsel."

Sarina gave a weak laugh. "I fear your faith in the Great Healer is misplaced. I will not survive this disease." Her face twisted in agony, giving credence to her words.

"Nay, do not speak thus. If you indulge in gloomy thoughts, you will surely bring about a fatal result. I shall aid you."

He spoke to her for a few more minutes, then sought the medic, a lean young woman with short black hair.

"What is being done for her?" he asked, as though his knowledge could help in this sterile setting of modern medicine. This world was full of wonders he couldn't wait to explore, but his duty was first and foremost to the Great Healer.

"We can only treat the symptoms," the medic said. "When her temperature rises, she slips into a delirium and mumbles incoherently. We give her medicines to lower the fever and lessen the pain."

"The blisters must be drawn," Mantra said. "May I assist you?" He told the medic what he required.

She gave him a strange look but obeyed. He'd survived the Farg, so perhaps his knowledge would be useful.

When Mantra returned to her room, Sarina had fallen into a state of insensibility. She rambled on about Captain Reylock and someone she termed the fat dog face. Even in her unconscious state, her countenance proclaimed the agony she endured.

Ripping away her covers, Mantra examined her body. He found one plague spot on the inside of her thigh and another ugly boil under her arm. Hastily drawing the blanket up so she wouldn't be chilled, he waited for the medic to arrive with the spirit of sulfur for the posset-drink he'd ordered, and the mallows, lily-roots, figs, linseed, and palmara oil to make poultices for her sores.

Sarina opened her eyes and fixed her gaze upon him. It was clear she did not know who he was, because she heaved a deep sigh and began talking to him as though he were Captain

Reylock. Mantra had wondered at their relationship. Was the Great Healer not betrothed to Lord Cam'brii? Had not their wedding been postponed because of her illness? He shook his head, puzzled.

The medic entered and silently handed him the requested items. "I had to create the alexipharmics you requested on the fabricator. Half of these things are unknown here, but the programming extends to Tendraa, so you are lucky."

The medic's speech was incomprehensible to Mantra. What was a fabricator? It did not matter, since he had what he required. Laying out the items on a table, he said, "I need some means to heat the poultices."

The medic pointed to an alcove inset in a wall. "You can use the fabricator in this room. Just place whatever you want in there and order it to raise the temperature."

Fascinated, Mantra asked for a demonstration. Truly, this was a miracle. You could create anything out of thin air. Pushing aside his curiosity, he focused his mind on the purpose at hand.

After applying the warm poultices to Sarina's tumors, he roused her long enough to get her to take the posset-drink. Then he gave her a dose of mithridate mixed with Venice treacle.

Placing a cool cloth on her forehead. Mantra sat back and waited. Not everyone responded to this treatment, as evidenced by the death rate on Tendraa. But Sarina was fortunate in that her illness had been caught in its earliest stages.

Within the haura, moisture broke out on Sarina's skin, a good sign. She writhed on the narrow bed, ranting and raving, as the sweat poured from her. At last she calmed and sank into a tranquil slumber. Mantra felt her forehead. Her skin felt cool. Rejoicing, he called the medic in to wash and change her. After the woman had finished, Mantra refreshed the poultices, reapplied them, and drew the covers over Sarina's thin body.

When she awoke, Sarina was so weak that she could barely lift her head. Her breathing had eased, and the terrible throbbing pain from her sores had gone. Mantra got her something to eat when she complained of hunger. He got a kick out of using the fabricator. While Sarina sipped a nourishing brew, he ordered a meal of Stuntorian stew and a carafe of ale for himself. He'd been so engrossed in caring for his patient that he hadn't remembered to dine earlier.

A commotion by the door made him glance up, and when he saw who was there, his face broke into a grin. "Ravi!" He stepped outside to greet his cousin.

The two embraced, and then Ravi introduced him to the rest of Teir's crew, who'd come to inquire after Sarina. They remained in the anteroom, safely outside the confines of the quarantine area. Nobody worried about Mantra carrying the disease, since he'd already been cured.

After a while, the others left, leaving Ravi and Mantra alone.

"How is your family?" Ravi asked. "I was sorrowed to hear of the passing of your parents and your sister Zunis."

Mantra gazed at him. "Alas, I would have thought no worse disaster could befall us, but now the Morgots are attacking the outermost planet of our system."

Ravi's jaw dropped in surprise. "The Morgots!"

"Glotaj has ordered the Defense League to muster a response."

"I've no doubt. He wouldn't want the Morgots to get the flavium resources on Tendraa. I'll have to see that we're assigned a ship to join the mission," Ravi said. "The battle will be a decisive one. Is that why you came, to request aid for your people?"

"In truth, I was sent to consult the Great Healer."

"The Liege Lord still refuses to participate fully in the Coalition?" At his cousin's nod, Ravi said, "He is a foolish old man."

"Not so foolish," Mantra replied, remembering the riches in the palace. "Just stubborn and prideful. I have set his daughter Tami to work on him to try to change his mind. In any event, it does not matter. A force will be sent regardless." He sighed heavily. "I did not wish to leave Kairi and Sita alone. I hope they will fare well. The Baynor has supplies delivered to them daily, thanks to Sarina, but they still must remain shut in the house."

"What did Sarina do on Tendraa that so impressed you?"

Mantra told him, and then their talk turned to the Great Healer's current condition.

"She's been grievously ill. In the height of her distemper, she kept crying out for Captain Reylock," Mantra mentioned.

"The captain is missing," Ravi said solemnly. "They were on Souk together. She fears he is either captured or dead."

"Why does she take so much interest in him?"

Ravi lowered his voice. "They have a tendre for one another. It was quite evident even when she was first aboard the *Valiant*."

"But she is betrothed to Lord Cam'brii. The wedding was postponed due to her illness."

"Hush, here comes her bridegroom now."

The two men fell silent as Lord Cam'brii approached, his stride long and purposeful.

"What is this news I hear? Sarina is recovering? If so, I shall be eternally grateful to you, Ambassador." Profound relief shone in his eyes. After donning a protective energy suit, he hastened into Sarina's cubicle.

Her eyelids fluttered open when she heard footsteps. "Rolf," she said, her voice low and strained.

"Are you feeling better?" he asked, concerned at how pale she still appeared. Her hair clung in moist tendrils to the sides of her face and spread about her pillow like a halo.

"The pain is gone, but I'm terribly weak."

"Rest easy. Everyone is asking about you. You must get well."

"Has anyone else become ill? Mara, Hedy, or yourself?" They'd been most directly exposed.

"No, and our researchers are puzzled. It was thought the pestilence was highly contagious. Yet no one else on Bimordus Two has succumbed. It is assumed you were infected when you went to Tendraa, and the incubation period was lengthy. It is possible that those of us who were exposed will become ill suddenly like yourself, but I for one hope that will not be true."

"I hope Teir isn't sick," she mused aloud.

Always her thoughts are for the captain, Rolf thought with a grimace. "You were both wearing the suits, weren't you?" If it didn't work for them, it might not work for him, either. Even though he'd already been exposed, he was hoping the contagion wasn't infectious until symptoms broke out. In that case, the suit should protect him if it worked.

"I shut mine off," Sarina confessed. "I'd wanted to test my healing power, and I thought the energy barrier might be obstructive. Teir kept his on the whole time. I hope he's all right."

"You can't ask him, can you?" Rolf snapped, then regretted his choice of words when he saw her stricken look. "Sorry, Sarina. I can't help it. We're supposed to be married soon, and all through your delirium, you kept crying out for Reylock."

"I did?" she asked in a small voice.

He nodded grimly. "Nonetheless, our wedding will be rescheduled. Eat and regain your strength."

Mantra shuffled in soon after Lord Cam'brii left. "What grieves you, Mistress?" he asked, seeing her melancholy expression.

"I wish I knew what happened to Teir." She studied him for a moment. "Mantra, would you do me a favor and send for Mara, please? I need to ask her something."

Mara came over as soon as she was free. "Captain Reylock is alive," she told Sarina right away. "I used my power while you were sick, hoping I would have good news for when you recovered. I didn't bother to *see* much, however. I'll do it again now that you're awake, and maybe it will give you a clue as to his location."

She returned that night with Teir's shirt hidden under her work clothes. Waiting until they were alone, Mara drew the white fabric to her chest. Closing her eyes, she swayed back and forth until the vision came to her. "I see what he sees," she intoned. "There is fire—a raging wall of fire. The heat blasts my face."

"Where is this?" Sarina asked, her throat dry

Mara didn't respond directly. She continued to speak in a deeper voice. "I am changing direction. Bubbling and hissing noises surround me. Oops, I nearly stepped in a pool of boiling liquid. See how it spits hot mud into the air."

Mara shook her head, her eyes squeezed shut. "The lizard man is watching me. He is suspicious of my behavior."

"Lieutenant Otis." Sarina shouldn't be surprised. The Crigellan was Bdan's second-in-command. He must have taken over when the slaver drowned in his moat.

"And there is another… a Souk with the face of an ugly bloodhound." Mara described his features.

"Cerrus Bdan? I thought he was dead." Shocked, Sarina asked, "What is he doing?"

"He is pointing at me and shouting. Now he flicks his wrist. Aargh, my throat constricts. Something is choking me." Mara snapped out of the trance, abruptly opening her eyes.

"A slave collar," Sarina whispered. "He lives but is restrained. Oh, Mara, what shall I do?"

"At least he is alive," Mara consoled her.

"Yes, but as Bdan's slave. I must help him." Tears threatened, but Sarina pushed them back. Weakness wouldn't help either one of them. "Has Teir's crew returned?"

"They've been back for some time and have quite annoyed the medics over you. I believe the Polluxite, Lieutenant Wren, sits in the anteroom with Mantra."

"Send him in. And Mara, thanks," she finished lamely.

Mara winked and left.

A moment later, Wren hastened into her room. "Sarina, you look much better," the ship's navigator said.

She got straight to the point. "Teir is alive. He needs our help. Cerrus Bdan still has him."

"How do you know this?"

"Mara used her special power. Can you go on a rescue mission?"

"To Souk?"

"Actually, I'm not certain of his location. The place is full of fire and bubbling pools of mud."

Wren rolled his eyes. "It sounds like Zor."

"No, it was outside, not a fiery underworld."

"I'll ask the others, but unless you have more specific information, I'm afraid it's not enough to go on. We've requested to join the fight against the Morgots in the Tendraan system."

"The Morgots are threatening Mantra's planet?" The Tendraan hadn't told her, but then, he was considerate enough not to worry her with additional problems when she was so weak. "When will you know if you've been reassigned?"

"Within the next few days. I wish we had the *Valiant*… and her captain."

"Me, too."

After Wren left and Mantra entered the cubicle, Sarina expressed her frustration to him.

"Mistress, you can do little else to aid Captain Reylock, but you can do much to help others," he told her, kneeling at her bedside. "Your words of wisdom have already wrought great changes on my planet. You are much needed here."

Emu came in and told her of the dissension within the government, dissension fueled by her indisposition. "You must show the populace you are well," said the Sirisian, stretching his rubbery face for emphasis. "It is time for you to assume your position."

"I have no superpowers," she told him bleakly. "Wouldn't I have healed myself if I did? The legend is a farce."

Healing Teir must have been a fluke. Either that, or her healing ability worked only on wounds and not on diseases.

"Do not be so quick to cast away your faith. It could be that your recovery is attributable to some innate quality within yourself. Many others have died on Tendraa using the same methods of treatment," Emu added. "And what of the long incubation period you experienced? Usually it is a matter of days, or even hauras. You must have been fighting the sickness all this time. And think about the method of transmission. If you were contagious, your friends would be sick by now. Some other factor must be involved in catching the disease. You have much work to do."

"His logic makes sense," Mantra told Sarina. "Use the resources available to you. Find out why your case was different. It could be because you are the Great Healer."

"You survived, Mantra. And you did the same things for me that helped you."

"Aye, but I got sick directly after exposure."

"All right, I'll discuss it with Glotaj," she agreed. They might have some valid points.

She sought a private audience with the regent a few days later, immediately after her discharge from the Wellness Center. Glotaj appeared to be unimpressed by her theories.

"Your blood and tissue samples were sent to the Timosian Research Station where our greatest scientists have gathered to study the Farg," he said. "I don't believe they found anything unusual."

"You can't explain how I healed Teir, either," Sarina pointed out, "but it did happen. I think my reaction to the disease deserves further analysis."

"It's possible you could contribute something new about the Farg with a fresh approach," Glotaj admitted. He studied her, thoughtful. "I suppose you'll have to go to Timos yourself."

"I'd be grateful for the opportunity," Sarina said, secretly elated by Glotaj's suggestion.

"Rolf isn't going to be happy about another postponement, but I think this is more important. I'll give you two weeks, no more." The regent paused. "It appears that the repeal of the execution decree is not going to pass," he warned her. "Daimon's supporters have grown in numbers. Immediately upon your return, the wedding must take place."

Sarina nodded her compliance, wondering how best to broach the subject that really concerned her. A flash of inspiration gave her the opening she needed. "What about Teir? Since I healed him, shouldn't he be part of this research?"

Glotaj gave an exasperated sigh. "He can't participate if he's not here."

"I might have a clue as to his whereabouts. I consulted Mara as you suggested." She described their session.

"By the moons of Agus Six, that place sounds like Taurus. If the captain is there with Cerrus Bdan, it can mean only one thing. Bdan is forcing him to retrieve the Blood Crystal. I must notify Admiral Gog at once."

"Why? What's wrong?" Sarina asked, alarmed by the panic on the regent's normally placid face.

"The Blood Crystal can predict the future, but its use is influenced by forces of evil. If the wrong people get hold of it, the results could be catastrophic. Reylock must be intercepted."

Chapter Twenty-Three

The *Valiant* reached orbit around Taurus eleven days and fourteen hauras after leaving Souk. A seething, hot volcanic planet, Taurus's terrain was known to be inhospitable and harsh.

In preparation for the shuttle departure, Teir was allowed on the bridge. Looking out the viewscreen for the first time on the voyage, he noticed an escort of two Souk patrol craft. They'd put a slight damper on his escape plan, but he should be able to manage. He dismissed them as being a minor inconvenience for now.

"We'll need special gear," he told Bdan, listing his requirements for the arduous journey ahead. The Souk stood beside him, gazing out at the cloud-covered globe below. Otis, sitting in the pilot's seat, had put the ship into standard orbit and was awaiting further instructions.

"The landing site is on a flat bed of rock some distance from the guardian," Teir told them. "The climb will be treacherous. I suggest you leave my friends on board the *Valiant*. They'll only slow us down."

"Very well. Lieutenant Otis, join us will you for the landing party. Vivak will stay on board. Flight training has he, and he can watch the elders as well. Geemus and Wyeth go with us. Help carry the equipment can the two Hortha guards."

Teir quickly totaled up the number in the landing party— three Souks, two Horthas, and one Crigellan, besides himself. It shouldn't be too difficult to elude them. He knew the secrets of the mountain. They didn't.

Vivak, a tall, lanky Souk, took over the controls while the

landing party made preparations. Once outfitted, they headed for the shuttle bay. Since the climate on the planet was hot and the atmosphere was tolerable, extra clothing wasn't needed. Bdan, however, changed into a tunic and baggy pantaloons to be practical. Still, Teir wondered how he'd get his bulk over the peaks and crevices below. Aside from Bdan, Teir was the only one not wearing a tool belt. Bdan wouldn't allow him to carry any equipment.

In the shuttle bay, Bdan grasped him by the shoulder and whirled him around. "R-r-remember, Captain, my prisoner are you. You make any attempt to escape, and I'll use an electrifier to punish you." He took the rod out of his tunic pocket to show Teir.

Teir gritted his teeth. "You're holding my friends captive on the ship. I won't step out of line." Of course, if his plan worked, they'd all be free as *hiimma* birds soon enough. But in the meantime, he had Bdan's unpredictable rages to contend with. He'd seen the heavy links of inertia manacles sticking out of the Souk's pantaloons pocket. If Teir acted up, no doubt those handcuffs would be slapped on his wrists in no time. It wouldn't matter how difficult they'd make his progress. The slaver would enjoy his suffering.

Teir opened the hatch to the shuttle and took over the helm. Bdan lowered himself with a grunt into the copilot's chair. Otis and the others filed in, taking seats in the rows behind them. After they'd fastened their safety restraints, the shuttle door hissed closed and locked.

Teir began the departure checklist. Pressurized air whooshed on, and the countdown sequence began automatically. The shuttle bay door slid open, revealing the black starry backdrop of space. With a neck-jerking thrust, they were out, soaring into the airless vacuum. Teir changed the heading, and the shuttle nosed downward. They dropped at top speed toward the planet's surface.

He made a smooth landing and powered down. After removing his harness, he stood and led the way to the hatch.

"Hold, Captain." From yet another pocket, Cerrus Bdan took a thick circular band.

"A slave collar! You wouldn't dare."

"On the contrary, Captain, gives me great pleasure does this."

With a nod from Bdan, the two Horthas gripped his arms. Teir struggled futilely as Bdan snapped the collar around his neck.

"Damn you," he yelled at his nemesis.

Bdan gloated gleefully. "Extra insurance is this. Trust you not, do I. You try any tricks, and—" He flicked his wrist and the collar tightened.

"You've made your point," Teir croaked when the pressure released.

Swallowing his anger, he opened the hatchway. A flight of steps automatically unfolded to the ground. The stink of sulfur wafted upward, and Teir wrinkled his nose.

Once his feet hit the planet's dry surface, he waited for the others in their party to catch up. Luckily, Bdan hadn't left any guards behind on the shuttle. That would have spoiled Teir's plan. As it was, it wouldn't be easy for him to escape his entourage.

The trek ahead of them would be perilous. Mountain ranges rolled and peaked in a terrain made gray and bleak by countless volcanic eruptions. Heavy rains had loosened the tons of ash dumped on the slopes, causing cement-like slurries to rush down streambeds in torrents called lahars. As a result, the landscape was barren, all vegetation having long since been obliterated.

Even as they stood, an eruption occurred in the distance. Plumes of superheated gas and ash spewed from the mountaintop, blackening the sky and shaking the ground with violent tremors. Lightning flashed overhead, strange streaks of blues, greens, and reds, while all around them rose pillars of steam, escaping from ground vents. Hissing and bubbling noises issued from pools of liquid mud, heated by the fiery magma beneath.

Bdan coughed into his hand. "This planet is cursed. Full of smoke is the air."

"We'd better move," Teir said. "This whole region is unstable, including the mountain we have to climb. We don't want to get caught in a pyroclastic flow."

He indicated the direction they had to follow. As protector of the Blood Crystal, he'd been to Taurus many times, but only once to this particular location. Twice an annum, he had made a solitary journey to check the seismic instruments placed near the guardian. If all was stable, he left until the next time.

During his last visit, he had seen signs of imminent eruption on the mountain housing the guardian, so Teir had changed its site. Although his primary assignment was to ensure the safety of the guardian's location, he also had to make certain no one else ever discovered it. The planet's desolate terrain had discouraged visitors, which made the last part easy—until now.

He took the lead, Bdan following him directly behind. They crossed a stream, scrambled over a bed of boulders, and passed through a narrow canyon lined by sheer towers of rock. Then they entered a relatively straight pass over bumpy terrain distinguished by towering hollowed lava trees.

"This part is easy," he lied, carefully choosing his steps. The gray rocks sprinkled with black dots were easily visible when you knew exactly what to look for, and Teir had placed the rocks himself in precisely this order for just such an occasion. He counted the seconds, waiting for the scream from someone in their party.

A crash sounded, then an unearthly howl. Whirling around, Teir feigned ignorance. "What was that?" The two Horthas were missing, he noted, suppressing a grin.

"They fell in." Otis pointed, looking stunned. A large hole yawned in the ground.

"It's a lava tube." Teir strode closer and peered into the black pit. "They must have broken through a thin spot. Watch where you're walking."

Bdan flicked his wrist, and Teir's throat constricted. "Trick us, will you? You lose any more of my men, and I'll manacle you." When Teir's breaths came in short, choking gasps, Bdan released him.

"I can't lead this group effectively if you question everything I do," Teir snapped, rubbing his neck.

"Lead on," the Souk commanded, waving an imperious finger.

Teir didn't waste time arguing. He'd noticed the gray ball growing just below the nearest peak. As it blossomed into a billowing pyroclastic cloud of hot gas, pumice, and ash, he warned the others.

"We'd better hurry. That doesn't look good." Another tremor shook the ground. He searched for a better route. "This way," he cried, leading the group through a pass toward the other side of the mountain. Glancing behind, he saw the rolling cloud of superheated ash race down the slope.

It took the better part of three hauras for them to reach the base of the mountain they needed to climb. By this time, earthquakes were coming fast and strong, and the yellowish sky had turned an ominous shade of slate. Ash fell like powdery beige snow. Teir insisted on having the slave collar removed before he went any farther.

"It's too dangerous from here on," he told Bdan, shouting to be heard over the claps of thunder. To their right, a fountain of flame burst out of a crack in the earth's crust. To the left was a steep incline, the path they were to follow.

"All right," Bdan grumbled, "but my electrifier will I not hesitate to use if you cause trouble. Understand?"

He choked Teir one more time, enjoying the sight of him falling to his knees and gasping for air. Abruptly, he released Teir's restraint. He grasped and pocketed it before Teir could think to grab hold. Hating the slaver more than ever, Teir resolved to push him off the nearest peak at the earliest opportunity.

Resuming his pace, Teir led them carefully through a section of boiling hot pools where heated mud spattered and spewed into the air. Their ascent began. Bdan sweated profusely under the strenuous hike. His bluish skin paled to a sickly color, and he nervously glanced at the path ahead as though a fountain of lava might erupt in front of them at any moment. The two Souk guards filed along in the rear. They were going to be a nuisance to Teir's plan.

He meant to reach the guardian, also known as the Cave of Crystal, then escape through the secret passage to the other side of the mountain and the sea below. Once on the beach, he could summon the shuttle using the hidden device in his vest pocket. But he had to get free of the others long enough to get there.

A blast rocked the air as part of the volcano blew apart. Red-hot lava cascaded down the nearby slope, exploding when it hit the sea on the other side of the range. The effect was a pyrotechnic show worthy of a miniature supernova.

Rocks rained from the sky, chunks of lava blown aloft and cooled into sharp-edged pumice.

"Take shelter," Teir yelled as glassy shards pierced his skin. He sidestepped to a ledge under an overhang, and they huddled there, waiting for the cataclysm to calm. "We should put on our breathing gear and night goggles," he suggested. Day had turned into night from all the ash and debris in the air.

"Are you leading us in circles, R-R-Reylock? As desolate as Zor is this place. I like it not." Bdan's jowls quivered as he spoke.

"We'll get there," Teir assured him, "unless a lahar gets us first. They can roar down the slope without warning."

Even as he shouted to be heard, a stream of basaltic lava flowed by like a river of fire. Cooling, it hardened into black glassy swirls. "Don't step there," he warned the others. "It's still hot."

They'd gone a few hundred meters ahead when Teir stopped and turned to Lieutenant Otis. "I need the surveyor's theodolite," he said to the Crigellan. The officer looked ill. His complexion, what Teir could see of it through his gear, appeared a sickly light green.

"What are you doing?" Bdan demanded as Teir set up the piece of equipment.

Teir focused the instrument on a palm-sized mirror he knew to be spaced higher up the mountain. Locking in on his target, he activated a small laser beam that leaped to the mirror and back. "I'm measuring the distance. It's forty-six hundred and eighty meters. That varies less than a few centimeters from my earlier measurements, meaning there's no dangerous swelling of the cone. We can proceed." He folded the device and gave it back to Otis.

After midnight, a light rain began to fall. Teir was genuinely afraid they might be caught by a lahar. He urged them on as pillars of steam rose all around them. Finally, the clouds of ash dispersed enough for a faint light from Taurus's two moons to brighten the climb. They reached the summit just as dawn broke on the horizon in a brilliant crimson display.

At Teir's advice, they packed away their breathing apparatus and night goggles.

"We have to descend into the crater." He pointed to the steaming, sulfurous caldera below.

"You're joking," Otis said with an expression of disbelief.

"I am not. I'll go first."

Teir inserted a thermometer into a crack that showed red just centimeters below. It was hot, but not volcanically feverish. He glanced down at the lava dome, smoldering like an ominous fuse.

"You see that opening?" he said, indicating the dark mouth gaping at the opposite rim. "It leads to our destination, the Cave of Crystal."

Bdan's corpulent body shook with fatigue. "We'll rest here, Captain. Go no farther can I r-r-right now."

"I could go down with Otis and bring the Blood Crystal back to you. He'll make sure I stay in line," Teir offered in a mild tone.

"Go nowhere will you without me. Trust you not, do I." He glared at Teir. "Soon shall we see if you have earned your rewards."

"What rewards?" Teir sank onto the ground's hard surface to gain a much-needed rest. His clothes were covered with ash, and his skin was encrusted with grime. He wiped his mouth with the back of his hand and then looked with disgust at the black dust that came off.

"Your friends will go free when we get back to Souk. Told you I'd keep my word, didn't I?" The smuggler gave him a sly smile. He plopped to the ground, his labored breathing audible.

"And what happens to me?"

Bdan grinned wickedly. "Have plans for you, do I."

Teir saw the direction of his glance. "They don't include pushing me into that pit of molten lava, do they?"

Bdan grunted his laughter. "I wish. No, Captain, a better idea have I."

Teir didn't ask him what it was. He didn't intend to be around long enough to find out. "We shouldn't spend too much time here. A strong quake could knock us into the caldron. There's only one safe way to descend."

Soon they began the final trek. The distance appeared to be short, but it took them a good part of the morning to reach the opposite rim. It was midday when they approached the opening to the cave.

"Flame torches or goggles?" Bdan asked, hesitating in front of the pitch-black hole.

"Flame torches will give us wider vision," Teir replied.

Taking the sticks from Otis and igniting them, he led the way into the yawning gap. The passage dipped ahead. They had to crouch, hobbling along half-bent until they rounded a corner and reached a larger passage. Here the path split in two directions.

"Which way?" Bdan prodded him from behind.

"We'll take the path to the right," Teir said, leading them over a flat slab of rock and into another tight corridor.

They continued to wind through a maze of tunnels, steam hissing from vents in the rock surrounding them. The temperature was hot despite the elevation, and sweat dripped down Teir's face.

For a moment he thought he'd lost the two Souk guards

bringing up the rear. He was rushing along as fast as he could despite the obstacles, and when he glanced back, only Bdan and Otis were to be seen.

"Captain," Bdan called as he tried to squeeze his bulk through a particularly narrow passage. "Go too fast, do you."

"I can't help it if you're not in shape," Teir said, hoping the two Souks were lost for good.

The smuggler grunted and pushed himself through the tight opening. "Halt," he commanded, waiting for Otis to catch up to them. "Leading us astray on purpose are you. I told you what the punishment would be for disobedience." He whipped out his electrifier.

Teir held up his hands. "Take it easy, Bdan. The path to the guardian is complicated. We must take the exact route."

"Take me to the chamber that houses the Blood Crystal."

"That's what I'm doing. We're almost there."

"Liar!" Bdan blasted him.

The shock threw Teir against the wall. He banged his head against an outcropping of rock and slid to the ground, dazed. His nerve endings burned with pain.

"Get up," Bdan shouted.

Just then, the two remaining guards staggered into view, one of them dragging the other.

"Sorry, master," said Wyeth as they rejoined the others. "Wanted to turn back did Geemus. Convinced him did I to follow orders."

"Turn tail, would you?" Bdan bellowed to his henchman. Flicking a switch on his electrifier, he aimed it at the quaking Geemus. As the Souk screamed, Bdan pushed the trigger. A crackling light shot out, and Geemus vaporized instantly.

He turned to Teir who watched, frozen on the ground where he'd fallen.

"Take us now, R-R-Reylock, or it's all over for you, too."

Teir put a look of defeat on his face. Heaving himself upright, he sighed, "Very well. This way."

Inwardly, he grinned. The odds were now three to one. The rest should be easy, unless Bdan decided to shackle him with those manacles dangling from his pants. He'd better appear cooperative.

At the end of a twisting passage, he stopped at a blank wall. "Now what?" Bdan said with a snarl.

"This is the entrance to the guardian." Teir fit his hands into two grooves carved into the rock face. A grinding noise followed, and a section of rock slid open in front of them.

Bdan gasped as a sparkling chamber was revealed.

"Behold the Cave of Crystal," Teir said and strode inside.

Stalactites and stalagmites of gleaming black crystal reflected the lights from their flame torches. Water dripped down the walls, adding to the dazzle, and silvery-white boloxite columns intersected the cavern. The effect was surreal in the artificial light.

Bdan indicated that Otis and Wyeth were to guard the entrance, more so that Teir couldn't run out on them than from fear of anyone following. Teir almost laughed. They didn't know the secret of the guardian.

With one push of a hidden control, he could move the entire Cave of Crystal to another preset location, using phase emission technology. The guardian simply vanished from one spot and showed up in another. That was how he had been able to keep the Blood Crystal safe from the cataclysms of nature. One hint that the mountain was about to erupt, and Teir changed the site.

Since Bdan and his cohorts were present, he'd use his private escape route, the one that would take him down to the sea. Now all he had to do was get near the chute.

"The Blood Crystal, where it is?" Bdan aimed the electrifier at him.

"This way." Teir strode across a river of cold flowstone and pointed to a raised pedestal in the center of the room.

Bdan joined him and squinted at the empty display. "I see nothing. Is this some sort of trick?"

Teir glowered at him. "A word of warning, Bdan. It is said that whoever uses the Blood Crystal is touched with evil."

Bdan laughed uproariously. "I'm already evil, Captain. Get it for me."

Glancing at the electrifier still pointed in his direction, Teir clenched his jaw. He'd hoped he wouldn't have to go this far, but there was no way around it. He couldn't make his move to get away just yet.

He set his palm on the flat surface of the pedestal. The blank whiteness lit with a momentary glow.

Standing back, Teir watched as an opening gaped and the gleaming black crystal slid upward into view. It was cone-shaped and streaked with veins of red that glowed in the light from their flame torches like rivers of blood.

Bdan lumbered closer and snatched it up. "Test it, will I." But as he held the glassy stone in his palm, nothing happened. "What is this? Why does it not show me the future?"

"Maybe it doesn't work with people who already have darkness in their souls."

Suspicion dawned in the Souk's beady eyes. "A decoy must this be. Where is the r-r-real crystal?"

Teir regarded him calmly. "You're holding it. You asked me to take you to the Blood Crystal, and I did. You didn't tell me to get it to work for you."

"Then do it."

"I don't know how. I've never touched it myself."

Bdan howled with rage. "You lie! Kill you, shall I."

As his finger moved on the electrifier, Teir threw himself into a flying somersault, snatching the crystal out of Bdan's hand before hitting the floor. He rolled toward the far wall as a jagged streak of electricity singed the air by his ear.

Teir slapped a raised knob on the ground and drew into a crouch as an ominous rumbling sounded. Bdan snarled and fired again, and Teir dodged to the side just in time. He charged for the section of wall etched with a barely discernible white circle. The last thing he saw before the wall crumbled and swallowed him up was the astonished look on Bdan's face.

Feet first, Teir slid downward in total darkness. He raced along inside a giant slide carved into the mountain's interior, straight down to the sea. Grasping the Blood Crystal firmly in his hands, he closed his eyes so he couldn't see the terrifying blackness below.

He landed abruptly. One moment he was hurtling through darkness, and the next he came to a bone-jarring stop on a bed of powdery volcanic sand.

Opening his eyes, Teir saw it was still daylight outside, though a gray haze obscured the ocean. He rubbed his face. His jaw was rough with stubble, and his eyes were gritty from dust. Blinking to clear his vision, he glanced at the object in his lap.

The Blood Crystal was cold and lifeless, albeit oddly beautiful. Was it true what Bdan had said, that this was a decoy? Had he, too, been tricked? Could this be merely a piece of ordinary volcanic rock?

Holding the black crystalline shape in his hands, he pondered its sleekness. Such perfectly even sides had to be of unnatural origins.

He remembered the worry stone Sarina had mentioned, although hers had been silvery-gray and rounded, with a pointed end. Thinking of her brought him pain. Where was she? Was she safe? Salla had said Devin was taking care of her. Had the youth managed to get her off Souk?

The first chance he got, he'd have to check on her whereabouts.

By the stars, he missed her. Viewing the bleak expanse of black sand beach, he felt an ache of loneliness so deep he wanted to cry out. He grasped the crystal tighter, clutching it against his chest as though it could conjure an image of her, showing him where she was.

And as his very soul yearned for her, the red streaks on the stone began to glow. The glow spread and expanded until it encompassed the entire black crystal. With it came a tingling sensation in his hands.

Stunned, Teir stared at the Blood Crystal. The haze around it shifted and shimmered. Through the growing brightness, he saw Sarina's image linked to his own in an aura of light.

His heart thudded in his chest. Was the Blood Crystal predicting the future? Were they to be reunited after all?

As he watched, Sarina's aura separated from his. Another image, this one a miniature version, glowed in her belly. The brightness radiated outward, and their auras joined Teir's in a halo of light.

Gods, could this be true?

He dropped the stone as though it were fire. Instantly, the vision extinguished, and the Blood Crystal lay lifeless in the sand.

Chapter Twenty-Four

Teir whipped out the remote unit from his vest pocket and activated the sequence to summon the shuttle. In less than ten minutes, it landed on the flat expanse of beach stretching before him. He grabbed the Blood Crystal and raced into the waiting vehicle.

His mission was clear. Salla had spoken of a quest, and now he knew what it was. He had to discover his birthright. She'd said it was he, not Lord Cam'brii, who was destined to marry the Great Healer. The Blood Crystal had shown this to be true. The proof was in his heritage. He had to visit his aunt on Alpha Omega Two to find out what she knew.

By now, Bdan and his cohorts would have dashed out of the guardian. Teir had sent the Cave of Crystal to its next preset location. Bdan would discover the shuttle was gone, but he wouldn't be stranded for long. One of the two combat vessels orbiting around Taurus would rescue him. Teir had no time to lose to put the rest of his escape plan into action.

After placing the stone carefully on the seat beside him, he pushed the throttle forward and lifted off. Once he took control of the *Valiant,* he'd blast those two Souk vessels out of the sky. Then the Souk smuggler would be trapped on the planet's volatile surface.

His jaw clenched as he imagined the pleasure he would get from destroying his enemy. The idea of annihilating Bdan thrilled him. His palms grew sweaty with anticipation, and he licked his lips with eagerness. And then his gaze fell upon the black crystal on the seat beside him. The red streaks glowed like burning embers.

By the stars, the thing was affecting him. It had worked its evil into his mind.

Aware he had no choice, he headed back to the planet's surface and touched down near the Cave of Crystal's new location. After making sure no one was inside, he returned the stone to its receptacle. It had shown him the future, but it had touched him with darkness. The stories about it were true. The Blood Crystal needed to be kept hidden until more could be learned of its origins.

Having seen no sign of his adversaries, Teir resumed his flight. He set a course straight toward the *Valiant.*

Days ago, he had keyed in a sequence on the computer that would allow him to access command functions on the ship. Now, seated in the shuttle, he sent the signal to open a channel to the *Valiant*'s command center. He requested that the computer use his digitized recording of Bdan's voice to order the Souk left on board to initiate docking procedures.

When his console lit, informing him this order had been carried out, Teir activated another preset sequence. This one would release a round of Nokout gas on the bridge. The Souk would be unconscious when Teir went aboard.

Teir would drop the fellow off, along with the Crigellans, at the nearest Coalition outpost. Then he'd head for Alpha Omega Two to visit his aunt—assuming she hadn't succumbed to the Farg. That possibility threw him for a moment, but he decided to deal with any obstacles as they occurred. As always, foremost on his mind was the need to check on Sarina. They shared a future together, if only he could see a path to it.

****

Sarina was on board the *Hornet* en route to the Research Station on Timos. Satisfied that Admiral Gog would pursue Teir's trail, she'd agreed to leave as long as she was kept posted as to his progress. When she'd requested Teir's crew accompany her, Admiral Gog had agreed. The *Hornet* had been on her way to join the force assembling against the Morgots, but they could drop Sarina off along the way.

"Ravi," Sarina said a couple of days into their journey, "did Teir ever talk much about his childhood?"

She'd remembered her conversation with Glotaj when the regent warned her not to inquire into Teir's background. Now she found it imperative to learn as much about him as she could. Somehow, she felt it was relevant to her future.

"Nay, Mistress. The captain wasn't one to dwell upon the past."

"When was he born?"

"I believe it was star date 2240."

"That would make him twenty-nine annums, the same age as Lord Cam'brii."

"Correct. He holds the unique achievement of being the youngest in the Defense League to reach the rank of captain."

"What else do you know about him?"

"His aunt and uncle raised him. When he was young, they traveled around. Later, they settled in a small village on Vilaran, and that's where he spent the rest of his youth. I gathered his relatives were of a reclusive nature."

"That village—what was its name?" Sarina asked.

"I'm sorry, *Mira,* I do not possess that knowledge."

"I think I'll study up on Vilaran history."

She accessed the files from the ship's database. According to what she read, the last hereditary king—the Preim of Vilaran—was a descendant of the House of Raimorrda and sovereign leader of the Retti dynasty. He ascended to the throne and ruled as a cruel despot until a bloody revolution overthrew the crown and established a republic.

Revolutionaries murdered the Preim and his entire family. The youngest victim, a great-nephew, was but a babe when killed, but the people did not regret their actions. They lusted for the blood of the Rettites who'd forced the populace into a life of poverty and toil.

Even now, annums later with an elected government in power, hostile feelings still ran high against the aristocracy.

Teir had been born the year of the revolution and raised after the Republic came into power. But how did that relate to things? Glotaj was hiding something. Had Teir committed a crime in his youth that could come back to haunt him? Was that why he'd run off to join the Defense League?

Wren interrupted her. She could tell he was excited from the way his wings unfolded and flapped at his back. "You have a message coming in from Command. Follow me to the Ready Room. You can take it in there. Maybe they've located the captain."

Her pulse racing, Sarina followed him into the conference room. She waited until he left, then sat at the long table and established a commlink.

Admiral Daras Gog's face projected onto the wall. "Our scout vessel landed on Taurus," he said in his gruff tone. "There wasn't any sign of Captain Reylock or anyone else on the planet's surface."

"What? How is that possible?" Her voice rang with disappointment.

"They did pick up a particle beam emissions trail that matched the one for the *Valiant*. We know she was there, and it appears a couple of Souk vessels were in the vicinity as well. Unfortunately, the trail for the *Valiant* has vanished, so we can't trace her."

"Could they have gone back to Souk?"

"I'm hoping the captain escaped in his ship and covered his trail so he wouldn't be found."

"If that's true, where is he now?"

"Your guess is as good as mine. If he's on the loose, he'd better report in to Command. Tell him so, if you hear from him before I do. It's unusual for Reylock not to check in. I've put our outposts on the alert. If anyone spots the *Valiant,* they're to notify me immediately."

Through the observation ports, Sarina saw the Timosian star system looming closer. With a sigh, she cut her communications and went to get ready for departure.

"If anyone can elude the Souks, it's the captain," Wren reassured her. He'd been distressed when Sarina said Teir hadn't been located. "The *Valiant* will show up. Give him time. He must have his own reasons for not contacting us."

"Yes, I imagine so." Didn't Teir realize how concerned she was about him? He could have at least sent a message that he was okay.

"You'll be riding down to Timos in a shuttle," Wren said. "Another ship can bring you back to Bimordus Two when you're done here. We're heading directly to Tendraa to join the fleet."

"Good luck," Sarina said, worried for him and his friends as they headed into battle.

****

Wagroob, the chief scientist at the Timosian Research Station, was less friendly to her. He gave Sarina a brief tour and asked what she hoped to accomplish by her visit.

"We're too busy to offer instruction," he advised her, apparently unimpressed by her status.

"I didn't come here to learn. I came to help find a cure for the Farg," she said, irritated that the man considered her presence a burden. "Glotaj thought you might want to run more tests on me since I'd recovered from the plague. It seems the long incubation period I experienced was unusual."

He eyed her with renewed interest. "I suppose there can't be any harm in testing you further. We might learn something new. Come this way to the laboratory, please."

Sarina fell in step beside him as he proceeded down a long corridor.

"After we're done there, I'll assign you a workstation," Wagroob said. "Do you have any background in microbiology?"

"Just what I've learned on Bimordus Two." She'd spent hauras in the study center using the subliminal learning device, reviewing data on the Farg.

"Sometimes I think we're too close to the material we're examining. It might be the one clue we're missing that would piece together the whole mystery of the Farg." Wagroob waved a hand. "You'll see what I mean if you review our findings. Someone like you with little background in science might actually present a fresh insight. If you need help interpreting the data, the computer can assist you."

Sarina was at her newly assigned workstation the next day when another call came through from Admiral Gog.

"We've just received word from an outpost in Sector Zero-Nine that the *Valiant* off-loaded two Crigellans and a Souk," the admiral said.

"What? Where is this place?" Sarina asked, her heart thumping. News at last!

"Not far from Taurus. The Crigellans are not being very communicative, and the Souk claims to have been tricked by Reylock. Unfortunately, the ship left orbit before security could get an explanation from her pilot."

"And now?"

"He could be anywhere." After ascertaining her safety, Daras Gog rang off.

Damn, why hadn't Teir contacted her? He was roaming the stars in the *Valiant* for purposes unknown to her, or to anyone else for that matter. Had he even inquired about her welfare? Didn't he care anymore?

Sarina turned back to her work but was unable to concentrate. Worry plagued her and clouded her thoughts.

****

Teir had managed to elude the two Souk combat vessels that were orbiting Taurus, fooling them with Bdan's voice as he'd tricked Vivak on the bridge of the *Valiant*. Afraid they might discover his ruse before he got out of sensor range, he'd used evasive maneuvers and maintained radio silence to cover his escape. He'd dropped the Crigellans and Vivak off at the nearest Coalition outpost, and then headed for Alpha Omega Two to interview his aunt.

Inquiring about Sarina was still uppermost in his mind, but he'd listened in on subspace frequencies and heard her name mentioned. Satisfied she'd made it to safety, he concentrated on his current mission. He needed something solid to go on regarding his heritage before contacting her personally.

Aunt Catharta was suffering from an infection of the lungs, and not the Farg, the healers told him at the Wellness Center. She looked considerably more frail than the last time he'd seen her. Her finely chiseled features were shrunken and pale.

When she saw him, a smile lit her face. "Teir! Back so soon?" she said in a weak voice.

"How are you, Aunt Catharta?" He stooped to kiss her wrinkled cheek.

"Much better, now that you're here. The nurses say I made it through the worst of this ailment." Taking a wheezing breath, she added, "I'm not sure that I can conquer it entirely."

"Nonsense, you've a strong constitution." Teir patted her hand as he seated himself at her bedside. The Farg having been ruled out, he didn't need to wear protective gear. "I've come for a reason. Tell me about my parents."

Catharta avoided his gaze. "There isn't much to tell."

"You said they died in a reactor accident. How old was I?"

She withdrew her hand from his grasp. "You were just a babe. But we've gone over this story before. Why now?"

"It's important." He fixed his eyes on her, waiting.

"Very well. You were eight weeks old."

"Where was I living?"

"In the city of Minna, where you were born."

"Who informed you of the accident? Were you and Uncle Jeb also in Minna at the time?"

"Aye, we were." She stared at a spot on the ceiling.

"And you were my mother's only living relative, is that right? So you were given custody of me?" When she nodded, he went on. "I was an only child, of course." He saw something flicker behind her eyes. *"Wasn't I?"*

Catharta directed her gaze at him. "Is there a reason for these questions, Teir?

"Yes. I've found my soulmate, but I can't join with her until I learn my heritage."

"I don't understand."

"She's the legendary Great Healer, Aunt." He told her how he'd met Sarina and how their relationship had progressed.

Catharta's eyes widened. "You're the one! I can't believe it. Yes, yes, I can. Listen—you must journey to Minna. The proof of your birth is there." Her shoulders sagged, and her expression saddened. "It's time for you to learn the truth. I'm not really your aunt."

"What?"

"Jeb and I were living in Minna. We'd just had our first child, a male. The babe wasn't two months old before he died in his cradle, the cause being unknown. It was a time of terror and strife in the land, the annum of the revolution." Catharta's hands picked at the covers, and her mouth quivered.

"Jannis, my sister, knew how we grieved for our lost child. She made us an offer that same afternoon. If we would entrust her with our son's body, she would give us a living child in exchange. We were to ask no questions but to raise him as our own. No one else knew of our tragedy."

"Where would your sister get another babe to substitute for yours?"

"She worked at the palace in Minna as lady's maid to the Preim's niece. But let me back up a bit and fill you in on Vilaran history. The Preim, a cruel despot, lived in the capital city of Theal. His brother, Gregor, lived in Minna with his wife, Ana. They had two daughters. Rite was the youngest. She married and had two sons."

"Rite's two sons were the Preim's great-nephews?"

Catharta nodded, her gaze distant. "Because of the Preim's cruelties, feelings against the aristocracy ran high. It didn't matter that some were innocent, like Rite and her family. All were branded traitors by the people. When the revolutionary fervor swept the land, mobs of angered citizens charged the citadels.

"My sister warned Rite, but the girl was too innocent to believe the people would rise against her when she had done nothing to harm them. But then word came that the palace at Theal had been stormed. The Preim, his wife and son, had been slaughtered along with all their servants. A horde was gathering in Minna that very day."

Catharta took a long, shaky breath before she continued. "That was the same day my beloved babe passed on. Jannis had an idea. She spoke to Rite, who'd recently given birth to her second child. Desperate to save her infant son, Rite agreed to the switch. It was done right before the mob broke through the gates."

Catharta closed her eyes at the pain of the memory. "The preimess was unable to save herself or her eldest son."

"They were murdered?" Teir still wasn't clear on how this related to him.

"Aye. When the revolutionaries charged into the nursery, they found a dead infant in its cradle. They assumed the babe died of natural causes, although some wondered about his brown hair. My sister urged Jeb and me to flee. Our babe now had hair as black as midnight, and some of our neighbors might notice the difference. It was you, Teir. You were that babe."

"But you claimed to be my aunt, not my mother."

"We traveled far from Minna, and I thought it would be easier to explain the difference in our looks. No one else would be the wiser in our new location."

"What about your sister? Did she make it out of Minna?"

"Jannis is there still. You must find her. She has proof of your birth. It has been a burden to her all these annums. Even the most distant relatives to the Preim were executed. To this day, an edict remains condemning the royal family to a death sentence. Memories last a long time."

"But the other members of his family weren't evil."

"It doesn't matter, Teir. You walk on dangerous ground if you return to Vilaran to seek proof of your heritage. You must do this in secret."

He nodded solemnly. "Where will I find your sister?"

"Jannis has a small abode in the bremen section of town—her last name is Reylock, by the way. I put out that you were her child but that she was unable to raise you on her own."

Recalling that it was Glotaj who had helped him be accepted into the Academy, Teir asked, "Tell me, Aunt Catharta, where does Glotaj fit into this?" He still called her aunt despite knowing the truth. She had raised him and loved him, and he'd always consider her to be his adopted aunt.

Sighing, Catharta let her head fall back onto the pillow. "Your great-uncle, the Preim, was a descendant of the House of Raimorrda. Because Glotaj was also a Raimorrdan, I sought his aid on several occasions. He knew your true identity. For your own safety, he kept silent. There are those on Vilaran who would see you dead."

"But why? I'm no threat to anyone."

"You are the only surviving member of the Retti dynasty. As such, you could be restored to power as the new Preim if the royalists predominated."

Retti… Rite… *Teir.* Jumble the letters around and that's where his name originated. But it was ridiculous to believe people would want to kill him over an ages-old revolution.

Something his aunt had said suddenly registered. He was a descendant of the House of Raimorrda.

"Did the aftereffects of the supernova reach Vilaran?" Teir

asked. Perhaps the same reasoning that applied to Lord Cam'brii could be applied to him regarding the sign of the circle. As a Raimorrdan, he might qualify under the legend as Sarina's mate.

But Catharta shook her head. "The only cataclysm on Vilaran that annum was the one caused by the people's blood lust. It still exists. You must be cautious if you go there."

"I'll be discreet in my inquiries. I have no desire to get embroiled in Vilaran politics," Teir assured her.

Catharta grasped his hand. "I love you as I would my own son, Teir."

"I love you, too." He squeezed her hand, then leaned over and kissed her on the cheek.

His eyes moistened as he got up to leave. He promised to contact her after his sojourn to Vilaran, but her health was fragile. This might be the last time they said good-bye.

As Teir made his way to the spaceport, the implications of what he'd learned reverberated in his mind. He was a Raimorrdan. As the only living member of the Vilaran royal family, he could consider himself to be highly placed. That left being born under the sign of the circle as the remaining requirement he had to meet to get the High Council's approval to wed Sarina.

He couldn't claim the same atmospheric disturbances that led to Lord Cam'brii's birth being interpreted that way, so what of his? He'd have to find out on Vilaran.

Contacting Defense League Command as soon as the *Valiant* left orbit, he was at once patched into Admiral Daras Gog's office.

"Captain?" boomed the Admiral's voice over the ship's comm unit. "Where in Zor are you?"

"I can't reveal my location, sir. It's imperative I speak to Sarina. Did she make it to Bimordus Two?"

"Aye. Her marriage to Lord Cam'brii was about to take place when she fell sick with the Farg."

"What?"

"Don't worry, she's recovered," the admiral said in a dry tone. Then a note of anxiety crept into his voice. "You haven't caught it, have you?"

"No, sir, I'm fine. Where is she now?" He had to speak to her and make sure she was all right. By the stars, her marriage hadn't already taken place, had it? He held his breath, waiting for Gog's answer.

"I'll give you her current location if you give me yours," the admiral offered.

"Dammit, where is she?"

Gog gave a heavy sigh. "This isn't general knowledge, Reylock, but she's at the Timosian Research Station. She'll be returning to Bimordus Two for her wedding in a few more days. When are you planning to report for duty? Maybe I can get you assigned to transport her."

"There's something else I have to do before I surface. I'll be in touch, Admiral."

"Reylock, wait! You blasted renegade. You don't have leave to take time off. I order you to report in for a debriefing—"

Teir severed the link, cutting off communications. He didn't want the admiral or anyone else to know where he was headed.

Leaning back in his seat, he thought about Sarina. She had suffered the plague. What a horror! If only he could have been with her. Storms of the sun, she'd nearly married Cam'brii. Their wedding had been delayed only because of her sickness. Now she was due to return to Bimordus Two and the marriage would go forth. He must prevent it.

Leaning over his console, he put in a call to the Research Station on Timos.

Chapter Twenty-Five

"I request permission to retrieve Sarina," Lord Cam'brii said. He stood facing Glotaj and the semicircle of councilors in the Council Chamber. A special session had been called because Sarina was requesting an extension of her visit to Timos. "You said she would return in two weeks, and our marriage ceremony was rescheduled accordingly. You can't change the arrangements now," he protested to the regent.

Daimon and his supporters in the Return to Origins Faction were becoming more powerful in Sarina's absence. Soon they'd have enough signatures on their petition to move up the vote calling for a dissolution of the Coalition. If that ever passed, all of Cam'brii's efforts against the Souks would have been in vain.

"I agree with Lord Cam'brii," Emu said, stretching his long neck. "Another delay is unacceptable. In my opinion, the Great Healer should not have been granted permission to leave in the first place. What has she accomplished at Timos?"

"Nothing!" Daimon exclaimed, his tone harsh. "The woman is a useless Earthling. I've told you before, she has no power. Nor has she made any contributions to our knowledge of the Farg. She dabbles in experiments beyond her ken."

"And how are you so well-informed?" Emu sneered. "Are you in communication with your friend Wagroob, who heads the station? I understand you're one of the largest contributors to his political fund, Daimon."

"That has no relevance to this situation. We've held far too many special sessions on account of this supposed Great Healer.

She fell sick and couldn't even heal herself. You're all nothing but fanatics, waiting for a Savior who doesn't exist. I'll show you the true way! If we go back to our original boundaries, we'll have a decent chance to fight off the Morgots. We won't need to rely on anyone but ourselves."

"You're wrong," Cam'brii said. "Even as you speak, a Defense League force engages the Morgot fleet in battle. We must remain united."

Tension filled the air as thick as fog. Glotaj motioned for Lord Cam'brii to be seated. "We are here to make a decision regarding Sarina's request," the regent said. "Is she, or is she not, granted additional leave?" He kept his expression impassive so his own opinion wouldn't influence the vote.

Seven to five voted against her remaining on Timos. Cam'brii voted against, and so did Emu.

Daimon cast his vote in favor of letting her stay, not because he felt she would accomplish anything on Timos, but because her return meant her marriage, and he didn't want that event to take place. It would increase her status and give added power to the Raimorrdans.

Daimon was solemn and thoughtful as he left the Council Chamber. In his private office, he summoned Ruzbee for a meeting. The short-statured Arcturian didn't take long in arriving. He'd been prowling the halls, trying to get news of the Great Healer. The Assembly representatives weren't aware of Sarina's location, only that she had left on a mission of import.

"We've got to do something," Daimon said, pacing his office with his maroon robe swishing at his feet. Stroking his beard, he faced the Arcturian. "Already the Earthwoman manipulates our central government. It is wrong, Ruzbee, wrong!"

"Where is she?"

"She's at the Timosian Research Station trying to find a cure for the Farg. She has requested an extension of her stay. It's been denied, and Cam'brii is being sent to retrieve her. He leaves within the haura. The wedding will take place immediately upon their return."

"So what is it that bothers you?" Ruzbee asked, wondering what Daimon was getting at or if he just wanted to complain.

"She is a thorn in our side. As Lord Cam'brii's bride, she will be perceived as supporting his goals. In that case, we may not get the votes we need for self-determination. We must ensure that she does not marry the Raimorrdan."

"What did you have in mind?"

The councilor's eyes grew crafty. "Lord Cam'brii is on his way to Timos. If he never arrives there, the matter would be resolved."

"You mean…?" Ruzbee pretended to look shocked.

"It's for the good of the people," Daimon assured him. "Our government has lost control. The Morgots and the Farg run rampant across the galaxy. We must save ourselves. The Coalition leadership leans strongly toward the Raimorrdans, and if this marriage takes place, they'll remain in control. Power must be restored to the people."

He drew a long breath and fixed Ruzbee with a glare. "Do you understand what I'm saying?"

Ruzbee nodded. "Might it not be better to wait until Cam'brii picks up Sarina? If they were intercepted on the way home, both would be removed as a threat."

"Good idea, but how? Too bad that Twygg assassin is dead. He might have given us some useful insights."

"Someone poisoned the poor fellow with mushgum, no doubt to silence him." Ruzbee tilted his head. "I might know someone else who could make the necessary arrangements for a price."

"There's always a price," said Daimon. "Do it."

"As you wish." Ruzbee bowed and hurried from the room. His Souk master would pay a generous bonus for this information. Ruel was lusting after another opportunity to get at Lord Cam'brii, and this setup would be perfect.

In addition, Ruzbee would pocket part of Daimon's payment to Ruel. Acting as liaison, he was entitled to a cut. And he'd make sure the trail led from Daimon to the Souks in such a way that the councilor would take the fall if their plan failed.

****

Cerrus Bdan looked forward to his next encounter with Captain Reylock. Bdan had just returned to his compound on Souk. He, Otis, and Wyeth had been rescued by one of the escort vessels orbiting Taurus, but only after a long and fearsome wait on the fiery surface. He didn't have anything to show for his journey, and that rankled more than anything.

"Waiting for you is a Morgot emissary, master," one of his lieutenants announced.

A spark of fear ignited in his chest. K'darr would be furious that he hadn't obtained the Blood Crystal. He'd have to tell the emissary that Reylock had led them to a decoy. Hopefully, the truth would be enough of a defense. K'darr did not treat failures kindly.

The emissary didn't look pleased when Bdan greeted him in the Reception Hall. Otis and Wyeth had come along, and Bdan could sense their apprehension. The Morgot was huge, towering over all of them. His opaque stare was as cold as the black rock from the cave.

"Where is the Blood Crystal, Souk? I must take it to my leader."

Bdan gave a look of confidence he didn't feel. "Have it not, do I."

"What! Why not?"

"Tricked us did Captain R-R-Reylock. He led us to a decoy."

"Where is he now?"

"Got away did he, but track him, we will." Bdan had tried to pick up the *Valiant* on his long-range sensors, but the captain's trail had been cold by the time he'd left Taurus. Now Reylock could be anywhere.

"What about the Great Healer? Do you have her for me to bring to K'darr?"

"Had her, did we, but she escaped. I'll find her, too." At Bdan's nod, his guards moved in closer. He feared what the emissary was empowered to do in case of failure.

"K'darr will be most upset. His Eminence would wait to confront you himself, but he is engaged in battle in the Tendraan system. He might have foreseen this event if you had obtained the Blood Crystal for him earlier. Our fleet's supply route has been cut off. K'darr may be forced to order a retreat. He will blame you, Cerrus Bdan, for not fulfilling your contract."

"Send troops can I to assist," Bdan said quickly, his jowls quivering. "Make good my word, will I."

The emissary shook his head, while Bdan's bodyguards encircled them, anticipating a hostile move. Unnoticed by them all, Otis slinked toward a side entrance.

"The price for failure is death, Cerrus Bdan." The emissary reached a paw inside his armored doublet. Instantly, the Souks drew their shooters. "You may kill me, but we shall die together."

He pulled out a round orb and held it up. "This detonator is set to explode in—" he checked the reading "—two point five seconds. The time for apologies is over, Souk."

Bdan's mouth gaped. The Morgot was on a suicide mission! They were all going to…

****

Otis stumbled through the archway into the next chamber just as a blinding white light exploded behind him. He didn't need to look to know his master and those surrounding him had been vaporized.

Otis was a Believer. He'd been the one who'd released the magnetic lock to Reylock's prison cell on the *Omnus* when Sarina was there to free him, and he'd been the robed figure who had assisted the captain in the palace. He was a Crigellan, and like

Salla and Etan, he worked toward making the prophecy come true. His position was dangerous, but it had served him well.

He'd get a new master now, but he still could be useful, feeding information to the resistance movement on Souk. One day, he dreamed of liberating his people who were enslaved here. But for now, Otis had to appear to be part of the Souk hierarchy, even if it meant going against his basic principles.

Devin would be his contact now that Salla and Etan had left. The underground movement still needed to establish a regular connection with the Coalition for intelligence purposes and support. He'd see what he could accomplish toward this goal in the coming months.

Otis wiped the smile from his face and put on a grim demeanor suitable to the terrible news he was about to deliver to Bdan's troops. A brighter day was dawning now that Cerrus Bdan was gone, but there was still much work to do.

****

Sarina reviewed her data at the Research Station on Timos. She hadn't yet been informed of the High Council's decision regarding her request for an extension, but she hoped she would be allowed to stay. She'd used an online tutorial to boost her knowledge of scientific methodology and then had begun to sift through the multitude of data gathered on the Farg. She felt as though she was close to a breakthrough.

She'd tried an unorthodox approach by overlaying the planets affected by the Farg with the ones conquered by the Morgots. It appeared these worlds were all rich in natural resources, almost as though the disease's targets had been selected on purpose by the warlike race.

Since planets of every size and geophysical configuration were visited by the pestilence, it was difficult to isolate the factors involved in disease transmission. Sarina, despite her findings regarding the Morgots, couldn't piece the two together.

The observation had been made that planets closer to their suns were less virulently attacked than those farther away. This led to the theory that heat might work in lessening the strength of the Farg. Yet when heat treatments were used, they had no effect on the victims. The only treatments currently available were palliative, not curative.

Superstitions remained in force, and nearly every culture claimed that a comet had preceded the dreadful pestilence. Yet astronomical observations could not confirm these reports.

The claims were confusing and too fragmented for any sense to be made from them. Sarina frowned at her console. The pieces of the puzzle were laid out in front of her. All she needed was one clue to fit them together.

Take those comets, for example. She wouldn't have thought people to be so superstitious in this age of interstellar travel. Yet people from every one of the planets involved had claimed a malevolent force was at work.

Perhaps so, Sarina mused, studying the graph on her screen. If those comets didn't show up on the astronomical charts, then where did they come from? Could one be traced? The reports claimed cosmic dust from the comet's tail seeded the atmosphere of the affected planets. What if that tail contained something more than ice and dust particles?

Her pulse accelerating, she summoned Wagroob. "It strikes me as significant that a comet appears over each planet right before the plague strikes. Have you found any evidence to support this claim?"

Wagroob looked at her askance. "No one can predict where the Farg will strike next, so how can we send a probe to take measurements?"

"The Morgots are in the Tendraan system now. Where would it benefit them to go next?" she asked, after explaining her theory.

"Why, Vilaran, I suppose. That system is the closest, and if your notion about natural resources is correct, Vilaran has deposits of piragen ore that would be useful for spacecraft construction.”

“Send a probe there, Wagroob, and let it wait for a comet. I’ll bet one will show up before the Morgots leave the Tendraan system.”

“I’ll see that it’s done, Mistress.” For the first time since her arrival, respect entered the scientist’s eyes. “I’ll let you know what happens.”

He stalked from the room just as Sarina got a call on her personal comm unit.

“Hello?” she said, hoping it was Glotaj with an answer to her request.

“Sarina, are you all right?” Teir’s voice came through loud and clear.

“My God, is that really you? Where are you?” She couldn’t believe her ears.

“Never mind. Tell me what’s going on.” His voice was gruff with worry.

“I’m fine, but I miss you. I need to see you. What’s been happening?”

“I escaped from the Souks. I’ve learned a lot, Sarina. You and I are meant to be together. You must stay there on Timos until I can get you.”

“But where are you now? What are you doing?”

He hesitated. “It’s my belief that I’m the Raimorrdan destined to wed you, but I have to go home to get proof for the High Council.”

“Let me come with you.”

“No, it’s too dangerous. Wait there for me. I love you.” The audio link went dead.

“Teir, no.” Sarina’s vision blurred with moisture. What had he said? *He loved her.* Dear God, she loved him, too. Why hadn’t he given her the chance to tell him so?

Then the rest of his words sunk in. He was the Raimorrdan destined to wed her. How could that be? According to the legend, she was supposed to marry a Raimorrdan who was highly placed and born under the sign of the circle. Rolf was the only one who met those criteria.

Or was he?

She remembered Glotaj's warning not to inquire into Teir's background. Now Teir was journeying home to Vilaran to get proof of his birth—proof that he was a Raimorrdan, too? But he'd still have to meet the rest of the criteria if he was the one in the legend. It made sense since she loved the man and had healed him.

Sarina rubbed her temples. What if she was right, and Vilaran was the next target for the Morgots? Would Teir be infected with the Farg when a comet swept by? She had to warn him.

Then again, why had he mentioned that going to Vilaran could be dangerous? Did he already know about the comet, or was there some other reason he wasn't sharing with her?

Oh God, Teir, I need to be with you so badly. She yearned to feel his touch and to hold him in her arms. How could she wait for him when they were meant to be together?

Her sojourn to Timos had been partly to investigate the Farg but also to avoid her marriage to Lord Cam'brii. She'd known in her heart all along that she couldn't wed the councilor. Now Sarina wondered how she'd be able to tell him.

Wagroob soon presented her with the opportunity. "I've received a message that Lord Cam'brii is on his way to bring you home to Bimordus Two," the scientist said at dinner. "His estimated time of arrival is twenty-one hundred hauras."

Sarina stared at him. So her request for an extension had been denied. Rolf was coming for her in person to bring her back for the wedding. She hadn't expected to have to face him so soon. How was she going to tell him the marriage was off?

"Thank you," she said in a meek tone, waiting until Wagroob left before covering her face with her hands.

****

The two geckos watched Cam'brii's small transport ship begin the descent into Timos's atmosphere.

"We'll wait until he picks up the Earthwoman, then we'll follow them at a safe distance," Orr, the one in charge, said. He rubbed his exterior shell, dented in several places from past battles. "When they're out of sensor range from Timos, we'll open fire."

"Agreed," said Pah, his copilot. He wasn't a big talker.

"I hope we don't have to wait long. I'm anxious to get home and replenish my nectar." Orr's antennae quivered in anticipation.

Pah gave a gruff laugh. "I had a long drink after we retrieved the *Omnus* for Cerrus Bdan."

"Yes, his bonus was generous, but his brother Ruel pays better. We'll see how promptly he rewards us after this job. He should be pleased once we succeed in this mission. Maybe we should continue to work on his payroll."

Orr returned his attention to the helm. Cam'brii obviously didn't suspect anyone was following him. It should be easy to blast the councilor and his bride out of space.

Chapter Twenty-Six

Booted footsteps from down the hall told Sarina that Rolf had arrived. She stood in her room and straightened her royal blue gown, then patted her hair into place. She'd braided a section off her face, twisting a matching-color ribbon through it. The rest of her hair hung down her back.

"Sarina, you look lovely." Rolf strode inside, beaming with approval. In two long steps, he stood in front of her and pressed his mouth to hers.

Sarina stepped back. "We have to talk. Computer, close portal." The door hissed shut behind them. "Please, take a seat."

Wearing a puzzled frown, he complied. "What's this about, Sarina? I thought you'd be happy that I came for you."

She sat on the edge of her seat and folded her hands in her lap. "I'm not returning to Bimordus Two."

"What?"

"I want you to take me to Vilaran."

"Vilaran? Why do you want to go there?" His eyes narrowed. "Wait a minute. Isn't that where—"

"Teir was born. Yes, that's right. I have a lot to tell you. It's time you learned the truth." And she proceeded to relate the nature of her relationship to Teir.

Rolf's emotions played across his face, ranging from anger to dismay to resignation. He'd always thought the two of them shared something special. He would never win Sarina's love now. He felt a flash of anger and jealousy directed at Reylock, as well as wounded pride, but then an odd sense of relief overwhelmed him.

Perhaps this was the way things were meant to be. He'd never really loved Sarina, and if he didn't marry her, he could remain faithful to Gayla's memory.

"So Reylock is saying he's the one destined to marry the Great Healer?" Rolf said. He was still concerned about the legend and its effect on his political goals.

"Teir claims he's a Raimorrdan. He's going to Vilaran to get proof. I wanted to go, but he told me it was too dangerous."

"Dangerous? Why?"

"He wouldn't say. Listen, Rolf, I came up with a theory about the Farg. All the infected planets were visited by a comet before the pestilence took hold, but none of these comets were recorded on astronomical charts. I think they may somehow be responsible for spreading the plague, and they're linked to the Morgots. Each one of the planets involved is rich in natural resources and would benefit the Morgots after a conquest.

"Wagroob and I determined that the next likely target is Vilaran. I don't know if this is what Teir meant, or if there's some other reason he wants me to stay away. Glotaj might know. He warned me not to inquire into Teir's background. I'm wondering if it's something to do with Teir's past on Vilaran."

At her request, Rolf put in a subspace call to the regent, using his personal data link as a scrambler.

"And so, the legend comes full circle," said Glotaj's resigned voice over the comm unit. "It is time for you to learn the truth. Reylock is the grand nephew of the former Preim of Vilaran. The entire royal family was wiped out in a revolution the annum of his birth. Teir was exchanged for a dead infant so the revolutionaries would think the infant prince had died. Meanwhile, Teir was raised by an adopted aunt who never revealed his identity because of the danger involved. It would be an instant death sentence if his heritage became known."

"A death sentence," Sarina repeated, listening over Rolf's shoulder. "My God, we have to warn him."

"He probably knows this already," Rolf said. "That's why he told you his journey would be dangerous."

"Teir can only be going to Vilaran for one reason," Glotaj added. "He's realized his destiny is to marry Sarina."

"But how is that possible? I'm the one who meets the criteria," Cam'brii replied.

"So does Reylock. I've never been sure which of you was the right one, but it seemed more sensible to choose you for the bridegroom. With your position and regal bearing, I thought it would be easier for the Great Healer to fall in love with you. Reylock is more rough-edged, and I felt he might not appeal to her as readily. Besides, he was unaware of his birthright. Just in case I was wrong, however, I threw Reylock and Sarina together so they'd have a chance to get to know each other. In the end, it would be Sarina's choice."

He paused. "Teir still has to come up with proof before the High Council will give their approval. I cannot do that for him."

"What kind of proof?" Sarina inquired.

"That is not for me to say. You mustn't go to Vilaran," Glotaj warned. "Return at once to Bimordus Two."

"I have another reason for wanting to go there," Sarina said in partial truth. "As I told Rolf, Wagroob and I have a theory about the Farg. If we're right, Vilaran will be the next planet struck by the pestilence. A comet will appear, as it has all the other times. Wagroob has sent a probe to take readings. If I'm on Vilaran, I can make on-site observations." She explained her findings regarding the Farg.

"You cannot go there. You'd be placing yourself in peril. Heed my words," the Supreme Regent advised.

"We'll keep you informed." Rolf terminated the link, then turned to Sarina. "I agree with you. We should go to Vilaran. Your theories about the Farg are valid and should be investigated firsthand. More importantly, Reylock may need our help. I want the legend to come true as much as you do."

****

Orr sat up excitedly in his seat. "Here they come." A small scout ship was just leaving the spaceport on Timos. Adjusting the controls, Orr moved his gunship closer until they were just out of visual range.

"He could pick you up on his sensors," Pah warned, his antennae bristling.

"So what? We could be part of the spaceport traffic for all he knows. Let's make sure of their heading before we take pursuit. Cam'brii will probably take the same route back to Bimordus Two as he used in getting here, but we don't know that for certain."

A few minutes later, Orr pointed at the viewscreen. "Look, they've broken orbit. Let's go after them." He increased speed, warming up the laser cannons at the same time.

"Wait, their ship is turning," Pah noted. "What the—?"

"Blast, they've changed direction." Orr punched in the new heading on the nav unit.

"This is not the way to Bimordus Two. We should see where they're going," Pah protested.

Orr shook his head. "Let's just get the job done." He pushed the control level forward to narrow the distance between the two vessels. Then he threw his head back and trilled a battle cry, a harsh shriek that echoed throughout the cockpit.

****

Unidentified ship approaching, Rolf's onboard computer warned.

"Shields up," the councilor ordered, scanning the sensor readings. "It has the outline of a gecko vessel," he told Sarina, seated in the copilot's chair.

She squinted at the visual display. The crab-like shape of the vessel was unfamiliar to her. "Could they be passing by?"

"I doubt it. Their weapons systems are armed. Hold tight, I'm going full about."

He pushed the button for a short burst on their side thrusters.

Sarina's safety harness tightened as she was thrust forward in her seat.

"They're firing," she said as a white flash erupted from the other vessel. A dull thud rocked the ship as the hit registered on their energy screen.

"Damage report," Rolf demanded.

Shields are holding, the ship's voice system replied.

"Look out, here comes another one." Rolf threw the ship into a stomach-wrenching turn.

"What kind of defenses do we have, other than the shields?" Sarina asked when she was able to speak again—that last round had knocked the breath out of her.

"This scout ship may be small, but she's well outfitted. Try to hail them on the comm unit. I'd like to know why they're targeting us."

Sarina tried but received no answer. Another flash of laser fire lanced out, pounding their ship. "They're gaining on us."

"I'm readying the torpedoes. We're not going to fool around." His fingers danced over the controls. "Okay, we're locked on target. Fire away."

The gecko ship evaded the missile. The torpedo hit a piece of space debris instead that had come between them.

Rolf cursed. Sweat beaded his brow as he saw how well the gecko vessel kept on their tail despite his best maneuvers. It reminded him of another time, another place, when he was also in a small ship being attacked. Only then, it was Gayla with him, and the Souks were the aggressors.

A red haze obscured his vision, and he heard Gayla's voice calling to him amidst the fury of battle. *"Rolf..."*

Gayla needed him. She'd been hurt.

"Rolf, pay attention," Sarina said sharply, drawing him out of his trance. "They're firing again—"

Another blast hit them, this time penetrating the shields. An alarm sounded. The hull had been breached, and an automatic shutdown sequence for the second level compartments went into effect.

"We need to go to warp speed," Rolf said. "I have to drop shields. We can't get away from them otherwise." Reylock would have known what to do, he thought. Although Rolf was a skilled pilot, the captain was better at escaping sticky situations. "I'm going into a dive. When we come out of it, I'll drop the shields. Can you activate the warp drive when I tell you?"

"Yes, let's do it," Sarina replied, her fingers hovering over the control console.

The tactic worked. Rolf went into a sharp dive, then when they were zooming out of it, he dropped the shields. Sarina pushed the lever and the space in front of the viewscreen blurred into star lines.

"We've done it." She sat back, her posture easing now that the unexpected conflict was over.

Rolf glanced at her after adjusting their heading. "I wonder how they got onto us."

She raised an eyebrow. "What do you mean?"

"Not too many people knew where you'd gone, and only the High Council members were aware of my journey. Add two and two together, and what do you get?"

Sarina shook her head. "I don't know. What?"

"A mole in the High Council. It's well-known that geckos do the dirty work for the Souks. Someone must have revealed our location to them."

"You think the Souks were behind this attack?"

He nodded grimly. "Probably. I'll check it out later, but I think this must be another attempt to impede the passage of the First Amendment. The sooner we get you and Reylock together, the better. The legend must unfold. I just hope he isn't running into trouble on Vilaran."

****

As one of the six founding members of the Coalition, Vilaran was a major scientific and cultural center in the northwest quadrant of the galaxy. Theal, the capital city, had undergone a transformation since the revolution, twenty-nine annums ago. Once mainly a feudal fortress, now it was a thriving modern metropolis with tall skyscrapers, people-movers, and marketplaces selling goods from the known worlds in the galaxy.

Teir flew into the spaceport and then caught a commuter flight to Minna. He didn't think there was any real danger in the *Valiant* being well-known. Those who knew him as Teir Reylock wouldn't question his background. The reason given for his visit was simple. He wished to see his mother, Jannis Reylock.

The only problem was, he had no idea where to find her. Catharta had said her sister lived in the bremen section of town. That didn't tell him much, so he walked into the comm center at the flight terminal and requested a local directory. There was no listing for a Reylock anywhere in Minna.

Teir grimaced. He should have known it wouldn't be so easy. Jannis's position in the palace might have put her in danger in the early days of the republic. She was probably used to covering her tracks. Either she no longer lived here, or she kept a low profile by not being listed in the directory.

He headed outdoors to continue his search on foot. The bremen section of town was an attractive area of tree-lined streets and individual residences painted in colorful pastels. Teir felt a warm glow of satisfaction to be home. The breeze freshened his face, and heat from the blazing sol warmed his skin. A perfumed scent from white keela blossoms floated in the air.

Under other circumstances, he'd have liked to linger and enjoy the sights, but not now.

The city's main marketplace was in a central location, so Teir went there first. Farmers from outlying organic cooperatives sold their produce in the glass-domed, climate-controlled food hall. Many people preferred to prepare their own nourishment instead of using fabricators, or else they wanted a break from the high-tech pace of life, so fresh fruits and vegetables were always in demand.

Teir strolled the wide path between stalls, admiring the mixture of modern and ancient techniques. Samples of the wares for sale were attractively displayed at each stall, but the items were actually obtained only when someone ordered them. Conveyors whisked the goods from warehouses to the point of delivery. This way, the natural produce was kept in ideal temperature storage until needed.

Colorfully dressed vendors loudly hawked their goods to the morning crowd. Teir glanced around, his gaze settling on an old woman wearing a scarf over her head like a refugee from Lutto. She might be able to use a few extra credits.

Sauntering over to her fruit stall, Teir pretended to admire a purple pommus. Round and shiny, it appeared to have a firm texture and smooth skin. "How much?" he asked, pointing.

"Five credits," said the old woman.

"I'll give you fifty if you have the information I need," he offered. "I'm looking for a woman named Jannis Reylock."

"Don't know her." The vendor's face closed.

"I'll double the price. One hundred credits." When the woman shook her head, Teir said, "One thousand."

The vendor leaned closer, bending over her stall. "You might ask Old Man Naggers. He's been around town longer than I have."

"Where can I find him?"

"Seek your answers where the water flows upward before it falls down."

"Huh?" He waited for a fuller explanation but it didn't come. Great, Teir thought as he strode away after giving the woman fifty credits for her trouble. Now what?

Getting hungry looking at all the food, he bought a salt bread and munched on it while deciding what to do next. His first task would be to find a body of water.

It was mid-afternoon by the time Teir discovered the steps. He'd been to several lakes and ponds, but none of them flowed upward, and no one answered to the name of Naggers.

He was about to give up when he reached the Centorium, the seat of the provincial government. It was across a wide square from the palatial Museum of History. In front of the long rectangular Centorium building was a fountain. A plume of rainbow-colored water cascaded onto a series of steps. The water on the steps flowed upward, into a pool surrounding the plume.

Teir glanced around but saw no one who bore the slightest resemblance to anyone called Old Man Naggers.

"Can I help you?" said a curt voice behind him.

Teir whirled, facing a uniformed sentry. "I was admiring the fountain. I'm a visitor here."

"Is that so?" The sentry gave him a keen look of appraisal. "You might consider visiting the museum across the square."

"Thank you, I'll try that later," Teir said, moving on. The flag flying atop the Centorium meant the provost was in residence, and apparently loiterers in front of the government building were not encouraged.

Vilaran was divided into provinces, each one ruled by a provost appointed by the central Parliamentary government, which was itself elected every eight years by the populace. The provosts had full authority to administer the laws within their realm. Each province, in turn, was divided into districts headed by a justice. An elected president was head of state for the planet.

Teir hadn't known Minna was the seat of the province, but the significance of it wasn't lost on him. That museum across the street might have been the palace where he was born.

He wandered toward a row of shops on a side street, looking for a place where he could query the local inhabitants, and soon found a saloon nestled between a data card supply shop and a jewelry store.

Chimes sounded when he pushed open the door. The atmosphere inside was stale, reeking of liquor. He made his way past a loud group of locals and took a seat at the bar.

"Do you accept universal credits?" he asked the bartender.

"Aye, that we do. New to these parts, are you? What'll it be?"

The bartender's long gray hair fell forward, shielding his face, but Teir glimpsed sharp brown eyes in a wrinkled visage.

"A cosh of your local, please." He handed over a data card for his banking credits to be debited. "I'm looking for a man named Naggers."

The bartender paused in filling Teir's carafe, but swiftly carried on until froth spilled over the brim. With a soft *plunk,* he put the carafe in front of Teir and handed back his data card. "What's the nature of your business?" he asked in a gruff tone.

"I was told Naggers could help me locate a lost relative."

Teir pocketed the card, noting that twenty extra credits had been charged. He took a long swig of the bitter brew, then nearly choked when the bartender said, "I'm Naggers."

"What? I'm here to locate a woman named Jannis Reylock," Teir blurted.

Naggers grabbed a rag and casually polished a brass fitting. "Who did you say?"

"Jannis Reylock. I'm Teir Reylock, her son," he lied.

The man's eyebrows shot up, and he gave Teir a sharp glance. "Never knew Jannis had no son."

"So you *do* know her." Teir leaned forward.

Naggers nodded slowly, his dark eyes sweeping the room to see if anyone was watching them. Groups of men sat around in clusters, drinking and talking. The loud chatter in the room would preclude their being overheard, and no one else sat near the bar.

"You saw my name when you charged my data card," Teir said quietly. "You know I tell the truth. I tried to locate Jannis at the comm center, but there are no Reylocks listed in this city." When Naggers didn't respond, Teir said in as sincere a tone as he could muster, "I was sent to live with my aunt when I was just a babe. Please, I'll be happy to reimburse you for your trouble if you help me locate my mother."

Naggers glared at him. "It's not credits I want, young 'un. I'll tell you what. I'll let Jannis know you're here. If she wants to see you, then we'll take it from there."

Teir looked at the man's set mouth and nodded. "When will I know?"

"Come back tonight at nineteen hundred hauras."

Teir finished his brew and left. He had no intention of hanging around for several more hauras. Checking the back of the saloon for alternate exits, he found an opening into a narrow alley and situated himself behind a public connector pole and waited. If he was right, Naggers should be coming out soon.

Sure enough, about fifteen minutes later, the older man hobbled out the rear door of the saloon. He'd drawn a cloak around his shoulders, but his scraggly gray hair was unmistakable. Teir followed him at a discreet distance. The man was good, as though he was used to evading shadows, but Teir was even better.

Naggers ended up taking a people-mover to a sparsely occupied section of town on the outskirts of the bremen section. There were no pretty rows of houses and well-tended lawns here. This area was desolate, almost rural.

Teir followed Naggers on foot some distance, leaving the paved roadway and walking across a meadow until he came to a small farm near a forest. A cottage stood amidst vegetable fields laid out neatly in the back. A flower garden graced the front lawn. On either side were groves of tall trees, dark and mysterious even in the late afternoon light.

Teir slunk into the shadows behind a tree and watched as Naggers announced his presence to an electronic door sentry. The door opened, and the old man disappeared inside the cottage.

Less than ten minutes later, he emerged and hastened away. Teir didn't bother to follow him, being more interested in the occupant of the cottage. This could be where Jannis was hiding.

When Naggers was out of sight, Teir approached the front door. "I'm a friend of Catharta's," he told the electronic sentry.

The door swung open. Facing him was a plumper version of his aunt, with blue eyes and silvery hair pulled back into a bun. She wore a comfortable work dress in a colorful print pattern.

"Who are you?" she asked, her tone curt.

"I'm Teir Reylock, *mother*."

Her mouth gaped open. "You can't be. Naggers said a man claimed to be him, but…" Speechless, she stared at him.

Teir held out his data link for her to confirm his identification. "Aunt Catharta sent me. May I come in?"

He glanced around. The surrounding trees seemed to be encroaching on the tiny house. An eerie feeling pricked the hairs on his nape. Surely Naggers hadn't figured he would follow and had set him up. Still, a feeling of foreboding accompanied him inside as he entered at Jannis's invitation.

"Why are you here?" she asked, closing the door and facing him.

Teir had expected her to be friendlier. "Aunt Catharta told me what she knew about my birth. I need proof of my birthright."

"You don't want it. It's dangerous for you to be here."

"What possible danger can there be now?" He surveyed the comfortably furnished living room, wondering if she'd invite him to take a seat.

"There are those who miss the old aristocracy," Jannis said in a low voice. "They would put you on the throne in an instant if they had the chance. By right of birth, you would be Preim."

"I don't want to be Preim," Teir said impatiently. "I'm happy with my position in the Defense League. Besides, the blasted government is a republic now. Why should they care?"

"The death sentence remains in effect. Any royals found are still under orders to be executed."

"That's absurd." By the stars, it reminded him of Sarina's situation with the High Council. How incredible that someone would want him dead now because of what had happened twenty-nine annums ago.

"Nevertheless, it remains a threat," Jannis said. "You must leave at once."

"After you give me the evidence I need."

Jannis put her hands on her hips. She was small like Catharta but determined in her expression. "Why do you want it?"

"Can we sit down?" At her nod, Teir took a seat in the living room. After Jannis sat in a lounger opposite him, he told her about Sarina, the legend, and where they both fit in.

"I've heard about the Great Healer," Jannis said. "Yes, yes, it could be true. You *do* meet the criteria, but I'd never have thought—"

She rose, rushing over to embrace him, and Teir stood and endured a crushing hug.

"I loved the preima as I would my own daughter," Jannis said with a sniffle after they stepped apart. "Ah, what a tragedy that befell us all. They killed the other servants, you know. I was lucky to have escaped. I feared they'd come after me, so I've stayed in hiding for many annums. The quiet life suits me. But even now, I often get the feeling I'm being watched."

She grasped his arm with a fond smile. "Anyway, thank the stars you are well and strong. I wish we had time to get to know each other, but you must not linger. The items you seek are buried out back. I have not looked at them since the day I took you from my dear lady and gave you to my sister."

He followed her outdoors and into a field where leafy greens grew in cultivated rows.

"I sell my vegetables to a vendor at the market," Jannis explained, stooping to pick up a small trowel. "It gives me an income that helps me pay my taxes."

The air cooled as the sol began its descent. Teir glanced at the surrounding forest as he and Jannis walked down a dirt lane between the rows of vegetables.

She asked him about his work, and he told her about his ship, his crew, and some of their missions. He stopped talking when his boots sank into a puddle of mud and he had to yank them out with a loud sucking noise.

"It rained recently and can be wet out here," Jannis said. "But don't worry. It's drier up ahead, and your valuables are well protected. In truth, I shall be glad to be rid of them."

They came to a break in the row of plants. Handing him the trowel, she stepped aside.

Teir crouched where she'd indicated and began digging. His heart raced. Was this the proof he so desperately needed? He'd soon find out.

The tool struck a solid object, and he cleared away the dirt to uncover a small metal chest.

"Lift it out. Don't worry, you can't damage anything." Jannis watched as he raised the chest from the hole. "Put it down. I'll open it, and you can take the contents. Then we'll rebury the chest. I don't want it in my house."

Teir placed it in front of her, then stepped back. An old keypad-style lock was in place, but Jannis knew the code. When the faint click sounded, she gave a grunt of satisfaction.

"Open it, Teir." She straightened her spine and gestured to him.

He bent to lift the lid. Inside was a waterproof pouch that held three objects. One was a heavy gold chain with a medallion. Another was a gold signet ring. And the third was a smooth silvery-gray stone with a lustrous finish and a pointed end.

"I understand the stone belonged to your maternal grandmother," Jannis said. "I have no idea of its importance, but the preima insisted I keep it for you. The medallion and the ring display the crest of the Retti dynasty."

Standing upright, Teir put the rock in his pocket and examined the other pieces in his hand. "What does this crest represent?" It was circular with spokes around the circumference.

"It is the sol. Originally, the preim's authority derived from divine right. The ancient people worshiped the sol, and they believed their preims were the sol god in human form." She paused. "The position of preim has always been hereditary, and you are the last of the line."

"I'm not interested in being any blasted preim. I just want to marry Sarina." Teir took the medallion and hung it around his neck, hiding it under his white shirt. The ring he put in his inner vest pocket.

"Don't let anyone see them," Jannis warned as he put the metal chest back in the ground and refilled the hole.

Together, they started back toward the cottage. Teir hadn't noticed how far out in the fields they'd gone. An ominous rumble sounded as they weaved through the narrow dirt lanes.

"What's that noise?" he said, his inner alarm bells ringing.

Jannis hadn't been paying attention, lost in memories of the past. Now as she heard it, she cried, "Speeders! The sentries must have found you. We must hurry."

Black dots loomed on the horizon and rapidly grew larger.

Teir increased his pace. "They may not be coming here."

But as he ran, a quick glance over his shoulder confirmed the speeders were definitely headed in their direction. There were at least a dozen of them.

Blast! If he had landed his shuttle, he could have used his remote unit to escape. But since his ship was at the spaceport, they were trapped.

"How could anyone know about me? Do you think Naggers told them?"

"Naggers wouldn't betray us. They must have been keeping watch using long-range sensors. I've always felt I was under surveillance." Jannis came to a standstill.

"Come on," Teir yelled, stopping and turning. The speeders were nearly upon them.

She sighed. "It's no use. I'm sorry, Teir."

He drew his shooter as the speeders landed, surrounding them only meters from the cottage. Uniformed sentries, weapons aimed, jumped out and encircled them.

"Lower your shooter," an officer commanded, stepping forward.

"I'm Captain Teir Reylock of the Coalition Defense League. You've no right to detain me."

"Drop your weapon," the officer snapped.

Realizing he was hopelessly outnumbered, Teir gave a grunt of disgust and threw his gun to the ground.

A couple of other speeders landed with civilians. Teir recognized at once they were men of authority.

"I am Provost of this province," said the portly gentleman with graying hair. He pointed to the tall man beside him. "This is the Justice of Minna. What is your business here, Captain?"

"I came to see my mother." Teir thrust his chin forward.

The provost nodded to a sentry who stalked over.

"Arms up," the sentry ordered.

"Go to Zor."

The clicks of triggers registered in his ears. Hastily, Teir complied.

The sentry frisked him, emptying his pockets and relieving him of his hidden blade and Nokout gas grenade. Teir was ordered to remain standing, hands on his head, while the two civilians examined his belongings.

"Data link, a set of data cards, one rock—and what is this?" The provost picked up his ring. "A signet ring with the royal crest! How very interesting, Captain."

Straightening, the provost strode to where Teir stood motionless. He ripped open Teir's shirt and gave an exclamation of triumph. "A medallion with the emblem of the Preim! So, you've come to claim your inheritance, have you?"

"Don't be ridiculous," Teir said, his blood rushing to his face. "Those are souvenirs, that's all. I'm just visiting Vilaran. Let me go back to my ship, and I'll leave at once."

"You might as well be truthful with us. We know who you are," said the justice, a malevolent-looking fellow with a thin face.

"Of course you do. I just told you." Teir lowered his arms. "I'm Captain Teir Reylock—"

"*Silence!* We always knew the infants had been switched. The dead babe had brown hair, not black like yours. We've been keeping watch on the preima's maid for annums, waiting for you to return. Now the death sentence can be carried out at last. The woman will be next. All traitors to the Republic are executed. Never again will the taint of imperialism contaminate our world. Prepare yourself, Captain. You're about to meet your ancestors."

"You can't do this," Teir shouted as the sentries dragged Jannis off to the side. The old woman didn't even whimper. Her expression of terror had changed to one of sad resignation. "I'm an officer in the Defense League. Glotaj, the Supreme Regent, will be enraged if you harm me."

"Glotaj and the Coalition have no authority here. This is a local issue," the provost said. He stood on the sidelines, content to let the judge do the dirty work.

"Ready," the justice said.

The sentries took aim.

"No!" Teir threw himself at the nearest trooper. The man's rifle butt caught him on the temple, and he crashed to the ground.

He lay there, despairing of his life and his lost future.

In another instant, it would all end.

Chapter Twenty-Seven

Sensing that something catastrophic was about to occur, Sarina had urged Rolf to go at warp speed to Vilaran. They'd arrived at the spaceport and checked through the dockmaster's manifest to find the *Valiant* listed.

Rolf had asserted his authority as a member of the High Council to gain entry to the vessel. Using the ship's scanners, which were programmed for Teir's molecular pattern, they were able to locate him on the outskirts of Minna. Sarina suggested using the shuttle to reach him.

"It's faster than surface transportation and is equipped with defense systems. We don't know what kind of situation we'll be facing." She couldn't help feeling an overwhelming sense of doom.

Rolf agreed. He had a bad feeling, too. Reylock should never have come here alone. If anything happened to him, it would interfere with the legend's fulfillment.

"What's going on?" Sarina asked as they approached Teir's position. Dozens of figures milled around in a field by a cottage.

"We'll find out soon enough." Rolf brought the shuttle down for a landing.

Sarina leapt from her seat and dashed to the hatchway. She hit the release and the hatch popped, the steps unfolding to the ground. Behind her, Rolf hollered out a warning.

She ran outside. Dear God, Teir was lying on the ground. Soldiers aimed weapons at him.

He caught sight of her, and she saw a flash of joy in his eyes just as a mean-looking official shouted, "Fire!"

Sarina screamed as the weapons discharged. Teir's body jerked and then he went still.

"Teir! Oh God, no." She crashed through the barrier of troops and knelt beside him.

The lasers had left scorch marks where they'd burned through his clothing and outer layer of skin. She scooped him up in her arms, cradling his broken body. His skin was ashen, his breath rattling in his throat. Sarina hugged him to her, sobbing his name.

Don't die, Teir. I love you so. Please don't die now that we're together again.

Tears ran down her cheeks. She couldn't lose him.

As she held him in her arms, conscious of nothing but her love for him, a strange sensation tingled along her nerves. At first it felt as though a charge of electricity were building inside her body. Her senses vibrated with an intensity she'd never felt before.

The feeling shifted to her hands. Her right palm grew warm, then fiery hot. Sarina looked down. The birthmark on her palm was glowing.

Without knowing exactly what she was doing or why, Sarina turned her palm toward Teir. A beam of light shot out from the glowing circle. It radiated over Teir's body, enclosing him together with her in a pulsating energy field.

Closing her eyes, Sarina let her aura bathe them both in the light of love. And then something incredible happened. All of a sudden, she was a separate entity, hovering in the air. She could see her body down on the ground with Teir. His aura was being pulled into hers, and they merged, one consciousness, one being.

And then they separated to rejoin their bodies, and the bright light faded.

Teir's eyelids fluttered open. A slow smile curved his mouth as he looked up at her, his head in her lap.

"Sarina," he whispered, awed by what he'd just experienced.

"I know," she said. "I love you."

"I love you, too." Aware that she'd healed his body, he drew her down and kissed her with all his pent-up passion, hungering for her taste and her touch. He never wanted to let her go.

Not caring who watched, she entwined herself in his embrace. His powerful arms enveloped her. His tongue probed inside her mouth and she met it with her own greedy thrusts. This wasn't enough. She wanted more of him.

They became aware of Cam'brii explaining the legend and their part in it to the astonished soldiers and their superiors.

"Forgive us, we had no idea," the provost said, throwing himself on the ground in front of them.

Teir and Sarina sprang apart, their faces flushed with embarrassment.

"Yes, yes," the justice said, his pallid complexion even more colorless than usual. "We didn't realize you were the Raimorrdan of the legend."

While Teir stood to accept their apologies, Sarina rose and faced Rolf. He gave her a deep bow. When he straightened, his gaze was full of wonder. "You truly are the Great Healer. You have performed a miracle on this day. I will do everything in my power to assist you and your chosen one."

"I owe you my thanks," Teir said, holding out his hand to the councilor.

Rolf took it, and the two shared a firm handshake. "Did you get the proof you need for the High Council? Although after I tell them what happened here, they shouldn't require it."

Teir retrieved his possessions. He pocketed the rock. Holding out the signet ring and the medallion, he said, "Here is the proof that I am highly placed. But I have yet to learn if I have been born under the sign of the circle."

"I can help you," said Jannis, who appeared at his side. "You were born in the preima's chamber at the palace, now the Museum of History. The answer you seek is there."

They set off immediately for the former palace. Teir and Jannis went with Rolf and Sarina in the shuttle. They landed on the wide lawn bordering the town square, followed by the sentries on their speeders who had now been assigned to act as their armed escort.

The museum was closed for the day, but the justice knew the combination to open the door. Commanding the lights to rise, he accompanied them inside.

"The preima had her chamber on the second floor," he explained, leading the way up a wide curving staircase.

Sarina gazed around in wonder. The palace was ornately decorated. It amazed her how the contents had been so well preserved.

The beauty of the preima's chamber took her breath away. Restoration work must have been done here, because the silken coverlet on the massive bed appeared in prime condition, as did the matching rose-colored drapes. But what caught her attention was the emblem on the wall above the preima's bed.

"This is where Teir was born?" she asked Jannis. Teir had introduced them earlier.

"Aye," Jannis said, staring at the same symbol that transfixed Sarina.

Teir frowned. "I don't get it."

"Don't you see?" Sarina pointed to the emblem. *"That* is a circle!"

"So what? It's the crest of the Retti dynasty and symbolizes the sol. See the rays coming out of the—" Then it dawned on him what he'd been about to say. *Out of the circle.* The evidence was right before his eyes.

No strange astronomical event had heralded his birth. He'd been born under the symbol that had served his family for eons.

"Storms of the sun, I think that's it." He turned to Sarina, his heart pounding. "Do you know what this means?"

She nodded, her face radiant. "Now we can be wed, my love. Nothing will stand in our way."

Teir addressed Jannis. "Will you come to Bimordus Two to be my witness, since you were present at my birth?"

"I don't think it's necessary for her to travel all that distance," said Lord Cam'brii. "If you record a mini-holovid with your data link, that will serve the same purpose. And you have the ring and medallion."

Teir now wore both, no longer afraid to display his heritage. No one would dare challenge him after what their leaders had witnessed.

"Then there's no need to remain on Vilaran," Teir said. "What of your transport?"

"We ran into some geckos on the way who weren't too friendly. My ship is in need of repairs. I suggest we all return to Bimordus Two on the *Valiant.*"

Teir gave him a nod then took Jannis's hands in his own. "I owe you a debt of gratitude. You saved my life when I was a child, and you kept my secret safe all these annums. What can I do to repay you?"

Jannis smiled, her eyes crinkling with happiness. "Seeing you alive and well is payment enough. I just want to return home."

"I'm sure that can be arranged." He released her and went to speak with the justice. "A sentry will take you on a speeder whenever you're ready to go," he told her a few minutes later. "Remember, if you ever need anything, call on me."

He walked outside with Sarina and Rolf.

"It got dark out fast," the councilor remarked, glancing overhead. "Is sol setting always so abrupt here?"

"I wouldn't know. Do you hear that strange noise?" Teir peered at the blackened sky. A strong breeze ruffled his hair, and an eerie whistling hummed in his ears.

"The sky looks weird," Sarina said with a shiver. She clung to Teir, her arm in his.

"Look," Rolf cried.

A bright dot became evident far above in the darkened sky. It grew larger, closer, and then became a glowing fireball streaking across the heavens. Behind it trailed a putrid yellow stream of cosmic dust.

"The comet!" Sarina's jaw dropped in horror.

"So your theory was correct," Rolf said. "Do you think Wagroob had time to launch his probe?"

"I hope so. Let's get to the *Valiant* and ask him."

They filed into the shuttle and hurriedly lifted off. Sarina explained her theories about the Farg to Teir on their way to the spaceport. Not much later, they secured themselves inside his ship and prepared for departure.

"I've got the Research Station on subspace radio," Teir said to Sarina on the bridge. Rolf sat beside him in the copilot's seat, and Sarina had moved to Wren's nav console off to the side.

"You're on Vilaran?" Wagroob said, his eyes wide as he stared at them on the viewscreen. "How in Zor did you get there? Never mind—did you see it? The telemetry readings are incredible."

"Yes," Sarina replied. "The comet streaked through the sky like a ball of fire."

"And it had a dust tail as predicted?"

"Correct. You could almost see the yellow particles falling from it like a light rain."

"That comet was an artificial satellite. And those dust particles carried the Farg," Wagroob pronounced in a solemn tone.

"What?" Rolf and Teir said in unison.

"We haven't been able to isolate the disease organism because it's not a naturally occurring phenomenon. Someone has used molecular alteration technology to change the microbe in such a way that it couldn't be detected using normal scientific methods. We ran an analysis of the cosmic dust. The infectious particles in the dust fall to the planet's surface, entering the water supply, and there you have it. An entire world is contaminated."

"My God!" Sarina exclaimed. "But who—?"

"The Morgots, my dear. You said yourself they benefited the most from these conquests. Each planet infected with the plague is rich in natural resources. It all makes sense. They've been manufacturing these satellites and disguising them as comets. These vehicles carry the seeds for the disease. The Morgots send them to the planets they want to conquer, where the satellite self-destructs after the planet's atmosphere has been seeded. Hence the astronomical charts show no trace of them. Comets have always been regarded as harbingers of evil, and these days are no exception. The Morgots have played to our superstitions."

Teir spoke up. "Now that we know how it's being done, what can we do to stop them from releasing more of these deadly missiles?"

"The battle in the Tendraan system has forced the Morgots to retreat," Wagroob replied. "I don't think we'll have to worry about another comet coming our way for quite some time." His voice deepened. "Sarina, if you truly are the Great Healer, you need to save the people of Vilaran. They have all been exposed to the plague, and so have your friends. Do something about it." With those words, Wagroob signed off.

Teir and Rolf both turned in their seats to stare at her.

"Me?" she said, feeling put on the spot. "What can I do?"

"You healed me with your love," Teir answered. "Do you think it's strong enough to heal a world?"

"We can find out. I'll need to go outside."

Teir powered down the ship. They proceeded to the exit.

"Now what?" Sarina asked. They'd moved away from the launchpads and stood on a patch of grass at the spaceport.

"Go ahead and do your thing," Teir said.

"Right here? What if nothing happens?"

Teir's blue eyes filled with faith and love. "You can do it. Try raising your palm, the one with the birthmark."

Sarina lifted her hand and closed her eyes to concentrate. After a few minutes, she cracked her eyelids open. "Well? Did anything happen?"

"The circle didn't even glow," Teir said with a note of disappointment.

She lowered her arm. "I don't know how to control my healing power. It works with you, but that's all."

Rolf gestured at them. "You're forgetting something. The legend states you have to wed your Raimorrdan. You and Teir have been joined in spirit, but not in name. Your healing power may have been activated by your love so that it works for Teir, but in order for you to aid others, you and he must be wed. Otherwise, the terms of the legend are not complete."

"But that means we'll have to return to Bimordus Two to get the High Council's approval," Teir objected. "It might take weeks. My people will die before we return."

Rolf appeared thoughtful. "We could request a conference call to resolve the issue. If the High Council gives permission, you can be married here."

Sarina grunted. "Do you really think Glotaj would agree after all the fuss he's made about my marriage?"

"Let me take care of it." The councilor requisitioned a speeder, and they departed for the government seat in the capital city. Once there, he told a sentry to summon the president.

A mature woman dressed in a business suit, President Lara Sanderson greeted them inside the parliament building.

"What can I do for you?" the planetary leader asked. She had apparently heard of their earlier adventures.

Rolf instructed her, and soon they found themselves seated in a conference room. A call was patched through directly to Glotaj. Rolf related recent events to him.

"Congratulations," the regent said, his holographic image projected on the table. "Captain Reylock, I hope you understand my reasons for keeping your secret all these annums."

Teir grimaced. "Considering the reception I got here, yes sir, I do."

"My best wishes to you both. Rolf, I hope you're not too disappointed?"

Rolf gave a wry smile as Sarina and Teir gazed at him. They sat together holding hands across the table.

"Sarina is a remarkable woman, and the captain is a lucky man to have her," he said without any hint of resentment. "Now what about getting the High Council's approval? We have to go forward with this matter quickly. Sarina and I were intercepted by a gecko ship on our way here. Someone in the government betrayed us. This means there's a mole among the High Council, Your Excellency. I am hoping that when the First Amendment passes, these assassination attempts will stop. The Souks must be behind them."

"Let's deal with one problem at a time," Glotaj said. "Hold tight. I'll get back to you."

They terminated communications. While waiting, Teir suggested they get something to eat. They had just finished their meal when Glotaj's call came through. This time, he was not alone. He sat in the Council Chamber with the other eleven members. The majority approved the wedding on Vilaran. Daimon gave the only objection.

Rolf promised to holovid the wedding so it could be seen live on Bimordus Two, and then Teir and Sarina received the blessings of the High Council before signing off.

President Sanderson beamed at them. "The Great Healer is going to be married here. The legend is coming true on our own soil. It's a great honor for us!" But then her fervor cooled. "I have already received reports of people falling ill. I pray you will be able to eradicate this pestilence. The arrangements for your marriage will take place at once."

Rolf accompanied the president from the room to assist in the preparations. He'd agreed to retrieve Jannis, who Sarina and Teir requested be present. The local justice would officiate. The holovid equipment had to be set up and the Grand Hall decorated. There was much to be done, and very little time in which to do it.

Left alone, Teir faced Sarina. They'd risen, and now he took her hands in his. "Are you sure this is what you want?" he asked. "I don't have Lord Cam'brii's aristocratic bearing. I might have royal blood, but I haven't been raised that way."

Sarina regarded him tenderly. How sweet that he needed reassurance. "Rolf can be too formal at times. Your lifestyle suits me better."

"Perhaps so, but you'll be expected to live on Bimordus Two. My job will keep me away more often than not."

"If my healing power works after we wed, I'll have a lot of traveling to do," she told him. "Many different peoples will require my services. I'll need an escort that I can trust. Besides, I want to see the galaxy. You don't think your crew would mind if I joined you on the *Valiant,* do you?"

Teir laughed. "They'll be thrilled to have you aboard. Oh, my sweet, I love you so." His head descended, and he kissed her.

Chapter Twenty-Eight

Sarina reveled in the pressure of Teir's lips and the masculine taste of him. She opened her mouth, letting his tongue plunder hers, meeting it with her own. Running her fingers through his hair, she thought about how much she loved him. She couldn't wait until they were alone to do this—and more—every day.

"Pardon," Rolf's voice said.

They broke apart and turned toward him questioningly. Beside him stood a young woman, obviously embarrassed to have come upon them in each other's embrace.

"This is Zeem. She'll help you get ready for the wedding, Sarina. I'll assist you, Captain," he told Teir.

Sarina hoped the two men would become friends. She said farewell and followed Zeem through a confusing maze of corridors. They ended up in a suite of rooms available for visiting dignitaries.

"I'll get dressed for the ceremony while you use the sanitary," Zeem told her. "Are you hungry? I can order you a snack if you wish."

"No, thanks. We ate earlier." Sarina went into the restroom to wash and remove her clothing.

By the time she came out clad in a towel, Zeem was already dressed in a jade gown. She wore the yellow yoke of office around her neck, signifying her status as a high government official. She'd twisted her shiny black hair atop her head under a tall green headdress with tiny bells that jingled when she walked.

"What am I to wear?" Sarina hadn't even thought about a wedding dress.

Zeem approached the fabricator. A few minutes later, she had produced a complete bridal ensemble, from a strapless bra down to a pair of ivory satin shoes.

"It's beautiful!" Sarina exclaimed, gaping at the wedding gown.

"Go ahead and put it on." Zeem held the dress up so Sarina could step into it. She fastened the back as Sarina stood in front of a mirror.

Threads of gold outlined the bodice that tapered to a narrow waist banded by sparkling crystals. The silken folds of the gown flowed to the ground. The gown's off-the-shoulder sleeves were lined with gold lame in rich contrast to the ivory color of the dress. Completing the effect was an ivory lace veil that Zeem draped over Sarina's head.

"This tiara will hold your veil in place." Zeem set the piece atop Sarina's head as a chronometer chimed the haura. "Just in time! The ceremony is about to begin."

Equipment had been set up to beam the wedding via satellites and deep space relays so everyone could see it on their holovid units. Billions of eyes would be focused on them, Sarina thought nervously, and then those same billions would be watching to see if her healing power materialized.

A hush fell over the assemblage as she appeared at the entrance to the Grand Hall. A long aisle stretched before her, and Teir stood at the opposite end.

Rolf, Jannis, President Sanderson, and the Minister of Justice waited beyond. Strangers stared at Sarina as she walked down the aisle, trying to absorb the moment. The surrealness of it took her breath away. Was she really going to marry Teir, the man of her dreams?

String music played softly in the background. She gave a radiant smile as she neared her bridegroom. Teir wore a white military dress uniform with gold braid, and she thought he'd never looked more magnificent.

"You're gorgeous. You look like a goddess," he murmured

as he took her hand. Together, they turned and approached the officiant.

Rolf and Jannis took up positions on either side of them, and the justice began the ritual. The ceremony concluded when Teir placed his signet ring on Sarina's finger and kissed her.

Loud applause broke them apart. Holding hands, they headed back down the aisle and emerged outdoors. Sarina grinned and gazed with adoration at her husband.

"We are married. I can't believe it."

"I know. You are mine, now and forever."

Responding to the cheering crowds, they raised their clasped hands toward the sky.

And from their joined hands shot out a glowing ray of light. It expanded, enveloping them in a pulsating energy field. The crowd gasped and fell into a stunned silence as the glow spread upward and out until it became a blinding radiance that surrounded the globe.

Sarina's body tingled and the hairs on her arms stood on end. Once again, their auras joined and melded into one. She wanted to stay united with her beloved, but there was work to be done. Reluctantly, she stepped apart. Their separation broke the circle of light and the radiance extinguished.

At Sarina's urging, the scientists tested their planet's water supplies and found those sources to be clean. No harmful plague organisms were evident.

A miracle had happened.

Sarina had cleansed Vilaran and all her people of the Farg.

****

On the way back to Bimordus Two, Sarina and Teir stopped off at Alpha Omega Two to heal Aunt Catharta. They brought Jannis along to stay with her sister during her convalescence. Their joyful reunion brought tears to Sarina's eyes.

From there, Sarina and Teir journeyed to Tendraa to practice their newfound power. Here they linked up with Teir's crew, who were patrolling the area after the Morgot defeat. They returned to Bimordus Two on board the *Valiant*.

Rolf had gone on ahead, taking his own transport back to the Coalition capital. He'd learned that Daimon had transferred credits via a middleman to the Souks right before the gecko attack. Since an economic embargo was in effect against the Souks, the transaction was illegal.

Daimon confessed he'd set up the ambush, hoping to prevent Lord Cam'brii's marriage from taking place. Forced to resign in disgrace, the R.O.F. leader admitted the legend was true, but it only reaffirmed his belief that the Raimorrdans were too powerful.

The Liege Lord of Tendraa sent a message to the Coalition that he wished full partnership. After the defeat of the Morgots and the visit by the Great Healer who had eradicated the Farg, he wished to proceed into the modern age. His petition was accepted and Tendraa entered into full diplomatic relations.

Mantra was offered the vacant position left by Daimon on the High Council. He eagerly accepted.

Several important votes took place. The execution decree that had threatened Sarina was declared invalid and struck from the legislative books. The R.O.F.'s proposal to dissolve the Coalition was voted on and defeated. And the First Amendment passed, much to Rolf's enduring delight.

The councilor wasn't totally satisfied, however. Rumors said someone on Souk still had a price on his head, and this was confirmed by another thwarted assassination attempt. Now that the First Amendment was no longer an issue, Rolf wondered why he was still a target.

Teir had told him about Bdan's demand to learn his personal routine. Who had made the request and why? Obviously, the Souks still had a mole in their government who was reporting on his movements. Daimon apparently wasn't the only one leaking information.

Souk pirate attacks on civilian vessels continued to take their toll of lives and captives. With his obligation to Gayla's parents in mind, Rolf determined to stop the Souks once and for all. When a communication arrived that the resistance leaders on Souk requested assistance, he volunteered to go to the planet and establish contact.

While on Souk, Rolf also intended to find out who wanted him dead. He had a chance to discover the identity of the mole there as well. Intelligence reported that the pashas were congregating at a special conference and the paid informant would be present. It was a chance to accomplish all of his goals at once, and he couldn't wait to leave.

He strolled toward the rotunda in the Great Hall along with his fellow councilors, Glotaj, Sarina, and Teir. Besides the regent, the legendary duo were the only ones aware of his secret mission to Souk. Once he left Bimordus Two, it would be a long time before he'd see them again.

"We have much to be thankful for," Glotaj said as they approached the Auricle. All of them wore dark glasses except for Sarina. "The Morgots have returned to their home world, and the Farg is finally being eliminated. Two major threats to the Coalition have been removed. We owe you a debt of gratitude, Sarina."

"Wagroob figured out why the Farg is sensitive to my power," she replied. "The disease organism reacts to radiant energy. Planets closer to their stars are less virulently affected—not because of the heat or visible light from the sun, but because of the invisible radiation, the same kind of electromagnetic energy that my healing aura provides. He thinks that is why my incubation period was so long. My body was trying to fight off the disease, but my aura wasn't strong enough yet to be successful."

Methods of treatment had already been devised. Hundreds of worlds were being irradiated with a form of energy that was harmless to the inhabitants but deadly to the disease organism.

Sarina had learned, to her dismay, that her healing powers were limited in effectiveness to those illnesses responsive to a specific band of radiation. Unfortunately, she couldn't cure every ailment that would ever exist.

At least she was able to use her healing aura alone, as it seemed to be strengthening with use. Uniting with Teir was like a booster. At first, she'd needed him to initiate her power. Now, it was no longer necessary for her to touch him physically. Their spiritual link was enough.

Calls for her services were frequent. The *Valiant* was assigned to transport her wherever she was needed. So far, Sarina had found her role highly gratifying.

Teir was happy because he was still able to perform his duty as chief troubleshooter for the Defense League. There were always areas of conflict or natural disasters that called for outside assistance, so they both had their work cut out for them.

Halting in front of the Auricle, Glotaj said, "This is where it all started. The Auricle glowed, and it led us to you, Sarina."

"Look, it's similar in shape to my worry stone. That's what I wanted to show you." She'd retrieved the lustrous silvery-gray stone from its hiding place on Teir's ship and had requested they all gather here. Now as she held it up, Teir drew out his own stone, the one left him by his maternal grandmother. Both his stone and Sarina's were similar to the amulet worn by Salla, the Crigellan female on Souk. Teir had told Sarina about Salla, wondering what the stones signified, and she'd replied that they'd find the answer here.

Clutching their respective rocks, Sarina and Teir held hands. To nobody's surprise, the Auricle's glow increased and a circle of light shot out from the monument. From within the blinding brightness, a holographic image of a woman's face materialized.

"My name is Malryn," she told them, waves of pure white hair framing her youthful face. "Welcome, Sarina. For eons, your coming has been foretold. I sent this herald to summon you and later to tell you this story.

"I come from a planet called Shimera. We were an advanced race of humans who sought to understand the complexities of the mind. We expanded our knowledge of brain function and improved our ability to control thoughts. And then, among a group of highly sensitive individuals such as myself, a new phenomenon emerged. We became able to manipulate our aura, the electromagnetic field that surrounds the body. We could even transfer the energy from our aura into another being. We began to call ourselves Auranians.

"Our difference frightened others who were skeptical of our power. This ability was not completely understood, and even though we used it only for good, such as to heal the sick, there were those who feared the power could be turned to evil.

"An atmosphere of fear and doubt prevailed, and a terrible persecution forced us to flee the planet. Terrified for our lives, we scattered among the stars. Search parties were sent to scour the solar systems and eliminate us, such was the fear of the power of the Aura, a fear that it could reach all the way back to Shimera itself to punish the aggressors. But we wished only to be left in peace, so we hid among alien populations, interbreeding and diluting the bloodline until we faded from memory.

"Through a mistake in navigation, Sarina, your ancestors reached the planet Earth. The small group settled in Salem, Massachusetts. When one female revealed her power by healing a sick child, she was accused of witchcraft and burned at the stake. The female was survived by a daughter. As a result of her mother's death, the girl believed the power to be a curse. She suppressed her own innate ability and warned her children against expressing any emotions that might trigger the power. As the gene passed down through the generations, so did her warning.

"For eons, the power lay dormant—until your birth. You were destined to awaken the collective consciousness, to rouse the other Auranians into declaring their heritage. Thus will begin a new era of love and peace."

Sarina broke in. "But how did you know this?"

"It was foreseen by the Blood Crystal," the woman's image replied.

Teir gasped at this revelation. "You had the Blood Crystal? Where did it originate?"

Malryn turned her somber gaze on him. "It comes from an otherworldly place not in our realm. It arrived on our planet and showed us what was to come, and it also predicted our destruction. But that was to happen later, after its evil spread and we Auranians were already gone."

"It survived the destruction of your world?"

"The Blood Crystal is not of this sphere of life, so it endured. What happened to it then and how you came upon it is beyond my scope of knowledge."

She addressed Sarina. "Since my power was particularly strong, I was selected to send you this missive. Knowing our world would someday be annihilated, we each took with us a token that would remind us of our heritage and act as a means of identification. Those are the glowstones you and your mate hold. Into this larger repository you call the Auricle, I embedded my message and sent it hurtling into space, knowing it would someday reach you. Now that my responsibility is fulfilled, I go to rest."

"Wait!" Sarina cried, but the image of the woman's face had already dissolved.

The Auricle's light faded. A long moment of silence ensued. Everyone removed their dark glasses since the protection was no longer needed.

Sarina turned to Teir. "I'm an Auranian," she said in an awestruck tone.

"Then I must be one, too. That's what Salla meant when she said, *We are of the people.* There must be others as well."

"We'll have to find them," Sarina determined.

Teir recalled the vision he'd seen on the planet Taurus. The warm light in Sarina's belly represented their child, a child who would be the offspring of two Auranians, the first such to be publicly acknowledged in ages.

"Malryn had said you would awaken the collective consciousness," he told her. "I think once other Auranians see it is safe to reveal themselves, they'll make open declarations of their ancestry. We won't have to worry about finding them. They'll find us."

He paused, taking her hand. "Through our child, the power of a lost people will be restored."

"Our child?" Sarina asked, wondering at the knowing light in his eyes. "What do you mean?"

"You'll find out soon enough, my love."

Epilogue

At last, Mantra went home. Dressed in his ambassadorial robes of office, he strolled down his street, greeting those neighbors who'd survived the terrible Farg.

How joyful it was to hear their laughter. How satisfying to see the doors opened wide to accept the clean, fresh air.

The last vestiges of the plague were gone, and the people no longer lived under a cloud of fear. The threat from the Morgots was past. Peace and harmony prevailed, just as it had in the beginning, and so it would in the end.

Life revolved in a circle, Mantra concluded, a circle of light. His work was to keep that circle revolving.

His journey had just begun.

THE END

Author's Note

Circle of Light began as a dream. It was so compelling that when I woke up, I had to finish the story. This title became my first published book and volume one in The Light-Years Series. It combined my love for science fiction and romance into a rousing adventure. I fervently wished I could step into the shoes of my heroine, Sarina Bretton. It was amazing fun to create new worlds and to let my imagination soar. I hope you enjoyed this imaginative romance and will look for the sequels, *Moonlight Rhapsody* and *Starlight Child*.

****

Thank you for taking the time to read my book. If you liked the story, please consider writing a review at your favorite online bookstore. Reader recommendations are critically important in helping new readers find my work.

For updates on my new releases, giveaways, special offers and events, join my reader list at https://nancyjcohen.com/newsletter. Free Book Sampler for new subscribers.

Moonlight Rhapsody Excerpt

Copyright ©1994 by Nancy J. Cohen

Here's a peek at Book #2 in The Light-Years Series

Rolf had never been caught in such a violent storm. His spacecraft, buffeted in all directions, was like a plaything to the terrible ionic gale raging outside. Sweat beaded his brow as jagged streaks of blue lightning flashed in the darkness, but he was unable to see anything on the viewscreen when the sky lit up except for roiling clouds.

He gripped the armrests of his seat and cursed his luck. His mission was dangerous enough without his ship being caught in a maelstrom. Unable to take a heavier vessel to Souk, he'd chosen a small, lightweight freighter meant for evading radar through swift maneuvers. But in this tempest, the ship was like a feather tossed by the wind. Updrafts and downdrafts battered his vessel, while his stomach wrenched with each thrashing.

He prayed the bursting ion streaks would avoid hitting him as he monitored the computer readouts. Since his descent into the atmosphere was unauthorized, he couldn't request emergency assistance from the Souks. Nor could he risk being detected as he neared the ground.

"By the stars," he cried as a loud jolt rocked the ship, straining him against his safety harness. An ion bolt had hit home. The lights went out, then flickered red as the backup system kicked in. Sirens wailed as a series of warning lights flashed on his display panel.

"Systems overload," warned the computer's impersonal female voice. "Switching off actuator valves one and two to reroute flow streams. Core fuel injectors remain operative."

The main power generator was out. Hopefully, the secondary reactor conduits would hold. He shouldn't worry about the blasted Souks picking up his approach. Concentrating on a safe landing was more important.

"Changing nose angle by point zero two five degrees," the computer intoned.

Sniffing, Rolf wondered at the pungent odor in the air. His eyes watered, and he blinked to clear his vision.

The helm didn't seem to be responding to the computer's command. According to the instrumentation, the ship was heading downward at an increasingly sharp angle.

As a bolt of charged ion particles lit the sky, he caught a glimpse of the planet's surface looming below. He scanned the nav readouts for the altitude. According to the instruments, he was at fifteen kilometers. But from the view, he'd put his altitude around nine. The navigational sensors must be off. By the corona, that meant he could have strayed off course. He'd been warned against flying over—

A lurch nearly tossed his stomach contents onto his lap. A loud claxon sounded as the red lights dimmed and then came back on.

The computer was down. Rolf suppressed a surge of panic and switched to manual override. Grabbing the control column, he yanked it back to raise the nose. The ship didn't respond, continuing its downward plunge toward the planet's surface.

Gods, the feed lines from the bimanthium crystal chamber must be inoperative.

Maybe he could reroute some of the remaining fuel. Sweat beading his brow, he nipped shut several switches and toggled others open.

The helm responded sluggishly. He fought the bile rising in his throat and checked the overhead panel. Sure enough, a couple of drive circuits were popped. Instead of seeing six rows of black buttons, he saw four black and two white. He pushed the white buttons to reset them and the secondary generator came back online. Now he'd have short periods of thrust with which to maneuver the ship. If he could make differential power adjustments along the way, the ship might not descend at such a steep angle.

Opening and closing the field relays helped him regain some control. But then a violent downdraft caught his ship and slammed it planetside.

Rolf coughed as the pungent odor on the flight deck grew stronger. White smoke stung his eyes. Burning filaments! He programmed the sequence for fire control, then remembered the computer was down. No time for other measures now.

Souk's surface was gaining, and his ship wasn't slowing nearly enough.

As he broke out of cloud cover, topographical features came into view—mountainous rises and rocky peaks. The lights of civilization glittered beyond the range.

Gods, he was going to crash into that cliff.

He activated the reverse levitators, forcing the screaming engines to break descent, but he was still coming in too fast. Using both hands, he yanked desperately on the control column. He had to exert all his strength just to move it back a notch. A small clearing was straight ahead if he could make it.

The impact came with the screeching sound of tearing metal and a bone-jarring series of thumps. His body strained against the safety harness. An explosion roared in his ears. Billowing smoke choked his nostrils and clouded his vision.

Finally, the vessel reached a shuddering halt.

Stunned, he sat motionless until the air grew too hot for comfort. As he unshackled his restraint, he noticed flames licking the rear. His head swam dizzily when he attempted to rise. He swayed on his feet, the hazy smoke confusing him.

Images of another time, another place, entered his mind. *We're under attack! Energize the laser cannon while I put out the fire... Shields are down... No, they've hit us again.*

His mind a disoriented fog of past and present, Rolf forced himself to stumble forward. Debris littered the cockpit floor. He weaved toward the exit, coughing and choking on the smoke. Heat blasted his face from the raging fire.

His throat clogged. He tripped across a fallen cable and toppled over. A crack to his head brought a white-hot explosion of pain.

The last thing he heard as he slid to the floor was a familiar female voice calling his name. *Rolf...*

****

The Souk officer's bluish skin quivered as he faced the smoking wreck. "Get the pilot out," he ordered his contingent of armed guards.

On patrol in the Beta sector, they'd heard the whine of engines before the spacecraft had become visible to the eye. The sleek vessel had broken through the cloud cover and plummeted toward the ground. At the last moment, the nose raised, and the ship came in nearly level. But it was going too fast, and the crash had been inevitable.

O'mon's floppy ears lifted as his men popped the hatch. A cloud of black smoke billowed from the interior.

"Fire!" Arg yelled, holding his snout-like nose.

"Move quickly," O'mon barked to his point man. "Salvage what you can."

A few moments later, the troops emerged, two of them carrying a limp human form. Arg held a pilot's dispatch case.

"The ship's logs?" O'mon asked.

"Burned are the filaments. The logs are lost. The data cards in this case are all that's left."

"Cargo?"

"None, unless it was concealed. We'd be risking our lives to do a more thorough search. Too intense is the heat."

"Let us r-r-remove ourselves then," O'mon agreed.

The soldiers laid the pilot on the ground in a wooded area at a safe distance from the burning spacecraft. O'mon ordered one of his troops to take a holovid of the ship before it was totally destroyed, as it might be needed for evidence later.

Clasping his hands behind his back, O'mon sniffed gratefully at the cool air. The spicy scent of jell berries was a welcome relief from the pungent odor of smoke. Normally he enjoyed these night patrols. Nothing much happened, and he could listen to the howl of the rabba and relish the breeze from the Upper Drifts. But not tonight. Tonight the peacefulness of the night had been shattered.

O'mon turned his attention to the pilot on the ground. Even unconscious, the human exuded a certain presence. He was tall and muscular. Straight black hair reached his shoulders. He had thick eyebrows, an aquiline nose, and a jaw that showed determination even when slack.

The human's manner of dress gave no indication of his identity. He wore a blue shirt that sagged open, revealing a broad chest and flat abdomen. The shirt was tucked into navy pants, skimming his polished boots.

"Check him for weapons," O'mon ordered. He watched while one of his troops frisked the human.

"He'd make a good krecker," Arg growled, reflecting O'mon's thoughts.

"Aye. We'll see what Bolt says. What could be his business in this sector?"

"Ask him yourself. Coming around is he."

****

Rolf returned to consciousness, gradually becoming aware that he was lying flat on his back on a lumpy, hard surface. An unfamiliar spicy scent entered his nose. Voices murmured around him, harsh barks and growls, but his mind was too foggy to pay attention. He put a hand up to his throbbing temple.

Remembering the crash, he wondered if he was among friends or enemies. Should he use the chemical mind block provided for him now while he had the chance, or should he wait?

The opportunity for this covert mission had come about unexpectedly. Rolf hadn't had time to learn more sophisticated techniques for resisting interrogation in the event he was caught. A memory molecule that only dissolved in saliva had been painted onto his fingernail. When he licked it off, it would provide twenty-four hauras of protection against a Morgot mind probe, the favored technique used by the Souks to make prisoners talk.

While under the influence of the chemical, Rolf would forget any important information that he possessed. But since he only had the one molecule, he'd wait to assess the situation before he used it.

He struggled to a sitting position, choking back a wave of nausea as his vision whirled. After a moment, he realized it was the dead of night, and he was outdoors on the ground. The moving shadows in front of him shifted and solidified.

Four Souks surrounded him, pointing shooters aimed at his chest. The dog faces wore gray uniforms with military insignia.

A frisson of alarm shot through him. He scanned the area, looking for a possible avenue of escape. The twisted shapes of trees came into view. Overhead, clouds scudded by in the nighttime sky. Distant streaks of lightning lit the heavens in fiery blue bolts.

"Who are you?" a gruff voice demanded from beyond his line of vision.

"My name is Sean Breslow," he said, giving his false identity. "Where is this place?"

An officer lumbered into the circle of guards. The Souk was large, his canine features fierce. "Your vessel crashed by the Rocks of Weir. What is your business on Souk?"

"I'm a trader from Arcturus. A client hired me to arrange a deal involving rubellis gemstones." Hopefully, his hastily created cover story would hold up under scrutiny.

"The r-r-rubellis quarries are on the other side of the Cobalt Wash," the Souk officer said with a snarl. "What are you doing by the Rocks of Weir?"

"My navigational system malfunctioned in the storm."

"Liar! Too far off course are you."

"I speak the truth. Examine my ship for yourself. You'll see the nav sensor array was damaged."

"What is the name of your client?"

"That information is confidential."

"His location?"

"I can't tell you."

"You try my patience, human. I do not believe your lies. A spy are you. We shoot spies," the Souk threatened. "Tell me the real r-r-reason you are here."

"I'm telling the truth," Rolf said, tasting fear in his mouth. It was an unfamiliar sensation. Shifting uncomfortably where he sat, he decided to try some inquiries of his own. "Where exactly are the Rocks of Weir?"

"It is I, O'mon, who will ask the questions," the officer said.

"I need to know how far off course I've strayed." His mission had a deadline, and he might miss it if he was detained. Even if he managed to escape, he had no idea how to get to his intended landing site from here. He needed specific information.

O'mon ignored his remark. "The pilot's dispatch case might prove useful. Arg, bring it to me." He leafed through the data cards in the satchel and plucked one out. Putting it in his data link, he grunted with satisfaction after reading the display.

"What is it? Is there a problem?" Rolf asked, hoping they'd accept his falsified documents at face value.

"Sean Breslow is your name," O'mon conceded. "Records of r-r-recent transactions and credit transfers are here. They confirm you are a trader from Arcturus." He scowled at Rolf. "Why is there no evidence of your deal involving rubellis gemstones?"

Arg spoke up. "The r-r-rest of the data cards are damaged. It is possible he tells the truth."

O'mon looked skeptical. "Let us deliver him to Bolt. The satrap may be able to loosen his tongue."

"Who's Bolt?" Rolf touched the back of his head. His fingers came away with a sticky substance. Blood. No wonder he had a headache the size of a boulder.

"Find out soon enough will you. Get up. You go to the pens."

Two guards tugged him to his feet, and before he realized what was happening, they'd whipped his arms behind him and bound his wrists.

"What are you doing?" he cried, wondering why they didn't let him go if his ruse had worked.

"You will speak when asked, human. You're a sumi now," O'mon said. Rolf spoke their language, and he understood sumi was the Souk word for slave. "Disobey, and you will be punished."

"How dare you? I have rights. I'm not a—oof." He grunted and doubled over as O'mon jolted him with an electrifier. "Damn you," he gritted, wincing at the pain in his gut.

"Wish you more, sumi? Come with us quietly will you." O'mon turned to his men and grinned. "A generous bounty will we get for this one." He pointed the punishment stick at Rolf. "Move, human."

Single file, they followed a winding trail through hilly territory dotted with twisted spirals of rock. Huge boulders dotted the landscape in a haphazard pattern while jagged cliffs stretched toward the sky. Traveling through the eerie landscape, Rolf stumbled several times but was forced to keep going, his feet tripping over the rocky paths, his arms bound at his back. Tree branches whipped his face as the night seemed to sing in empathy for him. A haunting whisper hung on the breeze, a melancholy note as the wind whistled through the leaves.

After passing through a short canyon, they approached a brightly lit enclave of buildings. Voices carried on the breeze, the wailing and crying of females, the shouts and curses of men.

As they neared the dusty town, Rolf's eyes widened in shock. A group of poor wretches was confined inside a fenced area guarded by two sentry towers at opposite ends. An energy field protected the perimeter. The stockade was roofless and he could easily see the captives milling about inside.

"Join the others," O'mon said with a chuckle. He thrust Rolf forward as a sentry opened the gate.

Rolf bucked against the large Souk. Suddenly a couple of bull-like Horthas bounded into view, swinging stun whips. One lash at his ankle and Rolf stumbled, crying out. With a final push, O'mon sent Rolf sprawling onto the dirt-packed ground inside the pen. The gate swung shut behind him with a loud clang, and a lock clicked into place.

Spitting the dirt from his mouth, he rose to a kneeling position and cursed.

"Save your breath," a weary voice said.

Rolf looked up into the soil-streaked face of a bearded man. "Who are you?"

"My name is Seth." Stooping over, the man undid the cord binding Rolf's wrists, then helped him to stand. The fellow wore a loose tan tunic cinched at the waist by a leather belt and matching leggings. His form appeared solid. Judging from the streaks of gray in his dark hair, Rolf guessed his age was forty annums, ten annums older than himself. He'd just celebrated his thirtieth birthday before leaving for Souk.

"We're situated in a remote mining district near the Rocks of Weir. It's part of Ruel's dominion." Seth gave him a keen look of assessment. "What's your name, friend?"

"Sean Breslow. My ship crashed in the hills, and O'mon's troops pulled me out of the wreckage." Rolf closed his eyes briefly to ease the throbbing in his head. "How did you get here?"

"We were captured in a raid. We're from the Alyte Garrison in the Omega sector." Seth waved at the cluster of men, women, and children huddled in a corner, bemoaning their fate, as the women clutched their offspring in terror. A few other species were evident in the pen as well—victims, Rolf assumed, of other raids or pirate attacks on civilian vessels.

Seeing the terrified captives brought a red-hot fury seething into Rolf's blood. His fists clenched. By the corona, he could throttle someone's throat. The rotten, liver-bellied Souks. All they brought was fear and misery to helpless victims. He'd come here to stop them, and now he was trapped, unable to carry out his directive. How he hated them.

The bearded man must have seen the anger in his eyes. "Go easy, my friend. There's not much you can do. No one has ever escaped from Souk."

"Yes, they have." His friends, Sarina and Teir, had managed to elude the clutches of the notorious Souk slaver, Cerrus Bdan. Their adventures had been the catalyst for his current mission. Rolf struggled to get his temper under control, then asked, "How long have you been here?"

"Two days, but it seems like two annums." Seth looked at Rolf curiously. "You said you'd crashed your spacecraft. Why were you coming to Souk?"

"I'm a trader from Arcturus."

"So you have a legitimate reason for being here. Why have they put you in with us?" Seth's eyes narrowed suspiciously.

"O'mon thinks I'm lying," Rolf confessed.

"Are you?"

"No." He fell silent, lost in anguish. How was he going to accomplish his mission when he was penned like an animal and doomed to a life of captivity? It was all the Souks' fault, like everything else in his life. Damn them! He had to escape. "What happens next? Do you know?" he asked Seth.

The older man nodded. "I spoke to a guard. Bolt is due to come on the morrow."

"Who in Zor is Bolt? I keep hearing his name."

"Bolt is the top military officer in the area. He holds the rank of satrap in Ruel's army."

Understanding lit Rolf's eyes, but he quickly hid it under

veiled lids. It wouldn't be wise to show his intimate knowledge of Souk affairs. "I don't understand," he hedged.

"Ruel is pasha of this territory. Souk is controlled by various commercial cartels led by individual pashas," Seth explained. "Together they form the Souk Alliance. Ruel is the most powerful pasha of all. He's the largest landholder, and his industrial interests extend into every corner of the planet. The Rocks of Weir, despite our desolate location, is important to him. It holds valuable deposits of piragen ore which are the main source of Ruel's wealth."

He saw Rolf's questioning glance and added, "I'm a geologist. Piragen ore is not a common commodity. I've surveyed its distribution throughout this sector of the galaxy."

"How does it relate to our situation?" Rolf asked.

"We could all end up as kreckers working the mines."

"Who makes that decision? Bolt?"

"No. A Dromo appointed by Ruel holds the position of authority here. Bolt merely carries out the Dromo's orders." Seth kicked at a rock on the ground. His face looked worn and weary. "The Dromo decrees who shall live and who shall die; who will labor in the mines or who will act as personal servants to the Souks. Bolt has the privilege of choosing women for his harem."

Rolf saw the direction of his pained glance. "Your wife?"

Seth nodded, not bothering to disguise the raw fear in his expression. "Aye. And my daughter yonder." He indicated a pretty girl of about fifteen annums sitting alone in a corner. She was combing her long blond hair with her fingers and staring vacantly at the night sky.

Rolf's gut clenched. "You don't think Bolt would—"

"I've heard stories," Seth interrupted, his tone grim. "Human females don't last very long when they're taken by a Souk, and Bolt is said to prefer females with light coloring."

"By the stars, I am sorry."

****

The night seemed to pass endlessly after that conversation, and when at last dawn came, Rolf stretched and yawned. He'd found a spare corner and lain on the ground, falling asleep instantly. He awoke cold and shivering, as were most of his fellow captives. They looked wan and pale in the orange light seeping over the horizon. His stomach growled, and he wondered if they'd be fed.

He went over to a small enclosure to relieve himself in the hole in the ground intended for that purpose. The area stank and swarmed with flies. When he came out, he studied his surroundings.

The pen was at the very edge of the town, which was situated in a narrow valley. The buildings were box-like concrete structures, functional rather than aesthetic, painted in a uniform muddy brown color. A paved street ran down the center of the town, and already he could see it was bustling with activity. The Souks, dressed in flowing caftans of bright rainbow colors, moved about their morning business, totally oblivious to the cries from the captives at the far end. Other dwellings, residences perhaps, branched off from the main avenue.

Atop a nearby hill stood a completely incongruous palatial structure. White with silver specks, it glistened in the sunlight, isolated from the town's drabness. No doubt that was where Bolt and his boss lived, Rolf thought. He wondered about the Dromo. Overseeing a work force of slaves in such a harsh environment was no easy task. The Dromo would have to be the most ferocious Souk around.

As he watched, a procession started down the hill. In the lead marched a brawny Souk wearing a gray military uniform devoid of any decoration. He had the meanest dog face Rolf had ever seen, a pudgy nose, ridged brows, and a perpetual snarl. He'd be a dangerous person to cross, Rolf figured, thinking this person must be the Dromo. The Souk was obviously in a position of authority. Rolf could tell by his autocratic bearing and by the obsequious attitude of the slaves running beside him to obey his commands.

His gaze switched to the slender figure striding alongside

him. Was that a human female? She must be either his willing consort or his slave.

As they neared, Rolf studied her further. Or rather, he couldn't tear his eyes away. Wavy auburn hair framed a face with such delicate features she could have been an artist's creation. Her brows were feathery arches the color of a fawn. He particularly liked the way her mouth was perfectly formed, with sensual pink lips.

His gaze trailed lower. From the fine bones of her face and her slender arms, Rolf would say she was slim, but she hid her figure beneath a rust-colored caftan. The way the garment fell over her body indicated that she possessed generous assets. Maybe that was why she dressed in such a drab fashion, so as not to attract undue attention. But who wouldn't be drawn to her startling beauty?

He realized the Hortha sentries were barking orders. Apparently, the captives were to line up, single-file, facing the gate. A long table was being set up outside the fence. The Souk and the young woman, who couldn't have been more than twenty annums, seated themselves in chairs behind the table. The Souk gave the signal for the gate to be opened.

"I am Bolt," he said in a loud voice. "You are to present yourselves in front of the Dromo. Keep your eyes lowered. You are not permitted to look upon her face. Anyone who disobeys will be punished."

Rolf nearly reeled in shock. Great suns! The woman was the Dromo in charge of this enclave!

He sickened as he watched each captive, head bowed, stand in front of the Dromo while Bolt pronounced his or her fate. The Dromo nodded approval, her lips tightly pinched, her back straight. Her eyes were blank as she stared straight ahead. How had she attained such an exalted status? Had she so pleased the pasha who ruled the territory that he'd honored her by putting her in command?

Yet this settlement was far from any major city. Wouldn't it be more of a punishment than a reward to be isolated here?

Screams and wails resulted when husbands and wives were separated. Anguished cries rent the air when children were torn from their mother's arms. The ill or elderly were condemned to die. Horthas stood by with stun whips, making sure the pronouncements were followed.

Groups began to form outside the gate. The strong and able were assigned as kreckers in the mines. Piragen ore could only be extracted by hand. It would be exhausting work with a high mortality rate for the work force.

Those less fit individuals were assigned as servers in the Dromo's household. And for some, a fate worse than death was prescribed. Bolt took the young adult females for his harem. Rolf assumed it was a perk the Dromo allowed him for his loyalty.

"What about the children?" Rolf asked the man in line behind him.

"They're sent away to the capital city of Haakat, where they are raised under strict supervision. When they're old enough, they receive their assignments."

"A life of slavery," Rolf stated, his face grim.

A woman screamed, and he glanced up. Seth's daughter had just been sentenced to join Bolt's harem, and it was her mother who'd cried out. Seth and his wife were being sent to the mines.

Rolf compressed his lips as his turn came. He stood in front of the table, his head raised proudly. He wasn't going to bow before anyone. He did, however, keep his gaze averted from the woman. Looking at her stirred something in him, even when he knew she was responsible for the people's anguish.

"Name?" Bolt barked, glaring at him.

Rolf stared back. "Sean Breslow."

Bolt wrote in a ledger with a computer stylus. "Profession?"

"I'm a trader from Arcturus."

Bolt's black eyes darkened. Against the blue of his skin, they appeared to be two opaque holes in his doglike visage. "You're the man whose ship crashed in the hills. I was not expecting a cargo consignment. What were you doing in this sector?"

"My ship's navigational system malfunctioned during an ion storm, and I strayed off course."

A small sound escaped the woman's lips. He risked a glance in her direction. She stared at him, undisguised interest in her expression. He returned the look, challenging her.

A stinging pain lashed his back and brought him to his knees with a grunt. One of the Horthas had caught him with a stun whip.

"Do not look upon the Dromo," Bolt snarled, leaping to his feet. "It is forbidden."

Rolf slowly turned his gaze upon the Souk. A half-smile twisted his lips. "It will take more than your whips to subdue me, Bolt."

"You will address me as master." Spittle formed in the corner of Bolt's mouth, and his face blotched with fury. "Punishment do you need, human. You are sumi here. Give him twenty lashes and then send him to the mines," he ordered the Hortha guards.

"Wait," the woman said, holding up a hand. "Don't you want to learn more about his background? If he is beaten senseless, we will gain little information." Her voice had the honeyed sweetness of keela blossom nectar. Again, Rolf wondered how she came by such a position.

"He needs to be taught a lesson, Dromo." Bolt's eyes bored into hers. "Do you not agree?"

A flicker of uncertainty shone in her forest green eyes. It was quickly clouded over as her expression went blank again. "Of course. Carry out the sentence," she ordered in a flat, dead tone.

A couple of beefy Horthas grabbed Rolf under the arms.

"This will be a good example for the rest of you slaves," the woman shouted to the terrified captives still in line. She got up and walked around the edge of the table until she stood in front of Rolf. The top of her head reached the bridge of his nose. Defiantly, Rolf met her gaze. Looking down into her cool green eyes flecked with burnished gold, he smiled.

She slapped his face. "Strip off his shirt," she commanded

the guards. "Let us see what manner of man he is when he feels the sting of the lash."

Rolf's shirt was ripped away. Guards dragged him a few meters toward a whipping post and yanked up his arms. Facing the post, he winced when his wrists were tightly secured to the wood.

"Give me that," the woman demanded from behind him. He twisted his neck and saw her grabbing a stun whip from a startled Hortha. She circled Rolf slowly, studying him like a she-wolf about to devour its prey. Her eyes shone with a feral light. "I will beat you myself, sumi. You will bend your head in submission before I am through."

"I'll never bow to you or anyone."

The lash whipped out, catching him on the upper back with electrifying force. A stinging pain like a thousand needles pierced his flesh. He bit his lip and bore the subsequent shocks in silence. But after that first lash, the others were lighter, as though meant to do no real harm. The Dromo screamed out, cursing at him, calling invectives on his name as though she were beating him to Zor.

Rolf pretended to be defeated by the whipping. He didn't know what her game was, but he would play along. Maybe she was saving him for a worse punishment later.

The whipping left welts on his back, but the painful shocks to his system weren't bad enough to knock him unconscious. If one of those Horthas had delivered the beating, he would have passed out after the first few blows. When it was done, and he hung half-limp from the post, his wrists were cut down. His legs buckled, and he fell to his knees. He'd been rendered weaker than he thought. A couple of Horthas caught him in their grasp.

"Take him to the mines with the other kreckers," Bolt ordered.

"Hold," said the Dromo, walking over to stand directly in front of Rolf. "Not so proud now, are you, sumi?" She reached up to gently brush his cheek.

Rolf jerked back in surprise. The tenderness of her touch had rocked him stronger than the jolts from the stun whips.

"Ilyssa, it is time to go," Bolt said with a pointed glance in her direction.

Immediately, she turned away. Her back ramrod straight, she left along with her underling. Rolf watched her retreat, instinct telling him they'd be seeing a lot more of each other.

Order Now at https://nancyjcohen.com/moonlight-rhapsody/

Glossary

Activators - Circuitry used on spaceships during landing sequence.

Actuator Valves - Valves in propulsion system of sublight engines.

Aguar Plant - A weed-like plant favored by K'darr. Crimson leaves, fuzzy texture. Secretes a digestive enzyme in the dark that eats through fur and skin.

Alexipharmics - Pharmaceuticals.

Alpha Gomaran Two - A volcanic planet.

Amplexus - The Yanuran mating embrace that lasts for several days.

Annums - Years.

Aramus - A creature that looks like a rug and loves to be trampled.

Arbiter - A mediator.

Athos - Planet where siren song originated.

Auranians - An advanced civilization on Shimera whose people developed the power to manipulate their auras. Persecution forced them to leave the planet that was eventually destroyed. Glowstones identify their descendants.

Arcturian Brandy - An expensive brand. Teir's favorite drink.

Auricle - Sacred stone in the Great Hall on Bimordus Two. It's a glowstone from an ancient civilization on the destroyed planet of Shimera. Legend says one of their descendants will arise again in a time of great need. This descendant will bring harmony to the universe.

Bangus Tree - Shady tree with hanging roots like a banyan.

Baynor - Mayor on Tendraa.

Belleek - An ugly sea creature.

Bimanthium Crystals - A fuel source.

Bimordus Two - The seat of the Coalition central government. Five biosphere environments inhabit this barren planet. The capital city is in the Lifestyle biome called Bimordus Central. There's a Nutrition Pod, Rain Forest, Marine Habitat, and Biogenesis Research Center.

Biome - Sealed ecosystem.

Blood Crystal - A mysterious rock that conveys visions of the future.

Boks - A board game with colored tiles.

Borks - Animals who'll rip each other's throats out over a piece of meat.

Brambid - A flying insect.

Bremen - An affluent section of town on Vilaran.

Bungrats - A derogatory term used on Tendraa, refers to a rodent.

Bzoran cat - Type of aggressive cat with sharp claws.

Calgonite Ore - A valuable mineral.

Carellian Clay - A sculpting clay used to make pottery.

Carzen - A large muscled animal that Souks ride like a horse.

Casement - Window.

Catarrhines - A monkey-type creature that lives in the rainforest.

Chirurgeon - Archaic term for a surgeon.

Circutia - Ilyssa's home world, a cultural and artistic nexus known for its friendly people. The Circutians are pacifists, abhorring all forms of violence.

Coalition - Coalition of Sentient Planets.

Coppenium - A mineral.

Cosh - A carafe of ale. A term of measurement, like a pint.

Crigellan - A species that is half-human and half-lizard.

Cr'ssian Soota Mud - A finishing polish for pottery sculptures.

Data Link - A portable data management device.

Deflector Shield - Ship's defense that protects against energy weapons and space debris.

Destiny - The vessel Rolf and Ilyssa take to Nadira. It's a Stinger-class ship equipped with warp-drive engines and two stabilizer fins attached to the main cylindrical-shaped body. The fins rotate horizontally for landings and lock vertically for combat and flight. Weapons include laser cannons, proton torpedoes, and concussion missiles.

Diamella - A clear crystal gemstone.

Dougger Gnat - A small, annoying insect.

Dromo - District leader on Souk appointed by Pasha.

Electrifier - Rod that emits an electrical charge used as a punishment device.

Eranus - Deitan Sage's home planet. People live on floating cities on vast oceans.

Fabricator - Matter synthesizer for food, clothing, and other essentials.

Farg - A deadly plague.

Field Relays - Circuitry controlling rate of descent in spacecraft.

Firestone - A brilliant, clear colored stone in gold, orange, or red.

Flamebrush - A bush with bright red thistles.

Flame lights - Torches powered by orellium gel.

Flavium - A mineral used in weapons production.

Flegymns - Fish that can devour a person in fifteen seconds.

Flyboard - Flying skateboard with handles.

Fodus Vine - A thorny swinging plant on Souk.

Fuel Capacitators - Storage for energy from charged bimanthium crystals.

Gecko - A creature with an exterior shell and antennae. They drink nectar for energy. They hire themselves out as mercenaries and often work for the Souks. Their gunships have a crab-like shape and carry laser cannons.

Gima - Mistress in Souk.

Glowstones - Stones that glow, like the ancient Auricle. These stones identify descendants of the Shimeran race who possess the ability to manipulate auras.

Halberd - A shafted weapon with a spike or axe-like cutting blade.

Haura - Hour.

Hazars - A pasha's private bodyguards.

High Council - Ruling body of the Coalition along with the Assembly.

Hiimma Birds - A high-soaring bird.

Holovid - A holographic video.

Hornet - A cruiser that takes Sarina to the science station on Timos.

Hortha - Bull-like creatures who use stun-whips as a punishment device. Speech sounds like buzzing noise. They act as guards for the Souks.

House of Raimorrda - Ruling class that crosses planetary boundaries.

Hovertram - Tram propelled by anti-gravity engine.

Humma bird - A songbird.

Igoob Leaves - Chew on them to repel insects.

Imperator - King on Nadira.

Imperatrice - Queen on Nadira.

Jaegger Beasts - Wild animals in the Uta Wastes, a desert plain on Vilaran.

Jakoon - Caretaker of the young on Yanura.

Jawani - Official Coalition language.

Jell Berries - Spicy berry on Souk.

Kather Sticks - A game with colored sticks and dice.

Katuba - A sport game involving a kick ball.

Kayoka - A white-faced monkey-like creature living in the Souk jungles.

Keela Blossoms - A white, fragrant flower.

Kookabur - A noisy type of bird on Souk that flies in flocks.

Koritah - A doctrine of proper social behavior for females on Souk.

Korions - An old enemy of the Coalition from its early formative years.

Kougra - A feline animal that likes to be cuddled.

Krach - Affirmative in Souk language.

Krecker - Souk slave laborer.

Krog - Battlecruiser and flagship of the Morgot fleet.

Lahar - A landslide of wet volcanic debris.

Lalith Leaves - An herbal remedy. When brewed like tea, it relieves congestion.

Landspeeder - A ground vehicle using anti-grav technology and turbo engines.

Laria - A term of endearment on Vilaran.

Laverbread - Seaweed mixed with oatmeal; a versatile food that can be prepared using various methods.

Lennox - A fat scavenger animal.

Levitator - Anti-gravity trolley.

Liana Vine - Tangled undergrowth vine.

Linear Actuator - A machinery part on a spaceship.

Lyphound - A beast on Souk. Used as a derogatory term.

Lypis Ice - A frozen fruit treat.

Marbelite - A white marble-like stone used in construction.

Mariculture - Agriculture in the ocean.

Marouche - A flying creature on Yanura that transports passengers.

Maug - A curse word used as an adjective.

Mediscan - Portable biomedical scanning device.

Meraninum - A lightweight, durable metal.

Merl - A type of seaweed that only grows on Yanura.

Mingka birds - Red jungle bird.

Mira - A respectful title for a female in Tendraan, like "ma'am" or "miss."

Mithridate - A fever-lowering medicine.

Moranian Flasher - A mixed alcoholic beverage.

Morgots - A warrior race from a distant solar system.

Mushgum - A quick-acting poison.

Mzips - Snake-like creatures.

Nadira - Lord Cam'brii's home planet in the Regulus star system. A lush, tropical world.

Nargot - A weasel-type animal.

Nutrium - An element that can combine with other elements in liquid form.

Omnus - Cerrus Bdan's ship.

Orellium - An organic substance used as a fuel because it burns for a long time and emits a cold light.

Oroxian Zinger - A mixed drink with fizz that tastes like cherries.

Pasha - Ruler of commercial cartel on Souk.

Parsec - A unit measuring distance.

Pastagillo Noodles - A pasta, like spaghetti.

Patima - Shawl.

Pest-House - A place where sick people are sent on Tendraa.

Petula - A term of endearment on Pollux.

Physio lab - Fitness center.

Piragen Ore - Metal used in spacecraft construction. Mined on Vilaran and Souk.

Pirium - A plastel used in spacecraft production.

Plastel- A strong but lightweight metal used in construction.

Platwhacks - Reedy plants that grow near marshes.

Pnimx Tusks - Contraband like ivory tusks.

Polluxite - Humanoid species with foldable wings. Home world is Pollux.

Pommus - A purple fruit, round and shiny like an apple.

Poultice - A soft, moist cloth filled with healing herbs applied to the body.

Posset-Drink - An herbal remedy on Tendraa.

Power Transfer Conduits - Part of a ship's propulsion system.

Preim - King of Vilaran. A descendant of the House of Raimorrda and sovereign leader of the Retti dynasty, the last Preim was overthrown in a bloody coup.

Provost - A governor on Vilaran; leader of a province.

Pyroclastic - Made up of fragments of volcanic origin.

Rabba - A wild animal on Souk.

Raker - Street cleaner on Tendraa.

Reeka Pears - A juicy pear with an expensive price tag.

Reflector - Mirror.

Reverse Levitators - Reverse anti-gravity field to slow aircraft on landing.

Rigelan Slug - A food delicacy eaten live.

ROF- Return to Origins Faction calling for secession of Coalition worlds.

Rorsh - A Tyberian monk.

Rubellis Gemstones - A ruby-like gem.

Sailbarge - Ground vehicle that flies with single propeller and sails.

Satrap - Military officer in Souk army.

Scramjet - A jet that travels at supersonic speeds.

Secondary Reactor Conduits - Backup system in sublight propulsion engines.

Sedit Beverage - Drink that induces calm.

Shimera - An ancient world with an advanced civilization whose people developed the power to manipulate their auras. These people called themselves Auranians. Persecution forced them to leave the planet that was eventually destroyed. Glowstones identify their descendants.

Shooter - A laser pistol with stun and kill settings.

Silverscreen - A filter that is impervious to sensor scans.

Sirisian - Race that has pink skin and an elastic body.

Siren Song - The power to mesmerize men through a woman's singing voice.

Skimmer - Surface vehicle with turbo boost engines and antigrav technology.

Slythian - A derogatory adjective for a low-life type of person.

Snipes - A freshwater fish eaten as seafood.

Snivel - Slithering creature like a small snake and just as lethal; lives in rock crevices.

Sol - Sun in Souk.

Solar Sailer - It's like a hot air balloon but with sails and a motor. A passenger basket is attached by cables to a rig of billowing sails.

Souk - A planet whose inhabitants have blue skin and dog-like facial features. They practice the slave trade and speak in guttural tones. Souk has two moons. Cerrus Bdan inhabits the

Nurash Desert on one side of the Koodrash Mounts. The Thicket of Bayne is a jungle at the foot of these mountains. His brother Ruel's territory is on the other side of the range.

Souk Alliance - A syndicate of commercial cartels in the mineral-rich Capellan system.

Speedcraft - Planetside transports smaller than skimmer.

Speeder - A form of land transport that holds up to four people and resembles a bullet-shaped car with a glass bubble. Can fly at low altitudes with its anti-grav engine.

Spiral Town - Residence of High Council members on Bimordus Two.

Sulu Berries - A mulberry-type fruit.

Sumi - Souk word for slave.

Tangent Beams - Energy weapons array on starship.

Taurus - A volcanic planet where the Blood Crystal is hidden.

Techno War - A war on Tendraa stimulated by too fast progress into the technological age.

Tendraa - Mantra's home world. Ruled by a Liege Lord. Capital city is Lazore on the coast of the Bazmayan Sea. The planet is rich in flavium.

Theodolite - A precision instrument with a telescopic sight.

Thrum - A man-eating plant from Antiguas Two.

Torgus Larvae - A live food delicacy on Yanura.

Torrock - A desert beast of burden the Souks ride like camels or horses.

Tractor Beam Wheel - Towing beam on a spacecraft.

Tupella Blossoms - Flowers on Nadira with orange and red petals.

Turbolift - An elevator that goes horizontal as well as vertical.

Twyggs - Tree people.

Tyberia - Mara's home world.

Vacchus - Living crystal on the planet, Athos.

Vilaran - Teir's home world. Vilaran is a republic and one of the six founding members of the Coalition. Theal is the capital city. Vilaran is divided into provinces, each one ruled by a provost appointed by the central Parliament which is itself elected every eight years by the populace. Each province is divided into districts headed by a justice. The Centorian houses the provincial government. An elected president is head of state.

Valiant - Teir's ship, a remodeled freighter with gunports. It has three decks with a warp drive, sublight engines, and deflector shield generators.

Venice Treacle - A home remedy from Tendraa.

Vermuchak - A derogatory term on Yanura.

Viewphone - A telephone with a video camera attached.

Viewscreen - Monitor window at the front of a starship.

Vorax - A scavenger bird.

Wagmint Tea - Mint tea.

Warp Drive - Faster than lightspeed propulsion.

Weri - Linen.

Wingboxers - Flying reptiles with yellow eyes, claws, and large wingspans.

Zandozor - A musical reed instrument.

Zor - A term for Hell.

Weapons

Armor Plating against projectile weapons.

Blaster Carbines - Laser Rifles

Concussion Missiles.

Deflector Shields - Ship's defense that protects against space debris and energy weapons.

Electrifier - Rod that emits an electrical charge. Used as a punishment device.

Halberd - A shafted weapon with a spike or an axe-like cutting blade.

Korion Fireball - A golden orb, it burns where it touches.

Laser Cannons.

Nokout Gas Grenades.

Photon Torpedoes.

Shooter - Laser pistol with stun and kill setting.

Stun-Whip - Whip that delivers electric shock. Used by Horthas as punishment device.

Tangent Beams - Energy weapons array on a starship.

Tractor Beam Wheel - Towing beam on a spacecraft.

Vibril - A lead-like substance impervious to sensor scans.

Vilaran Flamer - Mini-flame thrower.

Transports

Armored Hoverscout - Anti-grav ground vehicle with armor plating against projectile weapons.

Destiny - The vessel Rolf and Ilyssa take to Nadira. A Stinger-class ship equipped with powerful warp-drive engines and two stabilizer fins attached to the main cylindrical-shaped body. The fins rotate horizontally for landings and lock vertically for combat and flight. Weapons systems include two fire-linked laser cannon turrets, a proton torpedo launcher, and a concussion missile docket.

Flyboard - A flying skateboard with handles.

Gunship - Small fighter ship with high maneuverability and laser cannons.

Hornet - A cruiser that takes Sarina to the science station on Timos.

Hovertram - Tram propelled by anti-gravity engine.

Krog - Battlecruiser and flagship of the Morgot fleet.

Landspeeder - A ground vehicle using anti-grav technology and turbo engines.

Omnus - Cerrus Bdan's warship.

Sailbarge - Ground vehicle that flies with single propeller and sails.

Scramjet - A jet that travels at supersonic speeds.

Skimmer - Surface vehicle with turbo boost engines and antigrav technology.

Solar Sailer - It's like a hot air balloon but with sails and a motor. A passenger basket is attached by cables to a rig of billowing sails.

Speedcraft - Planetside transports smaller than a skimmer.

Speeder - A form of land transport that holds up to four people and resembles a bullet-shaped car with a glass bubble. Can fly at low altitudes with its anti-grav engine.

Valiant - Teir's ship, a remodeled freighter with gunports. It has three decks with a warp drive, sublight engines, and deflector shield generators.

About the Author

Nancy J. Cohen writes the Bad Hair Day Mysteries featuring South Florida hairstylist Marla Vail. Titles in this series have been named Best Cozy Mystery by *Suspense Magazine*, won the Readers' Favorite Book Awards and the RONE Award, placed first in the Chanticleer International Book Awards and third in the Arizona Literary Awards.

Her nonfiction titles, *Writing the Cozy Mystery* and *A Bad Hair Day Cookbook*, have also garnered numerous awards. These include gold medals in the FAPA President's Book Awards and the Royal Palm Literary Awards, First Place in the IAN Book of the Year Awards and the *Topshelf Magazine* Book Awards. *Writing the Cozy Mystery* was an Agatha Award Finalist.

Nancy's imaginative romances have proven popular with fans as well. These books have won the HOLT Medallion and Best Book in Romantic SciFi/Fantasy at *The Romance Reviews*.

A featured speaker at libraries, conferences, and community events, Nancy is listed in *Contemporary Authors, Poets & Writers*, and *Who's Who in U.S. Writers, Editors, & Poets*. She is a past president of Florida Romance Writers and the Florida Chapter of Mystery Writers of America. When not busy writing, she enjoys reading, fine dining, cruising, and visiting Disney World.

Follow Nancy Online

Website – https://nancyjcohen.com
Blog – https://nancyjcohen.com/blog
Twitter – https://www.twitter.com/nancyjcohen
Facebook – https://www.facebook.com/NancyJCohenAuthor
LinkedIn – https://www.linkedin.com/in/nancyjcohen
Goodreads – https://www.goodreads.com/nancyjcohen
Pinterest – https://pinterest.com/njcohen/
Instagram – https://instagram.com/nancyjcohen
BookBub – https://www.bookbub.com/authors/nancy-j-cohen

Books by Nancy J. Cohen

Bad Hair Day Mysteries
Permed to Death
Hair Raiser
Murder by Manicure
Body Wave
Highlights to Heaven
Died Blonde
Dead Roots
Perish by Pedicure
Killer Knots
Shear Murder
Hanging by a Hair
Peril by Ponytail
Haunted Hair Nights (Novella)
Facials Can Be Fatal
Hair Brained
Hairball Hijinks (Short Story)
Trimmed to Death
Easter Hair Hunt
Styled for Murder
Star Tangled Murder

Anthology
"Three Men and a Body" in Wicked Women Whodunit

Nancy J. Cohen

The Drift Lords Series
Warrior Prince
Warrior Rogue
Warrior Lord

Science Fiction Romances
Keeper of the Rings
Silver Serenade

The Light-Years Series
Circle of Light
Moonlight Rhapsody
Starlight Child

Nonfiction
Writing the Cozy Mystery
A Bad Hair Day Cookbook

Order Now: https://nancyjcohen.com/books/